I PROMISE
YOU THIS

ALSO BY PATRICIA SANDS

The Bridge Club

The Love in Provence Series
The Promise of Provence
Promises to Keep

PATRICIA SANDS

I PROMISE YOU THIS

BOOK THREE IN THE
LOVE IN PROVENCE SERIES

LAKE UNION
PUBLISHING

Published by Lake Union Publishing, Seattle

www.apub.com

Amazon, the Amazon logo, and Lake Union Publishing are trademarks of Amazon.com, Inc., or its affiliates.

ISBN-13: 9781503935723
ISBN-10: 1503935728

Cover illustration by Scott Collie
Map by Don Larson
Cover design by Mumtaz Mustafa

Printed in the United States of America

In memory of Peter McNeilly, who left us a legacy to love unconditionally and live life in the superlative.

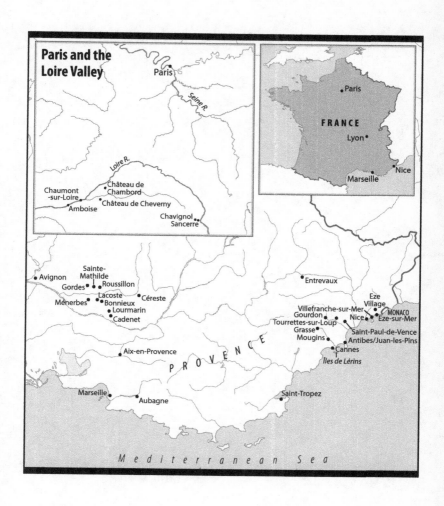

Paris and the Loire Valley

Paris

Seine R.

Loire R.

Chaumont
-sur-Loire

Château de
Chambord

Château de Cheverny

Amboise

Chavignol
Sancerre

FRANCE

Paris

Lyon

Marseille

Nice

Avignon

Sainte-Mathilde

Gordes

Roussillon

Lacoste

Céreste

Ménerbes

Bonnieux

Lourmarin

Cadenet

Entrevaux

Èze Village

MONACO

Villefranche-sur-Mer

Gourdon

Nice

Èze-sur-Mer

Tourrettes-sur-Loup

Grasse

Saint-Paul-de-Vence

Mougins

Antibes/Juan-les-Pins

Aix-en-Provence

Cannes

Iles de Lérins

PROVENCE

Marseille

Aubagne

Saint-Tropez

M e d i t e r r a n e a n   S e a

CHAPTER ONE

Rain pelted down.

The limo crawled along in a clog of traffic. For the most part, the rhythmic slap of the windshield wipers was all that broke the silence.

Philippe knew that Kat was struggling to keep her composure. He kept the conversation light and brief as they looked out from the backseat. "Now you see why I never take a taxi into Paris from the airport. At least with a hired car and driver, I don't have to watch the meter skyrocket if we get caught like this."

Kat nodded, expressionless, staring straight ahead. She thought it fitting that the weather was as gloomy and dark as the feelings she was fighting.

When the familiar landmarks of the Left Bank came into view, her mood began to lift. She leaned her head back against the seat, her hand nestled in Philippe's.

"This is reminding me of my visit here last June, and the words of Oncle François."

Philippe gently squeezed her hand and turned his head to her. Their eyes met. "Your lunch with him was the start of my good fortune."

Katherine felt the hint of a smile light her face, remembering how François's wise words on that early summer day had changed her forever. She could hear his kindly voice with its charming accent now, as she often did. "Life is full of choices . . . don't be afraid to make them . . . live it well."

It was her first cheerful thought since they'd received the phone call about Molly's life-threatening accident, not even twenty-four hours earlier. Molly was now in a hospital, in an induced coma. Philippe had accompanied Kat to Paris to put her on a flight to Toronto the next morning. He would follow later, once they knew more about Molly's condition.

"This is not the way I envisioned our first time together in Paris. We'll return in the spring when the trees are in blossom and we're happy."

"April in Paris," sighed Katherine, feeling a rush at the thought.

Philippe leaned into her and sang a few lines of that romantic old tune.

Kat laughed, in spite of herself, and thanked him with her smile.

He slipped his arm around her shoulder, pulling her close. "Who makes you laugh more than Molly? Just keep remembering that."

Swallowing back tears as her smile faded, Katherine nodded. "You're right. I'm going to try to do just that. I'm so frightened for her."

Philippe stroked her arm gently.

Once in their cozy room at the Hôtel Henri IV, Katherine slipped off her shoes and flopped on the bed. The room had only enough space on each side of the bed for a small side table, but the linens and décor were impeccable. The renovated bathroom had a deep soaking tub and thick soft towels, both of which were becoming more common in France.

"When I stayed here last June, I was so pleased you recommended the hotel to me. The location, the ambiance, the tiny perfect rooms . . ." Katherine smiled at the memory.

Philippe sat at the end of the bed and massaged her feet. "My grandfather used to bring me here as far back as I can remember. He knew the owner in those days. We would have great adventures in Le Jardin du Luxembourg. At least, they seemed adventures to me then, exploring the woods or racing our sailing ships in the pond. Sometimes we would visit an intriguing woman who lived nearby. He said she was a dear and special friend. She was beautiful and made the most delicious *madeleines*. I've never forgotten them . . . or her!"

Katherine smiled again. "Of course a favorite memory of yours involves food, even from childhood! I'm amazed it wasn't cheese!"

"Pourquoi pas?" Philippe chuckled and lightly tickled the sole of her foot before he stood up. "And speaking of food, we should get ready for our dinner reservation. But first, let's be *flâneurs*! Paris is the best city to stroll in when it is raining. I can't explain it exactly, but I believe you will love it. It will give you peace. *Je te promets*."

"Let's go, but I don't feel hungry yet. I'm not even bringing my camera. All I can think about is Molly and life and death. Hopefully a walk will replace this despair with hope. I want to savor every moment with you until I have to leave tomorrow."

Philippe nodded sympathetically as he opened the door for Kat and took her hand. "It's a terrible worry, *c'est vrai*. But let's try our best to think positive thoughts of Molly to get through this day. We'll help each other."

He collected an umbrella from the stand near the hotel entrance. Grasping its wooden handle, he put his arm around Katherine, and they set off through the narrow cobblestone streets of the bohemian-flavored Latin Quarter. The oversized green umbrella gave broad protection that was hardly necessary, as their bodies molded together.

The rain had lessened in intensity. The daylong soaking had created a palette of grays from the cobblestone lanes to the slate rooftops.

"You always told me Paris was romantic in the rain and now I see why," Kat said, snuggling even closer. "There's a softness in the air and everything seems to blend together. I feel like we're walking through an impressionist painting."

Katherine became caught up in Philippe's stories of the artists and philosophers whose lives had colored the history of the area. "*La rive gauche* evokes images of Toulouse-Lautrec, Matisse, Josephine Baker, Picasso, Hemingway, Stein, Fitzgerald—that amazing cast of characters of *les Années folles*."

"The crazy years. One of my favorite periods to read about. The arts were so alive." Katherine added. "Then things changed so dramatically after the war, with good reason. Existentialism and civil rights issues took over, with thinkers like Sartre, de Beauvoir, Camus, Baldwin. A rich time again, don't you think? I devoured Sartre's work when I was in university and love knowing all those luminaries walked these streets."

"I like discovering we shared the same interests in years past, although I must admit I devoured more cheap wine than philosophy in university," Philippe said. "Let me clarify—even though it was cheap, it was usually smooth and full-flavored! We were devotees of the vine." He grinned at the flood of memories.

"Another benefit of studying in France!" Katherine teased. Closing her eyes and inhaling deeply, she said, "And there's another benefit, the local *pâtisseries*! Everyone is lining up for the afternoon baguette . . . it smells divine."

Before long they spilled out onto the tree-lined Boulevard Saint-Michel, with its historic fountain. Groups of students were milling about in what was now a light drizzle, heading to the Metro after their day of studies in the university halls and buildings.

Philippe steered Kat through the busy crowd, toward the Seine. He told her the history of each bridge they passed, and Katherine expressed disappointment at the shuttered and locked green stands as they made their way along the river. "That rain was too much for even *les bouquinistes* today."

They stopped at the Pont des Arts, and Kat's eye immediately zeroed in on the mass of locks, of all sizes and shapes, attached to the chain-link sides of the bridge. "The love locks! I don't think there's room for even one more!"

"These *cadenas d'amour* just keep multiplying. They are on other bridges too," Philippe said, and then looked at Katherine apologetically. "Are you disappointed I didn't bring one?"

"*Mais non!* In fact, I'm glad you didn't. Now that we are standing here, I remember reading that part of this railing collapsed last year under their weight."

Philippe blew out a sigh of relief. "To be honest, I didn't consider it. I think it's gotten out of hand."

Soon they reached the ornate Beaux Arts–style Pont Alexander III, and Philippe steered them to the middle of it. "Every bridge has its own character. This one is exuberantly elegant," Kat murmured, admiring the cherubs, nymphs, and gilt-bronzed sculptures that graced the spans.

With his arm around her shoulder, Philippe turned their bodies to look across the river. "*Voilà, mon amour.* Drink this in."

Through the soft settling of dusk and the mist of light rain, not far in the distance stood the Eiffel Tower, ablaze with its festive lights. Katherine took a deep breath and sighed. As she lifted her face to Philippe's, his lips met hers with a long, gentle kiss. "*Je t'aime,*" he whispered, his tone soothing. "Carry this moment with you."

"I love you too," Katherine replied, her body tingling as she responded to his touch. The connection between them seemed even more intense because they were parting. "Thank you for bringing me to this view . . . this moment. I don't want to leave you."

He looked deeply into her eyes. "Minou, you are my everything . . . you aren't leaving me. You're going to help Molly and then you'll return."

Katherine's heart swelled with gratitude for all the romance Philippe built into their time together. Whenever she expressed this to him, he reminded her that solitude had been his companion for many years. He had convinced himself he could live without love until Katherine had—seemingly from nowhere—walked into his life. His tenderness had opened her eyes to how alone she too had been, in spite of having had a husband. Now their love was filling voids and creating a richer life than either had imagined just a year before.

She nodded, lost in his eyes and too overcome for words.

They stood holding each other in the thrall of the scene, under the umbrella, before Philippe raised his hand and hailed a cab. "Café Burq, Rue des Abbesses," he instructed the driver, who commented with a knowing "Ahhh."

They raised their eyebrows and grinned at each other as the driver took them on a backstreet tour that was at times hair-raising. He skillfully darted in and out of dense traffic on narrow streets, muttering oaths under his breath.

Philippe made certain Kat caught glimpses of some of the remaining Christmas-market huts and skating rinks that still dotted the *quartiers*, along with elaborate window dressings. "From *petite* boutiques to grand department stores," he said, "Paris does the festive season in fine style, and we've just caught the end of it."

As the taxi began to be slowed by ever more labyrinthian laneways, Philippe asked the driver to stop at the tiny carousel in the Place des Abbesses. "*C'est bien, merci.* The rain has slowed and we can walk to the restaurant from here. *C'est parfait.*"

"I recognize this. There's Sacré-Coeur up there; we're in the start of Montmartre, yes?" Katherine asked.

He took her hand as they threaded between shoppers. "Basically, yes, the Eighteenth. This area began to get trendy about ten years ago but has retained its own unique character. Les Abbesses is named after

Les Dames de Montmartre and the abbey that was here for centuries. We're pretty early, so the restaurant won't be crowded."

As they passed a long line winding out of a corner *boulangerie*, Philippe told her that the bakery had once won the award for the best baguette in Paris. They stopped to stare through the window at glass display cases filled with tantalizing pastries. Philippe pointed out a few.

"Besides their crisp baguette, the signature items are almond croissants and exotic flavors of *macarons*. After dinner, if the line is gone and the shop still open, we'll get some to take with you tomorrow."

"*Bonne idée!* They'll make delicious gifts. I hadn't even given any thought to that."

"Nor should you have . . . you have enough on your mind," Philippe reassured her. "But now we can do this."

A friendly young waitress seated them quickly in the dimly lit bistro with its swanky yet intimate atmosphere. The classic wooden chairs, checkered tablecloths, and blackboard menus reminded Katherine of the *bouchons* in Lyon. The tightly packed tables conveyed an air of conviviality, even with the room only half full at that early dining hour.

Katherine knew Philippe would have fine suggestions for their meal and wasn't surprised when they started by sharing a cheese appetizer. "This baked Camembert with honey is a must. They are famous for it!"

"Almost as delectable as yours," Kat teased.

She followed with *escargots* in cream, while Philippe rolled his eyes in rapture over the veal liver sautéed with figs. The waitress suggested an appropriate wine from their special organic list, and for a while Kat's worries were eased by the eclectic atmosphere and delicious meal.

Sipping her wine slowly, Katherine reminisced about their Christmas at Joy's manor house in Sainte-Mathilde and her immersion into the traditions of Provence. "It was like a dream. I keep reliving it all and don't want to forget any of it."

Philippe encouraged her to talk about other happy topics to help further distract her from her worries. They were supposed to be collecting a puppy at the end of the month, and Philippe assured Kat he would speak to the breeder. He also promised he would call her friend Simone, to explain her absence.

As they held each other close that night, Philippe whispered comforting words, and they talked about the possibility of bringing Molly back to France to recuperate. There was a sudden awareness they were parting.

Kat felt his body tense without warning. "I just had this terrible thought that you might not come back. *Mon Dieu!* I know you will be back. Why would you not?"

Katherine pulled herself even deeper into his arms. "Exactly. Why would I not? I can't imagine life without you. But before I return to France, you'll come to Toronto. It will be good for you to see that part of my life."

Her lips found his, and everything they knew about each other was expressed in that kiss. Though soft and sweet at first, it grew with intensity and excitement and quickly turned into hot passion.

Each had broken down walls deep inside that had shielded past hurts. They had built trust on the ruins of those walls. Trust that was strong and proven. They had bared their souls, and now they gave themselves to each other as they had so many times during the past few months. The euphoric feeling of passionate love was something Kat had thought was long gone in her life, but Philippe had awakened it just as he had won her heart.

At the departure gate, Philippe felt reassured. With a look of strong resolve in her eyes, Katherine held her head high and pulled back her shoulders as she took her boarding pass and passport from her bag. After a quick hug and *bise*, she nodded. "I'm off."

They both were only too aware it would be their first time away from each other for more than one night.

"Coming with me to Paris was such a fine idea. Thanks for getting me this far. I'm ready to be at Molly's side and to help in every way I can. I can't wait to see Andrea and the rest of my family too. Soon we can figure out when you should come."

Philippe rubbed his hand gently on Kat's cheek. "Go fix things, Minou. *Vas-y.*"

Katherine smiled. She loved the nickname he had for her and felt a glimmer of optimism at his words. Perhaps things would not be as bad in Toronto as she feared.

She boarded through the business-class line: another of Philippe's thoughtful surprises. When she had protested, he'd showed her the massive number of points he had accumulated, and that was the end of the debate.

She looked back one more time and waved. Philippe watched until she disappeared.

CHAPTER TWO

Katherine dozed her way through a couple of in-flight movies. Her dreams were interrupted by thoughts about Philippe and memories of her mother, as well as shattering images of Molly's accident.

This would be the first time in almost six months that Katherine was heading back to Toronto, ever since that fateful home exchange in Antibes the previous summer. Back to the childhood home she shared again with her mother for a few months after James had walked out on her. She suspected the memories of that special time before Elisabeth died might be overwhelming at first. It might not be an easy homecoming.

Comfortably nestled in the spacious business-class seat, her thoughts drifted back over those past months in France. A growing awareness came upon her that perhaps she was leaving her home now, not going home.

Taking her tablet out of her bag, she opened the photo file she had begun on that first day after Philippe brought her to his apartment from the airport. She had named it simply "Gratitude." Flipping through it regularly was as meaningful to her as written entries in diaries were to others.

Every day she chose one image to mark that date in a special way. Some days it had been an interesting challenge to choose just one. Other days, she quickly took a photo with her phone. Occasionally, that hurried shot turned out to be even more evocative than one carefully planned.

She took out her phone now and snapped a few shots. Framed by the oval window, the wing tip floated above a froth of clouds. The plane was about to begin its descent.

She was surprised to feel refreshed as the plane landed in Toronto.

As soon as the automatic doors parted and she entered the arrivals area, she spotted Andrea's husband, Terrence. Not only was her cousin taller than everyone else in the room, he was waving vigorously.

He rushed to the end of the walkway, scooping Katherine into his familiar bear hug. "It's so good to see you!" his voice boomed. "You look fantastic! Life in France is suiting you!"

Kat responded to his warm welcome before the conversation became serious and Terrence updated her on Molly's condition. Molly's transfer to a Toronto hospital two days earlier had gone without a problem, and she was now in the care of the top brain-trauma specialists in the country.

"The support has been outstanding. We're confident Molly is receiving top care but the staff will give you a detailed explanation. They see you as Molly's next of kin."

She nodded and her pace quickened with urgency. There was a sudden sadness deep within her of how alone Molly was in the world.

"Andrea is at Molly's bedside, waiting for you," he said as he reached over and took her hand. "We feel better knowing you are here."

With only her carry-on bag for luggage, they were out of the airport and on their way downtown to the sprawling hospital complex in no time.

"This is about the only time of day there isn't serious traffic gridlock anymore," Terrence grumbled. "You won't believe how bad it's getting. Reminds Andie and me how glad we are to live in the country."

He answered Katherine's questions as best he could. The details of Molly's car accident were straightforward. "Visibility was bad. The road was ice-covered at the corner. The other driver was young and inexperienced. It was no one's fault, just unfortunate timing when the young man lost control and crashed headlong into Molly's car. It's a miracle there wasn't a fatality."

They slipped into silence for a while before continuing with small talk. Katherine asked about her niece and two nephews, and Terrence brought her up to date on their activities. Then he attempted to entertain her with general observations about changes in Toronto and its disreputable crack-smoking mayor.

"Trust me, he will be out of office after the upcoming election this spring. He's been an embarrassment to the entire nation!"

"People were even talking about him in France!" Kat said as Terrence shook his head in disgust.

At first Kat felt disengaged from the recognizable urban landscape of Toronto as they drove into the city. It simply didn't draw the same response from her as driving along the turquoise waters of the Mediterranean on the Bord de Mer from the Nice airport.

Yet as the distinctive skyline came into view, there was a comfort in the familiarity of it that was almost disconcerting.

Anxiety set in as soon as Katherine entered the hospital. Her stomach was tied in knots. Her mouth felt parched.

Closing her eyes and taking a deep breath, she thought it odd how her former career had been health-related and she had attended many meetings in hospitals, but that had been the extent of her experience.

She had never known anyone who had been in the hospital for any reason other than childbirth, let alone a life-or-death situation.

Sensing her tension, Terrence put his arm around her shoulder. Kat gratefully patted his hand.

The elevator doors glided open without a sound. Katherine stepped into a soothingly sterile reception area painted in soft blues and white. Andrea was waiting there.

She and Katherine held each other in a long embrace before they stepped back.

"I'm so glad to see you, though I'm sorry for the reason that brought you home." Andrea's appearance was pale and tired rather than her usual healthy and fit demeanor.

"Andie, you must be exhausted. Terrence told me you've been here around the clock."

"Well, they toss us out at night—gently, of course." Gesturing toward a nearby doorway, she continued. "They've assured us she's not in danger now. It's just a waiting game." She took Kat's hand as she cautioned her not to be overwhelmed by her first view of Molly.

"She looks peaceful, like she's sleeping," Andrea said, softly, "but all of the equipment and tubes can be intimidating at first."

Katherine moved quickly to Molly's bedside and leaned down to kiss her cheek. Her hands trembled, and she felt a gut-wrenching stab of fear mixed with sadness. As her eyes took in the scene, they filled with tears.

With her face swollen and bruised, Molly lay on her back with her right leg in a cast. Bandages wrapped around her left shoulder and partway down her arm. There were tubes and devices everywhere, and her head had been shaved.

Kat's hand flew to her mouth, and she gagged as she quickly stepped back out to the reception area. Andrea followed to help her, and a nurse handed Katherine a glass of water as they eased her into a chair.

"It's okay, this often happens," a nurse comforted her. "Just sit here until you feel better. Take your time."

Andrea sat with her, motioning to Terrence for more water.

Katherine kept her head down and took slow deep breaths. She sipped the glass of water Terrence brought until she felt her symptoms subside. Closing her eyes, she gulped several times and grasped Andrea's hand.

"Let's try that again. I think I'll be okay now."

The nurse indicated that Andrea and Terrence could go in with Katherine, even though there was only supposed to be one visitor at a time.

Hand in hand, they walked back to Molly's side.

"This is awful," Katherine whispered. "What is all this equipment? Why did they shave her head? Are they going to operate or did they already? I didn't expect this."

"I know it's a shock," Terrence sympathized. "I should have described it more so you wouldn't be so surprised. We've gotten used to it. At the first hospital, they shaved her head. They thought surgery might be required, but then it wasn't—"

"And that was a good thing . . ." interrupted Andrea.

Katherine was accustomed to seeing Molly's thick dark hair in a wild mass of curls or pulled primly into a knot at the nape of her neck.

"She won't be happy when she wakes up and sees that!" Katherine mumbled as tears poured down her cheeks. Her voice hushed, she stuttered, "Th . . . that was a weak attempt at humor . . . Oh, poor Molly, this is so hard to accept . . ."

Standing next to her, Terrence wrapped his arms around Katherine as she sobbed. "It's so traumatic to take this all in."

After a moment, she pulled herself together, although she was conscious her trembling had simply transferred inward.

Terrence pointed out the ventilator to Katherine. "Depending on her progress, the doctors told us she might need a tracheotomy."

A collection of monitors and screens, some emitting low beeps and buzzes, surrounded the head of the bed. A nurse explained their vital sign–monitoring functions to Katherine. Her calm, efficient manner helped lower Katherine's anxiety.

"You will notice we only have one chair in this room. We hope you understand that visiting is strictly regulated in the ICU. There's a comfortable family-seating area in reception." With a smile, she nodded toward Andrea and Terrence. "We've gotten to know your cousins and they will fill you in on our requirements. Hopefully Molly will only be here a few days. Oh, here is Dr. Ponneri to speak with you."

A petite, attractive woman—who looked like she should still be in high school, Kat thought—introduced herself. She was brief and to the point. "Ms. Malone's condition is still precarious but the swelling around her brain is diminishing. Intervention was quick, so there is a strong chance of full recovery. We will do some further tests in a few days, when we can decrease medication and bring her out of this state."

Katherine plied her with questions, and the doctor explained, "With this type of brain injury, what happens is the metabolism of the brain has been significantly altered. You may have areas without adequate blood flow. The idea is to let us reduce the amount of energy those different brain areas need. If we can do that, then as the brain heals and the swelling goes down, maybe those areas that were at risk can be protected. The main thing about a drug-induced coma is that it's reversible. We are keeping her very safe."

She reached out to gently touch Katherine's arm. "As you can see, we are all here to help the family as well as the patient. Ask us any question, any time."

Kat felt tears slip down her cheeks. "I'm sorry . . ."

"Please. It's very distressing to see a loved one in such a state."

Kat nodded wordlessly but looked at the doctor with gratitude. Finally she whispered, "Thank you."

Dr. Ponneri smiled in an understanding way and moved on to the next unit.

Katherine, Andrea, and Terrence sat talking in the comfortable family area and took turns going in the room to be with Molly. Katherine cried every time she sat alone with her and decided she simply had to accept that until she got her feelings under control.

The entire experience was so foreign to her. It was hard enough to be in an atmosphere that was so calm and at the same time so frightening. To look at Molly and think she might die, or be adversely affected for the rest of her life, was more than Kat could handle. She struggled to make sense of it.

At 5:00 p.m. she called Philippe and related the details about Molly's condition.

"And you, Minou? How are you?"

Katherine opened her mouth to answer but instead started to cry again. "I'm sorry," she blubbered. "I've been doing this all afternoon."

Philippe offered calm words, his tone soothing. "Take your time . . . I'm here . . . Feel my arms around you."

Katherine sighed before she found her voice. "So far I'm not handling it too well. It's hard to get past the shock."

"Bien sûr," he sympathized. *"Je veux être avec toi.* Now I'm feeling like I should have gone with you."

"I think today will be the worst, adjusting to everything. I don't think you should come until something changes with Molly. Now that I'm here, I see that. Don't worry, I'll be fine. I'm just missing you already, and jet lag's kicking in."

She felt a gentle hand on her shoulder and realized she had dozed off in the chair next to Molly.

"Okay, Kat. Time to go home. We'll come back first thing in the morning."

Reluctant to leave Molly's side, Katherine straightened her back and rubbed her eyes. "Shouldn't we stay until visiting hours are over?"

"We felt the same way at first," Andrea said as they waited for the elevator. "But you'll realize that there is nothing more you can do today. We just have to hope that tomorrow brings some improvement. One day at a time."

"You're always the voice of reason, Andie. Thank goodness." Katherine slipped her arm through Andrea's as they waited for Terrence to pay for parking. "Now I'm getting anxious about going to my house. It feels like I've been gone a lifetime."

"Well, it's been almost six months, Kat. Hard to believe! The time just flew by."

Katherine sighed. "Everything in my life has changed—but in a good way. Such a good way!"

As they drove the familiar streets, Katherine once again experienced an unsettling disconnect with her surroundings. Although she had been happy growing up in her friendly middle-class neighborhood, she immediately missed the centuries-old streets of her new life.

She and Andrea kept up a stream of nonstop chatter, filling in small details that they hadn't shared during their regular Skype talks. However, the talk kept returning to Molly as they shared their worries about her present and her future.

When Terrence turned into Kat's driveway, welcoming lights shone from the living room windows. Katherine's heart filled with emotion as she anticipated her mother answering the door, like old times. It was still hard to accept she was gone.

Terrence set down Katherine's bag, unlocked the door, and stood back to let her go in first. She hesitated and then stepped into the entrance foyer. A wave of loss briefly engulfed her as she looked into the tidy living room, the furniture just as her mother had kept it for decades.

"Take your time, Kat," Andrea said softly, touching Katherine's back. "We'll wait in the kitchen for you. I put a stew in the slow cooker before we went downtown this morning. It will be ready whenever you are."

"I'll take your things up to your room and then whip up a salad," Terrence said as he disappeared up the stairs.

The house was filled with the savory aroma of onions, garlic, slow-cooked meat, and vegetables in red wine. Kat stopped, rolled her eyes upward, and inhaled. "Ahhh. I know that smell well. Would there also be your famous flaxseed bread to dip in that exquisite sauce?"

She smiled at Andrea's nod and then hesitantly walked down the hall into the room where her mother had slept during her last few weeks. She went straight to the carpet hanging on the wall and leaned her forehead on it, placing her hands gently against it. The carpet was a story in itself with the times of joy and tragedy it had been through.

Kat's emotions suddenly overwhelmed her. To her surprise they were feelings of strength mixed with the sadness of loss. She could sense the love her parents had always given her. All she knew about them now, after the letter her mother had written, poured into her thoughts. A rush of memories of her mother and her words went through her. "What doesn't kill us makes us stronger" had been her mother's mantra.

Kat could still hear her mother's kind voice, with its strong Hungarian accent after all those years. It would be a year in February since Elisabeth quietly slipped out of this life.

Kat rubbed her cheek on the worn silken threads of browns, golds, greens, and reds, feeling their softness. She had a sense her mother would be happy for her, proud of the way she had taken control of her life.

Power seemed to be transmitted into her hands as she pressed her palms against the carpet. Before she stepped back, she lightly touched her lips to this most treasured possession. *This will definitely come back to France with me.*

The intensity of the moment was fierce. She slipped her phone from her pocket. This was the time to capture the image. To forever remind her of the feelings she had just experienced. It couldn't wait. It was today's "Gratitude" shot, without question.

Katherine stood there for several minutes more, then slowly sat on a chair by the desk. The reality of being home suddenly hit her. When she had left for Antibes the previous August, it had been for a three-month exchange. Yet she had stayed almost six months. Going back next time might be for forever, and that shocking reality now took hold. She pushed fear into the back of her mind. This was not the time.

As she walked into the kitchen, her cousins glanced up with what resembled relief. "You look happy!" Andrea remarked, her eyes wide with surprise. "I thought you might be consumed with sadness by all the memories here."

"I'm as surprised as you are. Anyu obviously left good karma here because I felt only positive energy when I walked into her room. When I touched her carpet, crazy as it sounds, something rippled through my fingertips and deep into my core. I felt welded to the spot!" Her voice and expression left no doubt of her amazement and effectively buried the fear she had just felt.

"Neni was a special woman," Andrea said, using the Hungarian term for *aunt,* as Terrence nodded his agreement. "Her strength will always be with you, Kat. With all of us."

Katherine's jaw trembled as the wave of positive energy suddenly ebbed. "I'm going through such a roller coaster of emotions and I'm not sure where this ride is going to end."

Andrea put her arms around her. "There's a lot for you to deal with, Kat. Apart from Molly's accident, I'm sure it's a bit of a shock for you to suddenly find yourself back here. Want to talk about it?"

Katherine shook her head. "Not now. Not yet. Let's eat and try to talk about happier times."

Terrence brought the bowl of stew to the table and dished out generous portions. "A little of Andie's comfort food will help you feel better, Kat. It always does."

They shared memories of their families as they devoured Andrea's rich and appetizing veal stew. Andie's father and Katherine's father had been brothers from the same village in Ukraine as Elisabeth. They'd all kept the stories of their heritage alive. Yet it wasn't until the last year of Elisabeth's life—when she had written about the war years and its aftermath—that they all truly understood the traumatic events the family had endured.

Although Katherine's ex-husband, James, had frowned on her having any close girlfriends, Andrea's friendship and place in their life had never been negotiable, as Kat had firmly established with him from the beginning of their union. Andrea was family, after all. His complete disconnect from his own family left him incapable of valuing the feelings Kat shared with hers, but he tolerated them.

James had actually grown to like Andrea and Terrence. Their shared interest in cycling helped, and they all got together several times a year. A big deal for him. When James had been too busy with his law practice—which was most of the time—Kat often spent weekends in St. Jacobs on Andrea and Terrence's organic farm. She was close to their three children and their countless number of pets—past and present.

Now the three of them laughed until their sides ached as they tidied up after dinner, recounting tales of some of their more memorable pets. Kat was sure all the years of being exposed to so many cats and dogs had helped her welcome Picasso into her life during her exchange at the farmhouse in Provence. She felt she had learned significant lessons from that sweet yellow Lab.

"So when are you and Philippe picking up your new pup?" Terrence asked.

"Good question. We might have to wait for another litter. It was supposed to be this month, but we'll have to rethink that now."

Andrea nodded. "That was such a wonderful Christmas gift, though! Philippe has a way with surprises, doesn't he?"

"He does. That gift was totally unexpected! I can't think of anything I would love more right now; we're both so excited. We'd even been considering names for it over the holidays."

The talk turned serious as they pondered what the next days, weeks, or months would hold for Molly. They agreed this period of waiting was unbearable.

Andrea put a box of Laura Secord chocolates in front of Kat. "From Lucy! And here's a note she left. She's staying with her family to give us some time together."

Katherine smiled at the mention of Lucy, one of her colleagues from Dr. Henderson's pain management research group. When Kat had left for Antibes, Lucy had gladly accepted Kat's offer to house-sit since her own home situation was crowded and complicated.

"I'm looking forward to seeing her at some point while I'm here," Kat told them. "Hopefully I'll see the Hendersons too." Without realizing it, she toyed with the bracelet Philippe had given her.

"Oh, that's the bracelet you got for your birthday," Andrea said, taking Kat's hand. "It's even more beautiful than on Skype!" She examined each charm and laughed when she came to the piece of cheese. "Trust Philippe the *fromager*!"

Reaching for another chocolate and grinning, Katherine told her she seldom took the bracelet off.

Terrence left them chatting in the kitchen after he insisted on cleaning up. It wasn't long before Katherine was yawning and Andrea insisted she go to bed.

They held each other in a long embrace as they said goodnight. "Thanks for all you've done for Molly. I'm sorry that's what brought me back, but it's so nice to be able to hug you again."

Andrea stepped back and nodded, still holding Kat's hand.

"I love you, Andie."

"Me more," her cousin replied, as she had all their lives.

Lying in her old bed, the anxiety that had visited Katherine before rose to the surface again. *What am I doing? How can I simply walk away from everything? This is my home . . . Is my love for Philippe enough to leave all I've ever known?*

A deep sleep pulled the curtain down on the disquiet that had appeared, as if from nowhere, to fragment her thinking.

Jet lag wakened Katherine at 3:00 a.m., and she automatically reached for Philippe. It took her a moment to realize where she was, and she forced herself to turn over and go back to sleep.

Awake again at 5:30, she slid her feet into the fleece-lined slippers by her bed. *Papucs,* her mother had long ago told her was their Hungarian name. From then on Kate had called them papoochkis. Now Kat also wrapped herself in the cozy housecoat she retrieved from her closet. There was comfort in their familiarity.

A dim light glowed from the kitchen as she tiptoed down the stairs. She wasn't surprised to see Andrea making tea.

"There's nothing like farm life to make a person an early riser!" Kat said, followed by a loud yawn. "I was pretty certain you would be up."

Andrea gave her a hug. "I didn't expect to see you down here for a while. You were sawing logs very nicely as I walked past your bedroom door."

"Wha . . . ? I don't snore!"

Andrea chuckled. "*Excusez-moi!* I have news for you, cousin dear."

Kat sat down, rubbing her eyes with a sleepy look of surprise. "Damn! That's embarrassing! Philippe has never said a word about me snoring. I wonder if I do that often."

"At our age, it's more common than not," Andrea said with a shrug and a laugh. "Terrence and I end up in separate bedrooms half the time."

"Now I feel weird. What if I've been snoring and Philippe hasn't mentioned it?"

Andrea chuckled. "Give it a rest. If he hasn't mentioned it, it's not an issue. It's okay, Kat, you're normal. Here, I've made a pot of tea and even have the lemon sliced."

Before sunrise, they were dressed and walking through the quiet, snowy streets. Every once in a while, Katherine would moan about snoring and Andrea would shush her.

Katherine considered telling Andrea about the anxiety that had plagued her the night before but decided against it. She was hoping it was just some weird reaction to the hasty return to her old surroundings.

It was easier to walk on the road than to navigate areas where the sidewalk had not been shoveled. "I can't get over the height of the snowbanks this year. It's been a long time since I remember them being so enormous," Kat remarked.

"No question, this has been a winter like the ones when we were kids," Andrea agreed.

Katherine grabbed a handful of snow as they walked and tossed it in the air. "I have to admit, I missed this a bit in France."

"You love it because it's been so frigid that nothing has melted. It's still pristine and white. Remind yourself how messy it normally is and you might not miss it so much! Besides . . . was that a complaint about the French Riviera? Seriously?"

Kat smiled. "Why would I ever complain about anything in the South of France? Even the bad days are good!"

CHAPTER THREE

They were back at the hospital by 10:00 a.m., with a drive-through detour on the way for Katherine's café mocha.

"It didn't take long for you to slip back into that habit," Terrence teased.

"Hey! It's my first morning in town," she replied. "Give me a break!"

The first person they saw as they exited the elevator was Father DeCarlo, talking to a nurse in the hallway. He was formally dressed, his white priest's collar contrasting with the black suit.

He quickly excused himself to greet them, at first shaking Kat's hand and then giving her a reserved hug. "It's so good of you to come. I know how much it will mean to Molly. There are some important documents to sign. If you like, I'll go with you when the office is ready."

"Thank you, Father. It's nice to see you, and we all appreciate your assistance. I know it's because of your influence that Molly had pulled together the documents in the first place!"

There seemed to be no change with Molly, but the attending nurse assured them she was improving slowly. They spent the morning taking turns at her bedside. Today, Katherine's emotions were more controlled.

One new addition to Molly's treatment was a set of earbuds attached to an iPod. Music was thought to be helpful to patients in her condition, the nurse told them. The fact that music was such a large part of Molly's life, through her teaching at schools and her jazz singing at the Blue Note, made the idea even more appropriate.

Kat checked the playlist; she knew this was Molly's kind of music, and she wondered who had chosen the tunes. A nurse told her Father DeCarlo had brought in the music, after talking with the doctor about it.

Shortly before noon, the priest returned to say he had received a phone call to bring Katherine to the business office.

"Andrea, why don't you come along too?" he asked. "Then you will also know precisely what Katherine has signed. It never hurts to have another set of eyes and ears."

The documentation was straightforward, with Kat signing as power of attorney, since Molly was incapacitated. She initialed Molly's living will to confirm her signature.

Fishing in her pocket for a tissue, Kat wiped her eyes. "Sorry. I hadn't expected to be so emotional about this. But I also feel good knowing that whatever is being done is what she wants."

Andrea nodded. "Molly influenced us to do this too. It was interesting how relieved we felt once we had gone through the process. Plus, our kids were most appreciative. They said they were glad we had made the difficult decisions for them."

"I better get my act together too. If I sign the papers in Canada, I wonder if that will apply in France. There's a lot to look into."

"Have you and Philippe checked into what sort of documentation you'll need to move permanently to France?" Terrence inquired as they made their way to Molly's room. "I imagine there's a lot of bureaucracy involved—from what I hear about the French."

Katherine felt the same surge of anxiety as the night before. "I . . . um . . . we . . . They do make some things difficult when it comes to paperwork." In actual fact, she and Philippe had done nothing. She had changed the subject more than once, with unexplained jitters, when Philippe brought it up.

"And there have been worrisome reports about the economy, the political situation over there. No concerns?" Terrence continued.

Kat considered his question. "Philippe and I talk about all of that, and really, where in the world are there not problems like that these days? He's such an optimist and he's turning me into one too. I know we will deal with whatever comes along, one day at a time, if I do stay." She couldn't believe her ears.

Andrea looked at her in surprise. "*If* you stay? Are you having doubts? Has Philippe asked you to marry him?"

"I don't know why I said 'if,' Andie. It just popped out. I'm not thinking straight. Has he asked me to marry him? No. Has he asked me to spend the rest of my life with him? Yes. The marriage part really isn't an issue for either one of us. The commitment is."

"And . . . ?"

"I don't believe there's any doubt, on his part or mine, that we are bound to each other forever."

"Kat, I wish you could see the love that radiates from your face when you speak about Philippe. I have no doubt about your commitment either. I'm so happy for you and . . ."

"You mean, *we're* so happy for you," Terrence interrupted. "That includes me too, Kat, and the kids. They can't wait to go over and visit you!"

Katherine's face betrayed her confusion. "I've been happy for me too, since the end of October when I decided to stay. I don't know why I'm having these anxieties and being so weird about it now. I'm sure it will pass."

At home later that afternoon, Kat's phone conversation with Philippe was subdued. When he asked what was wrong, she simply blamed it on feeling sad and depressed about Molly.

"*Tu me manques*. I miss you more than you can imagine, Minou. I want to come to you."

"I miss you too, *mon* Chou. I'm struggling now in ways I never anticipated. Give me time and I will explain."

"Whatever you need, but you are making me worried. Is Molly getting worse? Is that the problem?"

"No, in fact, I think she's getting better but it's so upsetting to think she might not be the same Molly when she wakes." Her voice cracked as she spoke.

"Oh, Kat, it's hard not be beside you now . . ."

"I'm so tired I can't think straight. Let's say *au revoir*, good-bye, now and talk tomorrow. *Je t'aime*, Philippe, *de tout mon coeur* . . . all my heart and more."

Terrence was busy with spreadsheets on his computer. He had left the hospital earlier and picked up a load of packing boxes for Kat. Now Andrea helped Katherine sort through cupboards and pack up more boxes to go to Goodwill.

"This feels like the clearinghouse of my life," Kat muttered.

"You've got a big job ahead of you, Kat, if you really are planning to leave here forever. Everything is exactly as you left it last summer. Lucy lived around your stuff very effectively."

Katherine looked chagrined. "Since my first night back here, I've had a growing awareness that I've been living in fantasyland while in France. I fell in love with Philippe and Provence and our life there, but I truly didn't stop to look at the big picture. That fact has hit me smack in the face now."

Andrea looked at the growing pile of boxes. "Molly is the priority here, so don't let this get to you. You have other issues to resolve, my dear Kat. I'll come back to help you again next week. When is Philippe coming to join you?"

Kat's shoulders slumped, and she shook her head in despair. "I don't know. I just don't know what to do . . ."

Kat's body clock was still out of whack, and she woke at 4:00 a.m.

After lying in bed, attempting to sort through jumbled thoughts, she stretched out on the carpet and eased into a peaceful morning yoga routine. *I must find the carton with my yoga things in it. I need to do this every day.*

She could hear Andrea and Terrence in the kitchen as she tiptoed downstairs after a shower. Kat knew they were anxious to get back to their farm and catch up on missed work from the past week.

After they enjoyed another of Andrea's hearty breakfasts, Terrence persuaded Kat to let them drive her to the subway.

"You know we'll be back in a flash if you need us, Kat," Andrea said with their good-byes in the car.

"I'm fine for now," Kat assured them as they dropped her off. She had insisted there was no need for them to go back to the hospital. It was her turn to take over the watch. *I can do it.*

Kat was heartened that there seemed to be a small improvement in Molly's condition. The bruising and swelling appeared to be diminishing, and the nurses confirmed it. "You missed the worst of that."

With the background noise of beeps and whirs from all the equipment, Kat read the morning newspaper aloud to Molly. Then she reminisced about their time together in France, laughing softly and urging Molly to wake up and remember with her.

She looked at Molly, helplessly lying there, tied up in tubes, bristles of hair beginning to appear on her head, and Kat could not shake her thoughts about the randomness of life. How some people have bad luck and others don't. Molly had endured so much negativity in her life and yet she had always been a good person. She didn't need this—*but of course, no one does.*

Kat thought back to their school days: she, a studious introvert, and Molly, the class clown—they still had inexplicably been drawn to each other. From the first time Molly went to Kat's house after school, she became part of their family. Elisabeth had seen through the facade of laughter and recognized a frightened little girl. Through the years Molly had spent countless overnights, sometimes bringing her younger brother to escape their violent home life.

In spite of it all, Molly had grown to be a strong, smart woman, although always a little on the edge of conventional behavior. Their connection had been tenuous when Katherine was married to James. However, ever since James had left, Molly had been back in her life stronger than ever. Kat knew their special friendship had played a major role in her becoming the person she now was: strong, independent, confident.

There was something about schmoozing with a trusted girlfriend that lent itself to soul baring and laughter and understanding. It made Kat even more resentful of James, and annoyed with herself, to think she had missed out on that for so many years.

She took Molly's hand in hers again and kept talking, begging her to get better, enticing her with plans.

Father DeCarlo came by several times during the day. The more Katherine spent with him, the more she began to see beyond his clerical collar. She had often teased Molly about his dark good looks and accused her of going to Mass because the priest was a "hottie." Molly always had a flippant response that sometimes caused Kat to wonder vaguely what that was all about.

Now she simply appreciated his friendly manner and the spiritual care he was bringing to Molly's bedside, knowing it would mean a lot to

Molly. Molly had never lost her faith and sometimes teased Katherine for her lack of it.

From a conversation Katherine had with him, it was clear Molly had talked about Kat with the priest. "Katherine, your friendship with Molly has been so important to her. She sees you more as a sister—and that's very special."

Katherine had told him their friendship meant the world to her as well.

"Please call me Tony. The people in my parish feel better calling me Father, but I would like you to use my name, if you don't mind."

They'd chatted easily about many things and Katherine was glad for his company. His personality was engaging, and his passion for his street ministry was evident, as was his dry sense of humor.

The nurses also became sources of kindness for Katherine. They always stopped for a few moments to chat with Father DeCarlo and Katherine. As they went about daily care, they enjoyed Kat's stories about Molly. More than once, they expressed to Kat how nice it was to know the personal side of the woman they otherwise knew only as a patient.

The unit was busy and the atmosphere intense. Katherine sensed it was almost a relief for the nurses to pause in their demanding routine with a patient who looked like she would live.

The head nurse in charge of Molly's care, Roslyn, made certain to explain what they were doing and how they viewed Molly's progress. "You may not see the small improvements as we do. I know how it might look like nothing is happening, but she is coming along. I assure you."

As the hours slowly passed, Katherine was pleased to note she was doing a better job of keeping her tears in check. She had never considered herself a crybaby, but the specter of death at Molly's age had put Katherine's emotions into a spin. She'd never given much thought to her own mortality. Life just kept on going. But now, facing the possibility of death with someone so close to her had a profound impact.

She shared those feelings with Father DeCarlo that afternoon. Father DeCarlo . . . Tony—that was still hard for her—had said a lot that afternoon about the power of faith and positive thinking. She needed to focus on that. He had made a point that one did not need to be religious to draw on that power, although it certainly helped, he had added with a smile. And this made her smile, through her tears, when she lost it at that moment.

Their chat had brought back memories of her mother and her "what doesn't kill us makes us stronger" mantra. The priest had essentially been saying the same thing to her. She certainly knew her mother had lived a life of faith and strength without being religious. The role model was there, loud and clear. How Kat missed her.

As she paced the corridor for a change of scenery, Kat couldn't help recalling the crisis in her life when James walked out. A twinge reminded her how gutted she had been as she read his note that day in the kitchen. Their wedding anniversary. The beginning of the rest of her life. Dwelling on that thought, she nodded to herself and wondered how the next phase of Molly's life would play out.

"Please let there be one," she whispered out loud. "I'll be here to help with whatever she needs. I will not let her down."

With Wi-Fi in the reception area, Katherine took breaks to keep up with e-mails. She was touched to hear from some of the women in her expat walking group. There was even a message from Bernadette, saying she hoped all was well, and Annette had written to say the yoga class was sending their best wishes.

Her friend Véronique kept in touch regularly. Sometimes it was simply a philosophical thought or a photo of something she knew would be of interest. Katherine knew she was preparing some of her sought-after weaving for a Côte d'Azur art show in the spring.

In fact, Véronique had persuaded Katherine to consider entering some of her photography in that show. Thinking about it now, Kat was not sure she would even be there. Everything seemed so up in the air. Molly's well-being was her priority. *If I don't look after her, who will?*

Hearing from friends in France reinforced her sense of home over there. Kat felt annoyed for losing confidence in the choices she had been making in the previous months. She knew it had nothing to do with her feelings for Philippe. These sudden uncertainties were upsetting her.

Taking the subway early that evening, she tried to feel optimistic about Molly's recovery. She hoped it was not simply wishful thinking.

The motion of the train took her back to the many years this subway had been her daily transportation. *I've done a lot of thinking and read a long list of books riding the rails like this.* She was reminded of how she had loved her work, the intellectual growth it had involved, and the satisfying challenges of research—all left behind when she chose to stay in France. *But it was my choice,* she argued with herself.

There was leftover stew for dinner, after Philippe's call.

They Skyped this time but did not talk long, although they were happy to see each other on-screen. Words seemed not to come easily. It felt bizarre, they agreed, for their contact to be solely by phone, Skype, and text, after the intensity of their life together the past few months.

Philippe seemed a bit tense, as if something was on his mind. He denied it when Katherine asked, replying, "It's just strange not to have you here all of a sudden."

At the same time, Katherine was becoming aware that having some space between them perhaps was a good thing. There might be nothing wrong with her taking a long look at the changes in her life.

Her three-month home exchange had turned into a new life. A new her. *Was it real?* she wondered. *Have I simply been seduced by the lure of the narrow cobblestone streets, the history, and the beauty that surrounds me there? Is my attraction to Philippe part of the hypnotic spell under which I find myself? Why am I asking myself all of these questions now, when I've been feeling so strong and positive about my life in France?*

Blaming those thoughts on jet lag, she pulled herself into the present.

Alone in the house for the first time, she walked from room to room, pausing to soak in the memories, feeling like the child who grew up there. Every once in a while, she would become conscious of her age and see herself as her mother was at the same age.

That only served to raise more doubts. *Am I too old for all this? Too old to start all over? What if Philippe gets tired of me?*

In the past year, she had often found herself surprised to accept how her life could change at this late stage. It had become clear that anything could happen, no matter when, if she wished to make it so.

Her old bedroom brought back memories of Molly again. How many times had the two young friends whispered and giggled to each other when Molly had stayed over? How many nights had Elisabeth put her arms around Molly as she cried in fear, having run from her father's abusive behavior? And how many times had her young brother, Shawn, followed along behind Molly, asleep in a sleeping bag at the foot of the bed?

Kat stopped to sit on her old bed, surrounded by the furniture and ghosts of her youth. She had brought a few storage boxes up with her and began to pack things.

Then she went downstairs to her mother's favorite armchair. Upholstered in pale-pink brocade, it was soft and comfortable. Elisabeth had sat there and watched out the window for Kat to arrive for a visit. Now Kat closed her eyes, trying to channel Elisabeth.

Your spirit surrounds me, Anyu. I can feel it. How I miss you.

There was no one Katherine knew who faced stressful issues with more calm and wisdom than her mother had throughout her life. After all the horror and tragedy Elisabeth had experienced during World War ll and then the deep and loyal love she had shared with her husband, Jozsef, into their eighties, she had owned a sixth sense about life.

Kat's mind wandered, thinking how much fun it would be to tell Elisabeth about Philippe and France and everything that was happening. Then she thought how none of this would have happened if Elisabeth were still alive. Kat would never have gone on that home exchange in the first place. *Life does work in mysterious ways . . .*

Her gaze settled on a collection of photographs in silver frames on the small side table. Elisabeth had chosen the photos, then Kat had purchased the frames and placed the grouping for her to enjoy.

There was such hope and happiness on the faces of her parents as young immigrants to Canada from their small village in Hungary. In spite of the horror, cruelty, and betrayal they had witnessed and endured during the war years, their strong souls survived. Pure love radiated from their simple wedding portrait. Those same smiles, somewhat tempered with age, also shone from the photo Kat had taken at the intimate family celebration for their sixtieth wedding anniversary.

There were a few small black-and-white images of Kat as a child with each parent, holding poignant memories. One collage frame held three small photos with her proud parents on each of her university graduation days. Elisabeth had insisted on those.

Finally, she smiled at a selfie taken with her mother on their last Christmas morning together. She could almost hear Elisabeth's words. "My sweet Katica, always remember what doesn't kill us . . ." There was no need to complete the sentence. Mother and daughter had shared a warm embrace before Kat snapped the photo. "You will be fine, my darling daughter."

Those photos will all go with me . . . when I go . . . if I go . . .

An intense pang of loss shot through her. Coming home wasn't necessarily going to be easy. When she had been coping with the early days of grief—first with her marriage ending and then the loss of Elisabeth—she'd read somewhere that feeling pain could be turned into a positive thing. The strategy was to make each ache a reminder of pleasant memories. Kat was determined to work on that.

There's no question my parents left me with a lifetime of good memories. Being back in this house brings those memories alive once more. This is home. Toronto is home. Fifty-six years of home. Can I really walk away from it?

Checking her e-mail before going to bed, she discovered Philippe had sent her a message that contained only the audio of Ella Fitzgerald singing "All the Things You Are." They had played and swayed to it often in the quiet candlelight of their apartment. Philippe told her every word seemed to be written to express his feelings for her.

The sweetness of his gesture sent a rush of warmth through her. Kat tossed and turned as she tried to fall asleep in the midst of confusion.

CHAPTER FOUR

Kat peered out the window in Molly's room, thinking about Philippe and how the day they parted in Paris seemed so long ago. She had wakened eager to hear his voice after worrying herself to sleep.

Both of them were consumed with the emotion of the words from the song he had sent. Their morning phone conversation had been filled with passion and longing. After she hung up, Kat realized she had just engaged in erotic phone sex for the first time in her life. She put her hands to her face as a hot flush rushed to her cheeks while a smile played on her lips. *Better late than never . . .*

Snow was falling lightly again today. Katherine always felt a sense of peace watching the swirling delicate flakes.

She was startled at the sound of a familiar voice.

"G'day, gorgeous."

"Nick! I can't believe you're here!" she exclaimed as she spun around. "You're making a habit of turning up at the most unexpected moments!"

His customary dazzling grin was replaced with a subdued expression as his eyes flickered over to Molly from the doorway. Kat reached him quickly and welcomed his comforting embrace.

"I came as soon as Tim told me about Molly. I spoke to Philippe and he filled me in with a few more details. I was just across the lake in New York, and I thought perhaps I could help somehow . . . with my plane . . . or I can hire a Medevac to take her wherever the best treatment is. I also had to fast talk my way past Nurse Ratched just now."

Deeply touched by his concern, Kat began to cry, her head still on his shoulder.

Nick patted her gently on the back.

Fumbling for a tissue in her pocket, she stepped back and wiped her eyes. "It's so thoughtful of you to come. Incredible, really. Th . . . thanks. I needed that hug."

Nick walked over to Molly, leaning down to kiss her forehead as he took her hand in his. Kat went to the other side of the bed and slipped out Molly's earbuds.

"Hey, Moll, it's your Aussie buddy," he said. "Graham sends a big smackaroo too. I hope you can hear me." He looked across the bed and raised his eyebrows questioningly at Kat.

She shrugged, her face hopeful. "We're told Molly may hear us, so we keep talking to her. We're not giving up."

She motioned to two chairs in the reception area, and they sat down. In a quiet voice, she shared all the medical staff had told her so far.

"Her most serious injury is described as severe brain trauma, and they are keeping her in this induced coma to assist with reduction of swelling. This morning they were able to do a functional MRI to check her responses. Her hearing is fine. Her motor functions seem to be preserved, based on muscle response. What is still undetermined are her intellectual capabilities."

Nick listened thoughtfully. "What sort of tests have they done so far?"

"An EEG done at the same time as the MRI indicated an underfunction in the frontal lobe and temporal lobe. That has the doctors concerned. But as the swelling subsides, the function may improve. That's the hope, anyway."

"So what does 'underfunction in the frontal lobe and temporal lobe' mean, in layman's terms?"

"Speech and memory," Kat said with a frown.

They looked at each other and sighed.

"Time, Kat. Give it time."

She nodded, wiping away a rogue tear.

"As you saw, she also has a fractured femur and a combination broken collarbone and shoulder. She will need physiotherapy, but they are injuries from which she'll recover. It's the unknowns about the head trauma that are concerning."

"What do you think? Should I talk to the doctors about other treatment possibilities? I don't want to be pushy, but if there are alternatives, I could help. We can fly her wherever would be best."

"Sure. The staff here is amazing and the hospital specializes in head-trauma injuries. I doubt there is anything better, but it never hurts to inquire. Come to the nurses' station and I'll introduce you."

Roslyn listened as Nick explained his thoughts. She asked him to wait while she checked to see if one of the attending doctors was available.

The two friends remained standing beside each other. Nick took Kat's hand in his.

"What can I do for you?" he asked, his voice low and solemn. "Anything?"

She shook her head. "Thanks. All I need is for Molly to get better."

He squeezed her hand, and they stood like that until Roslyn returned to the desk.

In her brisk and efficient manner, the nurse said, "Dr. Primeau will be available shortly and suggests you go to his office."

"Want to come, Kat?" he asked, giving her hand a gentle pat as he let it go.

Roslyn interrupted, "Katherine, you'll have to sign a form giving Dr. Primeau permission to speak openly to Mr. Field about Miss Malone's condition."

"Absolutely. Nick, since I've just been updated yesterday, you go ahead and see what you can find out. I'll stay with Molly."

He gave her a wink and a nod and walked to the elevator.

"Thanks, Roslyn," Kat said. She appreciated the professional but warm attitudes of the staff attending to Molly. There was a sense that, in spite of its enormous size, this hospital focused on taking care of the family as well as the patients.

"Molly has great friends. Not everyone without family has that," said Roslyn as she gave Kat a sympathetic smile. "She's a lucky lady."

"We're the lucky ones. Just wait until she comes out of this and you get to know her."

Kat went back into Molly's room and took out one of her earbuds, holding it to her own ear. The mellow tones of Diana Krall crooned a favorite melody that Molly often included in her sets at the Blue Note.

"Come on, girlfriend. I want to hear you singing this song again soon," Kat whispered into Molly's ear. She continued to sit next to Molly, talking nonstop about her time in Antibes and her life with Philippe. As she spoke, her heart filled with gratitude for how her life had turned around.

Now if only Molly's would do the same.

After a while, she picked up a book of Nora Ephron essays they all had been taking turns reading to Molly. Andrea had brought it to the hospital when Molly was first admitted so people could do something rather than just sit in silence. She also knew that Ephron was a favorite of Molly's. It helped to laugh. Plus, the nurses had said it was a good idea for Molly to hear the voices of people she knew cared about her.

There were also books of poetry by Maya Angelou and Ogden Nash. Father DeCarlo had left those.

Since ICU visiting rules allowed only family, Kat was thankful the hospital had accepted Andrea and Terrence as kin. Father DeCarlo had vouched for them, and now she vouched for Nick.

Nick was gone for just over half an hour before he walked back into the room, carrying two Starbucks cups.

He gave Kat a warm, lingering look. "I remembered you moaning about missing your café mocha in Antibes, before Choopy's started making them for you. So I thought I'd grab you one now."

"Thanks! What a good memory you have! Oddly enough, when I got back to Toronto and rushed to have my first mocha, all I could think about was how I missed my *café au lait* at Le Vieil Antibes. Crazy how things change! What did the doc say?"

Nick began with a surprising chuckle. "Guess where Dr. Primeau studied for his medical degree? In Melbourne, Australia! So he was very happy to chat about how much he loved my homeland. It was the perfect icebreaker."

"Such a small world! But what did he say about Molly?"

"He's very optimistic. Said she was lucky that her skull was not fractured. He feels they will begin to bring her out of this induced state by the end of next week and then it will be clear whether there will be issues to address. He refused to speculate at this point. As he said, 'False hope leads to disappointment.'"

"That scares me."

"Kat, the bloke appears to go by the book. Very cut-and-dried. But very smart. I liked him and I think we need to trust what they are doing. He said there was nowhere that she would get any better care than right here. People come from all over the world to this hospital for their neurological expertise."

"I'd read that, and Terrence and Andrea told me that too. And the nurses say such positive things."

"So that settles that. Molly is getting the best care possible. Now, how about you? Are you getting the best care possible? You seem—not without good cause—pretty stressed."

Kat's face tightened, and she took a long drink of her mocha before responding. She nodded slowly. "I'm as okay as I can be. I'm worried about Molly, of course . . . nothing else matters at this point."

She swallowed and blinked back more tears. "Until her accident, I've never stopped to think seriously about how alone she is in the world."

"She must have other friends, people she works with . . ."

"Of course, there's the staff at the school and her music students and the people who love to hear her sing at the Blue Note, but they're really acquaintances. And my cousin Andrea cares about her, but Molly has never reached out to her unless I'm around, though I know that will change after this. Andrea had no idea Molly was so alone. It was such a coincidence Molly was visiting with them when she had the accident. I don't know what would have happened otherwise."

Katherine held Molly's hand and looked at her sadly for a moment. Nick walked over to stand silently by the window.

Katherine added, in almost a whisper, "The only other person I know she's close to is a Catholic priest. You'll meet him. He's very nice and when Molly's brother died, he stepped in and was a tremendous help and support to her. He comes by every day to see her here. But that's it. There's no one else who really knows what's happening in her life."

Nick's face took on a somber expression. "That's not good. Everyone needs people to share life with. To help each other, care for each other, laugh and cry with each other."

"She's always been a loner."

"I would never have guessed that about her. She's such a vibrant personality, so much fun to be with. What about guys? No one?"

"Y'know, she's had an ongoing affair for a few years—at least, she alludes to it from time to time. Friends with benefits, as she says, some hot Italian lover. But I have no idea who he is. I just know Molly is a straight shooter and if she says something, it's true."

"Maybe you should try to find him."

"I wouldn't know where to start . . ." Kat's eyes filled again. "No one should be this alone. All I know is that I'll stay here with her as long as she needs me. That's a given."

"She's lucky to have you, Kat. You're a true friend. Now, tell me how you feel about being back home. It's been a while, right?"

She smiled ruefully. "I'm feeling conflicted about being in my old house, without my mother and surrounded by memories of her and my father that make me both happy and sad. I think I'm caught up in a bit of grieving."

"No doubt. It takes a while to come to terms with losing our parents—losing anyone, of course. Grief is hard. It's different for every person."

Their eyes met, and Kat felt his sympathy before her face clouded.

"You've got to be a tad jet-lagged too," he said.

"For sure. On top of all that, I'm faced with the reality of the choices I've made about my life this past year and . . ." She paused.

"And? Any regrets?"

A light came back into her eyes. "No regrets. Just an awareness of how different my life has become. This trip is a reminder of what I am abandoning, and it's affecting me more than I thought it would. I realize I have a few issues to sort out without being under the mesmerizing spell of the South of France."

"You're carrying quite a load right now. How about letting me take you to dinner tonight and I'll attempt to lighten it a bit with my irresistible charm and wit?"

Kat snorted in spite of herself. Nick did have a way about him. "How can I refuse that?"

"Right. Besides, it would be pretty rude to turn me down after I flew here just to see you—and Molly, of course, " he quickly corrected himself.

Looking serious again, Kat suggested they make it an early evening before her jet lag kicked in. As if on cue, she stifled a yawn.

"Okay, let's stay here until you're ready to leave Molly for the evening. We'll go somewhere close. I'm sure you know some good places, and then I'll get you home. I've got a car and driver on call while I'm here. Or do you have a car?"

Katherine smiled to herself, shaking her head, as she was reminded of Nick's luxurious lifestyle. "No, I've been taking the subway back and forth. It's so convenient."

"Perfect. Now pass that book to me and I'll share my dulcet tones with the bald and beautiful Ms. Malone for a while."

"Read her some more of this Nora Ephron book. It's hilarious, and I hope with all my heart that somehow our words are reaching into the depths where Molly lies."

Katherine's cell phone vibrated while Nick was reading. Suffused with sudden warmth as she saw the call was from Philippe, she left the room. The misgivings and anxious thoughts that were gaining a foothold in her mind faded at the sound of his voice.

"*Ma belle*, how are you doing? Is there anything new with Molly? I miss you and want to put my arms around you right now."

Katherine swallowed a lump in her throat at the sound of his voice. "I wish that could happen, *mon amour*, but you are with me all the time. I never remove the bracelet you gave me—*jamais*—and it helps me feel you are here."

There was an electric silence for a moment before Katherine continued. "There's good news about Molly. The doctors say the swelling in her brain has lessened dramatically. They may begin to waken her in a day or so. Hopefully . . ."

She could hear Philippe blow out a sigh of relief.

"Oh . . . and Nick is here!"

"*Incroyable!*" Philippe exclaimed. "He is unbelievable. He called me yesterday. Tim e-mailed when I got back from Paris to see what had happened with the whole situation with Dimitri and Idelle. I told him about Molly's accident and he told Nick."

There was a pause before he continued. "And now Nick's there! He didn't mention he was going to Toronto."

"That's something, isn't it? He was just in New York, though, so . . . not so far . . ." She told him what the doctor had said to Nick about Molly and that they all agreed she could not be in a better place.

"Nick's reading to Molly right now. The staff think the sounds of our voices help her subconscious."

"Should I look into flights?" Katherine sensed a new urgency in his words as he continued. "I have meetings with Didier and his crew tomorrow; you will be very excited when I tell you how plans on our villa restoration are progressing! I should be able to come to Toronto in two or three days. *D'accord?*"

Kat was shocked at her hesitation. "Maybe not yet. There's nothing to do but sit here in the hospital. Stay and take care of things there for now."

Philippe's voice became softer and deeper. "These few days without you have been longer than I might have imagined. You've become such a part of me."

Katherine pressed the phone to her ear as the warmth of those words spread through her. The tone of Philippe's voice, the way he expressed his feelings, and that very sexy French accent always thrilled her.

"I feel the same. It's just not the right time to come," she replied, her voice heavy with indecision.

There was an uneasy silence before she continued. "Hold on and I'll put Nick on the phone. I miss you. We'll talk tomorrow."

She took the phone in to Nick and he left the room for several minutes. When he came back, he handed Kat her phone and said, "Philippe is one hell of a decent bloke."

"No question," she replied, feeling upset with herself over her less than satisfying conversation with him.

The nurses told them it was a good time to leave for the evening.

Katherine described to Nick how the staff would turn Molly and prepare her for the night. One of the nurses smiled when Kat motioned to the narrow glass vase on the table next to Molly's bed. "We're still trying to see if we can solve the red-rose mystery."

Katherine gave her a thumbs-up as she reached for her coat and scarf. Nick helped Kat on with her coat. "Meaning?"

She explained, "Each morning since Molly's been here, a fresh rose is placed in that vase and we have no idea how. No one is allowed in at night."

A nurse interjected, "We monitor everything and the only people coming in here at night, apart from medical staff, are the clergy. Rabbis, ministers, priests, imams, pastors—we get them all. They come to pray and offer comfort and are in and out at unusual hours. God doesn't have to worry about visiting hours."

The hospital was a few minutes around the corner from the office where Katherine had spent the last fifteen years of her professional life. She knew exactly where they should go for dinner. The family-run Casa Mia was a welcoming trattoria and the food was guaranteed to please.

Nick put his arm around Kat's shoulder, with an exaggerated shiver, and pulled her close as they walked. "*Brrr!* It's bloody frigid here! I'm expecting polar bears to come out of the shadows. Is your winter always this cold?"

Her breath coming out in frozen puffs, Katherine explained they were having an unusual subzero cold spell and that sometimes conditions were quite mild. "Not this year, though. Sorry!"

Welcoming the warmth of the restaurant, they were seated quickly. Crispy bread pulled straight from the oven, and two glass containers of olive oil and balsamic were set on the table immediately. After they had chosen their meals, Nick asked, "White or red, Kat? What's your pleasure?"

Katherine agreed with his choice of a bottle of Amarone and settled back in her chair.

"That was a big sigh," Nick exclaimed.

Katherine looked surprised for a moment and then answered with a wry smile. "I wasn't aware it was so obvious. This feels like the first time I've relaxed since I got here."

The waiter arrived with the wine and, after Nick approved the choice, poured each a glass. Raising his, Nick said, "Here's to Molly and to the friendship we all share. Yours with her has been so long and meaningful, and ours has been very short, but meaningful in its own way. May all of this long continue."

Katherine raised her glass in return and nodded. They continued talking about friendship and how life works in unexpected ways to bring people together. Kat inquired about Nick's close friend, Graham.

"Ah, the dear bloke and his family are all well. I'm hoping they will all come to France this summer. Just think, it was thanks to Molly that Graham and I got to meet you ladies that fateful night in Antibes!"

Laughing at the memory, Kat agreed, "Too true!" Then her expression changed to a concerned frown and she took a sip of her wine.

Nick reached over and took her hand. She could feel the emotion in his touch and his voice. In spite of his bravado, she knew he was a man who cared deeply. "It's so hard to see someone you love in Molly's situation. Trust me, I truly feel optimistic after meeting with the doc."

He patted the back of her hand and then changed the mood by giving her a wide-eyed look of delight as a plate of delicious-looking antipasto arrived.

They declared themselves ravenous and dug in as the focus of conversation switched to food. Kat reminded herself she needed to pay better attention to what she was eating. Her diet the past few days had been muffins and mochas.

The lighthearted combination of great conversation, laughter, and wine brought back memories of times they had spent together in Antibes. The intimacy of some of those moments caused Kat to avert her eyes and quickly change the subject. She felt unsettled as to whether it was embarrassment or remembered pleasure that was making her squirm.

We did share some moments . . .

After a decaf cappuccino, Nick called his driver, who was waiting outside when they left the restaurant.

"Katherine, this is Mohammed. He will get you home safely." Pointing across the street, he said, "I'm staying at the Marriott and have a conference call to make, so I'll dash."

As the driver held open the car door, Nick kissed Kat's cheeks lightly, in the French way. "This was a lovely evening, Kat. I've missed you." His eyes held hers, saying more than his words.

Kat glanced away briefly but smiled warmly. "Thanks for coming to Toronto, Nick. It's wonderful to see you. I appreciate you being here . . . and I know Molly would too."

"Hey. What are friends for? Call me when you're ready to leave home tomorrow morning and Mohammed will collect you."

As she began to protest, Nick put a finger to her lips. "Shhh . . . let me do what I can."

On the way home, she chatted with Mohammed, who told her he traveled with "Monsieur Nicholas" everywhere he went these days. At her urging, he disclosed he was from Syria and still had family in the midst of the raging conflicts. When she asked why they had not left, he explained that they were reluctant to leave their lives behind in the beginning; when it got so bad that they finally decided to flee, they could not get out. "I'm sorry," Kat said. "It's so difficult to find words to talk about the tragic events there. What a worry and sorrow it must be for you."

Katherine felt a tug at her heart and could not help but think sadly of the somewhat similar tragic experiences her parents' families had undergone in World War II.

They reached her house in what seemed like minutes, and the car sat in the driveway until she unlocked her door and waved. As she removed her layers of outerwear, she smiled and shook her head, feeling disbelief and pleasure at Nick's sudden appearance.

Katherine called Andrea and Terrence to fill them in on the day and said there was no point in them going back to the hospital just yet. They were relieved to hear that Nick was there to give her support. "We'll have to meet him one of these days, after all you've told us!"

Next, she found the box with her yoga gear and, after changing into yoga clothes, unrolled her mat on the living room floor. She had been thinking about it all day, missing that part of her routine. She stretched and warmed up before she focused on a solid hour of positions. There was an immediate calm she felt from doing yoga that was unique to anything else she did.

The exercise, combined with the food and wine from dinner, made her feel mellow. For the first time since arriving in Toronto, she slept through until her 7:00 a.m. alarm sounded.

CHAPTER FIVE

Katherine phoned Nick as she was going into the subway station.

"It's so easy, and I needed the walk," she told him when he admonished her for not using Mohammed. "I'll be at the hospital in twenty minutes."

She enjoyed the subway ride. It had been part of her daily routine for so many years. *Past history,* she thought as the familiar stops rolled by and she arrived at the hospital.

Stepping out of the elevator to Molly's floor, Katherine chuckled as Roslyn blurted, "Another rose!" Another nurse shook her head. "No one gets in here at night. It's bizarre!"

Father DeCarlo and Nick were sitting together in the reception area and motioned for Katherine to hurry to Molly's room.

There was a collection of white coats around Molly's bed. Dr. Primeau, the neurologist, nodded to Katherine and waved her into the room.

"We're beginning to bring Molly out of her deep sleep today. We're slowly reducing the dosage of her drugs, and in a few days she will be fully conscious. We're hoping for the best in terms of her function levels. However, we want to alert you that there are no guarantees."

Katherine's voice betrayed her anxiety as she asked what the outcome might be.

"It's still too early to say for certain. Today and tomorrow will be critical. No visitors. You and your friend can spend a few minutes with her now. Roslyn will text you with updates throughout the day. We have asked Father DeCarlo to look in on Ms. Malone, as her records indicate she is Catholic and knows him."

A nurse pointed to her watch and said to Katherine, "Ten minutes."

"Please ask my friend and Father DeCarlo to also come in."

As Nick and Father DeCarlo walked in, Katherine said, "Obviously you two have introduced yourselves."

They nodded. Katherine repeated what the doctor had told her as she held Molly's hand and lightly rubbed her arm. They spoke quietly and the priest assured them he would stay all day with Molly. "I'll keep you updated as the day goes on," he said, his eyes filled with compassion. "I know this won't be easy for you."

"Nor you. Knowing you are here with Molly makes all the difference."

Katherine was aware of a slight flicker in the priest's eyes that communicated he was as concerned as she.

Sitting together in the reception area, Katherine and Nick planned their unexpected day off.

Kat had just texted the news about Molly to Philippe when her phone vibrated in her pocket. Philippe was on the line, saying he intended to book a flight in a few days. "You sound anxious, Minou," he said. "Whatever is going on with Molly, I want to be there to support you, even if I only stay for a short time."

Kat wanted him with her but also felt increasingly conflicted about it. She was struggling with emotions that she couldn't quite identify. Something did not feel right.

Nick offered to send his plane for Philippe, speaking briefly to Philippe about arrangements. A direct flight from Nice would be a lot more convenient than having to go through Paris again.

"Nick, your generosity knows no bounds," Katherine said, touched by the earnestness of his desire to help.

His laugh was tinged with modesty. "I hope you'll take this the right way."

Kat looked at him with a puzzled expression as he went on. "I have so much money it's ridiculous. If I can use it to do something good for my friends, that's the most satisfying thing I can think of . . . along with the charitable foundation I established, of course. I didn't start off this way, y'know. I got very lucky, very early on with some big business deals, worked my ass off for many years, and the circumstances of my life changed."

"I remember you telling me your story when I was in Antibes," Katherine recalled. She also remembered being impressed with what a down-to-earth man he was, in spite of his immense wealth. Google had told her about his Field Foundation and its philanthropic work around the world. Brash as he might be, Nicholas Field was not a man to brag about his accomplishments.

Nick shifted awkwardly in his chair and changed the subject. "Okay, now we have the day free, so let's do something that takes our minds off everything else—especially our dear Molly. Let's hope today goes well in that hospital room."

Katherine nodded wordlessly, quelling an empty feeling in the pit of her stomach. She sent a silent plea into the universe that Molly would come through all this.

Nick's voice broke into her thoughts. "Okay, gorgeous. Show me your fair city . . . even if we are dressed like Nanook of the North! Gawd, it's bloody freezing! I'll call Mo and you direct the tour."

It did happen to be one of the coldest days on record, Kat told him. "I even put on my thermal underwear this morning. The car is a great idea." She was grateful for the distraction the day would provide. Her preoccupation with the unknowns of Molly's condition was consuming her.

The first stop was a nearby coffee shop. The rest of the morning was spent driving around the most significant downtown neighborhoods.

"The street scenes look dystopian," Nick commented. Clouds of vapor spewed from sidewalk grates into the frigid air. Pedestrians bundled in heavy, funereal winter wear rushed along, their faces obscured by scarves and fur-lined hoods pulled down to their brows. "Anonymity assured by the choice of clothing. Do you think they're heading to or from the Apocalypse?" he wondered.

"I've cycled through this entire city and know it like the back of my hand, but I've never stopped to observe it like this, or in weather like this," Kat told him, shaking her head. "It's a very different perspective."

She recognized immediately what was missing, compared to the South of France: color. "Everything is just so gray, so dreary."

They drove slowly through the almost-empty streets of the normally bustling communities of Kensington Market, Little Italy, Chinatown, and Little India.

"These areas are where we'll find some zest!" Katherine assured him. The vibrant signage and windows stuffed with flashy displays of everything from food to fabric to intriguing bric-a-brac demanded a casual stroll through their streets.

"Looks like I've got to return in warmer weather," Nick commented. "I could spend hours on these streets and the choice of restaurants appears endless!"

They also cruised through the exclusive residential areas of Forest Hill and Rosedale and other well-kept neighborhoods. Nick commented on the intermingling of mixed-income areas and street upon street of well-maintained aging architecture. "For the most part, it looks to me like a city that works."

"I must admit it's a great place to live—when the weather is good, that is. Minus the charm and history that seduces me in France," Kat said wistfully.

"You obviously know your way around, Kat. That's a sign of really appreciating what a community has to offer."

"I do love Toronto. It's safe and clean. There's great theater and excellent restaurants. I'm glad I grew up here."

She continued her running commentary while Nick kept her laughing with his droll observations combined with positive comments about the city in general. He praised the obvious multicultural blend of communities and insisted they get out of the car for a stroll when she took him by Graffiti Alley.

"Put your hat and mitts on, darlin'! What a fantastic idea this alley is!"

"I was biking around here the first time I happened upon it," she said as they walked along the alley. The walls and backs of buildings were covered in colorful and imaginative graffiti art. "It's awesome, isn't it?"

Nick stopped to admire and exclaim several times. "So many street artists are incredibly talented. It's tremendous recognition for the city to give them places to do their thing. We've got some spots like this in Sydney too."

The car was waiting for them at the end of the street. "Okay, that was fun," Katherine agreed, "but the next time you want to get out, you're on your own. I think we've hit a new low in temperatures today!"

Blowing on his hands and rubbing them together, Nick nodded. "Enough of that."

"I'm feeling rather proud of my hometown as I show you around," Katherine admitted. "But I don't get the same buzz I do from the ancient architecture, settings, and history from the villages in France. Glass and steel don't do it for me like the colors of Nice do, for instance."

At one point, Nick put his arm around Kat and pulled her to him. "Here's what I see. You may love your fair city, but you are *in love* with the South of France. It couldn't be more obvious."

With a faraway look in her eyes, Kat replied, "That's a good way of putting it. I think you may be right."

"We did have some fine times on the Côte d'Azur, gorgeous!" Nick reminisced. His gaze held hers a little longer than was comfortable. Katherine lowered her eyes before turning to look out the window. She couldn't help smiling.

"Yes, we did! Especially when Molly and Graham were with us," she agreed, choosing to be selective about the times she was remembering.

At 11:00 a.m., Kat received a reassuring text from Roslyn that simply stated: "Things are progressing normally. Next report at one p.m."

As noon approached, Nick surprised Kat by scrolling through some information on his phone. "I'm a huge fan of Anthony Bourdain's food and travel show, and I constantly make notes of where he eats. He raved about the pork sandwiches at Porchetta and Company—with crackle! In Toronto! Be still my heart! Are you game?"

"Something tells me I might not have a choice!" she said with a laugh. "But you're in luck because I do like pork. I've watched his show many times too. Quite a character. He reminds me of you, come to think of it!" They were soon perched on stools in a cramped space, trading superlatives about their meal.

Katherine's phone vibrated, and a repeat message from Roslyn appeared on her screen, with the next report to come at 4:00 p.m.

As they finished eating, Katherine asked, "What shall we do this afternoon? The CN Tower? We have a new aquarium or we can see what's on at the Art Gallery, the Royal Ontario Museum, or the new Aga Khan Museum. Your choice."

Nick's eyes lit up. "Niagara Falls! I haven't seen the Falls!"

"Um, that's a little over an hour from here, depending on traffic. I hadn't thought about leaving the city."

As he guided her out to the car, Nick was already making arrangements on his phone. "Take us to the Island Airport, please, Mo," he instructed as he continued to make calls. "Oh, wait! Kat, let's swing by your place to get your camera. You won't want to miss this opportunity to take photos from a helicopter. As I recall, you were seldom without your camera in France."

Katherine gasped, startled by the mention of a helicopter. She looked at Nick with such delight, they burst out laughing.

Katherine reminded Mo of her address. She ran into the house and was back quickly, camera in hand.

"Thanks, Nick. You're right! I would have been so frustrated not to have it. It's not every day a girl gets to take a helicopter to Niagara Falls!"

At the airport, they waited while the helicopter was sprayed with deicing solution before taking off. Katherine listened while the pilot and Nick had a conversation about the flying conditions. The pilot assured Nick he was absolutely right that the day would be fine for the flight, in spite of the cold temperatures.

Smiling to herself, Katherine wondered if there was anything about which Nick was not knowledgeable. He always amazed her.

As they lifted above Lake Ontario, Nick's eyes focused on the horizon. "Y'know, all the time I spend on my boat has fixated the horizon as something special to me. It's a soothing delight to my eye and rejuvenates my mind when my head is buzzing with other issues. It's a great escape. It might be obstructed or completely clear. The sun might be rising or setting. The horizon over water symbolizes freedom and adventure to me . . . there's such power . . ."

He nodded his head dreamily for a moment, lost in his thoughts. Katherine watched his expression. *In spite of his* bon vivant *lifestyle, he really is a thoughtful and philosophical guy.*

The aerial views were spectacular as the pilot swooped his machine closer to the ground. From the glass-and-steel forest of downtown's skyscrapers, across the vast, deep winter blue expanse of Lake Ontario, to the orderly rows of the Niagara Peninsula's orchards and vineyards against the pristine white backdrop, the vista rapidly changed.

"The rows of vineyards down there are making me homesick for Provence," Kat said, taking shot after shot from the unique perspective. "Although I doubt we would ever see that much snow on them in the Luberon."

Circling the waterfalls, the view was breathtaking. The subarctic temperatures had frozen large sections into abstract art forms.

Massive blocks of bluish-white ice encased cascades of water, as if stricken by a wizard's wand. Scattered between them, rebellious torrents powered over the drop into the river below. Plumes of mist shot skyward, sometimes briefly enveloping the helicopter.

"The strength and beauty of nature combined," Nick murmured, his tone reverent. Katherine watched his total absorption with the scene and was reminded of how he took such pleasure in showing her around the Riviera. He was the ultimate tour guide when it came to details about places.

During those early days in Antibes, before she and Philippe had had an opportunity to open their hearts to each other, Nick had charmed her at every turn. He had a sexual magnetism about him, along with sharp wit and intelligence, and his movie-star good looks didn't hurt either.

A memory of their cruise to Saint-Tropez on his yacht flashed into her mind. *That night at La Voile Rouge bordered on hedonistic . . . it was crazy . . . so out of character for me . . . and so much fun.*

She would never forget that it was he who had made her feel more attractive and sensuous than she had in decades. Nick had most definitely lit those fires. In spite of everything, she would always remember that night in Saint-Tropez.

She gave herself a shake now and put her camera back to work.

"You've got a rare opportunity here," the pilot told them. "The times this happens are few and far between."

Mist and spray from the Falls combined with the cold drifting winds. Nearby ornamental walls, lampposts, trees, and buildings were transformed into whimsical ice sculptures.

"I've never been here in the winter," she said. "It's such a different atmosphere from summer, and I honestly can't decide which season is more pleasing."

They put their heads together and took a selfie, catching a glimpse of the waterfalls out the window beside them.

This is one for my "Gratitude" journal, for sure. A dear friend and a most unique experience!

The pilot was a wealth of information about the Falls and surrounding area. He enjoyed Nick's spirited interest and probing questions, while Katherine's camera kept up a steady rhythm of shutter clicks.

By the time they disembarked back in Toronto, dusk was falling.

CHAPTER SIX

"Nick, what can I say? Thank you for that phenomenal experience. Talk about carpe diem—you certainly know how to seize the day!"

Putting his arm around her shoulder, he chuckled. "Y'know, gorgeous, I prefer to let the day seize me! You're right, though. That flight over the Falls was ace!"

Kat noticed she had missed a call from Philippe, but her return call went to his voicemail. She left a short message about the action-filled day she was having and about Roslyn's recent update. Nick commented that she should tell him his pilot would be contacting Philippe about the flight to Toronto.

When Katherine put her phone away, Nick pointed over her shoulder. "That's the CN Tower, right? Let's go do it!"

Katherine laughed. "Do you ever run out of energy?"

"Never when I have such fabulous company, my beautiful companion. Let's catch the sunset from there! I have to leave in a couple of days,, so I'm running out of time. Are you game?"

In less than fifteen minutes, they were on their way up the glass-enclosed elevator to the top of the tallest freestanding structure in the Western Hemisphere. "It was the tallest in the world until a few years ago when a couple of even higher towers went up in Asia," Katherine told him.

From their perch in the sky, they caught the sunset over the continually burgeoning urban sprawl. He commented on the islands, saying he never really thought of Toronto's waterfront personality.

"It's easy to forget when you live in the heart of the city," Kat agreed. "There's been increasing focus on developing lakeside parks, and bicycle and walking paths. In the summer, that part of the city comes alive. Extensive biking paths make Toronto a cyclist's delight."

"And how would you compare it to your biking experience in the South of France?" Nick bantered.

"Don't even go there," Kat shot back. "No contest." She felt a quick bolt of yearning for France.

"Oh, look." Nick read the information on an enormous poster. "Too bad the EdgeWalk doesn't open until April."

"Darn it anyway," Katherine replied, not hiding her relief about missing that part of the adventure. "Even your irresistible charm could never convince me to hang over that ledge." Nick threw his head back with laughter.

As they waited at the appointed pickup spot for Mo, back on the ground and watching the rush-hour traffic crawl by, Nick casually took Kat's hand and said, "At the risk of sounding food-obsessed, I would say it's time to think about a cocktail or two while we decide where to have dinner. Since I chose lunch today, it's your call this evening, Kat."

Sensing her hesitation, Nick added, "Would your rather go home and change? Or would you rather not go out at all? I've held you hostage today."

Kat laughed and acknowledged inwardly she really didn't want the day to end. "It's been an incredible day, Nick! Truly! I would love to have dinner with you. Why don't we compromise and go as we are so we can make it another early night. Feel like seafood?"

"Too right! Good plan!"

"Since we're in this end of the city, let me show you the Distillery District. It's a dynamic new area in the restored, red-brick Victorian-era buildings of the historical Gooderham and Worts whiskey distillery. This restaurant was one of my favorites. I hope it is still as good."

As they drove over, Kat gave the update from Roslyn's last message. "She said Molly is stable and the process is continuing . . . and they are removing the feeding tube tomorrow."

"Beauty! We'll toast to that!"

And so they did, with a perfectly chilled sauvignon blanc, before they shared an enormous seafood platter. Laughing, they simultaneously declared, "What a feast!" when it was placed before them on the table.

They lingered over the generous servings of mussels, scallops, shrimp, crab, and lobster before their cappuccino and espresso were served. There was no shortage of conversation, as Nick asked Kat about her adjustment to life in France and told her about his most recent adventures.

"The last time you and I shared a meal like this, we were in Saint-Tropez," Nick reminded Kat, his voice suddenly quiet and serious. She felt her face flush as the memory of that weekend returned. She looked away awkwardly.

Nick took her hand. His touch was gentle but his gaze was strong and deep into her eyes. "Kat, please don't take this the wrong way. You know how much I like Philippe. He's a great bloke. And I know the two of you have something special going. But I need to say this . . ."

He paused, his eyes filling with such emotion that Katherine felt almost fearful. "Ever since that night on the boat in Saint-Tropez . . . bloody pissed as I was . . . and I'm so sorry about that . . . I haven't been able to get you out of my mind."

Katherine felt her face burn with embarrassment, even as Nick made her laugh. With his inimitable humor, he reminded her of their dinner and all that followed at La Voile Rouge. "You said you had never seen so much champagne. We danced up a storm, didn't we—put those youngsters to shame!"

Kat's cheeks raged brighter, remembering her musings earlier that day. She recalled that night through a bit of a fog, but at the same time in vivid detail. It had been another turning point for her. Never had she dreamed of feeling so alive and sensual, at her age, as Nick had made her feel that night. He had made love to her like no one ever before. And then passed out.

With a wide grin, Nick went on, "Every time I hear 'You Sexy Thing,' I see the two of us boogying like there was no tomorrow. They wouldn't stop playing it, remember? I'll never forget it."

Then he sang, in a wacky falsetto with the most devilish look on his face. "I believe in miracles . . . where you from . . . you sexy thang . . ."

Kat laughed in spite of herself.

"Did you hear that the town shut down the club?" he told her. "Too many noise violations—we got there just in time!"

His amusement ebbed, and his change of tone now left no question of the depth of his feelings. Kat could not believe her ears.

"I'm in love with you, Kat. I need you to know this."

Flustered, Kat looked down and fidgeted with her napkin before she began to stutter a response. "Nick . . . I . . ."

Nick held up a hand to still her. "Wait, let me finish." His voice was warm, thick with feelings. "I think you're a fantastic woman and if there is any chance for me to win your heart, I want to do that. You've no idea how much I thought about you last year when I was waiting out that ridiculous Interpol issue. I looked at pictures of us in Saint-Trop . . . and other days we had on the boat . . . over and over again."

He cupped her hand tenderly between his as his eyes searched hers.

Katherine wasn't certain how to sort out the hurricane of emotions swirling through her mind. Disbelief was definitely high up there. She felt immensely complimented too.

She had been aware earlier in the meal that the last time she had eaten at the Oyster House had been with James, her ex-husband. That had caused some turmoil in her mind, but Nick made her laugh so often that she soon rid herself of that discomfort. Now she was feeling shocked and embarrassed—and special.

Was this really happening? This handsome, smart, articulate man who also happened to be sexy and fun and who would provide a lifestyle most people could only dream about—this man was gazing into her eyes and professing his love for her. She had not seen that coming.

"Nick . . ." she tried to begin again, but he interrupted once more.

"I'm sorry for putting you on the spot. Don't answer me now. Just think about what I'm saying." His eyes never left hers.

A shiver ran through her. She did care for Nick. Another flashback took her to those halcyon days on his yacht before he had to abruptly leave France. She remembered, though, that his advances had unnerved her at the time. She hadn't known how to handle them and was almost relieved when he had to leave so suddenly.

And then Philippe had won her heart, slowly and patiently.

Would things have been different if Nick had stayed?

She gulped, trying to find her voice. Finally, she answered, almost apologetically. "Oh, Nick. You are exceptional. You're such an amazing man in so many ways. I'm flattered. You're a most special friend."

"We could be so much more, Kat."

Yes, we could. She searched for the right words.

"I know there are many, many women, much younger than I am, who would love to hear you say those words."

"That's just it. Been there, done that. I don't want younger women. I saw how happy I could be with a woman like you, someone my age . . . full of life . . . beautiful inside and out. I want to spend the rest of my life with someone like you. Wait, let me correct that—I want to spend the rest of my life with you."

"I'm flattered, and I know you mean no disrespect to Philippe. You're good friends. But . . ." She could feel her heart overflow at that very moment, hearing her words. "I am in love with Philippe, truly, madly, deeply. Like a young girl, really. I'm quite stunned by it all. And very happy."

Nick nodded and patted her hand. Disappointment mixed with acceptance showed on his face. His shoulders dropped briefly with resignation. "That's all I need to hear . . . although not what I wanted to hear."

Picking up her glass of water, Katherine took a long sip, attempting to gather her composure.

Nick squeezed her hand lightly before pulling his back. "Know I will always be there for you. And promise me we still can be friends."

"Of course. The best of friends . . . always. And I know there is a special woman out there just waiting to be discovered by you. That would make me very happy."

Nick nodded slowly. His eyes signaled a certain resignation before he spoke again.

"Philippe is a fine man and I'm happy for you both. I needed to make sure you knew how I felt in case there was any chance at all for me. We Aussies don't give up anything without a major go at it. I reluctantly, but graciously, accept defeat—at least momentarily." He raised one eyebrow and gave her a cocky grin.

Feeling her poise begin to return, Kat said, "Well, you certainly surprised me." It was her turn to reach out for his hand. "I'm sorry . . ."

With a squinty look, he briefly scowled. "I will wallow in despair, but just for a moment or two. Because we all know despair is the solace of fools."

Katherine blinked at his somber words before he added, "I believe I got that from a fortune cookie," and they burst out laughing.

Beckoning to the waiter, Nick ordered a cognac. "I need a bloody stiff drink after all this. How about you, Kat?"

"I'm going to pass, but you go ahead. I'm still working on my cappuccino."

Katherine feared the rest of the evening might be awkward. However, in Nick's classic style of good humor and endless topics of conversation, he had them chatting effortlessly in no time. He encouraged her to describe how plans were progressing with the property on the Cap that she and Philippe were restoring and turning into a bed-and-breakfast inn. He assured her he would be one of their first guests, with or without his yacht in the harbor.

After dinner, when they pulled up in front of Kat's house, Nick stepped out of the car and held the door for her. "I'll walk you to the front door. What a sweet house, Kat. You grew up here?"

She nodded. "There are a lot of memories in its walls. I'm still unsure what I'm going to do with it. Sell, rent it, I dunno."

"The best thing with houses is to not make hasty decisions. See how things play out first."

"It seems I've been making a habit of hasty decisions."

At the door, Kat touched Nick's cheek as their eyes met. "Thank you . . . for everything. What a day."

Nick opened his arms. "Come here, gorgeous." Before she could react, he pulled her to him and held her tightly. Then he kissed her on each cheek. "Friends forever. Agreed?"

Katherine hugged him back. "Agreed."

"However . . . I will leave you with this. If you already know that you are in love with Philippe, I respect that. If you ever have any doubts, I'll be waiting."

Feeling flustered all over again, Kat said, "You don't give up easily, do you?"

"Nope!" And then he completely changed his tone. "I've got a meeting first thing tomorrow, so I won't get to the hospital until around ten. Shall I send Mo to pick you up or will it be the subway again?"

"Subway! See you when you get there. I'm excited and scared to see how Molly is coming along."

Once inside the house, she leaned against the wall. Her head was spinning, wondering what other surprises lay in store for her. Only fifteen months before, no man had been in love with her. Now there were two. Two very special men.

She hung up her coat and took off her boots before Kat noticed the message light flashing on the phone. She walked into the living room and picked up the phone, wondering why the messages hadn't been left on her cell.

One was from Lucy, saying her colleagues from her former job were planning a dinner for her and asking her to confirm an evening. She also suggested they meet for lunch in Chinatown the next day and asked for Kat's cell number.

Another message was from Andrea, saying they would pick Philippe up at the airport when he arrived. Kat knew he would be delighted to see them there. Andrea also asked her to call back and let them know what was happening with Molly. She asked if Kat's cell had a problem.

Kat called her cousin, and Andrea picked up immediately.

"Hey! Are you okay? I couldn't reach your cell all afternoon. It wouldn't even go to voicemail."

"You won't believe my day. But first let me give you the Molly update." She went on to say she would let them know as soon as Philippe's travel details were set.

"Nick is such a generous man. Can't wait to meet him. Terrence has been telling all our friends about him—we've never heard of anyone like him."

"Well, here's another tale Terrence can tell." Andrea listened in amazement as Katherine described Nick's impromptu helicopter escapade.

"What an adventure, Kat, and what a good friend he is to you and Philippe. How nice that he's been in town to keep you company these past few days. I hope it's helped you feel better about everything."

Katherine assured her Nick had been a great diversion. The rest would be her secret.

The third message was a shocker.

"Katherine. It's James. I would like to talk to you. I heard about Molly and that you were in town. Please return my call at least. Thanks."

Sitting slowly and heavily on the nearest chair, she was stunned. The surprise took her breath away. The sound of James's voice made her feel nauseated. It wasn't as if she hadn't thought about talking to him. She'd considered it from time to time but had always procrastinated effectively.

All of the communication—from the day he left her until their divorce was final—had been through their lawyers. She had not said one word during that time to the man she had allowed to monopolize her life.

"Classic James," she muttered as she considered his message. He might have at least said he was sorry about Molly's accident.

She would call him back. But not now. She wanted to think about it.

Taking her time packing a few more boxes, Katherine felt uncharacteristically on edge. An expanding to-do list incessantly ran through her mind. She would put in a call to the Goodwill pickup office in the morning. It was obvious that it would take more than a few weeks to get the house in shape to sell or rent. She needed to think about that too.

With a growing urgency, she lost herself in yoga for an hour, thankful for the relief of focusing only on that.

As she settled into bed, her mother's electric blanket kept her warm. Kat crossed her arms over her chest and looked up at the ceiling, her eyes wide open. Only last year, she had spent countless nights there wondering if anything else lay in store for her. Now surprises seemed to keep coming into her life.

Today had certainly held its fair share.

CHAPTER SEVEN

Waiting for Philippe's call was not an option today. After the events of the previous day, all Katherine wanted was to hear his voice, feel his love, and express hers for him. She phoned him as soon as she woke up.

"*Tu me manques, mon* Chou. I miss you more than ever today! I know you are still at the market but I couldn't wait to talk to you."

"*Moi aussi, mon coeur.* I miss you too," Philippe began and then continued to describe his feelings in French, his voice almost a whisper.

She loved to hear him say those words in that way. Her lips parted unconsciously and her breath caught. "You're making my heart sing. Can we talk now or are you busy?"

"We're still serving customers but when I saw the call was from you, of course I took it," he said, his tone changing. "How are you coping? Nick e-mailed me late last night to confirm that the plane will be in Nice in two days to bring me to you. He said you had quite an adventure yesterday, but he would let you tell me about it."

"An adventure for sure! I'll tell you about it when you get here. Go back to work and we'll talk this afternoon. I'm having lunch with Lucy. I think today will be pivotal for Molly. Talk to you later. *Je t'embrasse!*"

"*Moi aussi!* And I also have an adventure to tell you about. Simone sends her love and I will reveal all in person. A bottle of wine will be a necessity for the conversation."

"Oh my. How is Simone? Is everything okay? Did you meet her?"

"You must wait to hear the story. She is very well and said to tell you she and Victor Hugo miss you." His voice caught with emotion. "As I do, Minou. *Tu es ma joie de vivre.*"

The call was just the tonic Katherine needed after the emotional ride the previous evening. She couldn't wait to embrace Philippe and to hear about his visit with Simone. But she also knew she had to express her growing concerns to him . . . once she had them sorted out herself.

At the hospital, Katherine was disappointed to see that Molly still looked like she was in a coma. The encouraging news was that many of the tubes were gone and she appeared to be breathing on her own.

The attending physician explained that Molly might still need the ventilator at night for a day or two. "She is managing quite well on her own for several hours at a time. We're very pleased. She may be fully awake by the end of the day."

Katherine noticed the fresh red rose in the delicate vase next to Molly's bed. She was beginning to develop a strong suspicion about it, since there was only one other person whose presence was guaranteed every day.

She banished that thought for the moment as the heady perfume brought back memories of fragrant bouquets of roses James had given her each year on their wedding anniversary. She was working on replacing that connection.

Being back in Toronto was causing a plethora of nostalgic memories to resurface. As long as she was preoccupied with other people, Kat could banish the difficult recollections from her thoughts, but on her own, not so much.

She knew she had returned home a stronger, more confident woman than when she had left. She would confront the painful memories now, once and for all, and work through them to a place of acceptance, if not understanding. The positive history of her life far outweighed the bad, and that was what counted. She often felt she had already left her life here behind and walked into a completely new reality in France.

That's why she was so stunned now to feel uncertain about her choices. She had expected this time back home to be her opportunity to put her past behind her—in a good way. Somehow that wasn't how it was playing out.

She replayed the voicemail from James in her head. Maybe that was something she needed to deal with to help resolve these new feelings of uncertainty. But not yet.

Out at the nurses' station, she asked Roslyn, "What's the news today?"

"You can go in and out quietly a few times for short intervals, if you like. We're watching to make certain nothing interferes with the calm around Molly as she regains consciousness. These patients often wake with memories of terrible dreams or hallucinations and we hope to avoid that. Patience, my dear."

Katherine returned to be with Molly for her allotted time. She told Molly all about her helicopter adventure and about Nick's confession of love. She knew it would go no further.

She was sitting holding Molly's hand, willing her to wake up and be well, when Father DeCarlo appeared and suggested, "Let's go to the cafeteria and have a coffee."

He explained how he started his rounds at the hospital much earlier in the winter and left as soon as possible to get back to his street ministry. He said he had been spending more time at the hospital since

Molly was admitted, and Katherine thanked him profusely before he changed the subject.

"With all this cold weather, we're extra busy at the homeless shelter. A few of us take some vans and cruise around the streets picking up anyone who looks like they need help. Things have been very bad this year."

"Molly has told me quite a bit about your street ministry and how much she admires it."

He smiled warmly. "She's come along and helped us many times, often after her last session at the Blue Note. She's a good person, our Molly."

Katherine had never heard Molly mention being involved like that. She tucked that information away for now, along with the tone of the priest's voice when he spoke of Molly. Her intuition was getting stronger, the more time she spent with this handsome priest, even though she found herself anxious at what the reality might be.

The priest left to continue his rounds, and Katherine sat in the reception area in intervals, with her computer. Nick texted he was going to be tied up with meetings into the afternoon. He would check in then to see if there was anything new to report at the hospital.

She spent a while going through her photos from the day before, editing and storing, and was more than pleased with some of the images over Niagara. She felt eager to present them to André at his gallery back in Antibes and then began to fret about that decision. *I'll be sixty in a few years, and I'm walking away from an established profession. Really? Is that smart? What am I thinking?*

After stopping by the nurses' station to confirm Molly was stable, Katherine strolled the short distance to the Chinatown district. The sun was shining brightly, taking the bite out of the chilly air.

This had always been one of Kat's best-loved parts of the city. Close to the university where she had studied for so many years, the area was a student haunt. There had been many hours spent going over notes while eating spicy Szechuan meals accompanied by green tea or Chinese beer.

It had been great fun for her to point out her favorite restaurants and funky shops to Nick when they had driven through on their "city tour." He'd laughed when she told him she still had the best food steamer ever that she bought there thirty years earlier. "It's on my list to bring to Antibes when I ship my stuff."

Now Katherine walked into the Peking Palace and grinned as she saw Lucy leap up from a table. "Katherine! It's been too long! I'm so happy to see you!"

Petite and demure, Lucy was usually the picture of calm, dispensing pearls of wisdom from her Chinese ancestry and her lifelong study of astrology. A coworker in Dr. Henderson's medical research office, she had convinced Katherine to take up yoga after James had walked out.

When Katherine went to Antibes, she invited Lucy to house-sit, knowing the cramped conditions at her family's place. Lucy lived with several generations under one roof, and ever more relatives emigrated from China, so she was thrilled for the opportunity to be on her own. She insisted on paying the utilities in return for Kat's generosity. Little did either of them suspect it might turn into such a long-term arrangement.

Now, Katherine knew she needed to rent out the house in order to pay taxes and do repairs that inevitably would be required. In fact, she had scheduled a home inspection company for the following week. She felt badly having to give Lucy the news but it had to be done, and she was waiting for the right moment to raise the issue.

Before she could say anything, Lucy thanked her. "You've done me a big favor, Kat."

"It works both ways," Kat replied. "Thanks for taking such good care of the house."

"I'm the one to thank you. My brother thanks you too, since he got the extra bedroom with me out of the house. But first things first: how is Molly? I'm tracking her charts, and it's been troubling."

Katherine filled her in and then they ordered lunch. Lucy wanted all the details about Kat's new life and plied her with questions.

At one point, a strange look crossed Lucy's face and she blurted, "Omigod! I just remembered, I bumped into James last week at the courthouse. We didn't talk long because he was rushing to an appointment, but I told him about Molly. It was right after her accident. I said I thought you would be coming to Toronto. I hope that was okay."

"Of course. He already called the house and left a message. That explains it."

Lucy looked thoughtful. "You're going to see him. That's probably a good thing."

Katherine shrugged her shoulders and smiled. Lucy always had a touch of clairvoyance. "You would know."

Lunch arrived and Katherine finally had a chance to ask about Lucy and her family. To her surprise, her concerns about the house were banished.

"I have a proposition for you," Lucy told her, looking a bit hesitant. "My cousin, Li Mai, now has an excellent job, and we wondered if you would consider renting your house to us. We've been talking about moving in together and were looking around at places and we suddenly realized your house would be perfect. If you aren't moving back, that is."

She set aside her chopsticks, pausing for a moment and then asked shyly, "You are moving to France to be with Philippe, right?"

Kat's expression betrayed her bewilderment. "That was the plan. I thought it was what I wanted. I do think it's what I want . . . but I'm starting to feel that I'm making too hasty a decision. I'm worried I'm behaving like a schoolgirl in love instead of being rational and mature."

Lucy listened intently. "We don't always have to be rational and mature, you know. And maybe what you're thinking isn't rational and mature really is just that, with a slightly different set of parameters. You broke free of old constraints, Kat. You embraced new challenges."

Katherine rolled her eyes. "I'm in the beating-myself-up process right now, though."

"You're my hero, Katherine! Honestly! You've opened my eyes to the fact that there's a lot more of life to be lived at every age. I was feeling kind of stuck and resigned to my life. Now I'm looking at things differently. I've even been considering a dating site."

"Lucy, you've always been so serene, so calm. I'll forever be grateful to you for introducing me to yoga. I'm surprised to hear you say this about yourself."

Lucy sighed. "Don't get me wrong. I do feel positive most of the time, and I trust the stars and my charts. But it doesn't hurt to learn from someone else's experiences. That's what you've done for me. So thanks, my friend."

Katherine smiled. "That's what friendship is all about. I've learned that lesson this past year too."

Lucy's demeanor became serious. "I will say this, though. If you do decide to come back to Toronto—though I hope for your sake you don't—the new director I work for has told me he would always be open to talking to you. You left with your research reputation well intact."

"Thanks for sharing that. It's nice to know. I loved my job and am kind of surprised that I'm walking away from it. Every once in a while I have a moment of panic at all the changes I'm making in that direction too. You know, making photography my new career. But on the other hand, I'm really excited about it! See what I mean? I'm a mess!"

"Do you think you might change your mind? Maybe we shouldn't be talking about your house like this."

Kat shook her head. "Lucy, I've committed myself so far into this new world of mine, I can't pull the plug now. I'm just realizing that it may not be forever. There's still a lot to be determined. Maybe I am just taking a sabbatical . . . maybe . . ."

Lucy's eyes widened in surprise. "Go for it, Kat. You're moving from one life into another. We have a saying: 'Be not afraid of growing slowly, be afraid only of standing still.'"

"I think you're right—I've got nothing to lose. It's still scary, though. I feel like Philippe is my security blanket. When I'm with him, everything is right. Being here without him is causing a lot of concerns to arise within me. I need to know I can do this on my own."

They returned to talking about the house. Katherine was reluctant to discuss rent, but Lucy assured her it was not a problem with the combined salaries. "Li Mai's fiancé is doing his residency in China and won't be here for two more years, so we'll be good tenants! What do you think?"

"Lucy, you have an innate ability to solve problems," Katherine said with a chuckle. "I was worried about having to ask you to move out so I could rent the house. Just give me a little time to figure out what I'm doing."

"It's in the stars, Katherine, always in the stars, and so is your decision. The right answer will come to you! We don't need to know right away. Take your time."

An hour later, Lucy had to get back to work. They made plans for a reunion dinner with Laura from the office and the Hendersons. "Let's do it next week, and then Philippe can come too. We all want to meet him before you fly off for your new life with him . . . if you're going to, that is. I'm not going to make that prediction. My lips are sealed."

"I guess 'if' is the operative word right now," Kat replied. They hugged and headed in different directions.

Noting the traffic gridlock and dodging pedestrians on the crowded Chinatown sidewalk, Katherine nostalgically wished for a narrow cobblestone street.

She pulled her woolen toque from her pocket and jammed it on her head, making sure her ears were well covered. Clouds had hidden the sun, and the day had turned downcast. *Rather like my mood*, she thought as her final words to Lucy replayed in her head.

Katherine thought Roslyn looked tired, changing Molly's IV. "Don't you ever get a day off?"

"Actually, I've switched my days so I could be here while Molly is coming out of her deep sleep. I want to be here. She's been stirring today and breathing well on her own. I think she will be wide awake tomorrow morning."

Katherine called Nick and gave him the update. "I'm going home now. For whatever reason, I'm really tired and tomorrow could be a long day. I'll see you at the hospital tomorrow, okay?"

"No worries. I've been tied up in meetings all day. I still am. Why don't you let me have Mo take you home? It's snowing again out there right now. Say yes."

She did.

Once in the house, Kat brought in kindling and wood from the back porch and had a blazing fire going in no time. The comforting smell of the crackling logs took her back to her childhood. Sipping a glass of white wine, she settled in her mother's pink chair and thought how strange it felt to be home and yet simultaneously feel like she wasn't.

She had changed in the last six months. It was fact. There was much about her that was different from a year ago. But did it mean that she was going to leave everything behind forever?

Sitting in front of the fire, she ate the leftover Chinese food she had brought home without heating it up. *Another holdover from my student days*, she chuckled to herself as she refilled her wineglass and flipped on the TV to watch the BBC news. Afterward, she took the dishes to the kitchen and turned on the light-jazz radio station. Her thoughts drifted as she tidied up.

The world she was making hers in France was different in so many ways. She longed to be back in Antibes, even after this short time away. There was so much about living there that she loved. *But is it just a flirtation? Is Philippe the whole reason for making this move? What would happen if we don't remain together? Once bitten, twice shy . . .*

She knew she wanted to have Philippe here with her, but also she knew she needed to be honest with him about the thoughts she was having. *Time. I need more time.*

In the few days she had been back in her childhood home, she'd put together collections of small things she wanted to ship to France: books, photos, candlesticks. Nothing of much monetary value, but priceless in her sentimental connection. As the stack of boxes to go to France grew, so did Kat's doubts.

She retrieved one box and brought it to the living room. It had been a struggle to decide what to do with these particular items. First she took out the book her mother had so carefully handwritten, telling the story of her and Jozsef's life during the war and how they had survived.

Kat laid her hand lovingly on the cover as sadness rippled through her. She knew she could not open it or read those words again. It was simply too painful. And yet she would be forever thankful that she had read it once.

The details had become part of her psyche in a way she knew she would never forget. The reality of her parents' stories from the war had first crushed her with sorrow. Eventually, the gift they gave her was empowerment.

Thinking about it now, she made a decision. If and when she was back in Antibes, she was going to encourage Simone to tell her story. Family histories, like the one Elisabeth had reluctantly revealed, needed to be told before they died with the people who had lived them. Families needed to know and pass them on. The world needed to know.

From snippets Simone had let slip during conversations, Katherine knew there was quite a tale to be told.

She decided she would give the book to her nephew Andrew. He had shown how much he cared about their family's past when he had gone to what was now Ukraine to search for his roots. Memories flooded back to Kat. She recalled her surprise when she made a last-minute decision to go with him from Antibes. She shuddered at the memory of how unbearable that trip to her parents' village had been for her.

Next she opened a small silk pouch and removed a gold chain from which hung a delicate Star of David. Elisabeth's mother had pressed the pouch into her daughter's hand when Elisabeth had been secreted away to the convent that night in 1943. She had instructed Elisabeth to ask the nuns to hide it for her until the war was over. And they had done so.

It had belonged to Katherine's great-grandmother. Elisabeth told Kat she had never worn it again after the war, but she had always treasured it. Kat knew her mother had not been able to embrace her Jewish faith, or any other, for the rest of her life.

Kat's fingers slowly traced the pattern. She thought of all it signified and where this necklace had been. She thought about how the Nazis had intended to make it an emblem of shame that had only strengthened its significance.

Slowly, and with deep emotion, she put it around her neck and secured the clasp. *I will wear this to honor Anyu and her ancestors—my ancestors.*

She knew her niece and nephews would value the other mementos in the box and the stories would live on. That pleased her.

Kat felt a pang of regret that she was childless. There were times in her life when the reality left her feeling empty and bereft. But James had always become mute on the subject, leaving her to work through what felt like grief. It occurred to her now that the love Philippe was giving her filled the void that James had not. The emptiness was gone. She could let it go.

The thought of Philippe's daughter, Adorée, came to her. They would make a family unit, the three of them. With any luck, that little unit would blossom if Adorée married or had children. Something else to anticipate—if she stayed in France. That "if" apparently was becoming the elephant in the room.

The dying embers of the fire cast a soft, soothing glow and spread warmth into the room. Katherine turned off the lamps and then lay on the couch, drawn into the hypnotic flickering light. Tapestries of childhood moments appeared from the shadows. Swatches of her life and the people in it hung in the air before dissolving into the darkness. Waves of emotion washed over her, but she was determined not to feel sad. There was so much that was good to look forward to. So much to be thankful for.

As much as she mourned the absence of her parents, she felt blessed to have had them for as long as she did. She was acutely aware that this visit home might be her last for a very long time. Or would it? She knew these growing anxieties of hers would have to be shared with Philippe. Her love for him was not in question, but her commitment to living forever in France was becoming an issue.

Lying there, she willed the love and happiness of her life in that house to settle deep in her heart. The past was past. It had shaped her and there was much from it that would stay with her forever.

Once in a while a loud snap and spray of sparks in the hearth startled her, but soon she was asleep where she lay. At some point during the night, a warm throw her mother had crocheted found its way over her. She awoke to the alarm on her phone the next morning, with a slight crick in her neck.

CHAPTER EIGHT

The nurses at the station counseled Katherine when she arrived, giving her careful instructions about not making loud noises or sudden movements near Molly. When she inquired, she was told Roslyn was not in today. *A good sign*, Kat thought.

"Molly has actually been slowly waking for the past two days, which is why we've kept visitors away. Her functions are continuing to return, but it is best to maintain a calm atmosphere around her. We told her you were coming, and we could tell she's eager to see you."

The head of Molly's hospital bed was raised, elevating her to a sitting position. Her eyes were glassy as they met Katherine's, but soon brightened with recognition.

She smiled and nodded. Katherine hugged her gently, her eyes filled with tears. "Oh, Molly, you're back!"

Molly suddenly looked confused but said nothing. Katherine felt alarmed and kept talking as she sat beside the bed and held her friend's hand. Molly gripped hers in return, a veritable vise grip. Katherine could feel her fear.

The nurses had explained that Molly would be frightened upon waking up. "You need to speak to her in short, uncomplicated sentences and probably repeat a few times how she was in an accident. Dr. Primeau was here earlier when she first was alert and he also told her everything. And Father DeCarlo was here as well."

Kat followed the instructions, hoping to ease Molly's anxiety. Molly would squeeze her hand from time to time and nod. She seemed to grasp what had happened. Kat felt encouraged that she understood everything, hoping she wasn't fooling herself.

After a while, she noticed Molly had fallen asleep. Concerned, she told the nurses.

"She's going to keep doing that for a few more days until all of the drugs are out of her system. Don't worry, she's doing well. In fact, we're going to move her to a private room in the morning."

Sitting by Molly, Katherine considered how quickly life could change. How, suddenly, what was the norm was not anymore.

Her mind went back to the day James left and how afterward shock had been what she felt most strongly. She remembered how the word "alone" had suddenly come into her consciousness and held a more significant meaning than she ever might have imagined. It wasn't simply a word to her back then. It had defined her. She'd felt empty, angry, and afraid in her aloneness.

She thought next about the day her mother passed and how that word had come into her thoughts again in a different way. It had defined how she felt without her parents and caused her great sadness.

A sense of being alone had been with her on the day she arrived at the wonderful farmhouse in Provence. *That damn word again,* she'd thought as she sat on the step and cried that first morning, sad at being on her own in those incredible surroundings.

Yet she also remembered how being alone had become something that gave her strength and courage. Being alone had empowered her to take chances and grow. They were all important progressions in her life.

"Alone." She startled herself by saying it out loud now. Her reflections continued. She felt proud of the way she'd accepted being alone during those two weeks in Provence. She had learned to savor it. Well, not totally alone, she chuckled, there was Pico.

She couldn't help smiling as she recalled how that adorable dog had touched her aching heart in the most unexpected ways on that trip. His unconditional happiness at being in her company had helped her begin to live in the moment and be content with herself. It was impossible not to feel happy with his molten-brown eyes fixed on her and his non-stop wagging tail signaling joy with whatever they were doing.

Looking at Molly, she felt a surge of love for her friend . . . her first true friend.

That childhood friendship really didn't blossom again in adulthood until after James was gone. He had always discouraged it. *Why was I so stupid and accepting of his controlling ways?* She had asked herself that question many times over during the last year.

And if Molly and I didn't have this friendship, who would be here with her now? Kat's heart sank with that thought. It was a sharp reminder of how important it was to have others in your life to help. She felt almost ill for a second at the thought of her friend going through this on her own. There were times when being alone was not a good thing.

That brought her full circle to how life could change so dramatically in a heartbeat. She was glad to be there for Molly, and she would be with her as long as she needed her.

That whole thought process helped her make another decision.

She called James's cell phone and left a message, thankful for voicemail. "It's Katherine. I would like to meet you this afternoon if at all possible. I'm not certain I will have any other time while I'm in town. The cafeteria here at the hospital would work best for me."

She surprised herself but was glad she'd made the call. There would be no time to think about it and cancel. She was also glad to be getting this over with before Philippe arrived. She wanted nothing to detract from her joy of having him by her side.

Minutes later, Nick appeared in the doorway with Kat's café mocha and a bag of takeaway from the deli down the street. He set it down and gave Kat a quick hug. She put her fingers to her lips to signal Molly was sleeping.

"You look like you've seen a ghost, gorgeous! What's up?"

"I just arranged to meet James this afternoon."

"Blimey! That's your bleedin' ex, right?"

"The very one," she replied. "The last time I saw him, he kissed me good-bye in the morning and said he loved me. That was just hours before he left me a note—accompanied by a massive bouquet of roses, I might add—saying he was leaving me for someone else."

"What a dickhead!"

Kat nodded. "I would agree. I'm a little shocked that I made that call. He left me a message a few days ago saying he wanted to see me. I think it's the right thing to do."

"Are you sure? Would you like me to go with you?"

She smiled at his concern. "I'm going to be fine. In fact, I may tell him it was the best thing that ever happened to me . . . because it was."

Just then, her phone dinged lightly to announce an incoming text. It was from James. "I'll meet you at the cafeteria entrance at two p.m."

Nick began unpacking the bags. "Chicken soup with matzoh balls for all of us, especially Molly. I checked with the nurses and she can have the broth, not the balls—all the more for us. And pastrami on rye for the nonpatients. Sound good?"

"Sounds like my mother's kitchen," Katherine said with a smile. "Great idea!"

Molly continued to sleep. Nick and Kat enjoyed their lunch and talked about Philippe's arrival the next day. Kat watched Nick's face, wondering if their exchange the other evening had made any difference to his comfort level with Philippe. She saw nothing but genuine friendship and admired him all the more.

She told Nick that Andrea and Terrence would pick up Philippe. He had offered to send Mo.

"Ah, decent of them. Philippe will appreciate seeing familiar faces when he arrives. You're not going?"

"I want to stay with Molly. They're moving her out of ICU tomorrow morning, so she'll have more room for visitors, although we still have to keep things calm. Dr. Primeau was by earlier and told me he's pleased with her progress. He also said we should be patient about her not speaking."

"That's encouraging."

"I know. It's unsettling to not hear her voice, but he talked about spontaneous recovery from aphasia. Let's hope so."

"That's the first time I've heard her inability to talk referred to as aphasia. Scary. I hope Primeau is right with his prediction."

As they were finishing their lunch, Molly began to stir. After a quick check by the nurse, who raised the head of the bed so she'd be more comfortable, Molly looked more aware than before her nap and beamed at Nick. She obviously recognized him and looked surprised.

He went over and kissed both her cheeks. "G'day, princess! It's nice to have you back with us! We missed you. I gave you a big smackaroo from Graham when you were in your coma, so I'll deliver it again."

Molly nodded, her grin widening. She appeared ready to say something, and Kat and Nick held their breath in anticipation. But they were disappointed when nothing happened.

Katherine moved the tray table into position and asked if she could help Molly with her soup. Molly nodded and Nick provided an entertaining monologue while she slowly consumed half the bowl.

As the time to meet James drew nearer, Kat felt herself tensing up. Nick had been sitting on the other side of the bed and came around to her side. Putting his hands on her shoulders, he lightly massaged them. "Feeling a bit tense there, are we, gorgeous?"

"Just a bit," she agreed. "I think I'll freshen up before I go downstairs and get this meeting over with."

Molly tapped Kat's hand and raised her eyebrows inquisitively.

"I'm meeting James in the cafeteria here in fifteen minutes."

Molly's eyes widened and her brows shot up even more.

Kat kissed her on the cheeks. "I'll give you a full report when I come back up. You and Nick behave yourselves while I'm gone. No loud partying!"

"Party pooper!" Nick shot back. Molly laughed, and they all stopped dead at the sound.

"You laughed! Do it again!" So she did, and they all joined in. Katherine rushed out to the nurses' station to report the news, but they were already aware that Molly had laughed that morning—and also that she'd groaned aloud in pain.

She came back in and reported, "The nurse just told me this is an encouraging step and they've scheduled more tests in the morning."

Nick and Molly high-fived, and he promised to keep her laughing all afternoon. "I'll let the nurses be responsible for the other sounds."

"On that happy note, I'm off. See you soon."

Katherine went to the ladies' room to reapply her lipstick and run her fingers through her hair. Giving herself a quick once-over in the mirror, she liked what she saw.

All the cycling she and Philippe had done through the hills and the fact that she walked everywhere in her life in France had kept her fit. She'd let her hair grow longer and altered the color. She knew she looked different from the last time James saw her. She certainly felt different.

She nodded in approval at her jeans and the blue woolen turtleneck sweater that complemented her eyes. She had to admit she wanted James to think she looked good.

She thought how she had transformed since that first day she arrived in France on her own. Not without some moments of doubt and insecurity, she had become happy with herself. She had made choices, embraced change, and moved forward with her life. Philippe and the love they shared were the icing on the cake.

She went to the stairwell to go down the five flights. *Let me get those endorphins going. I can use the buzz.*

As she took the stairs two at a time, she repeated all the way down: "I've got this. I've got this. I've got this."

There were chairs in the elevator lobby, but she decided to go into the gift shop near the cafeteria. She wanted to be standing, not seated, when James arrived. She was feeling strong and hoped her resolve would not slip when she finally faced him.

Keeping an eye on the corridor, pretending to read the newspaper headlines, she saw him coming before he noticed her. He was in his standard business attire of a well-tailored, expensive-looking navy suit, coordinated shirt and tie. *He always was a fashionable dresser.*

Tall and trim as he was in the past, Katherine noticed he had put on a few pounds.

"Hi, James," she said, walking out of the gift shop as he reached the cafeteria entrance. She reminded herself to breathe.

"Katherine . . ."

The next moments were awkward. They stood facing each other, about two feet apart. James lifted his hands slightly, as if considering giving her a hug, and Katherine shifted back a touch as she felt herself recoiling,

"Let's go sit down," she quickly suggested, and she turned to lead the way.

The cafeteria wasn't particularly busy. They seated themselves across from each other at a table in a quiet corner.

"Would you like a coffee or something?" Katherine asked, hoping she sounded calmer than she felt.

James appeared pale and tense. His hands were clasped in a white-knuckled grip.

"No, but go ahead if you like."

"I'm fine."

They looked at each other. Katherine waited, wondering how he was going to handle things. Then she realized she was holding her breath and quietly exhaled.

James glanced down at the table and then back up at her. He licked his lips nervously. "How are you?"

Kat did an inner eye roll. *How am I? That's the first thing you want to say to me, you idiot?*

Her heart pounded in her chest. After a long pause, as she watched him shift uncomfortably, she replied with her voice as resolute as her gaze. "I'm very well, thanks. Better than I've ever been, as a matter of fact."

He stared at the table again. Without lifting his eyes, he mumbled, "That's not how I meant to start. Let me begin again."

He raised his head. "I'm sorry. I'm so sorry . . ." His voice trailed off as his face flushed and his lips twitched. For a moment Katherine thought he might burst into tears, which would have been totally out of character.

Briefly, she considered saying, "It's okay. It's all right. Forget it." Ever the peacemaker.

But it wasn't okay. It hadn't been all right. He should feel sorry. Very sorry. No matter how it had turned out. So she said nothing and instead looked squarely at him, seeing all the deceit, the lies, and the excruciating hurt he had inflicted.

She noticed a thin line of perspiration forming along his upper lip as he continued.

"I don't know how I can take back the hurt I caused you. I behaved terribly."

"Yes, you did." A painful memory flashed through her of crumbling to the kitchen floor with shock and disbelief. Kat drew in a deep breath and banished the thought.

James looked away and continued, his voice wavering. "I have really beaten myself up about it. Had to go to counseling. Knew I had to do this, to apologize directly to you. I'm sure you can't forgive me, but I hope you will accept my apology."

"You're right. I will never forgive you. But I will accept your apology." She tossed the ball back to him, realizing she wanted him to squirm. She knew she was behaving out of character, but it felt right. In fact, it felt good.

"I don't know what else to say. Whatever was going on, there's no excuse for the way I handled things." And again he repeated, his voice catching, "I . . . I am just so incredibly sorry."

Katherine knew he meant it. How couldn't he? They had shared a life for almost thirty years. Twenty-two of them married. She could tell he meant it, and she was well aware it was hard for him to be humble. He was never one to admit wrongdoing.

She found her voice. Her eyes never left his face. He lowered his often. The more she spoke, the stronger she felt.

"There's no denying the pain you caused me, from the shock of it all, from the deceit, from the obvious lying that had gone on, from the breach of trust, from the disrespect. All of that I will never forgive . . ."

His face flinched and he looked past her.

She wasn't through yet. "But things work out in the most unexpected ways sometimes. I have a life now in which I am happier than I ever could have imagined. I've discovered things about myself that never had a chance to surface in my life with you. Important things . . ." She paused.

His voice betrayed his inability to process what she had just said. He blinked rapidly as he unclasped his hands and wiped them on his thighs. "I called your house a while back and Lucy was there. She told me you were living in France."

"Yes, I am."

"I bumped into her at the courthouse last week. You remember her cousin was involved in that gangland slaying . . ."

Kat nodded. James continued to speak quickly, as if out of control.

"And it's still going on. Crazy business. She told me about Molly. That's when I called your place and left the message. I figured you'd be back. I'm sorry about Molly. How is she?"

"Not in great shape. It was a very serious accident but she is slowly recovering."

"That's good. I was sorry to see the obituary when your mother died last year. I wanted to call but then thought perhaps I shouldn't. I'm sure you miss her. I'm really sorry . . . sorry about everything . . ."

"Yes, I do miss her. But again, those months I had with her before she died were meaningful and special. That wouldn't have happened if you hadn't left."

James looked at her. A slight frown appeared on his face. Katherine knew her strength was throwing him off kilter. He was accustomed to being in control and dominating any conversation with her.

Katherine continued, feeling on a bit of a roll: "In fact, nothing that is in my life now would have happened if you hadn't walked out on me."

It occurred to her that it would be nice of her to ask how he was. To ask how he enjoyed being a parent. But she knew she didn't want to be that nice to him. Besides, she thought, she might end up asking him if he ever thought about how he had denied her that role. *What's past is past*, she reminded herself.

James began speaking rapidly again. "I want you to know I value the years we had together, Kat. You were a good wife. We had some good times. I have a lot of happy memories that I won't forget. I'm sorry I hurt you the way I did . . . I truly am."

She gave a curt nod, not missing a beat. "We did have some good times, you're right. In fact, I had no idea how much was missing from our marriage until I was on my own and discovered there was so much more to life, that there was so much more to me."

James stared down at his hands. His face was pale and there was an air of defeat about him. His voice was hoarse as he spoke. "I'm glad you're happy. There are times I wish I could take it all back and never have had all this happen."

Kat said nothing but was reminded of his controlling ways. *How dare he say this! Not just about my life, but what about his new wife and child? What does this say about his commitment to those relationships?*

She did not want anything taken back. She had dealt with the hurt and come out in a better place. He had lied to her. He had deceived her. Blatantly. All the while telling her he loved her. She did not want to hear how his life was. She realized she truly did not care.

He shifted awkwardly in his chair when Katherine said nothing in reply. James cleared his throat before speaking again. "So . . . I guess that's it, then. Thanks for giving me the chance to apologize. It means a great deal to me."

Katherine stood up and James followed, looking a little surprised that their conversation was over.

Looking across the table at him, she felt a certain calm come over her. With some inner surprise she heard her voice tell him, "I appreciate your apologies. You should be ashamed of how you behaved and the way you left. Life works in mysterious ways, and if it makes you feel better, I have never been more content than I am now with the life I have and the future that awaits me. I wish you all the best with yours."

She held out her hand and he shook it. He was never a hugger, but she could feel that was what he was looking for now. It happened quickly, and she stiffened as he put his arms awkwardly around her. Hers hung limply at her side.

In that moment Katherine knew she was saying good-bye. Good-bye to her past with him. Good-bye to all the years she didn't stand up for herself. Good-bye to the hurt he had caused.

Stepping back quickly, she felt as if a weight had lifted from her—a weight she had been ignoring. Her face was serene and her gaze strong, although she did not smile.

"You look happy, Katherine. You really do. Whatever you are doing agrees with you."

"Thanks, James," she replied matter-of-factly. And she meant it. "Good-bye."

She turned and went over to the coffee bar to avoid leaving with him. He walked out toward the elevators.

Placing her hands on the counter, she felt her knees weaken for a second. She took a deep breath. That encounter had not been as easy as she'd worked to make it seem. It was disconcerting to look into the eyes of the man with whom she had shared so much of her life and feel he was almost a stranger.

She stood there for a while, thinking.

After James had walked out of their marriage, Katherine had spent several months wondering if indeed they had ever really known "love" together. Had it simply been a case of comfort and convenience when they got married? The lust part had not lasted long.

When she was honest with herself, she knew there were numerous times when she had felt distinctly unloved, disrespected and hurt by his words and attitude toward her. She could remember thinking then that she should leave. She deserved better. But she never did. She never spoke with anyone about it. Certainly not to James, because she knew he would become angrier and meaner. So she swallowed the hurt and the dislike she felt for him. It faded but never truly went away. She retreated more within herself. They simply carried on as usual.

The difference between the love and respect she felt with Philippe and how she felt with James was like night and day. Finally, she had found love, and that love had changed her for the better in every way.

There was no question that her life with Philippe brought her confidence. But she also knew she had empowered herself as a result of those first trying months after James left her. That core strength and self-confidence defined the woman she was able to become. What Philippe gave to her sealed the deal.

She regretted nothing she had said to James today.

That chapter was over.

CHAPTER NINE

Molly was asleep when Katherine walked in her room. Nick was busy texting in a chair by her bed.

He quickly put his phone down and gave Kat a look of concern. "How did it go? Are you okay?"

"I am surprisingly fine, thanks. There were words I have thought about saying to James for a long time . . . and I did. He was apologetic. Done."

A nurse came in and said they were going to wake Molly to bathe her and change the linens.

"Let's go for a walk, Kat," Nick suggested. "I found a great pub near my hotel, and fresh air would probably do us both good. Besides, I could use a swig or two of the amber fluid! Let's go and lighten up."

Katherine grinned. There was no one who knew how to lighten up better than Nick.

They told the nurse they would come back to help Molly with dinner. Nick scribbled a crazy face on the whiteboard while Kat left a cheery note there for Molly to see when she awoke.

After a brisk walk, they stopped in at the King's Arms. The dark wood interior with stained-glass accents was welcoming and they paused at the wood-burning fireplace to warm up. Katherine was surprised how calm she felt.

After they settled into a cozy booth, Nick had the perky young waitress giggling as he questioned her about the craft beers she listed.

Katherine momentarily excused herself and sent a quick text to Philippe. She knew he would be wondering about her meeting with James.

Their drinks arrived as she put her phone away, and Nick raised his glass to her. "Cheers! Here's to moving on."

Kat nodded vigorously, raising her glass in return. "Cheers! I never admitted I was carrying around that baggage. Now that I've had my say, I know I was . . . and it's gone."

Nick was sensitive enough not to inquire any further about her conversation with James. Instead he talked about his impressions of Toronto. "Thanks for giving me the grand tour these past few days of your Big Smoke—erm, your fair city. It's a beaut!"

"It's a great place to live. It feels a bit strange to be back after almost six months in France. On the one hand, being back on my home turf is so easy: my familiarity with my surroundings, speaking the same language, friends and family with whom I have a history. I'm surprised how happy I feel to be home. Yet I miss my life in Antibes every day. I keep trying to analyze what I'm feeling. I haven't quite got it figured out."

"I hear you, being a nomad myself. Do you think it's simply that you miss Philippe? Lucky bloke!"

"I do miss him, no question. I can't wait to see him tomorrow. But another part of my heart is aching for the colors of the sea, the buildings, the sky of Provence. I miss the cobblestones and the shutters and the markets and . . ." Katherine rolled her eyes and sighed.

Nick grinned broadly. "You've got it bad, gorgeous. But I could see that when you were there. Every time we went anywhere, you were totally seduced by everything. Can't say I blame you. It's a very special part of the world."

Kat pointed her finger at him. "There you go. 'Seduced' is the word. Now I'm wondering if I've been realistic about the life I've been leading in France. What if it's just infatuation? What if the seduction starts to fade?"

Nick looked at her in silence, his eyes thoughtful. "Y'know, it sounds to me like you're having a classic case of cold feet. You've mentioned these thoughts to me one way or another every day since I got here. You're overthinking everything. I'm sure you'll feel differently again once Philippe arrives."

Kat hurriedly changed the subject. "Are you going to be able to spend time in France again? Is it indelicate of me to ask if your legal problems have been resolved? All restrictions lifted?"

Nick looked up to the ceiling and put his hands together, as if in prayer. "I may need a little divine intervention, but my lawyers tell me everything seems to be resolved. The travel restrictions on my passport have been lifted."

"Bravo!" They clinked their glasses together.

"You know, on my part it was much ado about nothing. Guilt by association. Being in the wrong place at the wrong time. But once a person becomes embroiled in a legal mess like that, it takes a while to get sorted out."

"We were all worried about you, and your presence was missed in Antibes. It will be good to have you back in the harbor."

"Speaking of harbor—I'm getting a new boat! I decided to return with a clean slate and a boat that looks nothing like *Searendipity*."

"That's exciting, although yours was a beautiful boat. Can you keep the name? It's such a catchy one!"

"How's *Searendipity II*?"

"Sounds like a plan."

Nick pulled out his phone and showed her photos and sketches of the boat he had ordered. "It's coming from America and Tim will oversee the delivery."

"This was a needed diversion," Katherine said as they finished their drinks. "You've got me thinking about summer in Antibes. It's a nice place to go in my head to escape the worry about Molly."

"I know, this was a terrible scare—more so for everyone else than our Molly. That's one good thing about being unconscious."

Katherine laughed in spite of herself. "Morbid humor, but true. We were worried if she'd even make it. Now she seems to be getting back to her old self. Talk about relief!"

They touched their glasses together again.

When Katherine was ready to return to Molly, they bundled up again to head out into the cold.

"Putting on all these layers and this thermal gear is another thing you don't have to worry about on the Riviera," Nick complained. "I hadn't anticipated freezing my butt off like this!"

Katherine's laugh was muffled as she pulled her scarf up over her mouth. She had to admit the weather was getting tiresome.

They walked back to the hospital in silence, enveloped in their frosty breath. Nick took Katherine's hand and tucked her arm through his. "Body contact helps to keep warm in this arctic air," he muttered.

Kat was surprised to see Mo and his car waiting outside the hospital entrance.

Nick hugged her good-bye, saying he had meetings for the rest of the day and evening. "I'll see you tomorrow, but I can't promise what shape I'll be in. I'm being taken to a Maple Leafs game tonight and I hear Canadian hockey fans party hearty!"

She chuckled as she waved good-bye. *He's one of those guys who'll simply never stop enjoying life! Too bad that can't be bottled.*

CHAPTER TEN

Katherine awoke the next morning energized with excitement. By midafternoon, Philippe would be by her side. For all her recent dithering, she couldn't wait to see him, to hold him, to look into his eyes and tell him how much he meant to her.

For a woman three years short of sixty, who just a year before had felt she would be on her own forever, there had been more than enough relationship issues in the past few days what with Nick's declaration of love and James's apologies. She was eager for the calm of her life with Philippe.

Although, come to think of it, there were a few months that most definitely were not calm last autumn. The raw emotional scar from the deceitful injury James had inflicted had revived terrible memories for Katherine when she realized Philippe was keeping secrets. It had taken a bit of work on her part and Philippe's to recognize he was attempting to protect her and not deceive her. She shuddered at the thought of all that happened and then shook it off. That too was over.

It would be great fun to show Philippe her hometown. She hoped he would gain a sense of her adored parents too. If she and Philippe really were going to be together forever, it was important to her that he know everything about her.

When Kat arrived at the hospital, Molly was sitting up in bed, eating oatmeal for breakfast. She smiled and nodded when Kat walked in, holding her good arm out for a hug. Then she pulled her earbuds out and motioned for Kat to sit on the bed.

"You're looking better every day, Moll," Kat told her, noting the color in her complexion and brightness in her eyes.

Molly screwed up her face and lifted her shoulders in an exaggerated shrug. Her frustration clearly showed.

Roslyn walked in at that moment and Katherine said how pleased she was to see her. She appreciated the fact that this was a nurse to whom you could ask questions and get a straight response. That wasn't always the case, she knew from comments others made.

"So how do things stand? What's next on my friend's recuperation agenda?"

"We're getting her up today. Right, Ms. Molly Malone?" She rubbed Molly's head lightly and commented how quickly her hair was growing in.

Molly grinned and saluted in return.

Kat looked thoughtful. "Um, that's going to be tricky with her leg in a cast and her shoulder bandaged like that. How's that going to work?"

"We're all about helping our patients become as mobile as possible as soon as possible. Molly is going to need wheels for a while." Roslyn nodded to a wheelchair folded in a corner of the room. "We're going to work on her shoulder today, but crutches may never be an option because of that injury."

She also explained that Molly would be having more tests later in the day to investigate the issue with her speech.

Fluffing up the pillows and adjusting the angle of the bed, the nurse continued, "Here's one thing we already know about our Molly: she's a strong woman with a ready smile. That's going to get her out of here sooner than anything else. And speaking of getting her out of here, this afternoon she'll be moved to a private room on the orthopedic floor."

Molly's eyes opened wide and she shook her head, gesturing for a notepad and pen on the table beside her. "No insurance coverage for private room," she wrote.

"Nick made all the arrangements, Molly. Don't worry about anything," Katherine reassured her.

Molly shook her head and wrote, "Unbelievable. Can't repay him."

"That's the last thing he would want, and don't try to argue with him. Nothing gives him more pleasure than helping his friends. Do you know he's flying Philippe over today in his private jet?"

Molly's jaw dropped in an exaggerated look of amazement.

"Okay," Roslyn said, "let's get this show on the road." Two orderlies appeared and gently moved Molly into the wheelchair. "Wave good-bye to ICU," she told Molly. Then she instructed Katherine to go sign the documents Nick had filled out for Molly's private room. "He pays, you sign—now, there's a deal."

Kat grinned and Molly gave her a thumbs-up.

Another good sign, thought Kat.

Katherine sat in a high-backed chair in Molly's new room while she waited for the tests to be completed. Sunlight flooded through a large window into a spacious area with four chairs for visitors and a small dresser, already covered in floral arrangements and cards. They were mainly from the staff at the school where Molly taught, but several were from patrons of the Blue Note and other people Molly would be surprised to know cared so much.

The underlying tension of the ICU, the accompanying noises of the lifesaving equipment, and the constant reminder of concern were lifted. Positivity filled the room.

Kat's book had fallen closed on her lap, and she was sound asleep when she heard "Minou" whispered in her ear. She opened her eyes and reached out her arms to be swept into Philippe's strong embrace.

Blissfully unaware of anyone else in the room, she returned his kisses and hugged him tightly.

After a few moments, there was a loud throat-clearing noise behind her. Laughing, she disentangled herself and turned to hug Andrea and Terrence. "Thank you for this special delivery!"

They grinned and bowed. "It was our pleasure."

Katherine slipped her arm back around Philippe, and he snuggled her into his body. "Oh, how I've missed you," he whispered in her ear.

"We've already introduced him to your coffee routine here, Kat," Terrence said as he set down a takeaway tray with four cups in it.

Philippe grimaced. "*Zut alors!* I think I'm in for a period of adjustment."

Kat laughed, recalling how she struggled to get used to coffee in France. Then she noticed Philippe's warm jacket, plus the toque and heavy gloves he had set down. "I'm glad to see you came prepared for our extreme cold weather!"

"These are all courtesy of Terrence! He e-mailed me to say he would have a Canadian Winter Survival Kit for me at the airport." He turned to Terrence now. "*Mon Dieu! À votre bon coeur!* I'm very grateful!"

Philippe pulled Kat into his arms once more. "We'll just have to spend a lot of time doing this."

"Yes, please," Kat replied. "Now, tell me everything I've missed. It feels so much longer than ten days. First of all, how is Simone and how did you finally meet her?"

"We're going to give you some time to catch up," Andrea said as she picked up her coffee and motioned to Terrence to do the same. "Text us when Molly comes back."

Philippe pulled the privacy curtain across the room and swept Katherine into his arms. They kissed long and hard before pulling apart.

"Ahhh, that's what I really wanted to do," he said, holding her in a tight embrace. "For starters . . ."

Kat nodded and buried her face in his shoulder. She breathed in the subtle scent of him, so familiar and pleasing. She felt a feathery-light sensation deep in her core and whispered, "I've missed your kisses, your touch, all of you."

Philippe's arms tightened gently, and he was silent. Kat felt him swallow before he held her at arm's length and smiled.

"It was thoughtful of Molly to vacate her bed for our reunion, Minou," he said with a teasing glance. Katherine rolled her eyes. They held each other close once again and then pulled back, sharing a look that promised much more to come.

Then they sat in the chairs by the window, holding hands and calming the electricity between them with conversation. The evening could not come soon enough.

After he received an update on Molly, Philippe gave Kat a full report on the Cap property.

"As you know, Didier's *équipe* began working the day after I returned from Paris. He runs a tight ship, so different from many other contractors I know, and they have already trucked away countless bins of plaster, rotting beams, and such. It's satisfying to see progress in such a short time. I'm encouraged."

Katherine felt herself getting caught up in his enthusiasm. "So exciting! I can't wait to get back and be part of it. And now, Simone— you finally met her. Why wouldn't you tell me anything more?"

"Simone made me promise to let her tell you the whole story . . . and what a story it is!"

Kat punched him on the arm. "That's what you told me before! You're being such a tease. Can't you give me even a little hint? Did you just go and knock on her door?"

"*Mais non!* I wouldn't do that. I phoned the number you gave me and left a message. She called the next day to invite me for tea."

"She's well?"

"Phénoménale." He pronounced the word the French way, knowing it would make Kat grin. "Simone is just as you described. She asked me to assure you she has fully recovered from her post-Christmas ailments. I took her a stunning orchid and two apples for Victor Hugo."

Kat leaned over and ruffled his hair. *"Bien fait!* Well done!"

They were interrupted by Molly's arrival back to the room and the flurry of activity as the orderlies repositioned her bed. A nurse smiled and excused herself as she checked Molly's stats and made sure she was comfortable.

Molly seemed weary at first, but her eyes sparkled as she accepted a gentle hug from Philippe. She nodded her head with excitement every time she looked at him after that and asked him a barrage of questions on her white pad.

Andrea and Terrence returned soon after. Another hour was spent chatting before Nick arrived and the party started.

He and Philippe greeted each other with warm handshakes and the standard *bise*. "Nick, *merci mille fois* for the flight here. That's certainly the best way to travel! I brought baguette sandwiches for the pilot and copilot along with a selection of cheese, and spent half my time in the cockpit. What a great experience!"

"Good on ya, mate! I'm glad it all worked out."

Before Kat could make the introductions, Nick turned to Andrea and Terrence. "The famous cousins! I'm mighty pleased to meet you at last." They were soon engaged in animated conversation.

Molly's eyes darted from one person to another. Her expression indicated her strong desire to join in, but the only sound she could make was laughter.

They kept her entertained while she ate her dinner, which had been upgraded to an omelette and fruit salad with ice cream. Nick excused himself partway through her meal to make some phone calls. "Some days it's just never-ending," he explained with a rueful expression.

Soon after, Father DeCarlo popped in and warmly welcomed Philippe. They chatted amicably, with Molly scribbling comments on her board.

As they all prepared to leave, Father DeCarlo was setting up Molly's computer so she could catch up on *Downton Abbey*. She happily waved good-bye.

"That's the biggest improvement in one day," Katherine said as they waited for the elevator.

Philippe's face registered relief. "I did not expect Molly to look as well as she does. She seems to be very lucid. But I'm glad you told me about her shaved head. Somehow it suits her, though."

After announcing he was suffering from the "mother of all hangovers," Nick went off to a business dinner but made arrangements to meet them for a sushi lunch the next day. "I've changed my plans and am going to stick around through the weekend to try and wrap up a few irons in the fire here."

Andrea and Terrence said they would stay for the lunch the next day and then head back to their farm.

On the way to Katherine's, they took Philippe on a little excursion down Katherine's memory lane, beginning with the University of Toronto and ending with the elementary school she'd attended. Kat's anxieties had initially vanished once Philippe was with her, but as the tour progressed, she felt the conflict between her past and her present again. Her trepidation crept back in.

In Andrea's usual manner, she'd made dinner the night before and brought it along. This time a thick and creamy chicken potpie—chock-full of juicy meat, peas, carrots, and potatoes and topped with a light, flaky pastry—was ready to warm up in the oven.

Before dinner, Katherine gave Philippe an emotional tour of her house. As she shared stories of growing up in those rooms, he held her hand tenderly.

When they stopped at Elisabeth's carpet, Philippe reached out and ran his fingers over the fine silk strands. "So this is your treasured carpet. It's beautiful. And truly there is a mystique about it. We will find a very special place for it in our home, Kat." He raised her hand to his lips. "Very special."

After a while, Philippe and Terrence banished the women from the kitchen. The men soon appeared in the living room with a platter arranged with one of Katherine's favorite *pâtés*, a bowl of tapenade, and fresh baguette slices. Accompanied by loud cheers, a cork was popped from a special bottle of French champagne Philippe had brought. He assured them he also had a selection of cheeses for the end of the meal.

"The joys of flying by private jet," he answered when they questioned how he ever got them through customs.

The evening was relaxed with endless conversation. Philippe had expressed his interest in their organic farm when he had met them in Antibes during Kat's exchange. During dinner, plans were made for Katherine and Philippe to visit overnight at Andrea and Terrence's, if Molly continued to improve.

"I'm excited to have a chance to see what you are doing," he told them.

"There's a fellow up the road from us who makes fine goat cheese and we can visit him too, if you like," Terrence suggested with great enthusiasm.

"Your time here is going to fly by, Chouchou," Katherine assured him. She felt conflicted, knowing there was going to be a difficult conversation ahead. *It would be so easy to forget all the feelings I've had this week and just sink back into the comfort of our relationship. But I know it all needs to be addressed. Just not tonight . . .*

CHAPTER ELEVEN

Andrea insisted she and Terrence sleep in the guest room at the far end of the hall. At first, she had not planned to stay overnight, wanting Kat and Philippe to have the entire house to themselves.

"I'm not even going to ask what you're thinking," Kat chided her, laughing. "We aren't teenagers planning to romp naked through each room. At least, not in these cold temperatures. Otherwise . . . maybe." She chuckled with a devilish look on her face.

"TMI, thank you very much," Andrea said with a snort.

"Of course you'll stay with us," Katherine insisted. "I promise we'll behave."

As they all said good night, Philippe thanked them again for meeting him at the airport.

Alone at last, Katherine lit a candle in the master bedroom.

"I feel like a schoolgirl, having you in what was my parents' bedroom. I've never slept with a man in this house. Imagine that. Silly, huh?"

"Remember the first time we made love?" Philippe whispered as he sat on the bed and drew her to him. He unbuttoned her blouse as he ran his tongue lightly across her lips and down her neck. Lifting his head, he studied her face, intimately tracing his fingers over her breasts.

Katherine leaned into him, pressing his hands on her breasts. Her eyes closed and her voice caught. "I'll never forget it. Our romantic box seats at the Nice Opera House and that sizzling performance of *La Bohème*."

They shared a look of pure desire before he grinned. "Then our unexpected swim in the Med . . ."

They laughed, remembering how Katherine had lost her balance on the pebbles and pulled him into the warm sea with her.

They shushed each other now and tried to control their voices.

Philippe's lips hungrily found her mouth, her face, her neck. He whispered in between kisses, "It began in the shower."

"Oh yes it did." Kat whispered back, between returning his kisses, her voice full of passion. She took his hand and led him into the master bathroom. He smiled, seeing a candle already lit in there too.

Still holding her hand, he reached in to turn on the water in the shower. "You went in first to wash off the saltwater . . ."

Their clothes fell to the floor as they kissed more urgently, their lips asking and taking. Their caresses touched all the right places. Philippe slowly turned her around, his eyes smoldering, *"Je suis fou amoureux de toi . . ."*

Katherine tingled with burning desire. Every nerve felt ignited. She smiled seductively, her voice throaty as she said, "And then I brazenly turned and beckoned you in. You made me crazy for you—like you are now."

Naked, she stepped into the shower and turned to press herself against him as he followed. She moved readily to his touch, their arms wrapped around each other.

"It's so good to feel you again," she sighed. Her hands moved slowly over his strong shoulders before her fingers played with the dark curls at his neck.

"I missed you so much . . ." Philippe ran his fingers through her hair. Their lips parted, and their tongues danced a slow rhythm together. His hands slid down her back, and her heart beat wildly before he gently grasped her buttocks and pulled her to him.

Steam enveloped them.

CHAPTER TWELVE

The following day, Molly was stronger and more focused. She put in a written request for sashimi when the others left for lunch. The rawness in her throat, from all the tubes they had removed, was much improved and she could eat most foods now.

She hugged Andrea and Terrence good-bye as they explained they were going home for a few days. Her eyes glistened as she nodded at them and scribbled a huge "Thank You!" on the whiteboard.

At the sushi restaurant, Nick encouraged Kat and Philippe to go to Andrea's farm that weekend while he spent time with Molly. "I've got to blow this pop stand on Sunday night. We're heading back to Oz via Tokyo and Singapore."

"We'll plan to arrive at the farm for lunch on Saturday and then come back for lunch with Molly on Sunday," Kat suggested. "How does that sound?"

"Take your time, mates," Nick said. "Why not plan to be back with Moll by supper time. Then you don't have to rush and I get more time to have her all to myself." He finished his sentence off with a sly wink.

"Nick, you're proving yourself to be an outrageous flirt. Your reputation preceded you and you're validating it in fine fashion!" Andrea teased as they prepared to leave.

Katherine enjoyed watching Nick and Philippe laugh and chat comfortably with each other. She'd been nervous that there might be some tension between them, but now berated herself for thinking she might be the cause.

This isn't high school, for heaven's sake! Still, it was awkward to think of herself as an object of desire at her age. Nevertheless, the proof was there—and she loved it!

The two men appeared to be the same good friends they were in Antibes. She was thankful for that. Philippe told Nick about the work that was going on with the villa, and they all made tentative plans for a summer reunion.

Nick discreetly left the hospital in the middle of the afternoon but insisted that Mohammed would drive them home. Katherine agreed that 6:30 would be fine so they could help Molly with dinner.

In the backseat of the car, Philippe caressed Katherine's hand and pulled her close to him. The sensuality of their reunion the night before still lingered. "Nick certainly knows how to live the high life! That hasn't changed."

Kat laughed. "Unbelievable, really! He's a genuinely decent soul, though, and his generosity is amazing."

Philippe agreed. "He's seriously wealthy, *bien sûr*. I've never known anyone like him."

The few silent moments that followed felt almost awkward to Katherine, but she quickly dismissed them. She thought it was simply her imagination that Philippe might feel jealous about the time she had spent with Nick.

Philippe changed the subject by engaging in conversation with Mohammed, and soon Katherine joined in. Traffic was light, and they were home in good time.

Once in the house, Philippe suggested he build a fire.

"That's a great idea! And let's eat in front of it when we get hungry. There are plenty of leftovers."

Lounging on the sofa, Philippe watched as Katherine opened a cabinet full of record albums. After taking out several, she lifted the top of the cabinet to reveal a turntable. She stacked the albums and flipped the switch.

"*Mon dieu!* John Coltrane . . ." Philippe took Katherine in his arms, and they slow danced for a moment before he walked her to the stereo cabinet. "You are the one full of surprises now, Minou. Who still has records and a turntable like this?"

"Isn't that something? It's my parents' stereo cabinet from 1965. They always loved music and had record players, but this was the latest technology at the time and my dad was so proud of it. When he turned seventy, we bought him an updated turntable. So this one is only fifteen years old."

"*Incroyable!*"

"On Friday evenings they would play music and dance."

"*C'est romantique!* Just Fridays?"

"Yes, Saturday is hockey night in Canada, come hell or high water." She laughed at Philippe's quizzical expression and explained what she meant. Then they sat down and she gave him a quick history of the Canadian obsession with hockey.

Philippe laughed at her description of fans' loyalty when the National Hockey League was small and everyone knew all the players like relatives. "It truly was a family tradition, with everyone gathered at the radio to listen—before television arrived."

Coltrane's music continued, and they sat on the floor with their plates on the coffee table, chatting and eating dinner.

Philippe insisted Kat remain where she sat while he cleared their dishes. Upon his return, with a wide grin, he presented a plate with a grand flourish. On it were sea salt crackers and a heart-shaped cheese that Kat recognized immediately. "Oh my! That's the same romantic cheese you gave me on my birthday. *Neufchâtel!* You brought it with you?"

He nodded: *"Séduisant!"* They laughed at the memory.

"Has any other woman been so wooed by delicious cheese?" Kat pondered, her eyes crinkling with delight. "This came by private plane with you, I presume?"

Savoring the delicate, creamy *Neufchâtel* slowly, they reminisced about Kat's birthday. Their bodies melded as they nestled into the down-filled cushions of the sofa. The melody of the mellow sax wafted through the room, and the pressures of the past week eased in both of them.

Katherine said softly, "My father often said music was their religion. I never thought about that comment until my mother wrote that letter to me about their life during World War Two. Her letter definitely gave me greater understanding about how they raised me and how they lived their lives."

"Of course, you told me about that letter before you went to their village in the Ukraine last summer with your nephew. I'll never forget how upset you were when you returned. You didn't talk much about it then, you know."

She nodded, and her hand went to her mother's necklace around her neck. "This was my mother's. I've decided that wearing it will keep her close to me no matter where I live."

Philippe admired the delicate piece. *"C'est joli.* It's so meaningful to know the story that goes with it."

Katherine was quiet for a moment. "Would you like to read her letter? I have it set aside because I'm going to give it to Andrew to keep. I never want to read it again. It's just too painful. But maybe you should."

Philippe hugged her. "*Absoluement.* That's an important part of your family history. You have been immersed in mine: the good, the bad, and the ugly."

Katherine went to get the binder that held the letter and arrived back with a bottle of wine and a corkscrew as well. Philippe poured them each a glass and he began to read as Katherine rested her head on his shoulder. She shut her eyes and let the smooth strains of the music envelop her.

Philippe closed the binder when he finished reading. He leaned his head against the sofa, took Katherine's hand in his, and said nothing. They sat that way for some time.

He wiped his eyes. His voice was subdued when he spoke. "There are no words, Kat . . . no words. But I thank you for letting me read that. It explains a vital part of who your parents were. We need to know those stories. I'm glad you shared it with me."

"While you were reading that, I was remembering when we drove with Mirella to Céreste. The stories that day were powerful."

"*Oui.* That was a most special day. There are so many tales to be told."

"That's the thing," Katherine said. "To me, that's a major difference between life in Europe and North America. Those stories captivate me. The history lives on."

They sipped the wine as they talked about their childhoods and families and the experiences that had helped shape them. Their histories and personal journeys had taken them down such dissimilar paths. It was a conversation different from any they had shared before, and it felt like a new depth in their connection to each other.

"Kat, this is all so meaningful: the music, the memories you're sharing with me . . ."

He had been sitting with his arm around her, but Philippe moved and made some space between them. His face grew serious and his eyes became downcast as he turned to her.

The puzzled expression on her face registered her confusion. "What's wrong?"

"The entire time we've been apart, I've been struggling with this, and now with you making our time here together so special—I'm concerned. You've been giving off some worrying vibes this past week."

Katherine's breath caught. As she reached for him, Philippe stood, increasing his distance from her. As though on instinct, her fingers rubbed her bracelet.

CHAPTER THIRTEEN

Kat broke the silence that settled between them. "You're right. I've been struggling with myself . . ."

Philippe interrupted, "Before you go any further, I have something I need to say. Something that has come back to haunt me since we've been apart."

Pacing, he took a while to speak again.

"I owe you an apology."

Katherine sat stunned, with no idea where this was going. She thought she was the one with a problem. Did it have something to do with Anyu's letter? With the evil Idelle and Dimitri, who had turned life upside down for Kat and Philippe last year? What was he talking about?

Philippe moved to the fireplace and added another log, poking the embers to revive the flames. Then he turned to face her. "Where to begin? I can't stop thinking how sorry I am for everything I put you through last autumn. I'm sorry for putting you in danger. I'm sorry for not being honest right from the beginning. I know how important honesty is to you."

"Where is this coming from? We were well past all of that mess before Christmas. We had an amazing time during the holidays. I thought we'd come to terms with all that adversity."

"I thought so too, but having time on my own to think about what happened made me worry that everything was at risk. On my own, I couldn't stop thinking about how lost I would be without you. I've never had this kind of closeness, such intimacy and openness, with anyone."

Still sitting, Katherine replied, "I would say the same thing. You know that. You have helped me become so much more than I was before. You've taught me to love with a passion I never knew I had. We're giving each other a second chance at happiness."

Philippe nodded slowly. His shoulders slumped. Katherine had seen him look this dejected only once before, when Dimitri was threatening them and he had feared for her safety.

Katherine got up and put her arms around him. "I love you, Philippe. Make no mistake about that. I know, without question, that I only want to be with you."

His voice was quiet now. "The more I learn about your life here, the more I realize how much you're leaving behind to make your life with me in France. I hope you still feel it's what you want. I'm sensing hesitation that wasn't between us before."

"You're right. Being here has made very clear what I'm leaving behind. I thought I would be fine with it. In many ways, I can't wait to get back to Antibes and my life with you. Every day, on the one hand, I feel more strongly about that, about starting over. I'll take wonderful memories from here with me and keep them forever. The bad ones I will leave behind. But on the other hand, I realize I need to know that I'm doing this for the right reason."

"And that is . . . ? Isn't the love we share the right reason?"

Kat knew what she wanted to say, but she floundered and said nothing.

Surprised by her silence, Philippe looked at her with disbelief. "Are you questioning our commitment to each other?"

The moment was difficult. Katherine could tell Philippe was hurting. She was too. This was harder than she imagined it would be. Her palms became clammy and her stomach twisted into a knot. She knew the moment had come.

Philippe sat beside her and took her hand. "Kat. *Dis-moi*. Whatever is causing you this distress needs to be shared with me. We're not kids. We can deal with this."

She began to speak, her heart pounding. "Being back here on my own was much more of a shock than I anticipated. Because it happened so unexpectedly, at first I really didn't think of anything except Molly. As I spent more time at the house and around the city, though, my sense of home came flooding back, and I was filled with all sorts of anxieties about moving to France for good, about making my home there."

Philippe listened intently, without making a sound. His expression was strained.

Katherine had found her rhythm. She continued, "I've been trying to make sense of what is confusing me. I think I have. This isn't about you and me. I'm in love with you, without question. I believe in what we have together. I just need to know that I'm not going to be wholly dependent on our love in order for me to be happy making my life in a foreign country. I need to know that France can be my home because I want it to be. Does that make any sense?"

Philippe blew out a long breath. Still he said nothing as he studied Katherine's face.

Her heart was beating even harder and she clenched and unclenched her hands. She wondered if he would understand or if he would feel she was diminishing their relationship. Nervously, she repeated, "Does it? Does it make any sense to you?"

At length he spoke. "Yes, it does. I'm just relieved that this is not about us. *Je t'entends.* I hear you, Minou. Tell me everything you are feeling."

Kat nodded. "I'm sad to be leaving all that is familiar to me and has been for my entire life. That hadn't truly registered with me until I came back. I'm afraid that I will be leaning on you entirely for my happiness."

"How can I help you? You can lean on me as much as you want or need to."

"I don't know. I don't want to feel I need to lean on you. Maybe I need more time here to work through this."

Philippe's silence worried Kat, and she had a flash of regret at spoiling things. She hoped he could understand her feelings and separate the issues of her love for him and her leaving her country.

The last record had finished playing. The odd crackle from the fire was all that cut through the stillness.

Philippe had been staring into the fire and now turned his head back to Kat, speaking softly. "You take as much time as you feel you need. I will be waiting. I want you to come home with me when you are ready."

"Thank you," Kat whispered, looking down awkwardly and feeling unsettled.

"Alors," Philippe said, standing. "Let's go for a walk. Fresh air always helps, even if it's as cold as it is in this city of yours. *Allons-y!"*

They put on their layers and walked through the quiet streets, hand in hand, saying little. At one point, Katherine told him, "Nick says I have a classic case of cold feet, and he wasn't referring to the weather."

"Pieds froids?"

"Yeah, cold feet. It means I'm afraid to stick to my decision, that I'm uncertain and fearful."

"Ah! *Tu as des doutes!* You aren't sure about what you are doing."

"I think he may be right."

Philippe nodded but said nothing more. They continued to walk in silence, except for the crunching of their footsteps on the snow, each lost in thought.

Back at the house, Philippe repeated his earlier words as he helped her with her coat: "You need to take as much time as you feel is necessary. You must be certain of your choices. I will be waiting. I promise you this."

Kat studied his dark eyes and strong face that pleased her so immensely. They hugged briefly as she nodded, unsure of what to say next.

Katherine felt a mixture of relief and nausea. She was glad she had finally said aloud the thoughts that had been plaguing her. She also felt terrible that she had hurt Philippe and caused him to feel uncertain of her love for him.

"I'm going to make some hot chocolate, Chouchou. Would you like some?"

They sat at the kitchen table, warming up with their drinks and talking intermittently about Molly. The elephant in the room was studiously avoided for quite a while.

Finally Philippe said, "Kat, there's no question you must stay until Molly is fully recovered. After that, you can decide when you will return to Antibes. For now, just focus on Molly."

Kat's responses were mostly nods. Now that she had let out all her feelings, she felt drained. There were long moments of silence.

"Let's go back into the living room and put on some more music." Kat went straight to the turntable before flopping down on the couch next to Philippe.

Ella Fitzgerald's velvet voice filled the room. Philippe smiled at Kat. "You put that on specially for me, didn't you?"

Kat gently pulled Philippe to his feet and they danced slowly. She desperately wanted to smooth the rift she worried she had created.

Leading her back to the sofa, he kissed her hand. "Next to Adorée, you are the best thing that has happened to me. *Tu es l'amour de ma vie.* I don't want my life to be without you."

"And you are the best thing in my life," Katherine responded, her words filled with emotion. "This is not about the love we share. Please believe me."

He ran his finger along her cheek, resting it on her lips as if to assure her those words were not needed. "I do. It took me a few minutes to understand exactly what your struggle was. I see how you feel about moving your life across an ocean, now that you are back here surrounded by all of your memories."

Their eyes met, and Philippe continued, "But let me say that I've watched you blossom in our time together in France. You've made my life complete by being a true partner, but also by being your own person. You've won over my friends and brought new friends into our life. You've shown yourself to be a talented artist with your photography and you're on the brink of a new career. *N'est-ce pas?*"

Katherine took a deep breath and started to speak. Philippe touched her lips with his fingers once again.

"*Attends* . . . I'm not finished. Because of you, we have a dream for the property on the Cap. Because of you, Adorée and I are a complete family again. So don't sell yourself short. You are a strong, unique woman who fell in love in France and with France. You belong there, with me, but only when you are ready."

Katherine reached for a tissue and blew her nose after wiping tears from her cheeks. Philippe's words went straight to her heart and her head. She knew he was right. She was strong and she was in love. She would be fine.

"Thank you for that. It's what I need to hear. I do want to be there with you. I just have to get past these troubling insecurities."

They sat holding hands, listening to the music, as a sense of calm finally settled upon them.

After many minutes, in a voice filled with love and intimacy, Philippe murmured, *"Entre deux coeurs qui s'aiment, nul besoin de paroles."*

Katherine translated: "Two hearts in love need no words. That's beautiful."

"That's us, Kat. I'm going to give you a book by Marceline Desbordes-Valmore. It's on our bookshelf at home. We can read her romantic poems together."

Katherine smiled as her heart swelled with love. "You know all the right things to say to ease my fears."

"Trust me, it's our love that brings those words to me. *Ne bouge pas, s'il te plaît,*" Philippe instructed her with a stern look.

"I'll wait right here," she assured him, wondering what he had in store.

He bounded up the stairs, two at a time. Returning in seconds, he sat beside her again.

Suddenly, he took a small velvet box from his pocket as he dropped down on one knee. "I didn't intend it to happen like this but . . ." he paused.

Kat could see he was collecting himself as he swallowed and looked directly into her eyes. His voice was clear and strong as he continued. "Minou, Kat, Katherine Elisabeth Price—*mon amour, mon coeur, je t'aime*—will you spend the rest of your life by my side and let me be the man who loves and cares for you forever? With no pressure about when you come back to Antibes . . ."

His voice trailed off. His eyes shone as they searched her face for her response.

Kat's pulse beat wildly. A lump rose in her throat and she felt almost faint. She had not seen this coming. Not when it seemed like she might have caused Philippe to lose heart. Not after she had acted as if she questioned her commitment to the life they were building.

Hesitation and uncertainty vanished.

The preceding days without Philippe, and all that had happened with James and Nick, only served to reinforce how right she knew her feelings were for Philippe. The issue of where home was had to be separate.

Speechless at first, her voice whispered back, "I love you too, and I want us to spend the rest of our lives together. Yes, *oui*—yes, yes, yes."

"And if it takes time for you to come to me, that's okay. And if you want to come back to Toronto to stay for a few months every year, that's okay too. We can make it all work. I simply cannot think of my life without you."

He sat beside her and slipped a stunning ring on her finger: a sizable cushion-cut pink diamond bordered by small white diamonds in an antique gold setting.

Katherine gasped, "It's so beautiful . . ." She looked at it carefully, her eyes sparkling, "I've seen it before, haven't I?"

"Almost—it's very similar to the ring Joy wears. I have heard you admire it. She gave me the name of the jeweler in Marseille and he brought stones to Antibes before Christmas. I chose this one and the setting. Do you mind? We can change it if you want."

Their eyes locked, and suddenly they were in each other's arms. Their emotions swept over them.

Tears streamed down Kat's cheeks, and she shook her head. "That's what I mean. You hear me. You notice what I say and how I feel and then you do something incredibly thoughtful like this. I love the ring! I love you!"

He told her the jeweler thought Philippe wanted the ring for Christmas, so he'd had it for almost a month. "I didn't want to give it to you on a holiday. I was saving it for a special moment. I didn't think it would happen like this, but . . ."

"This was special—very special. I thought for a moment we had a terrible problem."

Philippe looked chagrined. "That was bizarre. I had some kind of panic attack and then you revealed your anxieties. *Très bizarre!* And now here we are with the ring."

Kat laughed and let out a sigh of relief. Tremendous joy filled her. She felt happy, secure in their love. She could feel that emotion from Philippe too. The words "home is where the heart is" filtered through her mind from somewhere deep in her past. *Probably my mother,* she thought. *That's something Anyu would have said.*

She knew where her heart was, and she would try her best to follow wherever it led. "I can do this. I can do this."

There was something else on her mind as they listened to music. She had to take the chance.

In among her parents' albums were a few that had belonged to her. The Beatles, the Rolling Stones, Gordon Lightfoot, Carole King, James Taylor—even some Bob Dylan, which she was going to take to Simone.

There was one album in particular she had rediscovered this week. It was an LP titled *Avalon Sunset* from 1989. On it there was one song that had perhaps signaled a warning about James, which she had ignored. He'd always hated it and said it was the sappiest song he had ever heard. She'd never told him how she felt about it.

Now she put the album on the turntable and placed the needle to that song. "Tell me what you think of this," she said as Van Morrison began singing "Have I Told You Lately."

She turned up the music and took Philippe into her arms. They danced the slowest dance, melting into each other as the words of the love song filled the room. Nothing was said, but their bodies spoke with passion as they became ever more intimately entwined.

From time to time they kissed, but mostly they let the words and the music wrap around them.

"I've never heard that song," Philippe said. "It's beautiful. The words were written for us."

Katherine buried her face in his shoulder and held him tightly. "I always hoped someday that song would have meaning for me, because until this moment it never did. Even though I desperately wanted it to."

They played it again and again.

"I could never listen to it before without feeling sad," Kat told him. "Now it means the world to me."

Kat wondered if somehow the love her parents had shared as they danced to these songs was with them as she and Philippe began this new chapter.

"To think we might have missed all this," he whispered.

"What if I had never come to France on those exchanges? What would have happened to us?"

"Let's not even think about that."

They stayed on the sofa a while longer, listening to music and talking about how the next few months might unfold.

CHAPTER FOURTEEN

Katherine wakened slowly. A smile played on her lips before her eyes opened. Pure bliss was the only feeling she could identify. She slipped her hand from under the covers and held it in front of her as she admired the most beautiful ring she'd ever seen. She rubbed the band between her fingers and moved the ring up and down, examining it from every angle.

She wasn't sure what to call it. *Does an engagement ring confirm you are getting married? Is it a promise ring?* She didn't know and she didn't care. Philippe said they would be together forever. She had agreed. Nothing else mattered.

She felt more serene at this moment than any time she could remember. Her smile spread.

Murmurings of Philippe's voice filtered up the stairs. He'd kissed Kat's forehead lightly when he'd gotten up at 5:00 a.m. "Good old jet lag . . ." Kat muttered before she rolled over and fell back asleep.

Now she got up, wrapped her cozy robe around her, and slipped her feet into her fleece-lined slippers—her papoochkis. She chuckled.

"Good morning, Minou, *mon amour*, the woman I will love for the rest of my life."

"*Bonjour, mon* Chou, *mon amour,* the man I will love for the rest of my life."

Kat kissed him on each cheek and then twirled around, waving her hand to show off the ring. He reached out and pulled her into his arms.

"Is everything fine at the market with Gilles?"

"Yes, we had everything well organized when I left. I just spoke with him. *Pas de problème.*"

"Let's call Adorée and tell her our news!"

Philippe broke into a wide grin. *"D'accord!"*

Their conversation with Philippe's daughter was exuberant. "We're going to be a family!" Adorée cried with delight. "I'll come home for a weekend in February! Will you be back then, Kat?"

Philippe answered before Kat could speak. "We don't know, so don't plan anything yet. Kat has a lot to take care of here. Just be happy for us now and we will let you know what is going to happen."

"Whenever! I'm so thrilled for you both! *Félicitations, Papa!* Congratulations, Kat!"

After they hung up, Kat thanked Philippe for smoothing over what might have been an awkward moment.

"*Pas de tout!* There is no need to rush anything."

While Katherine prepared their favorite, poached eggs, Philippe went upstairs and returned with a file folder. "But then, speaking of rushing, I went online last week and found all the paperwork we must complete for you to live in France. Now I'm worried you will feel I'm pushing you."

Kat looked apologetic. "I'm sorry I put you on the defensive with all my earlier angst. Really, it was very thoughtful of you to do this."

"I've written the letter I need to give them at the French consulate here, and this is a list of what is required from you."

They looked over the list while they ate and made plans to visit the consulate in Toronto the next day. Katherine needed to photocopy a few documents, but otherwise the process looked quite simple.

"Ha! Knowing French bureaucracy," Philippe muttered, "we may have some surprises. We will hope for the best."

After a leisurely breakfast, Philippe got behind the wheel of Kat's car, and they began the hour or so drive to Andrea's farm.

The sky, gray and heavy with clouds, did nothing to dampen their high spirits. Katherine kept waving her hand around, admiring her ring from every angle and making Philippe laugh at her obvious pleasure.

"You make me feel like a young man again," he told her.

Speeding along on Highway 401, they became engrossed in their plans for the Cap d'Antibes property. Philippe gamely asked Kat to walk through every room of the villa in her imagination and describe her vision. Then he would incorporate his.

"How and when are we ever going to get it done with all these ideas?" Katherine asked, laughing at some of the more outrageous fantasies they were spinning. "Let's go back to our original idea of keeping it simple."

They had always envisioned a simple French-country look and agreed that had not changed. "You mean no crystal chandeliers, Persian carpets, and double-size Jacuzzi bathtubs with gold faucets?" Philippe said, attempting to keep a straight face.

Katherine snorted. "I guess we did get carried away just now. That is so not us!"

"We can have some weekend excursions to the antique markets in L'Isle-sur-la-Sorgue. We'll find some unique pieces there. You'll love it!" he told her.

Eventually there would be six guest rooms, but they would begin with two in the original part of the villa, along with public areas for serving breakfast and relaxing, plus their own private rooms. The remaining four guest rooms would be in the attached structure that had once been the barn. Philippe reassured Kat, "Didier says that part of the job will take another year, but it will not interfere with our use of the rest of the space."

Katherine's heart quickened at the thought of beginning this new adventure. Philippe's support and calm approach to her conflict about "home" were already helping her feel better about how things might work out. Lots of couples carried on long-distance relationships, so maybe that's what they would do for part of the year.

They spoke about financing and other realities that had only been touched upon in their short time together. Philippe had always told her he had everything under control and Kat had felt awkward about getting involved in the details when they were simply living together.

Now that they'd made this commitment to each other, she wanted that to change.

"I want to be included in every aspect of our life together, and that includes our financial situation. We are full partners now, and I want to contribute. *D'accord?*"

Philippe smiled in agreement. "Let's have a business meeting tomorrow night when we are back at the house."

In no time, they reached the turnoff to St. Jacobs.

"Agriculture is alive and well here, from small organic gardens to much larger farms," Katherine explained. "It reminds me a bit of some parts of Provence."

Record snowfalls and frigid temperatures kept the winter palette pristine in the countryside around St. Jacobs. No melting thaws had tarnished the whiteness of everything, cloaking the entire landscape in quiet and snow. There was a sense of stillness and tranquility across the broad expanse of farmland. Red barns and deep-green forests provided contrast in otherwise perfectly composed black-and-white images.

Philippe pulled the car over to the shoulder of the narrow road as best he could, given the snowbanks, whenever Kat spotted a scene she wanted to capture. "They are fields of inspiration today . . ." she murmured, looking through her lens.

He loved to watch her work with her camera, as he often told her. "I'm eager to get our website up and running to showcase your photos! Gilles and I began making a list of some cheese-making farms for us to visit too."

Kat laughed. "FromageGraphie! I've been thinking about it also. Especially during quiet times at the hospital. I can't wait to hear what you have come up with."

They were distracted just then by the sight of a horse-drawn buggy turning onto the road a little ahead of them. A black wooden cab protected the occupants.

Driving slowly over the snowy roads, Philippe was intrigued as Kat explained local Mennonite history. "Look at the wheels of the buggy," she told him. "See how they're steel? That indicates this family follows the religion to the letter."

Philippe shot her a quizzical look.

Kat continued. "The issue of metal or rubber tires is one that seriously divided the community. I'll get Terrence to better explain. They have good friends who are Mennonite, and I've been fascinated through the years learning about their culture."

"They live simply, do they not? We have Amish in the Alsace region."

"Exactly," Kat replied. "Terrence and Andrea's friend, Samuel, once explained that their religion was not relegated simply to written creed and church ideology. He said it was a sacred canopy that stretches over daily life. Isn't that a beautiful way to describe it? Even for a nonbeliever."

"Religion. It's hard to say what's best; it kind of speaks two languages. We have a similar situation in France. Only much more political. Adhering to cultural traditions speaks of community and identity—solidarity. On the other hand, it draws boundaries between the faith and the larger society."

Their conversation was interrupted by their arrival at their first stop. The St. Jacobs farmers' market was humming with activity, and finding a parking spot was a challenge. Kat described how shocking it was when the original extensive wooden structure had burned to the ground a year earlier.

The market had been a landmark for a century and a half. Now it was functioning under a massive tent until a new market was built.

"We won't have time to explore it all, but let's go check out some of the cheese vendors."

CHAPTER FIFTEEN

Just before noon, they turned onto the long driveway leading to Andrea and Terrence's farmhouse. The snowbanks lining the drive were so high that the normally protruding grasses and willow bushes were nowhere to be seen.

Katherine grinned as she pointed at the crowded activity around the bird feeders near the porch. Black-capped chickadees fluttered about, upside-down nuthatches waited their turns, and ground-feeding slate-colored juncos taunted the squirrels waiting to muscle their way through.

As they got out of the car, Kat pointed out tracks in the snow to Philippe. "Andrea and Terrence must have been out snowshoeing this morning. I tried that once and was a total flop at it. I literally spent as much time lying in the snow as I did walking on it. Give me skis anytime."

Philippe laughed. "All this snow is making me think we should plan a ski trip next year. I promised to take you to the Haute-Savoie for *tartiflette*."

"Oh, let's do that! Denise and Armand can join us—without any stress this time!"

"*Bonne idée!* We will make it happen."

The side door opened, and two border collies roared across the porch and down the stairs to wildly circle the visitors. Terrence stepped outside and blew a whistle. The black-and-white blurs dropped to the ground and didn't move. Then he blew another command and the dogs hustled into the house.

Katherine and Philippe laughed as Terrence said, "You just met Frick and Frack. They have an endless abundance of typical border-collie energy. Fortunately they are great about responding to whistle commands."

"Cool! Those are the rescue dogs I met on Skype, right? They were much quieter for the camera."

Philippe was busy giving the dogs a good rub as Andrea said, "They're very good in the house. But as soon as they go out the door, they go crazy and think they need to herd everything and everyone."

The topic of excitement switched immediately from dogs to diamonds when Katherine—shy but joyful—presented her hand to Andrea. Lunch was a celebratory affair as they toasted the surprise of Kat's stunning ring and talked about the future.

"We're so happy for both of you," Andrea and Terrence told them. "The story of how you came into each other's lives is like something out of a romance novel. You've renewed our faith in life offering wonderful opportunities no matter what age we are. We can't wait to see what happens next."

"As soon as Molly is stable and we know what the rehab plan is for her, Kat promises she will come back to France," Philippe told them. "I have to return next week, but I haven't booked my flight yet. I want to make certain everything is fine here first."

Katherine looked pensive. "Dr. Primeau told me that Monday will be a critical day for Molly after all the test results are in. They can't figure out why her speech is so affected. He told me she will have to be in a wheelchair for a while. Her shoulder injury won't allow her to use crutches."

Much of lunchtime was consumed by talk about Molly's injuries and how they might have an impact on her future.

"I've never been more aware than right now of how alone Molly is," Katherine admitted. "She has no family. I'm the only person she is close to—except, I guess, Father DeCarlo, and then you guys."

"Terrence and I have talked about it," Andrea said, "and we will do whatever we can to help her. We can even bring her here once she's discharged."

They all nodded thoughtfully, and Terrence smiled. "Well, let's see what happens tomorrow."

Kat and Philippe went on to describe their plans for the villa. "We know the restoration work will happen in stages and that it won't be finished for a year or two. But we hope we might be able to open with two guest rooms in the autumn."

Philippe explained that there was no question they would have their own small organic garden. "Practically everyone in France, even with just a little patch of property, has a *potager*. We're only going to serve breakfast at our inn, so we want herbs and a few vegetables. We'll keep it simple."

"I've learned that the French have always been masters of the kitchen garden," Katherine said.

Philippe added, "They've intermingled veggies, herbs, fruit, and flowers since medieval times, kind of like an English country garden, except the focus is on veggies rather than flowers. The *potager* is more about a complicity with nature rather than a need for order."

"And chickens! There will be chickens for our fresh eggs!" Kat's eyes lit up, and her voice crackled with enthusiasm. "I don't know why I'm so excited about that, but I am! You know I've always loved your chickens."

Philippe laughed as he enjoyed Kat's elation. "She's turning a project that could easily be filled with frustration into an exciting adventure. She's making me feel like a kid again!"

"So you'll have to bring your gardening expertise with you and help us get started. Promise you will!" Kat and Andrea locked pinkie fingers to seal the promise. Philippe gave them a quizzical look, and they explained their childhood tradition of sealing a promise.

After lunch, the men went on a tour of the barns and greenhouses. The minute they were out the door, Andrea turned to Kat. "What a surprise your ring is! How're you really feeling about it? Did you confess to Philippe how you were worried about moving to France for good? I hope you got those feelings out of your system!"

Katherine gave her the short version of their talks. She explained how Philippe had been understanding and supportive. "And then, in that sultry, sexy French-accented English of his, he told me he understood. He really tried to soothe my fears. Honestly, I've come out the other side of my angst feeling stronger than ever."

"But you haven't talked about marriage? Isn't this an engagement ring? What about a wedding? I guess I'm still too old-fashioned, but . . ."

"Marriage isn't as big a deal in France as it is here. To be honest, we haven't even talked about it. What we do talk about is the depth of our love for each and our commitment to staying together forever—and he did bring all the documentation we need for me to live in France."

Her cousin nodded thoughtfully and shrugged. "That sounds like commitment to me. You're right. The bottom line is what is important to both of you."

"I remember a conversation I had with Molly when I was first falling in love with Philippe. He hadn't said he loved me, and I was all hung up on that. Molly made a valid point about what she called the 'L word.' I've never forgotten her reminding me that people often tell someone they love them while they are screwing around with someone else. She said it's not the words but the actions that count. Another lesson learned the hard way. She was right."

"Yes, she is," Andrea agreed.

The remainder of the day was spent relaxing by a roaring fire in the massive fieldstone fireplace in the family room. Katherine insisted Andrea pull out old photo albums and family videos going back to their childhoods so that Philippe could be fully indoctrinated into their family history.

Before dusk fell, they drove Philippe around the area, pointing out landmarks of the Mennonite community, including the quaint covered bridge of West Montrose. "This is about the best we can do with ancient history around here," they explained with a chuckle.

They stopped at a local inn on the main street of St. Jacobs for dinner. Philippe was introduced to some traditional dinner selections that involved a lot of melt-in-your-mouth pork dishes and sauerkraut, accompanied by crispy-crusted warm bread. To top off the meal, they ordered one slice of sweet and gooey shoofly pie, with four forks, for dessert.

Sunday morning Philippe was treated to a full farmer's breakfast, with fresh eggs, homemade sausage, and smoked bacon, accompanied by home fries cooked in duck fat. "The secret to the best-tasting potatoes," Terrence said, adding, "I believe your countrymen introduced that to Canada, Philippe. *Merci beaucoup* for that."

Philippe agreed that this was no secret in France.

Kat and Andrea shooed the men out of the house again. Terrence was taking Philippe to visit the goat cheese farm up the road.

The women settled into the cushions of a window seat in the kitchen, steaming mugs of tea in hand. "Honestly, Andie, this situation with Molly's accident has made me so aware of how we need to make certain we have people in our life who truly care about us. It's reinforced the need to establish meaningful relationships throughout our life, inside and outside our families, because families can change as time goes by. "

"Yup! We should always have someone who can advocate for us and vice versa. No question," Andrea agreed.

"It's also caused me to be vividly aware of how quickly the years are flying by. I've been feeling like a real boomer through all this. I'm so glad Philippe is here; age becomes meaningless with him."

Andrea smiled. "Age is just a number. Especially when we're blessed with the healthy genes we appear to have. Don't ever forget that, and don't worry about Molly. Thanks to her friendship with you, we'll always be here for her. I had never thought about how alone she was before."

Katherine hugged her. "That makes me feel better."

Taking her cousin's hand in hers, Andrea asked, "I'm sorry to be a pest about this. You said this morning that you were feeling less anxious about moving away for good. I just want to be reassured."

Katherine patted her hand. "Don't worry. I know I still have some work to do. Philippe gets how difficult it is for me to make this break and is completely supportive. What I feel now is a clearer understanding that rather than leaving things behind, I'll be taking them with me. They will always be part of me."

Andrea's eyes glistened. "Exactly, my sweet Katherine. Home is where you want it to be. What you want from the past will stay with you, and you'll build on that. We'll miss you terribly, but as we know, time passes quickly. And we'll visit each other every year. Promise?"

"Promise! And I'm not leaving any time soon, so don't make this sound like good-bye!"

Andrea laughed. "I didn't mean to do that. Honestly, I'm excited for you. I hope you don't take too long to make up your mind!"

Kat left her mother's letter with Andrea, who assured her that Andrew would treasure it. Kat had already spoken with him on the phone about it and was pleased with her decision. Elisabeth and Jozsef's story would live on.

On the drive back into the city, Katherine asked, "Is there anything specific you'd like to see in Toronto? Anything special you want to do?"

He listened thoughtfully and then replied, "Even though we're building a life together in France, Toronto is always going to be part of your past and your future. We'll come back every year, if you like."

"There you go being thoughtful again—and next time we'll come in warmer weather!"

"Here's what I suggest. Let's not worry about touring now. We can save that for our next visit. Going out into the countryside, as we just did, was great! Plus, I'm getting a decent look at the city as we go back and forth to the hospital."

With an impish grin, Kat added, "And besides, you would rather not have subarctic conditions. *N'est-ce pas?*"

Philippe mimicked intense shivering, and Katherine laughed in agreement.

"*Honnêtement,* visiting St. Jacobs was very special. It was an interesting contrast to the busy streets of Toronto. I could feel the organic connection between community and land, even under all that snow, and I liked it very much. *Tu as raison,* there's a feeling of Provence there."

Kat was reminded how different Philippe's approach to travel was in contrast to Nick's. Nick knew all the facts and historical details. Philippe knew a lot about that too, but focused more on the philosophical and organic connection of the French to their culture, the land, and virtually every aspect of life: their *art de vivre*. The *terroir*. It was about the loving care that goes into the *pâtisseries*, the wine, the markets, high fashion, and of course cheese, as she learned so well from Philippe.

"All about *le plaisir et la séduction*," as Joy had explained so well when Kat had first arrived in Provence.

CHAPTER SIXTEEN

As Kat and Philippe neared the city, the sun was beginning to set. Arriving at the hospital, Katherine admitted she was feeling a little anxious about not having been with Molly since Friday.

"I'm so thankful Nick was around. What a support he's been."

Philippe added, "And don't forget Tony."

"I can't quite get used to everyone calling him Tony. He's been Father DeCarlo to me for so many years that I have a lot of trouble calling him anything else."

Philippe said nothing for a few moments. "There's a special relationship between him and Molly, *n'est-ce pas?* I'm not sure what it is, though. Has she ever said anything to you?"

Kat shook her head. "No, but I'm feeling the same way you are."

Philippe looked thoughtful. "At first, I thought I was imagining it. After all, he's a priest."

Silent for a while, Kat then told him that she knew Molly had a secret lover for quite a few years. "I say 'secret' because she wouldn't divulge any information about him. The most she ever told me was that they were friends with benefits."

"Friends with what?" Philippe asked.

Laughing, Kat explained what it meant, and then said, "Oh my gosh, she did once let slip his name was Antonio. Hmm, Father Anthony DeCarlo—could he be the mysterious Antonio?"

"I think you just figured something out."

Kat's eyes were as big as saucers. "Can it be? I mean, I know I've sort of wondered before, but it's beginning to make sense."

Nick was with Molly when they walked in her hospital room. Her eyes lit up as Katherine presented the container of Andrea's chicken soup and some carrot muffins.

"You knew there was no way I would come back empty-handed from Andrea's kitchen, right?"

Molly nodded vigorously and then looked at Nick with a strange grin.

"Ready, Molly Dolly?" he asked and then surprised them by singing, "Thank you for the chicken soup" very slowly, going up the musical scale. Molly joined in with just a bit of hesitation, her articulation somewhat unclear.

"What's going on?" Katherine and Philippe asked in unison.

"We've had quite the weekend," Nick said as Molly nodded. "Dr. Primeau was here yesterday with a speech therapist. He explained that the medical team was stumped by their findings because there was no clinical explanation for Molly not speaking. Her brain functions all test normal. The speech therapist suggested that melodic-intonation therapy might work, given Molly's musical talent."

He went on to say that Molly had responded quickly to the therapy over the weekend. "Because Molly doesn't have any brain damage, they think she'll regain her normal speech abilities with a continuation of this therapy."

Crossing her eyes, Molly spread her arms apart in a questioning gesture.

Katherine hugged Molly gently, ever aware of her shoulder injury. "I see your attitude is on its way back as well. This is good news, Moll!"

Molly nodded, her lips skeptically pursed. Nick sang, "I'm feeling very happy," to the same notes and then Molly repeated it with him, tapping her good hand to mark the syllables.

"This has been bloody fascinating," Nick said. "The therapist helped us get used to fitting syllables to the musical scale. We just have to come up with simple words to fit the rhythm. Right now she has to hear it and mimic it, but she should advance before long."

Molly waved her left hand around in a "whoopee" gesture that made them all laugh.

That evening felt like a turning point. Katherine declared it as the best time she'd had since the first shock of the news of Molly's accident. There was an air of optimism and progress. Molly seemed strong and focused.

Thrilled by Molly's progress, Kat momentarily forgot her own happy news. Nick was the first to notice. "Ahem," he said, with an exaggerated clearing of his throat. "It appears that the two of you have something to share with us."

Philippe proudly held up Kat's hand to show the ring as her face split into a grin. In spite of her joy, somewhere deep inside she felt a small spasm of sadness for Nick.

Nick offered warm and sincere congratulations. Katherine was touched by his emotion. Clapping her hands somewhat awkwardly, Molly beamed.

Then she beckoned for Kat to sit on the bed and held her hand as she carefully examined the ring. Looking at Philippe with her eyes sparkling, Molly nodded repeatedly and then reached to plant a kiss on both of his cheeks.

Katherine, Philippe, and Nick went to dinner together at Casa Mia and discussed a few different scenarios for Molly's ongoing care. Nick explained that Dr. Primeau's office would call Katherine in the morning to arrange a time to meet and make some decisions.

Nick explained he had to head back to Australia. "Here's what I'd like to put on the table for you to consider. Although nothing concrete was disclosed to me, it sounds like Molly could be discharged for rehab. I want to take care of whatever isn't covered by your wonderful health-care system, if anything."

Katherine nodded. "Definitely one of the great benefits of life in this country. I'm pretty sure Molly is covered for everything. I looked over her insurance plan."

"So how long do you think you'll stay here, Kat?"

"Well, Molly seems to be improving daily. If the plan is to discharge her to rehab, Andrea said she'll come and stay at the house for as long as necessary. She can see Molly each day and make sure everything is being handled properly. Lucy and her cousin Li Mai will also be at the house, and they've offered to visit with Molly too and give Andrea a break."

Nick nodded. "Tony told me he'll check on her every day too." He gave Katherine a strange look. "Do you think Molly and the priest have more than a pastoral relationship?" Without waiting for a response from her, he added, "I definitely do."

"Well, now that you say it out loud, I have to confess—pardon the pun—we were just talking about that very topic on our way back to the city."

They all looked at one another and nodded, eyebrows raised.

"Who are we to judge?" Nick remarked. Nothing more was said as the waiter arrived to clear dishes and offer coffee and dessert.

Kat changed the subject. "If they do discharge her to rehab, and Molly is well looked after, I may be going home with Philippe." She realized she kind of liked the sound of that.

"It seems there's no urgency to be here now, and I've managed to get other matters organized with the house. I will come back in a couple of weeks when Molly is ready to go home. I can probably be of more help then."

Though Nick had been listening intently, he now seemed lost in thought for a moment before he spoke. "Well, it sounds like you've got that case of cold feet under control, Kat! I'm glad to hear it!"

Her face flushing, Kat nodded. "I'm sorry I subjected you to my anxieties! I'm coming to terms with my feelings, and Philippe has been incredibly understanding."

Nick gazed at them both. "Somehow I believe you two will make it all work. Now, about our Molly Dolly—I've got an idea simmering. What do you think of this?"

Katherine and Philippe listened, astounded at what he was proposing.

As they were parting, he said, "I'll pop in to say good-bye to Molly tomorrow and we'll see what Dr. Primeau has to say about our little plan."

"Nick, I think it just might work. You met with him before and you've been involved in Molly's care, so he knows you're part of the family, as it were."

Nick gave both Kat and Philippe a grateful look. "Thanks. It makes me feel good to know that I'm helping. You certainly know I care about her. About all of you."

CHAPTER SEVENTEEN

A phone call to Simone to share their good news was the first item on the list before they left for the hospital the next morning.

"It's three-thirty in the afternoon in Antibes, so she might be in the kitchen having a cup of tea," Kat confirmed, checking her watch. "Or covered in paint in her studio. You just never know." She chuckled affectionately as she thought about Simone's lust for life.

They put the call on speaker phone and Simone picked up immediately.

Not one for long conversations, she was delighted to hear from them and thrilled to learn of the ring Katherine now wore. "*Magnifique, mes chérs!* I've been waiting for this kind of good news from you!"

Simone inquired about their *"amie"* and was pleased to hear things were going well.

"I miss your company, *chérie*," she said to Kat. "But you are doing one of life's most important tasks: being the best friend possible."

She teased Philippe about being the best friend possible too, since he had gone to Katherine's side in spite of the frigid temperatures.

They laughed as he described the layers of clothing required before setting one foot outside. "No exaggeration!"

"You forget I am from the north, Philippe. *T'sais?* I know cold too! That's why we all choose to be on the Côte d'Azur! *Oui?*"

"*D'accord,*" said Simone. "I'm going to prepare a light dinner and get back to my painting. I have something new in the works that I'm very excited about! Let me know when you return. *Bisous* to you both."

Kat and Philippe barely had time to say good-bye before the line went dead. They laughed as they hung up. "No small talk with Simone!"

When they arrived at Molly's room, Dr. Primeau was making his rounds. He explained how satisfied the medical team was with Molly's progress. The consensus was that she could be transferred to a rehabilitation center by the end of the week. Her leg injury was healing well, but her shoulder and collarbone issues were more complicated and would require extensive physiotherapy.

"Now that the swelling in your brain has subsided and your functions—for the most part—are back to normal, we would like to operate to reposition bone fragments in your collarbone."

Molly looked taken aback; the doctor patted her hand. "Don't worry. The surgery is standard and does not take long, but it is essential for an effective recovery."

Picking up her whiteboard, she wrote, "When?"

"We have a cancellation in two days, as a matter of fact. You could be out of here and at the rehab center sometime next week. What do you think?"

Katherine asked about Molly's shoulder and how it would be affected by the operation.

"She has a type-three shoulder separation that does not appear to require surgery but will probably need at least twelve weeks of physiotherapy."

"So Molly is not going back to work for a while."

"I would say she is out for this school year . . ." He paused. "Of course, that is dependent on her speech returning. We are completely stymied by that aspect of her recovery. There is no discernible reason for her condition. In fact, we're documenting it in detail."

Molly hummed *The Twilight Zone* melody, and everyone laughed.

"That's about it," the doctor concluded as he closed his file folder. "You're a model patient, Molly. I'm certain you will be back to a hundred percent in a few months."

She smiled and nodded. Looking at Kat and waving, she sang, "Bye, bye, bye, bye, byeeee," going up and down the scale. Her responses were becoming much more varied.

Dr. Primeau held out his hands and laughed as he shrugged.

Nick asked if he could make a suggestion about Molly's ongoing rehabilitation. "How does this sound: if Molly's collarbone surgery goes well and she's moved to rehab next week, Andrea will stay in town with her. Am I correct about that?"

"Correct," the others chorused.

"At the same time, Molly will continue with the melodic-intonation therapy."

"Yes," Dr. Primeau agreed.

Nick paused for a moment as a smile slowly spread across his face. "What if I fly Molly to Nice once everything is going well, and if we can put the same treatment into place there? Then she can continue her rehab with Kat and Philippe."

Nick outlined what they'd talked about at dinner the night before. Now they watched Molly and Dr. Primeau closely to gauge their responses. They were pleased to see Molly's face brighten with surprise and excitement.

Once Dr. Primeau agreed to approve the health care Nick arranged, the whole idea was a go. "We have connections with hospitals around the world. I will put in a call to my colleagues in Nice and see what I can find out about the best clinic," the doctor informed them. "Let me know if you need any other information."

Molly grabbed Katherine's hand and squeezed it tightly. Her eyes were ablaze.

In addition to her whiteboard, which was handy for quick comments, Molly had requested a thick writing pad for more detailed conversations. Now she made a list of questions about her job, her apartment, her inability to speak. There was certainly nothing lacking in her desire to communicate.

Katherine reassured Molly that they would find answers to all of her questions. "It will all work out."

Dr. Primeau addressed the speech problem again. "Molly, we are all mystified. The fact that you're beginning to articulate words with the music therapy is encouraging. I wish I could tell you more. Every once in a while, we run into the most unusual conditions and simply have to keep investigating for answers. We will continue to search. Trust me."

Molly's feistiness was returning. She wrote, "I need to get out of this bed and get on with my life! I appreciate everything everyone is doing but I'm getting ANTSY!"

Dr. Primeau laughed. "That's the best sign yet that you're on the road to recovery."

Nick continued. "I'll get my people investigating the rehabilitation support we can arrange in Nice or Antibes and report back to you, Dr. Primeau. Sound like a plan?"

Everyone nodded, and Katherine threw her arms around Nick. "This is incredibly generous, Nick. Very exciting!"

"I told you, I do it for my pleasure. I'm really a very selfish guy."

Philippe shook his hand and then they did the man hug kind of thing. "*Merci mille fois*, Nick. After you mentioned this to us last evening, I e-mailed Didier to check the doorways in our apartment and our ancient elevator to make certain Molly's wheelchair would fit. He did it this morning. *Pas de problème.*"

Dr. Primeau stood up and shook hands all around. "This is definitely a first for me . . . but a very good first. Nick, let me know what you discover and we will see how we can make this work."

He picked up his files. "Molly, this afternoon the nurse will confirm that surgery will be scheduled for the day after tomorrow. You won't be able to have anything to eat or drink after eight p.m. the night before. I'll see you in the operating room. And don't worry—this is standard stuff. You will be in and out in no time."

Nick also said his farewells. "The world's a small place these days, and we can settle these arrangements no matter where we are. I'll be in touch."

Nick sat beside Molly and sang up the scale, "I'll see you in my dreams." Molly sang the words back.

Her face radiated gratitude and love as she handed him a note. He kissed her cheeks and gave her a gentle hug. After reading the first line of her note to him, Nick blinked rapidly and folded it into his pocket. "Thanks, Molly Dolly, I'll read this where no one can see me sniffle. I'll talk to you soon."

CHAPTER EIGHTEEN

Two days later, Molly's collarbone surgery was at ten o'clock. Three hours later, she opened her eyes and saw Kat sitting beside her in the recovery room.

"Is it over?" Molly whispered.

"All done," Kat said, patting Molly's hand. "Dr. Primeau said it went like clockwork and he will see you later toda-a-a-y." Her jaw dropped. She stood up abruptly, almost knocking her chair over in shock, and looked at Molly in astonishment.

"You just spoke!"

Molly smiled dreamily and drifted back into a deep postsurgery sleep.

Katherine texted Philippe, her hands shaking as she told him the news. He'd sat with Kat until Molly was out of surgery and then had left, city map in hand, to do some investigating at the city's food markets.

Trying to remain calm, Katherine asked the recovery room nurse to page Dr. Primeau. Then she promptly texted the news to Andrea and Nick.

Checking a schedule on her desk, the nurse informed her that the doctor was in the operating room for the remainder of the day. She would leave a message for him.

At 2:30 p.m., Molly was in her room, still sound asleep. Katherine asked the nurse on duty to tell Molly that she and Philippe would be back with dinner. Before her surgery, Molly had written her order for Chinese food for dinner at 6:00 p.m. and even specified a restaurant. Her appetite was back in full force. She also wrote that Father DeCarlo would be joining them.

Katherine left to meet Philippe for their appointment at 3:00 p.m. at the French consulate to go over all the paperwork required for Katherine to live in France. The previous day they had gathered originals and photocopies of her birth certificate, passport, and divorce papers, along with banking information, in case that was required. Everything had been translated into French, and the birth certificate had the apostille seal document attached.

There were two forms the consulate had to supply to them: a *certificat de coutume*, or a customs certificate stating that one's home country's marriage customs were similar to those of France—for example, one could not have seven wives), and a *certificat de capacité matrimoniale*, stating that one was indeed single.

In the papers Philippe had brought with him from France was a brochure titled *"Guide des futurs époux."* "You know you have to marry me if we follow this guide because it calls you my spouse," he teased her.

They had both laughed—Kat a bit nervously—when he added, as he took her in his arms, *"Voilà!* I said the M word out loud."

"Yes, you certainly did. I heard it too."

"Well, what do you say, Madame Scaredy-Kat? Molly wrote me a note and said that's what I should call you, by the way. Tony explained the word to me. Do I hear a *oui*?"

Katherine had not been entirely surprised at her hesitation. Her insecurities of the past couple of weeks were lingering, even though

Philippe's understanding of them had eased her anxiety. She knew there was no question about her feelings for Philippe. Those were crystal clear.

Am I worried that if we are married, we won't behave the same way? Am I worried that once we are married, there is something to end?

Sensing something was not quite right, Philippe had said, "*Ne t'inquiète pas, mon amour.* Don't worry. No pressure." He gave her such an irresistible smile she couldn't help but smile back.

"What's wrong with me? I'm not worried. I just feel afraid to say yes."

"Then don't say yes. Say *oui*! Maybe you will feel better about *le mariage en français. Oui?*"

Katherine had squeezed her eyes shut but couldn't hide her grin. *What* is *wrong with me? Why can't I just say yes?*

"We can do whatever you like. A big blowout affair. A church wedding. A quiet appearance at the Hôtel de Ville. *Qu'est-ce que tu veux?* What's your pleasure?"

Katherine face had paled slightly, and she felt a nervous flutter in her stomach. "Do I have to decide now? Let me adjust to the shock that we're doing this . . . period!"

"You have six months before some of these documents will have to be resubmitted. Enough time?"

Katherine fought to quell her jitters. *Behave like the mature woman you are!*

She'd closed her eyes for a moment and then said, "Okay. *Oui!*"

"*Oui* what? *Oui* to waiting six months?"

Taking a deep breath, Katherine replied, in a voice just above a whisper, "*Oui*, let's get married . . . maybe in six months."

Philippe then picked her up and whirled her around.

As he set her back down, Kat had continued, "Let's plan on sometime between now and the six-month deadline, when the spirit moves us. But for now it will just be our special secret. *Bonne idée?*"

"*La meilleure idée*, Minou! The best! *Oui!*"

They'd collapsed in laughter on the sofa and then went out to Merlot, Kat's favorite neighborhood restaurant. They'd toasted their decision with a glass of champagne and ended the celebratory meal by sharing a *crème brûlée*.

Today they were fully prepared with paperwork and looking forward to having all the preamble taken care of.

Except for the last-minute jitters.

This morning, Katherine had suddenly become paranoid that somewhere in the jumble of bureaucracy, something would prevent her from returning with Philippe. He had calmly attempted to reassure her, but even he found himself getting anxious today.

Giddy with happiness and relief, they left the French consulate arm in arm. Their bulging envelope contained all the documentation they needed to build a life together in France. Their *dossier de mariage* was complete.

"This calls for another bottle of champagne," Philippe told Katherine. "Too bad we can't pop the cork in the hospital with Molly— we have so much to celebrate with her. I can't believe she started speaking again. Just like that!"

"I know! We'll set aside a bottle for that express purpose once she's out of the hospital. Now, that will be a party!"

As they walked along, they went back over all that had transpired at the consulate. To their great surprise, the process had been quite simple since they had already done their homework. The administrator who had assisted them commented it would make everyone's job much easier if all potential candidates were as well prepared.

They were a bit early to pick up dinner for Molly, so they stopped in at a small coffee shop on the way. Philippe entertained Kat with some funny stories of his visit to the St. Lawrence market and how one of the cheese vendors happened to be a cousin to a supplier Philippe had known for years near Toulon. That immediately qualified him as honorary family, and a bottle of rosé was opened.

"This being Canada and not France," Philippe told her with a chuckle, "we drank it from coffee mugs behind the counter. Not quite the same."

Katherine smiled in amusement. Then she took out her phone. "Look at this e-mail from Nick. Whoever he has looking into Molly's situation has done a fantastic job. I didn't realize that the St.-George Clinic in Cimiez was so high-tech."

Philippe said, "Oh, yes, it's been rated the number-one medical facility in France in many polls."

"Well, Nick's helper—for want of a better word—got contact information for every kind of therapy Molly might need. Though who knows, she may not need the speech therapy after all. I can't wait to get back to the hospital and see what's happening."

"That makes two of us," Philippe responded. "But no matter what, it will be fun to have Molly stay with us. Of course, I am much happier that we can help her at our place rather than you having to come back to Toronto. It's, as you say, a wiener, wiener."

Katherine patted his hand. "Close. It's a win-win situation."

"You'll have me speaking perfect English yet, Minou! How long do you think Molly will stay in France? It would be nice if we could keep her with us through the summer."

"I agree. I just realized I forgot to tell you that someone from the private school where Molly teaches got in touch with me. He brought some insurance documents to the hospital for me to sign and told me that the insurance will pay Molly's rent while she's on medical leave. As long as she's receiving treatment, that cost will be covered."

"That worked out well. That's something else she does not have to worry about."

"I'm not sure if you know, but Molly has no savings. She spent every cent paying off enormous drug rehab bills that her brother ran up through the years. So this insurance is a real lifesaver. Now if we could just find her a good man, all would be well. What do you think about introducing her to Gilles?"

Philippe gave her a strange look. "Oh, I don't know about that. But to change the subject, I'm starving. Let's go pick up dinner and get back to Molly."

Along with their dinner order, they added extra spring rolls and a deluxe order of a vegetarian noodle dish to leave at the nurses' station. Katherine knew the nurses deserved treats once she'd seen the care they dispensed day and night.

CHAPTER NINETEEN

Father DeCarlo and Molly were deep in conversation when Katherine and Philippe walked in. Katherine noticed he was holding Molly's hand but quickly slipped it gently back on the bed.

Molly was talking as though nothing had ever been wrong with her voice. The tone was thin and raspy, but she was speaking.

Katherine and Philippe stood in the doorway, not believing their ears.

"They don't know why," Molly said, in answer to their barrage of questions. "Something to do with the anesthetic is the only explanation they've come up with so far."

"Dinner is served," Kat announced as she opened the containers and set them on the dresser. "Molly, point to . . . wait, no, tell me what you want and I'll fix you a plate. It's so good for me to hear your voice again."

"Katski, it's good for me to hear my fuc . . ." Molly stopped in midsentence.

Three sets of eyes stared wide-eyed, waiting.

"Uh . . . my voice again!" she continued. "Ha! Had you worried there for a minute, right? So was I!"

"With or without f-bombs," Kat said. "Seriously, I'm glad to hear your voice either way at this point!"

"Well, before the accident you pretty much had those f-bombs under control. We just didn't know what would happen after your voice came back," Tony said.

Kat declared, "Now that you've called me Katski, I finally feel like life is returning to normal. No one else calls me that."

"*Bon appétit!*" Philippe wished everyone as they all filled their plates.

Their dinner conversation was lively and laughter-filled, with Molly adding comments in her usual flippant way. A way that had been sorely missed, they all agreed.

Tony DeCarlo was good company. It was really the first time Katherine felt she had truly relaxed and talked to him as a regular guy and not a priest. She was aware of how considerate he was of Molly, making sure she was comfortable. But then, he was also that way with her and with Philippe, she realized. *I guess that's his compassionate nature and nothing else,* she tried to convince herself.

"Molly tells me she may stay with you in France for a while to finish her convalescence," Tony said to them. "What a great idea. Nick is certainly a take-charge kind of guy—and I mean that in a good way."

"Yes," Katherine agreed. "We were all flabbergasted when he first mentioned the idea."

"Flabber what?" Philippe asked. Without waiting for an explanation, he said, "We're happy about his idea," flashing Molly a smile. "We've already got a long list of chores you can do."

Molly's eyes twinkled, "With pleasure, as long as there's wine and cheese involved. Oh, and nougat!"

"And Kat already has started thinking about matchmaking, so prepare yourself."

A noticeable silence fell over the room, and then a nurse came in. "Whom do we thank for the delicious Chinese food?" she asked.

Molly pointed at Kat and Philippe, and the nurse told them how much everyone had enjoyed the treat. By the time the woman left the room, the atmosphere was back on an even keel.

Shortly after they finished eating, Father DeCarlo—Tony—received a phone call and said he had to go to another part of the hospital. He told Molly he would see her in the morning.

Katherine and Philippe stayed a while longer, but Molly was beginning to fade.

"This has been the best day since I got here, Moll! It's such a relief to see you back to normal," Kat said as she hugged her good-bye.

"*D'accord,*" Philippe said after kissing Molly's cheeks. She waved as they disappeared out the door.

When they neared the elevator, they heard their names being softly called and saw Tony beckoning them down the hall.

"I'm glad I caught you. I thought I might be too late," he said, a little out of breath. "Sorry, I just ran up three flights of stairs!" He gestured to a door. "Have you got a few minutes?"

"Of course," Kat and Philippe replied in unison.

They walked through the door into a small chapel. The room was wood-paneled with secular images of nature carved into the light oak. Two stained-glass windows in a modern motif softly glowed with moonlight shining through. There were six rows of pews and a simple altar at the front.

"We have one of these on every second floor," Tony said. "It's surprising how often they get used by all denominations as well as those simply looking for a peaceful place to process their feelings. Please, have a seat."

He remained standing and gazed intently at them both for a moment before clearing his throat. "Katherine, you are truly Molly's family. She has no one else."

Kat nodded. "I know. She's always been like a sister to me, and never more than at this point in our lives."

"Precisely," the priest continued. "Your love for each other is obvious, and that's why I feel it's appropriate to have this conversation with you. And you too, Philippe, since you and Kat are together."

He continued hesitantly. "It's . . . it's . . . rather ironic we are meeting in a holy place. I have a confession to make—a bit of role reversal here, with the priest doing the confessing . . ."

He stared up at the ceiling for a moment. Katherine reached for Philippe's hand. She felt a deep sense of foreboding but didn't know why.

Bringing his gaze back to them, Father Anthony DeCarlo quietly admitted, "Molly and I are in love with each other. We have been for many years."

No one said anything.

After a pause, he continued. "I know this is a bit of a shock, but please hear me out. As you can well imagine, I've been deeply conflicted about this. It's a complex struggle about trying to do what God expects, what the church expects, and what my transformed heart expects. Deep inside, I have known my true desire for some time. When Molly had this accident, I realized how close I came—we all came—to losing her. It was the impetus for me to take action."

Silence filled the small chapel before Katherine spoke in almost a whisper.

"What are you going to do?"

"I'm going to do what Molly doesn't want me to do. I'm going to leave the Catholic Church."

Philippe shook his head. "We never know what life is going to put in our path."

Katherine didn't know what to say. She continued to sit quietly, her eyes never leaving Tony's. In her heart, she felt happy to know that Molly had this love in her life instead of some random lover.

Tony continued, "So true, Philippe. It's strange how things happen. Molly going to be with you in France for a while is the best thing that could happen for our situation. I have actually begun the process of leaving the church. In fact, I have not offered the sacraments for several years, and my role has more and more evolved into our street ministry program. My bishop and archbishop have met with me several times and persuaded me to stay. Now they reluctantly agree it's best that I leave."

"I can't imagine the conflict you've faced," Philippe repeated, at a loss for the right words.

"It's been gut-wrenching because my love for my religion has guided my life since I was a teenager. I never anticipated being in a situation that would dishonor my promises to God. I have never wanted to offend my church. And let me be clear, I am not doing that now. But that is the perception of my superiors, sadly."

Shifting somewhat uncomfortably where they sat, Katherine and Philippe could see the pain etched on the priest's face. His voice broke as he continued.

"However, my love for Molly is stronger than any other love I have experienced. In spite of my love and commitment for the ministry God called me to, I have been struggling for years, feeling I was missing the core of the human experience. A life with Molly is most important to me. For many years we tried to have a simple friendship, but that became impossible."

"You said Molly doesn't want you to leave the church," Katherine said.

"Molly thinks she would not be able to stand the guilt of being the reason I left the church. I don't want her to feel that—ever. I believe once I have officially made the break, she will be able to accept it because I will still be in a ministry."

"What will you do?" Katherine asked.

"I've been invited to be a priest with the Church of England. It's really quite ironic—there are some married Anglican priests who have been accepted into the Catholic Church, but because I began in the Catholic Church and took the vow of celibacy, I cannot be married and stay. Hopefully that will change one day. I know other priests who have left the church to marry and who would have gladly stayed if it had been possible."

"Pope Francis appears to be an extremely forward-thinking man. Perhaps things will change," Katherine offered.

"We live in hope. In the meantime, with Molly overseas with you, I can finalize all I need to do and spare her any guilt or anxiety. The most important thing is for her to get better."

"And today is really the first time that I feel she is truly making progress," Katherine said.

"Yes, there was a time when that wasn't a certainty, and that's when I realized what a loss she would be to me. Please don't tell her about this conversation, but I felt it was time you knew the truth."

Philippe reached out to shake the priest's hand, "Of course we will keep this between us. We wish you good luck with all you have to face in the coming months. Please let us know if there is anything we can do, besides taking good care of Molly."

Katherine stood, not quite knowing what to do. Suddenly she blurted, "Um . . . just one thing. Those roses?"

Tony nodded and then broke the awkwardness by reaching out to hug her. Kat hugged him back, feeling strong affection for him and this tumultuous situation he faced.

As they prepared to leave, he said, "I hope I'm not putting you in an awkward position and that this hasn't been too much of a shock."

Katherine shook her head. Her thoughts were swirling. In spite of the suspicions she'd had, it was still a surprise to sit there and hear him say it out loud. She felt as if she had contributed nothing intelligent to the conversation, but deep inside she also felt pure happiness for Molly.

Looking intently into Tony's eyes, Katherine saw nothing but raw emotion and honesty. "No, Philippe spoke for both of us. We only want the best for you and Molly."

CHAPTER TWENTY

In the elevator after leaving the chapel, Katherine and Philippe studied each other in silence. Katherine shook her head repeatedly. Philippe bit his lip. His eyes were wide with astonishment.

"Life does get strange at times, doesn't it? Don't bother answering, it's rhetorical," Kat mumbled.

It was Philippe's turn to shake his head. *"Incroyable . . ."* he muttered. "I don't know what to say."

"Well," Katherine continued slowly, "I guess for now there is nothing to say. Father De—um, Tony—took us into his confidence and we have to respect that. It's quite a sto—" She stopped in midsentence.

Philippe stared, waiting for her to continue, as they stepped into the parking garage.

Kat stared back, her mouth wide open. "Oh my God. Pardon the expression, but the light just went on. Father Tony DeCarlo—Father Anthony DeCarlo—has got to be Molly's hot Italian lover! Even though the thought crossed my mind from time to time, I really did not expect it to be true."

Philippe still said nothing.

"Seriously! Now it all makes sense! They've had a relationship for years! And the good news is that he loves her. He loves Molly, and she won't be alone!"

Katherine was leaping about the pay station area while Philippe fed the machine.

When he was finished, she grabbed him and hugged him. "Do you see what I mean? This is serious business about him leaving the church, but he loves Molly! They'll be together! They have been together! They are together!"

Other people got off the elevator and looked at her strangely. Laughing, Philippe put his arm around her and guided her to the car.

"Minou, settle down and tell me what you are talking about."

And so she explained as they drove home. As the story unfolded that this was Molly's friend with benefits, he understood Kat's happiness for Molly's future.

"But now you have to reign in that excitement of yours. We have to keep Tony's confidence in us a secret until he indicates otherwise."

Kat nodded, becoming serious, "I can do that. It's such a relief not to worry about her future."

"And you don't have to do all that matchmaking you were planning," Philippe said.

Katherine giggled. "I still think Molly and Gilles would make a good couple. But of course, I wouldn't do anything to jeopardize her future with Tony."

"Somehow I don't think anything will put that love in jeopardy . . . and besides, I can't believe it never dawned on you that Gilles is not interested in women."

Katherine looked at Philippe in disbelief. "What? Gilles is so gorgeous and charming, all the women love him . . ."

Philippe chuckled. "And your point is?"

They talked all evening and made plans for the rest of the week. "Once we know Molly's treatment plans, we can book our flights back to Nice," Philippe said. "You know, this is the longest I've been away from the market in years. In fact, the only other time, you were involved too. Remember?"

Katherine thought about it for a moment. "Do you mean when we first met in Provence?"

Philippe grinned. "That's right. When I met you at that lunch at Joy's, I had been there for a few days looking after Oncle François after his episode. You never knew that the reason I stayed through that next week was because I wanted to get to know you."

"I'm so glad you did."

The remainder of the week seemed to be over in no time.

One day Katherine took Philippe to her favorite Middle Eastern restaurant, Jerusalem, and they debated whether it was better than their favorite Les Pins d'Alep in Nice. Finally, they agreed it was a draw. Both were excellent.

In between visits to Molly, Philippe took charge of much-needed repairs around the house. Katherine sorted and purged, clearing out everything she forced herself to admit was unnecessary to keep. At the end of each day, they would open a bottle of wine and feel very satisfied with their progress.

One morning, they got a late start and stopped in at a shop Katherine had discovered in her university days after her study-abroad trip. The love of French cheese she developed during her six-week stay in Villefranche-sur-Mer demanded that she investigate further than the local grocery stores when she arrived back in Toronto. She was thrilled when she discovered this "epicurean emporium," as they called it on their website.

Within minutes of entering the atmospheric shop—its floor-to-ceiling shelves crammed with a vast selection of products ranging from ordinary to artisanal—Philippe nodded his approval to Kat.

She was delighted to see their *maître fromager* behind the counter and introduced Philippe to him. They had an engaging conversation, and he invited Philippe to return at the end of the day to take a personal tour of their prized cheese vault. Exchanging cards, they agreed to stay in touch.

"You're right, Minou," Philippe said as they walked out to the car. "That's an exceptional store. It's like a mini Provençal market in one spot. No wonder you love shopping there!"

"Now, wait a minute—nothing here compares to the Provençal markets. *Rien du tout!* But it is a special shop, that's for sure."

When they got to the hospital, Philippe told Molly where they had been and how impressed he was. He handed her the small package of three exceptional cheeses he had chosen for her.

"Oh, I love that shop!" Molly chirped with delight. "Thanks so much! That's my favorite place to buy cheese—until I discovered your market stall, of course!"

"We're going to leave a little early today, Moll, so Philippe can have a personal tour of their cheese vault. I knew he would be intrigued."

"Does all this cheese talk make you eager to get back home, Philippe?" Molly asked.

Philippe gave her a warm smile. "The only thing I'm eager about is you getting better. The cheese can wait. It will always be there."

"And soon you will be there with it, Molly!" Katherine piped up, the thought lighting up her face. They spent the remainder of the day making plans for the time they would spend together. Molly asked them to go to her apartment and collect a few books about the South of France that she had purchased after her visit there with Katherine the previous summer. She also asked for her iPad so she could catch up on reading.

"The one good thing I can say about being in the hospital, now that I'm conscious again, is that it's a great opportunity to whittle down my to-be-read list."

The next evening, Lucy organized a dinner at the Peking Palace with Laura and Dr. Henderson and his wife, and two other of Katherine's former colleagues.

Katherine would always be grateful to Dr. Henderson for being the first to encourage her to return to France for her initial three-month exchange in Antibes.

"I've never forgotten how you and Susan inspired me to do it," she said, hugging them both. "In fact, if I remember correctly, you not only encouraged, but I believe you insisted, Susan!"

Susan laughed her cheery, infectious laugh and wheeled her chair over to where Katherine could sit as well. "I was about to correct you there, Katherine! I would have put you on that airplane back to France myself if I had to! And look what has happened. Your entire life has changed. Now, let's meet that lucky man who's stolen your heart!"

Katherine looked around for Philippe, who was standing at the end of the table, absorbed in conversation with Laura and Lucy. Inspired by Katherine, Laura was excitedly explaining that she had just booked her first overseas trip. She was going to Paris with a women's group and was asking Philippe to give her some sightseeing tips.

Katherine was about to interrupt, but Susan stopped her. "They look like they're having a good chat, Katherine. Introduce Philippe to me later. In the meantime, let's stay sitting here. I want to hear all about your new life in France. You're living my dream, you know."

"Oh Susan, you're so well-traveled. Nothing has ever stopped you and Dr. H. from visiting far-flung places. I've always admired that."

"You're right. Travel has been our addiction since we were first married, no matter how difficult it became for me to get around. You have to be married to a special guy to do that, and of course, our whole family has pitched in to make some of our voyages such joyful experiences."

Katherine reached over and hugged her again. "Your family inspires me."

"Well, I have to admit that it gets more difficult each year as this damn illness progresses, but we're not about to stop making plans and seeing them through as best we can."

She took Kat's hand in hers, and their eyes met. "Katherine, you are fortunate to be blessed with good health. Take advantage of that as you follow your own dreams. You never know when things might change. I don't mean to sound pessimistic, just realistic. Seize the day, my dear, and count your blessings—and stay in touch with us."

Katherine's admiration for this woman knew no bounds. In spite of the increasing challenges Susan faced as time went on, Kat had never known her to complain or be anything less than cheery. She was a fine role model of the proper way to approach life and how to deal with the increasing challenges of multiple sclerosis.

Kat smiled warmly. "Thanks for those words of wisdom. I've been struggling with doubt and insecurity lately, so your message comes at the right moment. I hope you know your family has a standing invitation to visit us any time—as soon as the inn is ready. I'll be sure to keep you posted."

"I think we might just take you up on that! You know how we loved visiting that part of the world so many years ago. Say, Katherine, you should start a website so we can follow your progress."

"That's a great idea! In fact, I'll get Molly to help me when she's with us."

The rest of the evening passed quickly. Philippe spent a lot of time fielding questions about life in France and his career as a *fromager*. He and Kat shared their plans for the future, and Philippe showed them all photos of the Cap property on his phone.

On the way home, he told Katherine how much he enjoyed her friends and that he looked forward to return visits. "In spite of the fact I'm speaking English nonstop!"

Molly continued to improve. The next step was to move her to a rehab center early the next week.

"How lucky is that?" Kat asked Molly when they discovered the facility was conveniently located within easy access of Kat's house.

Tony continued to be a constant presence. Since their talk, Katherine told Philippe she felt much more comfortable calling him by his first name, as some of his priestly aura had given way to a less-ministerial persona. They invited him to have dinner with them on Friday night.

Andrea and Terence planned to come back to the city on the weekend so they could have a last visit with Katherine and Philippe.

Lucy and her cousin prepared to move into the house right after Katherine and Philippe vacated.

Boxes had been shipped in a crate to France, while a few were stored in the basement. Several loads had also gone to Goodwill. Katherine was increasingly crossing her emotional hurdles and feeling more content that "home" would be wherever she was.

She had been deeply touched by the emotion Philippe showed in arranging the shipment of Elisabeth's carpet. He had insisted they have the carpet professionally handled by a top-notch Persian rug company. Once cleaned and carefully packaged, they had sent it by priority mail to Véronique and David to keep for them.

It all seemed to have happened so quickly. Even though Nick was making his way back to Australia in his private jet, he had offered to organize another for them.

Both Katherine and Philippe politely declined this time. They assured him they appreciated what he had done for them, but they didn't feel right taking his charity when there was no emergency.

"You're doing way more than anyone could imagine for Molly. That's where it really counts right now," Kat said, her eyes shining with conviction. "It's time for us to get back to the real world."

CHAPTER TWENTY-ONE

"On our way home . . ." Katherine murmured as the plane lifted off.

Philippe took her hand. *"Oui. Chez nous."*

"Chez nous—I love the sound of that. Home is wherever we are. I'm working on that."

Philippe squeezed her hand and smiled. "You're doing a good job. I believe you just might convince yourself. I already know it's true."

The simple fact she could fall asleep in her seat with his arm around her gave her peace. She reveled in that sensation before she felt it replaced by a new empowerment: the knowledge that they were truly committed to a future together. All she had to do was shake the insecurity that crept in at times.

When she had seen the early flight check-in details, Kat knew they were not going directly to Nice from Paris. The connecting flight Philippe had booked was two days later.

"There's a little business I want to take care of not far from Paris. You and your camera will just have to tag along. Do you mind?"

From the twinkle in his eye, there was no mistaking Philippe was up to something. Kat recognized that look. She also knew she would have to be patient. The man she loved enjoyed his surprises.

They didn't have to wait long for their luggage and were through to the car-rental desk quickly.

"Are you going to tell me where we're going now?"

Making a trumpetlike sound, Philippe announced, "There's a saying, *'La douceur de vivre est pour les amants'*—the sweetness of life is for lovers. So get ready to taste that sweetness in"—he lowered his voice to a sultry level—"*la vallée de la Loire* and . . ."

Katherine's excited words interrupted him. "The Loire Valley! I've always wanted to see that area and those *châteaux*! Oh, Philippe, how wonderful!"

He grinned with satisfaction. "Somehow I thought you would have that reaction. It's only an hour and a half or so south of here, so why not. It's a romantic place to celebrate the beginning of the rest of our life."

Katherine beamed silently at Philippe for a moment. "You are amazing. That's all. Just amazing."

"This is going to be a quick look at the area. We'll plan a longer trip for another time," Philippe told her. "There are so many parts of my country I want to share with you. First we're stopping near the town of Amboise to check into a hotel, and then we'll drive about half-hour to the Château de Chambord. Here you go." He handed her a Loire Valley travel book.

Katherine happily absorbed the history, sharing snippets as they drove along.

The early-morning Paris traffic was stop-and-go. Commuters on cell phones mingled with a steady stream of trucks as kamikaze motor-cyclists cut in and out with their own set of rules.

"You know, when we drive through these kind of surroundings, with apartments and commercial businesses and crazy traffic, I feel like we could be anywhere. It's not Paris to me," Katherine said, looking around.

"You've never forgotten the France you fell in love with as a young woman. Nothing was like this then. That's why."

Kat grinned. "I guess all those years of soaking in the bath and reliving my memories of six weeks in Villefranche-sur-Mer made me a hopeless romantic about France. Is that a bad thing? I know I'm not being realistic."

Philippe looked serious for a moment. "Perhaps we all need to be a little more unrealistic about where we live? I've learned to love a lot about my surroundings since you came along and let me see things here through your eyes."

Kat smiled and flipped her guidebook closed while Philippe continued talking.

"It's not like you're unaware of the politics or the societal problems and issues, but you choose to focus on the beauty around you, the small details, the history. You bring places to life for me. You would rather be in the *vieille villes*, or the historical *centre ville*, than in the newly developed areas."

"You know, now that you mention it, I rarely go into the newer parts of Antibes or Nice. I wonder if that will change as time goes by. Am I living in fantasyland?"

Philippe shrugged. "What if you are?"

"If so, that's exactly where I want to stay. I thought about it a lot while I was sitting with Molly. I like where I am in my life now."

"So do I—like where you are in your life now," Philippe said and they laughed.

Katherine buried her head back in the travel book. She was glad to learn where they were headed and, from time to time, she read details out loud.

"The main springs of the Loire bubble up in the Massif Central and the river changes a few times before it flows into the Atlantic Ocean in the northwest. It's the longest river in France, and the *vallée* stretches for about two hundred eighty kilometers along the middle, lining the river with vineyards, orchards, and crops like artichokes and asparagus."

"That's true. *Le jardin de la France*, the garden of France. Or sometimes *le berceau de la France*, the cradle of France, because some consider it to be the true birthplace of French culture and language."

Looking at a map, Kat said, "It says here that the easternmost region, the Berry, is the geographical center of the country. Another distinction!"

Philippe nodded but was still caught up in singing the praises of the Loire Valley. "To say nothing of its architectural heritage! We have nothing really in the south to compare to what you will see here. *C'est unique!*"

"And the south has its own particular beauty that you can't find here, so it all evens out."

Philippe grinned as he reached over and pinched her cheek lightly. "Seriously, I think you should take a job with France Tourisme. Who loves Provence and the Côte d'Azur more than you?"

The manufacturing and commercial buildings that dotted the A10 began to give way to vineyards, farmers' fields, and thick forests still in their winter state of undress.

"This isn't the prettiest time to visit this area, but we won't have to worry about crowds of tourists," Philippe remarked.

"And if the weather stays like this with such a bright-blue sky, the light will be perfect for taking photos," Kat said.

Philippe pointed out a typical sightseeing sign that alerted drivers to historic sites or areas, with the graphic of a castle and the wording "Val de Loire."

"Here we go, Minou. Get your camera ready, as if it isn't already," he said with a chuckle as they turned onto a secondary road. He found it amusing that she rode in the car with her camera on her lap, battery well charged, wherever they went.

"Can't wait, but I'm confused," Kat told him. "Why does that sign say 'Val de Loire'? I know that *val* is masculine, so it would be Le Val de Loire . . . but my guidebook says 'Vallée de la Loire,' which is feminine for *vallée*. Why does the French language do this to me? Just when I think I am getting it, I'm not."

Philippe chuckled and agreed there were more than a few exceptions to rules and just plain illogic in his language. "Either of those is right. Isn't it nice to have a choice? But my interpretation is that Val de Loire is this specific part of La Vallée. Is that good enough?"

"Makes sense. So, Val de Loire it is." Kat said, putting the book aside to enjoy the scenery. She picked up the map, resting it on her camera. "You know, as great as the GPS is, I still love to follow along on a road map. Somehow it helps to put it all in perspective for me."

Philippe nodded. "Look to your right. Quick or you will miss it."

Kat clicked on her camera and brought it to her eye. Ornate wrought-iron and gold gates indicated the entrance to a long driveway. Philippe checked that no one was behind them and slowed the car.

In the distance through the gate, Katherine could see a majestic sprawling *château*. The shutter clicked several times.

"It's a little one that obviously belonged to lesser nobility," he told her. "And still privately held, from the look of it. The big ones, of course, are mostly owned by the government now and open to the public."

Katherine snorted. "Size is all relative, isn't it?"

The road ran along the river. Suddenly, Katherine gasped. Dramatic pointed turrets on a massive castle roof appeared high up on the hill as they came around a bend. "We're in Chaumont-sur-Loire." Philippe said. "Isn't that a beauty? I checked and it's closed today, *malheureusement*."

From the road below, Katherine snapped away as Philippe turned between the stone walls bordering the steep street. Thick, twisted stems of wisteria vines climbed the walls in several places, and Kat could imagine the frothy mauve display that spring would provide.

"Oh, promise me we'll come back in spring! Maybe we can come here again when we visit Paris in April."

"Bonne idée!" Philippe agreed. "The Val de Loire requires more than one visit."

At the top of the hill, they parked the car near the *château* and got out to walk around and examine the building and grounds.

"The photos will be awesome, whether the *château* is open or closed. How dramatic! Imagine living with that in your neighborhood."

Listening to the camera shutter click, Philippe teased Kat about running out of space on her chip. "That's the beauty of digital," she replied, without taking the camera away from her eye. "I can always delete, and as you well know, I always have an extra chip with me. Learned that lesson long ago!"

Back in the car, they drove out of the picturesque village and back to the road meandering along the river. The midday sun shone brightly, but the temperature remained cool along the water.

At the edge of the village, Philippe pointed out unusual-looking flat-bottomed boats with tall masts tied to docks. A sign read "Balade sur Loire" with a phone number. Three men bundled in heavy jackets and caps sat on a wall, smoking. An overturned barrel served as a table for a couple of thermoses and the inevitable wine bottle.

"They wouldn't go out today, would they? Isn't it too cold?"

"You never know—the sun is shining. Those boats are called *toues*, and there are still a handful of enthusiasts that keep the era of ancient boatmen alive. It's very idyllic to see them sailing along the river on a warm sunny day. Want to go?"

"I'll wait for the warm sunny day! But I'll definitely take some photos of them."

They pulled over, and Philippe strolled down to chat with the men while Katherine walked over to the boats.

Soon Philippe was beside her, followed by the three men. "Katherine, meet some of the men of the Loire."

The three nodded to her, each offering a *"Bonjour, madame,"* saying their names too quickly for her to catch. With Philippe translating, two of the men proudly used what English they knew to tell her how the same style of boats had been carrying people up and down the river for centuries.

The oldest fellow, who appeared to be in charge, puffed his chest out and stood a little taller as he assured Katherine, *"Oui, madame. Tout au longue d'année, nous allons de l'aube à la nuit, tout au longue du jour."* The other two grinned broadly.

She was amazed they would go out every day, all year long, from dawn until nightfall.

Philippe said, "These men have a fleet of eight boats in full use in all seasons."

"C'est la Loire qui en decide," the grizzled, middle-aged member of the trio piped up. With a nod toward the river, he shared some strong words with Philippe. He hadn't said anything in English but seemed to be following the conversation.

"The Loire decides if they go or not. Apparently this river has a mind of its own," Philippe repeated. "They said it was surprising how some people want the experience even on a cool day. Spring and summer are most popular, though, with picnics on the sandbanks or small islands. The route is mainly between Chaumont and Amboise at this time of year."

Katherine complimented the men on the simple beauty of the boats. Using gestures and words, all three indicated how the flat bottoms allowed them to easily go into difficult docking places. Philippe explained how the shifting currents created ever-changing sandbanks and long, sandy islands.

The next thing she knew, their new friends insisted on demonstrating how they handled the ropes to unfurl the single large sail and control the directions. "Nothing changed from 1600! Even before many *châteaux* were here!"

Beaming, Katherine asked if she could take the men's photos with the boats, and they were only too willing to oblige. She admired their obvious pride and love of their vocation. This was France to her.

Once back in the car, Kat and Philippe continued along the road with the river on one side and rocky cliffs now on the other. They chuckled at how they had to politely refuse the men's offer of a glass of wine, convincing them they were on a tight schedule. Their new friends seemed genuinely disappointed Kat and Philippe could not linger.

Katherine was checking her photos when Philippe stopped the car on the other side of the road. They were staring at the face of a cliff with a massive double door on it. Large signs offered *"Degustation de vin."*

"Wine tastings here? What the . . . ?" Kat questioned.

"Troglodyte dwellings," Philippe said, "There are thousands of caves like this throughout the valley. Soft pale tuffa stone, or *tuffeau*, was dug from these caves to build everything, including the *châteaux*. Peasants saw opportunities for their own shelters. Many are still lived in or are used as wine cellars or mushroom farms. With a steady interior temperature of around thirteen degrees Celsius, conditions are perfect for all of those uses."

He turned off the engine and beckoned her, adding, "In some places they are even becoming trendy real estate."

Kat picked up her camera and followed him, her curiosity aroused. The heavy-looking wooden door opened surprisingly easily, and they walked into a brightly lit wine store inside the enormous cave.

After a warm welcome, they chose a couple of different wines to taste and were entertained with stories of other unusual cave communities to visit. One whimsical example that a shopkeeper mentioned was in the Samur area: facades in the soft tuffa stone that mimicked turreted manor houses, some of which had been turned into unique hotels and guesthouses.

"And don't forget that entire underground village, Rochemenier, also near Samur. The chapel is very special," said the shopkeeper. "Excellent wines there too. Here, taste this one!"

Along with the wine, there was a small buffet with baguette and a simple *charcuterie* platter. Kat and Philippe realized they needed something to eat, and this was just enough to satisfy their hunger.

When they were back in the car, Kat quickly turned to the pages about the caves in her guidebook and marked them to read later. "More reasons to return!"

"And now to our own *petit château*, before it gets dark," Philippe announced. "Unless there is something else that draws us to pull over again. We don't want to miss anything!"

Thanks to the GPS, they turned up a long driveway not ten minutes later. A pair of horses grazing near the road raised their heads and lazily watched the car drive by, adding to the romantic vision that lay before the new arrivals.

Perched on a terraced slope sat a majestic tower-flanked *château* that took Kat's breath away. The light-gray stone with white accents around the windows and a black-slate peaked roof gave the former medieval stronghold a stately appearance. A welcome sign noted that the chateau dated back to the early thirteenth century.

"This is where we're staying? It's magnificent—out of a historical romance novel!" Kat leaned over impulsively and kissed Philippe's cheek.

"I thought you might like it," Philippe said, looking pleased. "We can check in and then dash out again to visit a *château* down the road that is *plus grand*, to say the least."

After admiring their spacious room and four-poster bed, they quickly inspected the manicured terraced gardens that led to a protected swimming pool area. "We'll definitely make another visit in warmer weather," Philippe noted. "In fact, I'm thinking about a cycling trip through here. What do you think of that?"

"Brilliant idea! Yes! Let's do that!"

"The Loire à Vélo route is at least six hundred kilometers and is going to be eight hundred when they finish. We can pick what part we want to do . . . or we can do the whole thing."

"That would be a blast. Long and beautiful, but not terribly challenging—just right for warm weather. I can imagine how spectacular this area would all be once these gardens and the woodlands are in full bloom," Kat agreed, her camera clicking incessantly as she captured the *château*, gardens, and quirky images that presented themselves.

"Leonardo da Vinci lived just a few miles down the road for much of his life," Philippe told her. "How's that for a neighbor?"

The rest of the afternoon was spent in full tourist mode, driving through farmland, woodlands, and vineyards dotted with the elaborate hunting lodges of the wealthy and royalty of centuries before.

They first toured the stunning and immense Château de Chambord, with its elaborate rooftop, which Kat commented was even more beautiful and impressive in reality than in photos.

"Simply fascinating," Katherine repeated excitedly as she listened to the detailed audio guide describe the history, as well as intriguing bits of information about everyday life there through the centuries. They learned that it was the largest of the Loire *châteaux*, started by King Francis I in 1519, and now containing more than 440 rooms and 282 fireplaces. It had often been abandoned, though, and during World War II art treasures from the Louvre and Compèigne were stored there.

"Simply drafty too," they agreed as the brisk winter air filled the massive, mostly empty rooms and chambers.

Philippe shook his head. "Imagine how much wood had to be burned to even begin to warm up these spaces."

After a thorough tour spent completely enveloped in the historical ambiance of Chambord, they wound their way through back roads to the exquisite estate of Château de Cheverny, built a century after

Chambord was begun. This was a fine example of luxurious aristocratic life, with the furnishings and décor remarkably well preserved.

They were just in time to see the feeding of the more than a hundred hunting dogs. The barking and baying from the kennels could be heard well before the hounds came into view. "Pico would not be happy having to share with this many!" Philippe joked as they watched the mass of toned bodies and wagging tales fill the kennel courtyard with canine energy.

"Imagine a property owned by the same family for six centuries. That just boggles my mind," Kat commented, her face filled with wonder as they toured the elegantly furnished rooms. "How fascinating and completely appealing to have such complete knowledge of your family history."

Philippe nodded. "It's not uncommon here."

Looking at her watch, Katherine said, "I can't believe we managed to fit both of those *châteaux* into the afternoon. They were fabulous . . . and so different."

"Now let's go back to soak in that cavernous bathtub and rest up for a very special dinner in our *château*'s Michelin-starred restaurant."

CHAPTER TWENTY-TWO

They wakened to a symphony of sweet-sounding birdsong, and Katherine opened the tall windows framed by rich, silk draperies. Set in the thick stone wall of the *château*, the window ledge provided a perfect seat. Through the leafless trees, she could see the Loire flowing at the foot of the terraced property.

"This could well be a definition of sublime," she sighed, breathing in the crisp morning air and firmly fixing another unforgettable moment in her memory.

Philippe smiled with satisfaction.

After a sumptuous breakfast served with the same elegant efficiency as the exquisite dinner the night before, the travelers were off on another mission as a light rain fell.

Besides introducing Kat to the Val de Loire, Philippe wanted to visit a cheese supplier of his and show Katherine the charming tiny village of Chavignol. When he first told Kat they would go there, she smiled broadly. The delicious goat cheese, Crottin de Chavignol, was among her most loved cheeses—particularly the very small nuggets.

Philippe had often called it her addiction and had teased her about it being named after goat dung. "Well, it looks like it, doesn't it? And you know what the word *crotte* means!"

As they drove past the turn to the hilltop setting of Sancerre, they voiced regret for not having enough time to visit that grand medieval town.

"That's the thing, isn't it?" Kat sighed. "Wherever we go, we could spend days exploring all of these intriguing villages without going far afield."

Endless vineyards, farm fields, and walnut orchards covered the rolling hills. Although the hills were bare in their winter wardrobe, it was clear the crops thrived in this specific *terroir*.

Goats grazed, their rich brown coats gleaming from dampness, seemingly oblivious to the light drizzle. Bright-yellow ear tags bobbed as they chewed.

"There's a sense of promise here," Kat remarked. Her gaze brushed across the landscape, eagerly absorbing every detail. "Or is my imagination working overtime? I feel something special in the air."

"*D'accord*, I have always felt that too. The products from this area are of the highest quality." Philippe had introduced Kat to a sauvignon blanc from Sancerre at dinner the night before, and they both agreed it would become a favorite of theirs.

"Wine and cheese have been the outstanding products of this particular area through the ages," Philippe told her. "This was also a regional command center for the Resistance; Simone will tell you about that."

"I'm so anxious to hear her stories," Kat replied.

Only three kilometers further, Chavignol was one of the smallest villages Kat had ever visited. Its simplicity charmed her immediately. "Blink and you're through it!"

"We will come back here after we visit the goat farm and you can take pictures to your heart's content. Our flight to Nice is early tomorrow, so we will have a few hours before we have to return the car and check in to the airport hotel." Giving Kat a light nudge, he couldn't resist teasing, "Unless, of course, you don't want to shoot any more photos."

"Hey, it's France. It's impossible for me to stop taking photos."

Just outside the village, Philippe turned onto a bumpy dirt road that led to an even bumpier dirt lane, then stopped in front of a farm that might have been straight out of a sixteenth-century painting. Outbuildings surrounded what looked to be the original structure. A jumble of attached additions created an illusion of a horizontal stone sculpture.

A barking dog of questionable heritage heralded their arrival and greeted them with a wildly wagging tail after they parked the car.

Katherine gave the dog a good scratch around its ears as an elderly man moving slowly with two canes appeared in one of the doorways.

Greeting Philippe with obvious affection, he invited them into a cavernous space warmed by a roaring fire. Gesturing for them to sit at a long wooden table, he disappeared into a back room. Philippe explained that the first time he came to this *chèvrerie* was with his own father, who had been friends with this proprietor, Monsieur Fortin. This family had been producing their famous Crottin de Chavignol for six generations. Philippe's father and now Philippe were among the select few to whom their product was distributed.

The elderly man returned to the table with a young woman he introduced as his granddaughter, Céleste. She carried a tray with warm baguette, several types of *chèvre*, and a lightly chilled jug of white wine.

After chatting and toasting *"santé"* many times, Monsieur Fortin spoke slowly with Katherine, his eyes twinkling flirtatiously, before he asked Céleste to take them on a tour. He apologized for being unable to move around well these days.

Katherine was fascinated by the explanation of the entire cheese-making process. Céleste told them that new regulations by the European

Community made their work more labor-intensive and frustrating these days. She translated for Kat: "Fortunately our results haven't changed and our customers are happy. Our herd of alpine goats numbers around one hundred and fifty, and they must be fed cereal and only locally grown grass grown to comply with the AOC."

She paused and looked at Kat to make certain she understood.

Kat indicated she did with a nod. She was well aware, from Philippe's business, of the strict French regulations based on the concept of *terroir*. They were granted to certain French geographical products like butters, wines, cheeses, and other agricultural products that were held to a rigorous set of clearly defined standards. "It's what makes them so special," she said.

"*Absolument!* The work here is all by hand and very intensive at times, but we love our goats . . ." Céleste smiled proudly. "And that's one of our secrets."

Philippe explained that the farm was a small but exclusive supplier compared to others, and there was always a waiting list to become one of their customers. A sharp, pungent smell wafted out of the cheese-making room, where the wet cheese glistened in wooden molds. Sold at different ages, the smell and color changed as it matured, and now Céleste offered them samples from various stages.

Céleste looked pleased as Philippe told Kat, "The older cheese from this farm is renowned for its particular odor of undergrowth. That's another one of their secrets."

When they returned to the table, more wine was poured and several selections of *chèvre* tempted them on a thick board. Sliced sausage and *jambon* appeared, along with olives and the typical salad of fresh greens accompanied by fresh baguette. A warm *tarte tatin* sat to the side as the final touch for dessert. Lunch was served.

Philippe explained how Katherine was addicted to their *crottin*. She sighed with pleasure and smiled broadly as she enjoyed some of the samples. The old man cackled with delight. Katherine later told

Philippe she was convinced that every one of the numerous lines on Monsieur Fortin's face was the result of laughter.

Before they left, Céleste invited Katherine to photograph whatever she wished and accompanied her around. They went outside to where some of the herd was grazing nearby. Katherine found herself mesmerized by the innocent faces of the goats, whose widespread eyes made them appear to be full of curiosity and bursting to say something.

She was charmed as Céleste told her the names of many of the goats and saw the gentle way they responded to her.

Meanwhile, the two men sat at the table and carried on a conversation filled with uproarious chortles and guffaws. Philippe told Kat later that the old man had endless amusing stories about local characters and some of his own youthful escapades. "He's a sheer delight, that fellow! Always has been!"

They ended their visit with Katherine taking photos of grandfather and granddaughter, which she promised to send to them. It was easy to see the family tradition of cheese making was in good hands.

The rain stopped by the time Katherine and Philippe left the warm hospitality of the *chèvrerie*. As promised, Philippe returned Kat to Chavignol and turned her loose with her camera. He waited in the local bar, reading a book and sipping an espresso in front of the embers left from the morning's fire.

They spent the rest of the afternoon driving narrow back roads. Philippe suspected there would be many places Katherine would want to stop as they happened upon estates and vistas too inviting not to photograph. He loved watching her work.

They ended their Loire Valley excursion with a hearty daube at a small country *auberge*. The menu blackboard boasted that the ingredients were from the latest local hunt and from surrounding farms. Philippe nodded as Katherine declared they could not have found a better spot.

Driving to the airport hotel, Philippe said, "I know it's frustrating to be this close to Paris and not go there. But we've got the first flight out tomorrow morning, so I figured this would be a better plan. No traffic worries."

"Definitely a good idea. We can sleep longer! This visit was a very special excursion, Chouchou. Thanks so much for thinking of it, and for planning it for me."

"I did it for one reason," Philippe said with a smile.

They looked at each other with wide grins and in unison said, *"Le plaisir!"*

CHAPTER TWENTY-THREE

Katherine could almost taste her anticipation as the plane banked for its descent. Visibility was bright and clear, and the early-morning sun threw a vivid splash of light over the landscape.

She relished the view of the snowcapped Alps backing the ocher-colored villages and rooftops tumbling down to the turquoise waters of the sea. Even the massive high-rise construction of Monaco could be forgiven in that light. Her shutter clicked away; as she told Philippe, she could never have too many of these shots from the air.

He leaned over for a glimpse and kissed Kat's cheek. "As you say, 'ome sweet 'ome."

Bernadette and her taxi waited at their usual spot. She greeted them with the customary *bises*, accompanied by her bright smile and her delightfully thick Marseillaise accent, and wearing—as only French women of any age could—five-inch-high scarlet stilettos. Katherine smiled as she noticed that Bernadette's wild mane of gunmetal-gray hair was vividly streaked with mauve highlights.

"I am so 'appy to 'ear zat Molly goes well," she told them.

Her smile widened as Philippe told her Molly would probably be coming to Antibes before too long.

As Bernadette steered them quickly onto the Bord de Mer, knowing this slower route was their favorite, she provided a running commentary of the latest news during their absence.

"Marc-Antoine's wife 'ad twin girls, and the *boulangerie* made special double *beignets* to mark zee occasion. Paul, zee *poisonnière*, is enlarging 'is store and 'is wife Giselle will sell 'omemade fish soup and frozen *entrées*. *C'est un peu scandaleux*—everything is always fresh at fish markets, and now zee other shopkeepers' wives are feeling zee pressure to come up with similar 'to-go' ideas."

Philippe and Kat chuckled. They were home indeed.

As they passed the familiar scenery of the pebble beaches bordering the turquoise water of the Mediterranean, the more content Katherine felt. The usual number of fishing poles dotted the beach, and the snack trucks were surrounded by patrons in their folding chairs sipping espressos.

Bernadette continued her news broadcast.

"*Oh-là-là, vous avez de la chance*—you are wiz ze luck!" she continued, her voice dropping to a lower and more dramatic tone. "You missed *le déluge*! But you must check your place on *le Cap*. The rainstorms 'ave been *terrible*."

She pronounced *terrible* in French, which Kat always felt sounded entirely stronger than in English. Apparently there had been much flooding and damage. As Bernadette continued to describe the problems of all that rain, it made Toronto's snow and frigid temperatures insignificant.

Philippe assured both women that Didier had been keeping a close eye on the property.

"Ah, Didier is doing zee restoration work for you? 'E is okay—for a Frenchman. *Je te donne le feu vert*," Bernadette said, always quick to state her disdain for her male countrymen.

Kat swallowed a snort at Bernadette giving them the green light for Didier. Philippe discreetly rolled his eyes at Kat and shook his head.

As they *bised* with Bernadette in front of their apartment, she suddenly reached for Katherine's left hand. Her face aglow, she admired the ring. "*C'est magnifique!* More news, *mes amis?*"

"*Comme tu veux,*" Philippe replied with an enigmatic smile. "As you wish."

Grinning, the taxi driver drove off down the wide boulevard with a final elaborate wave out the window.

"*Et bien!* That news should be all over town by the time *apéros* are served!" Philippe declared.

As they entered the lobby of their apartment building, Philippe led Katherine to the antiquated elevator that they seldom used anymore. "Let's do this again, like the day you came back with me from the airport. Now it will be even more official."

They kissed their way to the next floor, then Philippe scooped Kat up into his arms and through their open apartment door. "Across the threshold, just like last time," Kat laughed, "but I don't think we'll leave a trail of clothes to the bedroom this time."

"Well, we could . . ." Philippe answered with a sly grin.

"Oh sure, leave it up to me!" Kat laughed as he looked at her with an exaggerated puppy-dog expression. "I know you're dying to get to the market to meet with Gilles and get caught up. Besides, you have a case of Crottin de Chavignol you need to put in the cooler! *Allez, zou!*"

Philippe carried her to the closet that held their biking helmets. "And I know you don't want to wait another moment to hop on your bike and go see Simone! *Oui?*"

As Philippe set her down gently, Katherine pinched his cheek lightly. "You're absolutely right about that. What a difference a few months make in a relationship!"

They looked at each other with comfortable confidence.

"You know how it goes, Chouchou. Now I've got the ring—that's it for sex!"

"Meet me at the market after your visit and we will discuss that further," Philippe instructed, eyebrows raised. Then, with a quick *bise*, he was out the door.

Katherine stood still for a moment holding onto that last *bise*— such a simple thing—and thinking how happy Philippe made her feel.

In the kitchen, she gazed down the lane after she opened the window and unclasped the shutters. Leaning out, she breathed in the cool air and then ran her hand up the wooden slats of the shutters as she fastened them back to the wall. A smile played on her lips as she took in the scene.

A dog barked and another replied. Voices of children coming home for lunch would soon bounce off the uneven walls of the timeworn buildings lining the cobblestone alley. Clothes hung on lines across windows. As the colorful items fluttered in a light breeze, Kat noted the pleasure this scene always gave her.

Yes, it's small things that help make this home to me. I should feel this is home. I want to feel it. I've got to let go of my fear once and for all.

She pressed Simone's number on her phone. It rang only once.

"*Chérie! Bienvenue!* Welcome back!" Simone's happiness rang in her voice. "I have missed you. How is your friend? Were you happy to be back in Toronto? Wasn't it too cold for you? How did Philippe like his first Canadian experience? *Mon Dieu*, I have so many questions for you . . . come, *viens!*"

"I've missed you too. You've been well? *Ça va?* I'll answer all your questions when I see you!"

Kat smiled to herself as Simone's voice rose above the Bob Dylan music in the background. She could picture the diminutive artist in her studio.

"*Très bien, merci!* All the better now that you are back! When can you drop by?"

"I'll hop on my bike and see you shortly. May I pick up anything for you?"

"*Non, merci.* You are all I need. I will prepare a salad for us for lunch and put on the kettle and tell Victor Hugo you are on your way. He has missed you too!"

Although the sun was dazzling and the sky its wintery deep Provençal blue, it was cool and would be even more so in the wind along the water. She decided lined cycling tights and a windproof jacket would be more than enough to keep her warm. As an afterthought, she tucked biking gloves into a pocket.

CHAPTER TWENTY-FOUR

As Katherine bumped along the cobblestones in the back laneway, her body tingled with happiness at the familiar, intimate feeling of the narrow alley. Turning onto the paved street along the shoreline, she couldn't help being filled with satisfaction. The sea shimmered in the sunshine before the light wind whipped waves up along the rocky shoreline. Wispy clouds scudded across the brilliant, clear blue Provençal sky.

Ahhhh, home. Chez nous. *Keep saying it.*

It wasn't long before she clicked into a lower gear going uphill toward Simone's home on the Cap, taking a slightly more circuitous route that led her past Philippe's property. He continued to encourage her to refer to it as theirs, not just his, but she knew that would take a little practice. From this vantage point, it wasn't possible to see the renovations.

Passing the partially hidden driveway, she rode a little further and put her bike down at the side of the road. All the grasses and shrubs were still withered by winter. A row of cedars separated the field from the fence.

"Coucouuuu . . ." she called as she stepped over to the fence. There was a bustling noise before she parted the branches to peer in. She laughed as she came almost nose to nose with Victor Hugo, turning her head quickly as he emitted a loud bray directly at her. Donkey breath was never pleasant!

Pulling an apple out of her pocket, Katherine rubbed it on her sleeve out of habit and offered it after giving the donkey's nose an affectionate rub. His head bobbed up and down with joy, and saliva sprayed as he crunched the apple in a few short chomps.

He turned sideways so Katherine could give him a good scratch through his thick winter coat. After a few minutes, she said, "Okay, *allez chez toi!* I'll see you up at the house!"

She remounted her bike and pedaled up the hill to the open front door of Simone's home. As Kat leaned her bike against a pillar, Simone appeared with her arms open wide. After enthusiastic kisses on each cheek, the tiny woman enfolded Katherine into her arms.

"You know I never do this, but I am hugging you! *Je suis très, très heureuse de te voir*—so happy to see you!"

They stood locked in an extended embrace and Katherine said, "Simone, this isn't like you."

When Simone released her, Katherine stepped back. She was pleased to see her friend looked as serene as ever and that her bright-blue eyes had not lost their sparkle.

"*Chérie*, I realized while you were gone how very special our friendship had become to me. Then, after I was reconciled with Philippe, I knew what we have is something much greater than friendship. Now it feels right to embrace you."

Katherine looked puzzled. "You were reconciled . . . with Philippe? You knew him? Whatever do you mean?"

"*Mon Dieu*, come in off the step. We're so silly, standing here nattering. Come into the kitchen, the water will be boiling by now. I will prepare the tea."

"Your magic *tisane*, I hope."

"*Bien sûr!* But of course!"

"I know I won't get any more information from you until we are sitting and sipping our tea," Kat said, scrunching her face in a mock frown. "In the meantime, tell me what you've been doing. When I left, you had not been well, and then you were entertaining your friend, the art dealer from Paris, and his wife. How did that go?"

Simone pressed her hands together at her chest in a prayer position and bowed over her fingers. "Namaste. It went very well. I am always amazed to discover new people who want to purchase my art."

"Let me get the kettle," Katherine offered as she pulled out a chair for Simone. She walked over to the counter where the kettle was plugged in and whistling. "I drank a lot of café mochas while I was away. It will be a nice change to sip your soothing blend."

They passed a few moments trading news back and forth. Simone was fascinated by Molly's condition and asked many questions.

Finally, Katherine reached over and took Simone's hand. "I'm so curious about the visit you had with Philippe. He was very mysterious about it. What's going on?"

Simone's eyes glistened. Her face softened and pleasure filled her voice as she looked at Katherine's hand. "*Chérie*, it is for you to tell me what is going on. *Quel joli bijou!* I haven't seen this ring before."

Katherine smirked. "You are an expert at diversion!"

"It's a long-established trait," Simone replied with a twinge of irony. "You will have to be patient. I want Philippe to be here so we can tell you the whole story together."

Katherine shook her head. "Mystery and intrigue. Life is never dull with you, my dear friend."

"Please serve the salad, and tell me everything. I will slice the baguette."

As they enjoyed their light lunch, Kat related the story of how Philippe had surprised her with the ring.

Delighted, Simone asked, "So, *chérie*, would you say this stunning ring is *une bague de fiançailles*—an engagement ring? Will we be planning *une fête de mariage*?"

Kat felt embarrassed as she explained her nervousness about an actual wedding. "Words like 'engagement' and 'wedding' still cause me to get twitchy. Can you explain that? At my age, it's kind of silly, *n'est-ce pas*? Especially when I love Philippe like I do."

Simone's face wore a wise expression that Kat had come to recognize, a mixture of serenity and experience "*Chat échaudé craint l'eau froide*. What is that English expression—once burned, twice shy? I suspect you are still holding onto the fear of hurt from your broken marriage. You need to let that go. I know you can, in your own time."

Kat nodded, not surprised that Simone had picked up on her feelings. She hadn't realized there was a similar saying in French to the English one. "Well, my own time is a bit under the gun. Based on the documents we have in place, I have less than six months to get my act together if we are to get married. I made a commitment, though. I did say yes to Philippe's proposal, and that was a big step forward. Now I have to take one more step and just do it. "

Smiling, Simone simply responded, "*Ce qui sera, sera*. What will be, will be."

Katherine smiled back, filled with gratitude for the presence of this treasured friend in her life. Deep inside, though, she wrestled with frustration. She had felt her stomach tighten with anxiety during that exchange with Simone. *This flip-flopping of feelings has to end*, she told herself.

She was pleased to see that Simone appeared to be completely recovered from the illnesses that had plagued her during the holidays. She looked healthier than ever to Kat, who yet again thought how no one would come close to guessing Simone's age.

When they parted, Simone urged Katherine to let her know when she and Philippe could come for lunch. "I promise you full disclosure. Now that it is time for the story to be revealed, I'm eager to tell it. Somehow I never dreamed I would live to see this day."

Back on her bike, Katherine inhaled the sea air as she accelerated through the twisting turns that took her back to the coast. She had been away only three weeks, but it felt much longer. She and Philippe hadn't been on their bikes since well before Christmas, but she was pleased to discover that the crisp winter air was not too cold for cycling.

"*D'accord*, Minou," Philippe agreed when she arrived at the market and suggested they plan a ride that afternoon. She could see the line was moving slowly at his counter. Many of his regulars knew he'd been in Toronto and were curious to hear his observations. They would not be ready to close up shop for a while.

Gilles greeted her warmly from behind the counter and then came around to offer her heartfelt *bises*. "I understand congratulations are in order, Katherine. I am very happy for you both. I'm glad your friend is getting better too."

Suggesting to Philippe that she wait for him at home, Kat gave him a flirtatious wink. Then she parked her bike in his storage unit at the market. Taking the extra *panier* they kept for just such occasions, she considered what to buy as she perused the stalls. It was time to get life organized once more.

As always, the market bustled with color and energy. Overflowing with a vast assortment of veggies, fruit, cheese, meats, olives, and flowers, it was a veritable kaleidoscope of sights, smells, and sounds. Kat found herself wrapped in the ambiance as she made her way up the aisles, selecting greens and fruit to refill their larder.

Other vendors offered similar sincere wishes as Gilles. *"Les bonnes nouvelles vont vite par ici!"* They teased her. "Good news travels fast around here!"

Grinning and thanking everyone, Katherine wondered if she would ever outgrow blushing.

She enjoyed the quieter atmosphere in the market. With far fewer tourists in the winter, the vendors had time to chat about the weather and politics or suggest recipes. Others in line were quick to add their tips and kibitz as to which of them prepared the best dish.

"Don't forget to add extra onion," said one.

"*Mais, non!* More garlic, not onion!" answered another.

"*Écoutez-moi! Les deux, les deux!* You need more of both. Trust me!"

Laughter always accompanied this lighthearted banter.

By the time Kat stopped at the bakery and fish store on the way home, her *panier* and heart were both overflowing. Putting away the food, she marveled once again at how much her traditional woven wicker basket could hold and never feel heavy. *Such a simple thing turns buying food into a completely different experience than wobbly shopping carts and plastic bags. I love my* panier!

Then she checked her e-mail to see what news had arrived from Toronto. Andrea had promised to write every day and there was a quick message saying she had talked to Molly. Apparently the rehab was going well, and Terrence was in Toronto today installing voice-recognition software so Molly could e-mail. The therapists had told Molly they didn't want her using a keyboard just yet, as it might interfere with her shoulder healing. Molly was feeling good and told Andrea she was planning to Skype Kat and Philippe.

The next two hours were spent unpacking from the trip, reorganizing, and finding the right spots to set the special framed photos Kat had brought back with her. The crate she shipped would take a couple of weeks to arrive.

Kat was just beginning to wonder what was keeping Philippe when he burst in. "Sorry to keep you waiting. We had one thing after another to deal with—and a lot of curious customers! Still want to cycle? I rode your bike home. Let's pick a route and then end at the villa. Didier wants to meet us there and introduce his *équipe*, as he called it."

Laughing as she got ready to ride, Kat said, "His team? It's all go, isn't it? I can't wait to see what's happening on the Cap."

"Don't get your hopes up!" he cautioned. "Best to be pleasantly surprised. The way repairs and renovation go in France, there's never a guarantee about anything."

They chose a short hour-long route that would take them west toward Cannes, but not up to a challenging elevation. "We better take a while to ease into those hills, *ma belle*. This will be a good beginning."

They put their heads down and focused on cadence and breathing. Kat's legs responded to the challenge as they picked up speed. She wondered if she would pay a price the next morning after more than a month without any exercise. She had already promised herself she would get back to her yoga class the next morning and had left a voicemail for Annette to say they should do lunch after their session.

Now she felt the familiar buzz of elation and liberation that cycling always gave her. Philippe led the way, his powerful legs pumping rhythmically. Kat was pleased to see she was keeping up better than she expected, but knew she had some training to do.

CHAPTER TWENTY-FIVE

The gate to the property was ajar, and they cycled straight in.

The gravel tracks of the driveway looked a bit worse for wear—proof that there had been quite a bit of activity while Katherine was gone. She held her breath as she neared the end of the shrub borders and the villa came into view.

She wasn't certain whether to be pleased or horrified as she viewed the scene before her. Two dumpsters were filled to overflowing with all manner of building materials. The exterior of the villa looked as sadly deteriorating as when she had first fallen in love with it.

Philippe indicated they should lean their bikes against a large oak tree. They unclipped their helmets, hanging them on the handlebars. Kat bent down and shook her head to tousle her hair, running her fingers through it.

Philippe playfully reached over and ruffled her hair. "*Ne t'inquiète pas.* You look beautiful even with helmet hair! You taught me that phrase, you know."

They laughed together as they walked to the villa, hand in hand, and Katherine tried to quell her disappointment.

The double main entrance doors swung open, and Didier stood before them, covered in dust from his hardhat perched on top of his beret to his work boots. His smile beamed even more brightly than usual, in contrast to the gray of his plaster-covered skin and clothing.

"Bienvenue chez vous!" he called, his arms wide open in welcome. "Wait until you see what we have done!"

He walked over to Katherine and reached for her hand. "May I?" he asked as he bowed and kissed it in the most polite way. "Close your eyes, *s'il vous plaît*! Let me bring you in."

Didier slowly led her into the entrance foyer and then turned left, which Kat knew would take them into the main salon. The last time she stood in there, the space had been rubble-strewn with plaster and wood that had fallen from a crumbling wall. Judging by the evidence left behind, a family of critters had also taken up residence. Some windows were broken, and leaves had mixed in with the detritus on the floor.

"Voilà! Ouvrez les yeux! Ta-daaaaa!"

Katherine's eyes widened as they swept around the transformed space. The walls had been repaired and replastered. The beamed ceiling now made a stunning statement where before it had been barely noticeable. Broken windows were replaced, revealing the panoramic view in its splendor.

"Minou, now we can enjoy the results of all that clearing, cutting, and trimming we did in the garden. We can look right to the sea and across to the *vieille ville* and the hills beyond, once again!" Philippe drew beside her, slipping his arm around her shoulder.

"Magnifique!" Kat murmured. Then she turned to take in the rest of the room. It definitely did not look finished, but was so improved that it surprised her.

Didier swept his arm around the room. "We wanted *le salon* to look somewhat like it will when it is finished so you would feel encouraged about the outcome. It's going to be a very special room. Now, be careful and follow me."

Philippe took Katherine's hand as they walked into the spacious hall that led to the other main-floor rooms. Most of the rubbish that had filled the dining room, library, and three bedrooms had also been cleared.

The kitchen—which Philippe and Kat had used occasionally in the autumn when they were clearing the garden—was in the process of being transformed. The wall separating a large storage area had been knocked down to create a spacious food preparation section that would eventually contain an expansive island and counter space.

An adjoining room that had once contained a double-size ice cupboard and cold storage was being turned into a pantry. They had also created a door so groceries could easily be brought directly in from a side parking area.

"This will be a dream kitchen," Katherine exclaimed, picturing the finished product.

Didier suggested they make an appointment to walk through the space and decide on some smaller but important details, like electrical outlets and lighting.

Most of the debris had been cleared from the remaining rooms, but nothing further had been done elsewhere. "We have been rebuilding the walls in preparation to plaster in the next week or so. First we want to finish replacing the windows and the roof so that the elements won't be a problem," Didier explained.

His face flushed with pride as Katherine and Philippe complimented him on the work. Then he blew his whistle and called out some names.

Two handsome young men appeared, also dust-covered. They were tall, with smoldering dark eyes and olive complexions. Didier introduced them as Alfonso and Alesander from a village in the Pays Basque. Greeting her with courtly bows and shaking Philippe's hand, they appeared to be as charming as they were handsome. The conversation quickly became one Katherine could not follow.

CHAPTER TWENTY-SIX

As the week progressed, Kat's leg muscles continued to feel the pain of getting back into cycling shape.

She hadn't really been shocked to discover the aftereffects of not being on her bike for well over a month. She had gone through that once before. After James had left her, she had been so bitter she'd packed her bike away for months. That was after she had viciously dismantled his expensive, treasured bike and left it stuffed in a garbage can in the driveway.

She still couldn't believe she had behaved so badly. On the other hand, at the time it had given her great satisfaction. It was the only way she could think of to hurt him back.

When she'd met Philippe, there was no question that cycling would be a big part of her life again. And memories of cycling with James had seldom entered her mind. It was another good example of how she had moved on.

Her two yoga classes that week had helped immensely to stretch out those aching muscles. The studio was her kind of place: relaxed but truly dedicated to the union of mind, body, and spirit. Anouk, the petite and personable yogi, welcomed Katherine back. "Beau *le boucher* mentioned you had to help a friend in the hospital in Canada. I hope she is getting better."

Katherine was touched by Anouk's sincere thoughtfulness. She smiled to think that even the butcher was thinking of Molly. She nodded as the words "It takes a village" flitted through her head.

She'd also pushed herself to get back out cycling twice more during the week when it wasn't raining.

Today she was looking forward to seeing Annette at yoga. They had talked earlier in the week, but Annette had said she wouldn't be at class until today, as she had been fighting the flu. It seemed the cool, damp air was causing a lot of sniffles around town. Fortunately, Simone was avoiding the germs, and Kat had been lucky so far.

Before walking to yoga, Kat phoned Simone to make lunch plans on Monday, when the market was closed and Philippe could join them. "Honestly, Simone, I can hardly contain my curiosity. Philippe keeps giving me these crazy looks with wild raised eyebrows every time I mention you or our lunch date. No matter how much I plead, he's not telling me anything until we are with you."

Simone clucked softly. "Patience is a virtue, *chérie*. Now, tell me about the progress on the work at the villa and meeting Didier's work crew."

With a grin, Kat corrected the wording. "You mean Didier's *équipe*—his team!"

"Ha! And why this term?"

"Apparently Didier views his projects as sporting events! Seriously! He even wears a whistle around his neck, like a coach. He may not approach his work like a typical general contractor, but I hear he gets results."

"Bravo for him. You know how I approve of people who think out of the box!"

"You'll like him when you meet him—and the rest of them. Didier's family originated in the Pays Basque, and he always wears a beret to honor that history. However, he seems to have inherited the stature of his Norman ancestors on his mother's side, and he's almost as wide as he is tall."

Simone replied, "I can relate to that. The short part, at least!"

Katherine continued thinking about the conversation with Didier as she walked to yoga. She had missed most of what was said and felt extremely embarrassed asking Philippe to translate when they got home that day.

She would have to get back to her French lessons with Ida. It wasn't that Kat didn't have plenty of eager tutors. Often she forced herself to stumble through chats in French with Annette. She still felt shy about speaking the language with Simone, even though Simone had offered to help her many times. Philippe was a great help at encouraging her to speak it with him, but Ida had a more pedagogical approach that was extremely effective.

At the yoga studio, Kat didn't see Annette. When Kat asked Anouk about her, she learned that her friend had not been attending class regularly the previous weeks. Katherine hoped she wasn't still sick. She took off her shoes, laid her yoga mat in her usual corner spot, and began some warm-up stretches. Just as the class was preparing to begin, Annette slipped into the back of the room and gave Kat a little wave as she was rolling out her mat.

The room fell under the spell of Anouk's serene voice leading them through the calming breathing exercises and then from one pose to another for an hour. Today they also chanted the Gayatri mantra and ended with Anouk playing a soft shamanic-like drumming rhythm on a gong. The vibrations soothed and relaxed them into their cool-down stage. Katherine felt these were the best yoga classes she had ever taken.

"Kat! *Bienvenue!* Welcome back to Antibes!" Annette greeted her with *bises* before they rolled up their mats, but there was a heaviness in her voice as she plied Katherine with questions. "I'm so glad you are back. Shall we go for our *thé au citron* and you can tell me about Molly?

Was it strange to be in your old home? Were you happy to come back here?"

"You're full of questions! The short answer is that I'm more than happy to be back—I'm ecstatic! Molly is getting better and may be coming here soon to finish her recuperation. And you? How are you?"

It did not escape Katherine's notice that Annette avoided the last question and focused on Molly.

"*Formidable!* Molly is coming to Antibes? Tell me more!"

"We're excited at the possibility, but it's just that at the moment. She's in a rehabilitation center where they are working on her leg and shoulder. She had surgery on her shoulder before we left, and that went very well. They think she may be ready to leave in a couple of weeks."

Katherine was glad to see her friend but sensed her upbeat tone seemed forced. She was also concerned about Annette's pale complexion and what looked like a heavy application of makeup around one of her eyes. Looking more closely, Kat could see that her cheek was swollen and bruised.

This wasn't the first time alarms had sounded in Kat's mind about her friend, but she had never directly addressed them. She would try and find the right moment over tea. During some of those hours she'd sat at Molly's bedside, this had been one of the decisions she'd made. She realized how much she valued the friendships in her life and felt a responsibility to say something.

At the café, it wasn't warm enough to open the walls of windows, so Annette suggested they settle into a cozy corner table that offered some privacy. There were only a few other customers, and Félix, the oldest waiter, brought their order without asking. The hint of a smile and an almost imperceptible tilt of his head toward Katherine gave a clear welcome-back message. Kat gave him a megawatt smile in return that had him turn abruptly as his face flushed a deep red.

"*Santé!*" the women toasted with their teacups.

There were snippets of gossip to be shared. Kat chuckled as Annette mentioned that their favorite butcher had been the source of most of the information.

Months ago, at Philippe's suggestion, Kat had begun buying her meat from Beauregard, known far and wide as Beau *le boucher*. His family had owned the old *boucherie* for six generations, and little had changed in the shop's appearance or in the way he conducted his business. She had been amazed that he wrote nothing down when a customer placed an order. If you were local and a regular customer, you paid no money until the end of the month, when he issued a statement. He knew everyone and everything, and shared the latest gossip—*les cancans*—at his counter every day, in the friendliest way.

Annette nodded in agreement when Katherine said, "It's one of the many reasons everyday life here is an experience. There's nothing routine about it for me."

Then she gave Annette a serious look. "*Quoi de neuf*, Annette? What's new with you?"

Annette's eyes flickered away from Katherine's for a moment. Katherine had a sense she was about to say something revealing, but then Annette shook her head and said, "*Rien de tout*. Nothing at all. Busy at work."

Kat wrestled with her thoughts, but her mind was made up. "Forgive me if this is too personal, but I'm worried about you. We've known each other a while now, and I need to ask you this: Is someone hurting you? Do you and Thibaud have a problem?"

Annette lowered her eyes as her shoulders slumped. Again, she shook her head quickly.

Katherine forged on. "You wouldn't be the first, you know. You need to tell someone. I've seen bruises on you before, Annette, but this mark on your face is bad. Someone punched you. That's obvious."

Annette pinched her eyes closed and bit her bottom lip. Her voice was barely more than a whisper. "*Oui. C'est vrai*. It's true. There is a problem . . ." She stopped in midsentence and looked at Katherine with an expression so filled with agony that Kat felt herself wince inside.

"But it's not what you think."

Katherine felt disappointed, anticipating what she had read about so many battered wives: excuses and rationalizations. But she was mistaken.

"It's not Thibaud. It's . . . *ma mère* . . ." Annette barely voiced the final two words, and Kat missed them completely.

"I'm sorry. I didn't hear what you said. Who is it?"

"*Maman*. My mother," Annette said, her voice catching, her face consumed by sadness.

Katherine flinched inside as she reached for Annette's hand. "I'm confused. Your mother has been giving you these injuries?"

"Yes. My dear, sweet mother who would never hurt a fly. My *petite* mother who looks like an angel—well, she used to—and is barely one hundred fifty centimeters tall."

Katherine was speechless. Her heart went out to her friend.

Annette continued. "Since Papa passed away last year, Maman has been deteriorating. Now she's an angry old woman, partially deaf, slipping in and out of senility."

"I'm so sorry, Annette."

Annette grimaced. "I never really gave a lot of thought to getting old before, and certainly did not expect this of my mother. We had some elderly women I thought were crazy old ladies in our village when I was growing up, but I never, ever, thought of them as someone's mother. Now I think of them all the time."

She tilted her head and looked at Katherine matter-of-factly. "There. I've told someone besides Thibaud. He knows, *bien sûr*, but I've had to demand he stay out of the matter."

She paused for a moment, and Katherine could see she was wrestling with her emotions.

"How did Thibaud react to that?" Kat asked, more to fill the dead space of the conversation than anything.

"It's created tension between us. It's very upsetting for him, and he feels we need to report this. So far he has agreed to let me handle it, but he's having a difficult time with that."

Katherine shifted in her seat and exhaled loudly as thoughts swirled through her mind. *Who would have ever guessed this? What on earth would I do? How heartbreaking!*

Annette continued as her sad expression changed to anxiety. "He hasn't seen my eye because he is out of town on business until tomorrow. I'm hoping I can ice down the swelling today."

Katherine was wide-eyed with distress. Her heart went out to her friend. "This is terrible. I'm so sorry for you—and for your mother. Do they know about this at the residence where she lives?"

"*Non!* If they discover she is being physically violent, they will move her from her little studio apartment and admit her to the extended-care wing. They might put her in restraints or medicate her into oblivion! I couldn't bear that. Anyway, it doesn't happen all the time."

"I'm stunned. I don't know what to say. How awful for you. And she doesn't do this to anyone else?"

"It would be recorded in her file if she did. Thibaud insisted on coming with me when this began. Maman would be as sweet as *meringue* in front of him, but she would not let him touch her. Then she would ask me to help her to bed or to the toilet and pinch me or squeeze my arms with unbelievable strength. Even if he was looking, she might kick me in the stomach or in the back and then smile sweetly at him. It's bizarre. I know the true side of Maman would never do this. This side of her is a completely different being. I can't bear to report her, and I asked Thibaud to stop coming."

"And . . . ?"

"He grudgingly agreed but does not like this arrangement one little bit. I lie to him and tell him it is getting better, but when he sees my eye, I'm afraid he is going to insist on getting involved."

"Do you think your mother realizes what she's doing?"

"Most of the time, no. Every once in a while, her face will soften after she has hurt me and she will cry and beg my forgiveness. That's the hardest time of all for me. She was the best mother: kind and loving and always supportive. She would be aghast to think she had done anything like this. It tears me apart to see her this way, and I will deal with my bruises to help her maintain some vestige of dignity."

Katherine refilled their teacups after Félix brought another pot of tea. They sat quietly. She couldn't help thinking about Elisabeth, feeling grateful for the dignified manner in which her mother had spent the latter years of her life. Then she thought of Simone and felt gratitude again. *You just never know.*

Kat and Annette talked about aging and how there were so many variables over which people had no control. "It's really frightening me," Annette said with a sigh. "I can't stop thinking about it these days."

"I understand. Listening to you is causing me to feel very fortunate for the way my mother was right to the end. Even though she spent a few years caring for my father as he became increasingly an invalid before he died, she lived eight more years, quietly making the most of each day."

Annette told her that two years before, her father had died suddenly of a cerebral hemorrhage, and that had been when her mother's anger began. Their married life had always been simple and contented, and her father had spoiled her mother with pleasure. "She never got over him leaving her like that!"

Kat nodded sympathetically. Annette continued, "Then I moved her to the seniors' residence after a year because she was not happy alone in their big house. At first she was okay with the idea, but after we had her moved, she became even angrier. My brother is no help, so it all falls on me."

"It's the luck of the draw whether we're dealt a hand with senility or Alzheimer's or whatever else," Kat speculated. "This is all a reminder to seize each day as it comes."

"I couldn't agree more," Annette told her. With a pleading look in her eyes, she asked Katherine to help her. "Now that you know, perhaps there is someone you can think of who might be able to offer some advice."

They talked and sipped and sometimes just quietly watched people passing by.

"I have to admit . . ." Katherine began and then hesitated. "Please forgive me for my assumptions, but I thought Thibaud was hurting you. I noticed your bruises."

Annette's eyes were sympathetic. "That's the natural suspicion, isn't it? But that is not the problem. I mean, we don't have the best relationship—he is very aloof—but he is caring in his own way. Although right now he is upset with me for not letting him interfere with this problem with Maman."

They sat quietly again, lost in thought, and then Katherine had an idea. "Are residents allowed to have pets in your mother's building?"

Annette nodded, "As a matter of fact, they are. Why?"

"Has your mother ever had pets?"

Annette nodded again. "We always had cats when I was growing up."

"I keep reading how pets are a positive addition to the lives of seniors. I often thought about getting a cat for my mother but never got around to it. That's one of those things I look back on with regret."

"But do you really think your mother would have liked it in her later years?"

"I do. I think a small dog would have been too much work for her, but cats are so easy. I think it would have been good company for her after my father passed. I should have done it."

"Hindsight is a wonderful thing, Katherine. *La recherché du temps perdu.* Don't be too hard on yourself."

Katherine smiled. "We can't undo the past. But now I wonder if a pet might make a difference to your mother?"

"You know, you might have an idea there. A kitten. Or, wait, maybe a more mature cat that would be a bit docile."

A few seconds of quiet passed. Annette was clearly considering the idea. "I could get it from the animal shelter." Her voice became more excited. "I'm going to phone the residence right now and check this out with the *directrice*."

"You never know. It might not work, but it's worth a try. Let me know if you're going to the shelter and I'll go with you."

Annette took out her cell phone. "*Pardon*, I'm going to call right now."

Katherine sipped her tea and thought about where the local animal shelter might be. She couldn't recall having seen one. Checking her watch, she was startled to see how much time had passed. She had an appointment with André to talk about the exhibit he was planning in March—they were going to finalize what pieces Kat would enter.

Annette was speaking French at lightning speed, but Katherine could tell from the looks her friend was giving her that the conversation was going well. As she ended the phone call, Annette gave her the thumbs-up signal. "*Oui! C'est bon!* In fact, she said it was a good idea, as she thought my mother was very much a loner and could use company. She said to be sure the cat is up to date on shots and has been neutered."

Katherine grinned as Annette thanked her effusively. "I'm going to give this a lot of thought, and I'll let you know what I decide. I'm excited to think it's something that might make my mother feel happy again."

After they exchanged *bises*, Katherine took Annette's hand. "I'm so, so sorry you had to experience this with your mom."

Annette blinked back tears. "Thanks for pushing me to tell you about it. I appreciate that more than I can say."

They waved good-bye, and Katherine hurried home to shower and change.

Her friend Véronique had left a voicemail message. She said that she and her husband, David, were looking forward to having dinner with Kat and Philippe at their *pied-à-terre* in Nice on Saturday night.

Katherine smiled in anticipation of catching up with those dear friends. She would always be grateful to Véronique for encouraging her to become more serious about photography and consider exhibiting. Meeting Véronique in Entrevaux the previous November had been the good part of that fateful day with the terrifying car chase. That autumn day had been the only time Kat had truly feared for her safety. A secret from Philippe's past had surfaced, and unsavory criminals had disrupted Katherine and Philippe's life together. She suddenly shuddered at the memory.

Now, after a quick bowl of soup, Kat packed up her laptop and notebook for her afternoon with André.

The prospect of exhibiting her photography was scary and exhilarating at the same time. She knew André was extremely talented with a well-established reputation, and Kat was flattered he wanted to include her in the show. Véronique had also talked her into exhibiting in a mixed-media art show in Nice in the spring.

On the way out to meet André, Kat grabbed an umbrella from the stand by the door. The drizzle had turned into a downpour, so she put on her flashy rubber boots with colorful patterns. If there was unpleasant weather, those boots made her smile in spite of it.

The walk was just a matter of minutes, but it gave her pause to consider winter in that part of the world. *I have to admit, I didn't expect to be wearing these boots as much as I am in Antibes. Winter has its bad moments even here in paradise.*

Then, as if to emphasize those thoughts, her umbrella blew inside out.

CHAPTER TWENTY-SEVEN

"Am I glad to see the rain has stopped," Katherine said as she stretched and took her time getting out of bed on Saturday morning.

It was still dark as Philippe prepared to leave for what was always the busiest day of the week at the market. Kat had decided to walk over with him and then carry on to the beach a few minutes further to capture some sunrise shots.

Earlier in the week, when she and André met to discuss her photography, Kat became acutely aware that she had nothing to show from France at this time of year. She was excited about the challenges of working with the winter light now as she packed her tripod and a variety of lenses in her backpack.

The quiet stillness accompanied them as they walked along Cours Masséna. It was a little too early for the restaurants to begin their morning routine of setting up heaters and seating on the terraces. Most of the market vendors would not arrive for another half hour.

Philippe and Gilles used this time to drink an espresso or two, review how the week had gone, and plan for the next. The two old friends' partnership was easy and flexible.

"I'll come by when I'm finished shooting," Kat said, kissing Philippe lightly on the lips. "Remember, I'm going to the animal shelter with Annette this afternoon. I might not be back home until around four."

"D'accord," Philippe said with a smile, "That reminds me! Now that we're back, I'll call the Lab breeder about a pup. She said they would keep a pup for us out of the next litter, scheduled for this summer."

"Good plan," Katherine agreed. "It's too bad we missed out on this last litter, but who knew how long I would be in Toronto. Anyway, by summer we'll be organized and hopefully living on the Cap with all that garden for the pup to play in."

They had talked about it on and off all week. Since it was certain Molly was coming to France, they didn't have to be concerned about getting the pup and then having to leave to return to Toronto. They could focus on that busy initial puppy potty-training time without interruption.

Now Katherine turned into the narrowest of winding streets in the *vieille ville,* her most favorite part of Antibes. She pictured herself walking the same route in the autumn with her very own dog at her side. She smiled inwardly as she carried on through the cobblestone laneways, past the Musée Picasso and down to the waters edge at the Plage de la Gravette.

Memories of her walks with Pico filled her mind, and she wondered if they would be able to train their dog to walk without a leash like he did.

She couldn't wait!

Annette swung by to collect Kat at 1:00 p.m. In the backseat of her car, she had a cat carrier along with a crate filled with a litter box, cat food, and toys.

"Well, you are clearly serious about this. What if they don't have exactly what you're looking for?"

"*Mon amie*, I'm not in research for nothing. I did my homework, and that's why we are going to the *refuge des animaux* near Mougins. I made a lot of phone calls in the last two days. This one has a two-year-old female tabby that sounds perfect."

"I just had a thought," Katherine said. "What if your mom has pet allergies now? It happens sometimes as people age."

"If that happens, they will take the cat back. It's on a trial basis. I had a long conversation with a worker at the refuge, and then we did a Google Hangout so I could see the cat for myself. Unless I am very wrong, she's adorable. I even heard her purr!"

"I'm happy you are so enthused about this," Katherine said. "Wouldn't it be wonderful if adopting a cat became a way of helping your mom . . . and you."

Annette gave Kat a hopeful look. She maneuvered the winding, switchback corners in a way Kat had come to understand only locals could do. "You know, Annette, someday I hope to drive these roads half as smoothly as you do."

Annette laughed knowingly. "I've had a lifetime of practice."

Traffic was heavy on the scenic drive up the meandering road to the medieval hilltop village of Mougins, just fifteen minutes north of Cannes. "There must be something special going on, which is not unusual for this active community!"

"I love this drive, in spite of the traffic," Katherine told her, admiring the sweeping views down to Cannes and the sea beyond. "And cycling here is even better—especially the ride down. I've spent so much time at the museum of photography here, they've told me I'm definitely the winner of the Most Frequent Visits award!"

"I can imagine! That Picasso photography exhibit is unique, isn't it? Such an intimate look at his personal life. I guess you know that Picasso lived just outside Mougins in the *mas* Notre-Dame-de-Vie for the last thirteen years of his life and that his old studio is the tourist office in town now."

"Villers's photography of Picasso living his life is unbelievable," Katherine raved. "But there's also the iconic photographic portraiture of so many avant-garde European artists, writers, and intellectuals. It's a fascinating place for me. There's always something new to discover there."

"Have you been to the new Museum of Classical Art here? It's supposed to be amazing as well, but I haven't made it there yet. Even though this village is small, there's a lot to keep you here."

"*D'accord!* We haven't been there yet, but it's on the list," Katherine said.

She made a mental note that the village would be a good place to bring Molly once she could walk again. She knew Molly would be thrilled just to know Edith Piaf had once hung out there and had owned a home nearby for years.

Kat pointed out, "This is another village that holds its history in the ancient buildings still in use. Even though the restaurants draw a crowd, there's still a feeling of authenticity here, don't you think?"

Annette nodded her agreement. "Driving up here isn't as much fun as it used to be, because of the traffic, but once you're here, it's definitely worth it."

"L'Amandier is my favorite restaurant, sitting out on the terrace with that panoramic view in the other direction across the valley and forests and over to Grasse . . ." Kat's voice trailed off.

The road climbed, passing through the modern urban spread that lies below the original village. Soon the stone buildings perched on the hilltop came into view.

As she parked the car beside the former olive mill that was turned into a *refuge des animaux*, Annette worried aloud, "I hope I'm not disappointed!"

Katherine had never been to an animal shelter before and didn't know what to expect. She anticipated something noisy and smelly. This one was immaculate. They walked into a small office to be greeted by a young woman with exaggerated black eyeliner and lipstick, and more tattoos and piercings than Kat had ever seen. She was wearing serious goth attire with fishnet stockings and leather boots, towering on high wedge heels.

Kat hoped she wasn't staring as overtly as Annette. It was hard not to, she had to admit.

Annette quickly recovered her manners. She explained she was the woman who had called the day before about a cat for her elderly mother.

The young woman's eyes lit up immediately. "Wait just a moment, dear ladies, and please have a seat. You want to meet Felicette! You will love her."

As they sat and waited, Katherine looked at the posters, in French, English, and Russian, along with photos of dogs, cats, birds, rabbits, and mice that adorned the walls.

Grinning, she read out loud, "Adopt me. I'm pawsitively perfect."

Annette was still getting over her first reaction to the young woman. "Have you ever? I couldn't stop staring! I didn't think she would be able to put two words together or to articulate properly with all of those piercings around her mouth. Yet her English is as good as her French, and she seems like the sweetest, most polite young lady. Fascinating!"

Katherine nodded and was about to respond when the girl returned with a healthy-looking gray tabby in her arms. There was something about the way she held the cat that gave a sense of innate affection for the animal. She sat beside them and said, "Meet Felicette, one of the sweetest cats we have ever seen. All she wants to do is cuddle, *oui?*"

With that, the cat stretched her head up and affectionately rubbed underneath the girl's chin, purring loudly. "See what I mean?" she laughed, and then asked Annette if she would like to hold the cat.

Katherine could see that Annette felt very comfortable with the animal as Felicette settled in a ball on her lap.

"She is adorable, and her coat is as soft as silk," Annette said, stroking the cat's back. "Plus, she's a nice size. Not too big. I think she might be just what we are looking for. What do you think, Katherine?"

Kat agreed that the cat seemed very sweet. The girl gave them her background and explained she had belonged to an elderly woman who had died. The woman's family had allergies and couldn't take the cat, so she had ended up at the refuge. "We were hoping someone would take her and here you are! I love happy endings."

Smiling inwardly, Kat thought again how first impressions are so wrong sometimes. This young woman's manners were expressed with warmth and sensitivity. She was absolutely delightful, not at all what one's first glimpse of her suggested.

"I've never been to a pet shelter," Katherine told her. "How many animals do you have here? It's so quiet—I don't imagine there are many."

The girl chuckled. "Come with me."

Looking up from the floor, where she was playing with the kitten and a piece of string, Annette said she would wait there.

"My name is Delphine and I hope to be a veterinary technician one day," the young woman introduced herself as she pushed open a heavy door and they walked into the immaculate room. The sound level was definitely at a higher volume.

This area was much larger, with a white tile floor and white walls lined with shelves of animal crates. A few were empty. But inside most of the crates, curious furry faces pressed against the wires. A chorus of meows and barks greeted them.

At a quick glance, Katherine estimated there were thirty animals in the room. Her heart felt sad suddenly to think all these animals needed homes.

Delphine had treats for them and called them all by name. A few cats and dogs were sleeping deeply, and some kittens were too busy wrestling with each other to pay any attention, but even so, Delphine stopped to leave a treat or offer a gentle scratch as she passed by.

"You seem to love working here with all of the critters," Kat said.

Delphine's face lit with a sparkling smile. "It is the best place to work. I come every day after school and on weekends. I adore animals and want them to feel loved. Some of the pets that come here have never felt that, we can tell. So what a sweet job I have to deliver that kindness to them. We keep every one until they have found a home."

"Cats and dogs—oh, and a rabbit and turtle—in the same room. That's not a problem?" Kat asked.

"Not at all," Delphine assured her. "Do you have a pet?"

"We're getting a pup, a yellow Lab, once the litter is born in a few months."

"Labs are such fun. We have some here, though not purebred, of course." Delphine stopped by a large crate in which two balls of chocolate brown fluff were having way too much fun, leaping on and nipping each other and tumbling about. Kat knelt down, and two wet noses immediately protruded through the wires. "They're so cute and so funny," she said as they quickly resumed their rough-and-tumble routine.

"Here," said Delphine, spreading a throw sheet on the floor, "we can let them out."

Katherine squatted down to pet the pups and was instantly bowled over by them charging into her. Laughing, she attempted to scoop the wiggling bundles into her lap. They bounced around, trying to lick her face and scramble all over her.

Delphine joined her on the floor to play with them. "These two were from a litter of ten, and they were the only ones alive when we found them. I heard the heartbreaking tale. So these are a feisty pair, brother and sister, with a strong will to survive."

Looking around the room, Katherine said, "It's hard to believe that people can mistreat such innocent creatures or simply abandon them."

"*C'est la vie,*" Delphine replied with a rueful expression. "We do our best to fix that."

Annette came through from the front room, the cat still comfortably ensconced in her arms. "What's all the hilarity in here? I didn't want to miss out."

"Look at these two fluffballs! Aren't they adorable? Oh, this makes me so eager to get our pup!"

"Why wait?" Delphine asked. "Take one of these."

"Well, no. I mean . . . well, what do you know about them?"

"I know their mother was a chocolate Lab. We don't know what the father was, but they seem to have all the strong Lab characteristics. We found them when they were very young, so they have been with us for just over two months. They were too young to be adopted until now. That means they've been well treated by us, and not abused like some older ones that arrive here."

Annette spoke up, "What do you think? How do you think Philippe would feel about a rescue dog?"

"I'm sure he likes the idea of adopting pets, but I also believe he has a commitment with a breeder." In spite of herself, she took her phone out and shot some video and a few stills of the pups to show Philippe.

"Bring him for a look, if you like! I will be here tomorrow from noon to five and all day Monday. Come back with your husband."

Katherine started to say, "He's not my husband . . ." but then caught herself in time. She had liked the way that sounded when Delphine said it. "*C'est possible,*" Kat answered, but in her heart she was pretty sure Philippe would want to go with the breeder.

Annette was looking at all the other crates and making sympathetic comments as little paws poked through the wires or noses pressed against. "There are so many adorable animals here, how does one choose?"

"I know," Kat agreed. "It's so tempting. Maybe we should have a cat too!"

"So how about Mademoiselle Felicette?" Delphine asked Annette. "Do you think your mother would be happy with her?"

"Yes, I do. I will take her to visit my mother and tell Maman I am looking after her for a while because she needs a home. Then I'll see what happens. Hopefully she will have the idea herself. Wouldn't that be perfect?"

"Good idea! Since you talked with Monsieur Albert yesterday, he had me get all the papers together about her shots. She is ready to go home with you right now, if you like."

"I might want to keep her myself," Annette said, handing the docile cat—now purring contentedly—to Katherine. "I'll go out to the car and get the travel carrier for her."

CHAPTER TWENTY-EIGHT

All the way back to Antibes, Annette kept thanking Katherine. "I can't believe how that worked out! All because of your good idea. Thanks, Kat!"

Felicette had settled into the carrier in the backseat and occasionally emitted soft mewing sounds. Katherine reached back from time to time and rubbed the top of the cat's head with her fingers.

Katherine smiled. "It was someone else's good idea, but I'm glad I thought to mention it. See you next week at yoga, and I hope there will be no new bruises."

"Well, I guess we can't expect that to stop instantly . . . or can we? Anyway, I'm taking your advice to have Thibaud go with me when he can, and hopefully, one way or another, the situation will improve. Thank you for encouraging me to be more open in talking to him."

When they arrived in front of Kat's apartment, Kat got out of the car and told her, "Fingers crossed, as we like to say in English. Let me know what happens. I can't wait to hear all about your mother's reaction."

Katherine took the stairs two at a time and was disappointed that Philippe was not home. A note on the table said Didier had called him over to the Cap and he would be back soon.

She checked her e-mails and was pleased to see one from Molly that was full of her zany humor. The rehab treatments were to begin the next day. Molly sent a copy of the schedule that included arm and shoulder work in the morning and speech in the afternoon.

"Important news about my leg," she wrote. "I'll be getting a walking cast in two more weeks and will only need to use the wheelchair for long distances. I should only need the walking cast for two weeks and then will require physio to strengthen the muscles. I can't wait to get back to my completely perfect and awesome self. Hahaha!"

She also told Katherine that Nick had the rehab schedule as well and would e-mail them both when he heard back from the treatment center in Nice.

Her message ended, "I can't wait to come to Antibes! Counting the days!"

Katherine and Philippe were looking forward to having Molly stay with them.

In addition, while they had been at the hospital with Molly, they'd gotten around to talking about the FromageGraphie website they were planning to set up, and Molly had offered to help. She had become quite adept at establishing websites for her serious music students during the past couple of years and thought she could at least get their idea started online.

Philippe walked in to the apartment as Kat was writing her reply to Molly's message. "Tell her to give our love to Tony," he teased.

Katherine squinted her eyes and shot him a look. "Don't joke about that. We can't mention it to Molly yet. I just hope it all works out for them."

Katherine and Philippe were still trying to process their conversation with Tony at the hospital.

"That was heavy," Philippe had commented to Katherine on that particular day and many others thereafter.

Katherine agreed. "It's clear how we tend to forget priests are normal people too."

Katherine had downloaded a book written by a priest in Florida who had gone through a similar situation. She remembered reading about it in the papers a few years earlier. She told Philippe she thought the book was well written and gave tremendous insight into the whole delicate quandary.

They both agreed that there had been no doubt in their minds of Tony and Molly's love for each other. Their interactions during Molly's hospital stay had made that obvious.

"I like Tony very much," Philippe told Kat, and she agreed. "Time will tell what happens, but I want to give them all the support they need. Everyone deserves to be happy."

"No question, I wish everyone could be as happy as we are!" Kat said, reaching up to kiss Philippe's cheek.

"Do we have an arrival date for our Molly yet?" he asked.

"Not yet, but they're working on it. What's happening at the villa? Why did Didier call?"

"He wanted me to look at a new idea he has for the kitchen. It involves taking down another wall but will give us some very nice extra space. I told him to wait until you take a look too, but I think you are going to be pleased with his plan."

They chatted a bit about Didier's unconventional approach to construction and renovation. "Somehow he just seems to know what to do, even when he looks like he doesn't. Dust and debris can be everywhere one day, and the next, he and his Basque brigade are making order out of chaos," Philippe said. "But I also know he's very well trained and comes highly recommended."

"We'll just have to trust he's up to the task. He has the sweetest nature, and I love how he always wears his beret and blows his whistle when he wants the other guys' attention."

"Maybe I should start wearing a beret," Philippe suggested.

"*Non, mon amour*, you are already too irresistible to me! Let's get ready to go to Nice. I can't wait to see Véronique and David and collect Anyu's carpet from them too."

Philippe reached for her hand. "Hanging the rug will be a memorable moment for us."

Katherine felt herself fill with emotion at the thought. She nodded silently. Then she said, "Oh, and I have an interesting story to tell you on the way."

Philippe chuckled as he headed for the shower. "When don't you have an interesting story for me, Minou?"

As they drove slowly in the heavy traffic along the Bord de Mer, Katherine talked about how her priority was to prepare for André's photography exhibit, just three weeks away.

"What do you think about the pieces we've chosen to show? We haven't had much of a chance to talk about them."

Philippe praised the choices, and Katherine said that tonight she and Véronique were going to explore how they should best be mounted. Ultimately, the decision would be André's, but Katherine wanted a second opinion.

Philippe nodded. "With all of Véronique's experience in the arts, I'm sure she will have some good ideas. Are you going to enter the spring exhibition in Nice that she mentioned to you?"

Katherine admitted how nervous she was about taking this new step with her photography. "I'm going to wait until André's show is over and see how I feel about it."

Philippe patted her knee. "I believe you are going to be pleasantly surprised at the response. Just you wait and see! And Molly might be here for it too. Even more fun!"

They drove in contented silence for a few minutes, except for the occasional sigh of pleasure from Kat at the passing scenery along the coast. She always said there was something special about the way the pinkish rays of the setting sun brushed the sea. Finally she murmured, "I'm never going to get tired of this. Never, ever, ever. *Pas de tout!*"

Philippe smiled, inside and out. He said nothing but knew in his heart Kat's insecurities were melting away. He loved how she loved this land he loved.

"Oh, oh, oh!" Kat cried. "How could I forget to tell you my story? You know how I went to Mougins with Annette this afternoon?"

"Yes, of course. You went to see about a cat for her mother."

"Well, first of all, it was wonderful just to do that drive again. It's been a little while since we were there."

"Mm-hmm," Philippe agreed. "We should go again soon. Lunch at L'Amandier, *oui?*"

"*Bonne idée!* How about tomorrow after the market closes?"

"You're not wasting any time!"

"Well, there's something else I'd like to show you while we're there."

"*C'est quoi?* Or is it a secret?"

Suddenly she blurted, "I can't keep it a secret—and maybe you aren't even interested—but . . . well . . ."

"Minou, you're keeping me in suspense. Let me guess, you visited a gallery and there's a painting you would like us to buy."

"No."

"Some antique furniture?"

"No."

"There's a house you would like us to buy."

"Now, that's just silly."

"I've got it! An original photograph of Picasso in his underwear!"

"Very funny." Kat laughed. "But now I'm not telling you. It'll have to wait until we get there."

For the rest of the drive, Philippe teased her with ever more imaginative guesses. Soon they were pulling into the underground parking garage near Véronique and David's *pied-à-terre* in the *vieille ville* of Nice.

They had become close friends with the Johnstons and spent many a pleasant evening sharing one of David's gourmet meals. He was the chef in the family and loved to entertain.

"*Bienvenue*, Katherine! Welcome home! You were missed."

"Let's begin with champagne to toast the news about your friend Molly's recovery. We're looking forward to meeting her when she comes to France."

Katherine and Philippe told them about their time together in Toronto. Philippe raved about the cleanliness of the city and the efficient transit system. "Of course, with the subarctic temperatures, it felt like dogsleds would be more fitting. *Mon Dieu!*"

American-born David teased Philippe about some aspects of life in Canada that differed from France. Philippe laughed and admitted his greatest challenge was understanding conversations since everyone spoke so quickly.

"The shoe was on the other foot," Kat agreed sympathetically.

"And what about *la Saint-Valentin*? *Mon Dieu!*" Philippe exclaimed to David. "It was January and there were already valentines all over the place. Shop windows were full of hearts and flowers and treats. It looked more like *la fête de Noël*."

David shook his head in disgust. "It's out of control in North America, like all the holidays! In France it's a low-key expression between you and your true love, with no kids involved and no anxious moments with schoolchildren checking to see if they got as many cards as everyone else!"

Nodding agreement, Philippe added, "Here we just take our loved one out for dinner or give flowers—preferably a red rose."

Véronique snorted, "Oh, we know about that. *Oui*, David?" Turning to Katherine, she said, "He gave me yellow roses on our first Saint-Valentin together—and they represent infidelity!"

"I didn't know! I thought they were beautiful," protested David. "And she still won't let me forget!"

They all laughed and raised their glasses to love.

Since David had been caught up in business affairs all day, he hadn't been able to cook. "So we're going over to the *vieux port* for *moules frites*. How does that sound? And since rain is still threatening, I'll drive."

They all agreed they would never turn down a good feast of mussels and *frites* down at the lively old port.

As they were saying good-bye at the end of the evening, Philippe said, "We're planning to go to Mougins for lunch at L'Amandier tomorrow. Why don't you join us? I'm going to leave the market a bit early."

"We haven't been up to Mougins for ages," David said. "I miss that foodie heaven, now that you mention it."

Kat and Véronique enthusiastically agreed in unison.

"We'll swing by and pick you up just before noon," David suggested.

Katherine wondered how they would all react to her surprise.

CHAPTER TWENTY-NINE

Kat met Philippe at the market for a brisk walk home. "It will prepare us for the gustatory challenge ahead," Philippe teased.

"I think it was Julia Child who stated something to the effect that eating in France is a serious art form as well as a national sport," Kat said.

Philippe chuckled and nodded in agreement.

"Even though the weather looks good today, that drop in temperature tells me something nasty might be blowing in," Philippe said as he took Katherine's hand.

"Your predictions are usually correct, Monsieur LaMétéo."

They were waiting outside their building when the Johnstons arrived to collect them.

Lunch at L'Amandier was always a special event, and the four friends were excited to be on their way.

Blue sky and bright sunshine were the perfect combination for the drive up to the medieval hilltop village. The women oohed and aahed at the vistas before them, and the men agreed it was worthy of their gushing.

"Sometimes we take these surroundings of ours for granted," David commented. "Don't ever lose your enthusiasm, Kat. You can see Véronique never has!"

They all agreed that coming to Mougins was a fine idea and then plied Katherine with questions as to when she would reveal her surprise for them.

"First we dine," she replied with a teasing grin, "and then we shall see what we shall see."

The *cuisine de soleil* menu focused on the scents of the *garrigue* and featured fine traditional recipes from Nice and its surroundings. There was always something new and enticing on the menu, as well as favorites that people returned for time and time again.

David described some of the experiences he'd had in their famous cooking school and explained some of the history to Kat when she asked. "It started with the renowned chef Roger Vergé in 1977, and then Alain Ducasse took over. Many of the world's top chefs spent time here learning Provençal cooking methods. Now new owners are carrying on the traditions."

Véronique added, "Actually, Vergé had opened Le Moulin de Mougins a few years before L'Amandier, in a nearby sixteenth-century mill. It often took months to get a reservation at the small *auberge*."

It was too chilly to sit on the terrace, so the foursome sat at a table in the main dining room, with its intricate mosaics and fine Provençal materials. Near the windows, the panoramic view across the rolling hills could still be appreciated from inside.

"This room fills me with such rapture," Véronique murmured, looking around fondly. "The first time we came here . . ."

"At least thirty years ago, I might add," David interjected.

Véronique smiled nostalgically. "So true! I was so inspired by the combination of colors and textures—they were a major influence in one of my earliest weavings. Even though renovation and redecoration have occurred through the decades, the mood has never changed."

David and Philippe agreed that through the years, they seldom came to the restaurant after dark. "Like so many experiences in the South of France, the light and view are equally important factors. Coming here during daylight only enhances the experience."

They all selected the *menu du chef* and were not disappointed. A delicate *amuse-bouche* of poached quail egg with a sliver of smoked salmon on its own spoon began the meal. Next they were served classic stuffed zucchini flowers with creamy mushroom butter. The main course, risotto *milanese* with grilled prawn and fennel sauce, was presented with a flourish as silver lids were lifted simultaneously from the four plates.

"I may faint from the heavenly aroma wafting up from this plate," David commented, to murmurs of agreement around the table.

Dessert was a fine lemon tart with caramelized *meringue* and a dollop of triple-cream vanilla ice cream that sent them all into euphoric exclamations.

Even the cheese tray received accolades from Philippe.

As they began to drive out of the village, Katherine asked David to slow down and make a left turn at the *"Refuge des Animaux"* sign. They all gave her a strange look, but David followed instructions.

"Come with me, please," Katherine invited them once he had parked.

They stared in amazement as Katherine was warmly greeted by Delphine, whose attire and makeup were even more dramatic than the previous day.

"I was hoping you would return!" Delphine burbled with pleasure. She nodded politely as Katherine made introductions. "Would you like me to bring the babies out here?" she asked. "It will be more comfortable for all of you."

David was suddenly eager to see everything. "Let's go back and see all of the animals. I've been thinking about getting a pet lately myself."

Véronique nodded and said, "This is very coincidental. We've been talking for ages but haven't gotten around to doing anything."

Kat explained she had come with Annette. "She's been talking about adopting a rescue cat for a while and asked me to come with her."

Turning to Philippe, Kat said, "This is the surprise. No pressure, *honnêtement . . .*"

Philippe wore a startled expression. "I never would have guessed this was your secret in Mougins! I was certain you had your eye on some art! You want to get a cat?"

Kat replied somewhat nervously, suddenly worried that this hadn't been the best idea. "Not a cat. But possibly the gift you offered me at Noël."

Delphine proudly led them into the back room.

A chorus of animal sounds greeted them. The Johnstons paused to look at and coo over each animal. Kat took Philippe's hand and led him to where Delphine was opening a crate.

With a one-handed flourish, Delphine dropped the throw sheet to the floor.

Kat and Philippe both knelt down as the pups barged out and made the rounds with nonstop licks and wagging tails. Everyone laughed with delight at their antics and adorable squeaking noises.

Philippe picked up each little brown bundle of fluff and examined it closely, pumping Delphine for more information about their history.

He looked at Kat and chuckled, "No pressure? *Comment puis-je dire non?* How does one resist these?"

"I know you were going to place another order with the breeder because we missed getting the pup from the original litter. It never occurred to me that I would look at any dogs here."

Philippe smiled warmly. "I think giving a rescue dog a home is a great idea—I don't know why it didn't cross my mind before. I just automatically thought of going through a breeder."

Going into the office, Delphine returned with some pages stapled together. She addressed Kat. "After you left yesterday, I put together all the information we had about these two, and I spoke with the administrator here to make certain I didn't miss anything."

She blushed a deep red through her pale makeup as they all commended her on being so efficient.

Kat said, "What do you think, Philippe? Honestly, it's up to you, being more knowledgeable about dogs. If you think we should wait for the litter at the breeder, I'll certainly agree."

Philippe was quiet for a moment, except for the sounds he was making to the pups as he snuggled one and scratched the belly of the other. "*Non*, it's what you think, Minou. This is your gift, and you have to choose."

Katherine hugged Philippe. "*Mille mercis!* I want one of these, as long as you feel they're healthy and of good stock. Choosing one won't be easy, however. Should I go with the male or the female? Unless I pick them up, I can't tell them apart."

"Well, I'm sorry," Philippe said with a wide grin, "but you have to make a decision."

Véronique and David watched with amusement as Katherine cradled first one pup and then the other. After a while, she said, "Okay, I'll take the female. I hope she won't be too lonely without her brother."

Delphine told her that most pups get separated from their siblings. "It's more the humans who agonize over the parting, not the canines."

"So it's final, then, *mon amour*? That's your choice?"

"Yes," Katherine agreed, holding the wiggling bundle in her arms.

"*Eh, bien!* Then I will choose her brother. *Merci beaucoup.*"

Katherine gave him a confused look. "So you're saying you want us to take the male instead of the female?"

"No, I'm saying you take the female and I will take the male. *En fait*, we will take them both home!"

Katherine handed the pup she was holding to Véronique and threw her arms around Philippe once more. "*Vraiment?* Really? Both pups?"

With an ear-to-ear grin, he nodded. "Both pups. We will be a two-pup family!"

Delphine wiped her eyes, smudging eyeliner down her cheek. "Bravo! *C'est formidable!* I was hoping they would not get separated, in spite of what I told you about it being okay. *C'est trés cool!*"

"We can be the dogparents!" David suggested. Véronique nodded enthusiastically.

Delphine cleared her throat and excused herself for interrupting the celebration. "I have a responsibility to give you information about raising the pups together. You do not want them to develop littermate syndrome. They must have separate crates and be trained separately or they will become too dependent on each other. It will be twice the amount of work."

Katherine and Philippe looked at each other and nodded. "*Allez!* We're up for it, Delphine."

The young woman continued, "We have been treating them this way already, though we sometimes put them in the same crate to play, and they are responding very well; they will soon be potty-trained, if you continue the same routine. They also have been socialized with the kittens here. It's all in the papers I will give you."

Philippe nodded. "We will go shopping for crates and food and some toys today—all the supplies we'll need. Then we'll pick up our pups tomorrow afternoon. Does that work?"

"We're having lunch with Simone tomorrow, so we can come here directly after that," Katherine reminded him, consumed with excitement. "Or we could come in the morning since it's your day off."

"But we wouldn't want to leave them alone right after we get them home. So after lunch it is!"

The Johnstons took photos of several cats and promised they would seriously consider returning.

They all went back to Kat and Philippe's apartment, where they took their time choosing the best wall location for Elisabeth's carpet.

Having their friends help in the ceremonial hanging of this treasure of Kat's made it all the more meaningful to her. Véronique and David did not know the details of the history. When emotion overtook Katherine, Philippe was able to continue the narration.

It was a powerful ending to a lovely day—one Katherine would never forget, and one that brought her another step closer to seeing she was indeed home.

CHAPTER THIRTY

The next day, it felt strange to arrive at Simone's home in a car. But blustery winds and heavy rain left them no other option. This was winter weather on the coast at its worst.

Simone phoned to suggest they postpone their lunch date if Kat and Philippe would rather stay home. Since it was Monday and the market was closed, she was concerned about them leaving the dry indoors for a visit with her.

Without hesitation, Kat had replied, "Simone, my curiosity is piqued to the limit. If I had to crawl through quicksand in a typhoon to get to your house, I would."

Though Kat could barely contain her excitement about the pups, she wanted to concentrate on much more serious matters for the time being. She would save that news for the right moment.

After greeting her guests at the door with lingering *bises*, Simone graciously invited them into her main salon. As usual, she was dressed in white, but not her usual cotton yoga gear or perfectly pressed linen. Today she wore a full-length cashmere cowl-necked knit dress with long sleeves. She looked elegant and relaxed as she sank into the colorful deep cushions on her white sofa.

A well-tended fire warmed the room. Delicious aromas wafted from the kitchen and filled the air. A silver tray rested on the coffee table with a bottle of Veuve-Cliquot nestled in ice. Three delicate cut-glass flutes waited to be filled.

"Philippe, would you mind serving the champagne?"

"Avec grand plaisir," he replied. Katherine was aware of a tone of great affection for Simone. It was all she could do to keep herself from begging them to begin sharing their secret.

Simone raised her glass, and they joined her. "We have much to toast today. First, your return to Antibes, along with the beautiful ring Philippe has placed on your finger, Katherine."

Smiling, they raised their glasses toward each other, eyes meeting as they sipped.

"Next," Simone continued, "I wish for us to toast the memory of Gregoire Dufours and our son, Jean-Luc Garnier."

Philippe repeated the toast and Kat joined in, wishing she knew what was going on. Wasn't Gregoire Dufours the grandfather of Philippe and the father of Oncle Francoise and Philippe's father? She felt most confused, and that obviously registered in her expression.

Philippe gave her a tender smile. "It will all make sense in a few moments."

"Shall I begin?" Simone asked, looking to Philippe for a response.

Bowing his head with great respect, he said, "It is your story, whenever you are ready."

"Bien. Je dois commencer . . . it is time. Katherine, you may recall I mentioned that during my years in the Resistance, I fell in love with someone. That someone was Gregoire Dufours, *le grandpère de* Philippe."

Katherine blinked in surprise. Philippe reached for her hand.

Simone continued. "He was ten years older than I was when we met in 1942, and was married with four young sons. He was sent to

Normandy from Antibes to help train those of us who were working in the communications group of *la résistance.*"

She nodded to Philippe. "*Mon chèr*, why don't you explain a bit more about your *grandpère's* expertise."

Katherine sat spellbound.

"My grandfather had been in the military from a young age, and his specialty had been espionage. As the technology of the 1930s progressed, he specialized in electronic surveillance—such as it was. The main task was to disrupt German lines of communication and send reports to Britain to aid in planning their offensives."

Simone broke in: "I was born with extremely sensitive auditory acuity. In some ways it plagued me as a child, and in other ways it defined me. Maman called it my gift."

She paused, as if lost in a memory. "Finally something that had seemed to make me an oddity for much of my life became a valued skill. I could make out conversation in spite of terrible static and other interfering noises. Monitoring garbled radio messages from the enemy, between their divisions, provided invaluable information—as you can imagine."

Katherine became more and more intrigued.

"We also were responsible for breaking into German transmittals and sending incorrect information to them. Gregoire was a master at this, and his German was impeccable."

She stopped for a moment and sipped her champagne. "Oh, *chérie*, there is much to be told, and one afternoon will not begin to cover it. Let me move on to tell you Philippe's involvement and how we are more closely connected than you might ever have imagined.

"When the war ended in 1945, there was fear and trepidation mixed with urgency to return to our families, hoping they had survived. We were so afraid to see what had become of all we held dear. But more than a few of us had fallen in love. Working together under constant threat of death, with our only goal that of defeating a brutal enemy we despised—well, emotions ran high. It's impossible for anyone to even begin to imagine the volatility of our lives during those times."

Katherine nodded, fascinated. "I believe you. It is unimaginable."

"Gregoire and I became lovers. We denied it for months and then succumbed to a passion that was strong and true. I believe it kept us alive. Our commitment to each other and to our cause inspired us, kept us determined to defeat the terrible enemy. When the war was over, we could not bear to part. He went with me to see my family, and we discovered the worst of my fears there. Our peaceful simple farm, my home, our entire property, was a mess of craters from bombs. My brothers were missing, and so was my mother. No one could possibly live there, and I wondered if they had all died there. Gradually we came upon neighbors and villagers who knew much of the story."

Philippe moved to refill their glasses. Simone covered hers gracefully with her fingers. "*Merci. Non.* One glass is more than enough for me."

She cleared her voice and brushed back a strand of hair that had fallen across her face as she continued. "My brother Marcel had been taken away early in the Occupation. Remember, I told you we had slaughtered a cow and he insisted on saying he alone was responsible? He never returned. From that moment on, my poor father's heart was broken and his health began to fail. My two other brothers became *maquisards* at the first opportunity."

Katherine looked confused for a moment, and Philippe interrupted politely to explain. "Another name for resistance fighters, who were particularly active in the north and south of France."

Simone nodded her thanks to Philippe. "I wanted to join them, but they laughed at me and said it was no place for a silly young girl. But they were mistaken. When they learned what was being done at the listening posts, they knew I might be very useful indeed, with my extraordinary ears. We had to steal off secretly, and soon after, unknown to me, my frail mother was disguised as a nun and driven by the priest to Paris to live with relatives."

Finally, Katherine found her voice, filled with compassion. "Simone, please promise me that you will record your story, one way or another. I will help you. It must not be lost."

"*Oui, d'accord. Je te promets.* I give you my word on that." She drew a cross over her heart. Kat smiled inwardly, thinking she hadn't seen anyone do that since she was a youngster. "But now I want to tell you about after the war.

"Gregoire was one of the heroes of the Resistance and of the terrible period, *l'epuration sauvage*, at the end of the war . . ." She stopped speaking with a noticeable shudder.

Again, Philippe explained: "There was a brief period of hysteria then against collaborators, as you can imagine. There was a wave of public executions, shamings, women who had or even were suspected of having romantic liaisons with Germans had their heads shaved . . . or worse. *Grandpère* was a strong voice of reason and calm in ending this."

Simone took up the story again. "He received accolades and medals and a small cottage on the sea near Deauville. He was torn by his desire to see his sons, even though he admitted he felt no love for his wife. Their marriage had been fueled by family connections, not emotion. He wanted to stay with me forever. After a bit more than a year after the war ended, I realized I was carrying his child. I kept it a secret from him, all the while trying to convince him to go to his family. His boys were the twins Guy and Gaston, then Denis—Philippe's father—and finally, François."

Philippe interjected with a thoughtful, serious expression. "Papa was a little older than Oncle François and bore some painful memories about his father missing a lot of their childhood. Guy and Gaston were that much older and very bitter. Even though my father understood later what a hero his father had been, sometimes, for a child, that still doesn't make up for a parent's absence."

It was Simone's turn again. "Finally he agreed to see his family, but promised he would return soon. You must remember too that in France, it was not uncommon for a man to have a mistress. Particularly in those times. Indeed, it was quite accepted. But I did not want to be a mistress."

She toyed with a wide gold band on her third finger. "As soon as he left, I stole away to my aunt in Corsica and hid my whereabouts. Jean-Luc was born there, and it was the most peaceful and soothing place for me. There was much healing to be done after the unspeakable horrors of the Occupation. I could not have been in a better environment in Corsica. Have you visited there, *chérie*?"

Kat shook her head, and Simone told Philippe he needed to take her there.

"Corsica is rugged and mountainous, with beautiful bays and white sand beaches along its coastline. In some places the golden hue of the rocky cliffs contrasts with the particular blue of the sea there, in a way unique to the island.

"At different times of the year, the air is perfumed with myrtle, lavender, heather, and other wild aromatic plants that create a dense thicket of undergrowth over the hills and valleys. Chestnuts are a staple."

Philippe elaborated. "Today it's still like going back in time—except for the summer traffic jams. But forget that for now. Imagine how untouched it was seventy years ago. It was occupied by Italian troops under Mussolini during the war, and then by German troops after Italy surrendered. But the history of the island has been more Italian than French, and you feel that."

Simone returned to her story.

Her voice dropped to almost a whisper as she described life with her infant son. Katherine felt a lump catch in her throat. Even though she had not been a mother, Kat sensed the bittersweet mix of love and despair that filled Simone's memories about Jean-Luc. About the son she had loved so deeply and tragically lost in a car accident. The pauses between thoughts were heavy with emotion.

"Let's refresh," Philippe said gently. He stood and refilled their champagne glasses. After refusing earlier, Simone acknowledged that a splash might be a good idea after all.

Kat lowered her head to compose herself. She had felt a powerful message about life in Simone's words. Particularly when she said, "No matter what obstacle or heartbreak is put in our path, we alone choose to be happy. No one else makes that choice for us."

They expressed their sympathy to Simone. She nodded graciously before she collected her thoughts and continued the story.

"It was so tranquil. Living a simple life was the reality. There were few cars, and the road system was rather terrifying. People stayed in their villages, or walked or rode horses and donkeys from one place to another. That's part of the reason the island is such a hikers' haven today. There are footpaths everywhere."

"Would we be happy cycling there?" Kat asked Philippe.

He grinned. "We would be very happy there on the Ducati, *je t'assure!*" he said, referring to his cherished vintage motorcycle. "It would be perfect with all the hairpin turns that lead to the breathtaking views."

His comment caused Katherine to look away quickly. An unexpected flashback had her nerve endings tingling, recalling the erotic sensations of her body pressed to Philippe's the first time he took her for a ride into the hills above Nice.

After they had become a couple, Kat had told him how on that ride, with her arms wrapped around him, she'd had carnal desires that she hadn't realized she possessed. Philippe had grinned, knowing every ride after that pretty much guaranteed passionate lovemaking to follow.

Kat caught her breath, feeling again like a schoolgirl, and brought herself back to the present. She stuttered, "Yes . . . yes . . . *bonne idée!*"

She couldn't disguise her pleasure as her face glowed, and she shook her head with embarrassment as Philippe's eyes met hers.

Simone's face registered a wise and knowing smile before she continued. She'd been there. She knew those feelings.

"Jean-Luc flourished, and we were content in our primitive life. He was a healthy, happy baby, surrounded by loving relatives who all wanted to spend time with him. I thought perhaps we would stay there forever . . . and that perhaps some day the burning ache in my heart might fade."

"Oh, Simone, you were very brave."

"I'm not sure that 'brave' is the right word. It was the only way I could think of to ensure that Gregoire stayed with his family. I couldn't bear to be the woman in the middle. No matter how much I loved him . . ." Her voice trailed off.

They sat in silence for a few moments before she continued. "And his boys needed him. I knew that. Every child should have their parents in their life. But one day, as I sat outside shelling chestnuts with my aunt, there he was. Gregoire. *Grand, bien, et beau.* So tall and handsome and strong . . ."

She stopped in the midst of that thought. The emotion in the room was electric. "He swept me into his arms, and I had no desire to resist. I wanted him as much as he wanted me."

Her voice, expressions, posture—all became ageless as she spoke.

"We slept together for weeks, taking Jean-Luc for long walks in the hills, making love in flower-filled meadows while our son napped in the shade. It was idyllic, truly a time of passion and romance."

Kat and Philippe exchanged meaningful glances. Simone had transformed from a gracious lady of almost a hundred to a rapturous young woman living a passionate life through the images she was painting with her words. Her eyes radiated peace, and a luminous aura seemed to envelop her. Her lust for life, for her lover, for their son and the moments they all shared was palpable.

Simone had been sitting on the edge of the sofa as she told her story, but now she leaned back, almost collapsing into the cushions. For the first time, she appeared suddenly spent from her recollections.

Philippe moved to help her, but she waved him away. "*Rien, rien, c'est rien.* It's nothing. I'm fine. . . . just so many memories."

Katherine swallowed the lump in her throat. She did not want to cry.

Simone's voice relaxed a little now, her ardor somewhat tempered. "We talked and talked and argued and finally reached a conclusion. Jean-Luc and I would go to Paris and live in my mother's apartment. She was ailing at this point. Did you know most Parisians lived under near-starvation conditions during the Occupation? I had been wanting to help her, but there was still much to be done in the countryside . . . and I was with Gregoire. She had been shocked when I had told her I was with child, but gradually she accepted the reality, and I thought that Jean-Luc would bring some joy back to her heart—which he did."

"Did Gregoire choose to leave his wife then?" Kat asked.

"I insisted I would only go to Paris if he remained with his family. But I ultimately agreed to be his lover. I wanted no one else. And so it was. And that was in 1949. Gregoire had many influential connections after the war, and he was a valuable person within the government. He sat on many committees and was consulted by top officials—all of which meant he often had to spend time in Paris. He made certain he did. My mother would look after Jean-Luc so I could slip away with Gregoire. Other times, we would have him with us. Gregoire loved him very much and doted on him. This simply became the fabric of our lives."

"When did you come to Antibes? To this property?"

"Gregoire inherited the property when he was young, long before the war. He loved it but also had a house in the old town of Antibes. His wife preferred that house and disliked being on the Cap. When Jean-Luc was ten, Gregoire separated this section and deeded it to us.

This house was a shepherd's shelter originally, and he turned it into our love nest."

Her eyes looked around the room momentarily. Katherine was almost embarrassed at the raw emotion of the story. Philippe's gaze dropped to the floor.

"I continued to live in Paris but came here for holidays, and we were often included in the whole family's social plans. Many people thought it was his way of thanking me for all I had done during the war, and some people kept that story alive. Others knew we were lovers. *C'est la vie.*"

Simone looked at Katherine with some concern. "Can you understand this?"

Katherine's voice was soft when she responded. "Yes, I believe I do understand. It was a different time."

She reached over and took Simone's hand in hers.

The spell was broken, as Simone said, "*Eh bien.* I believe we could all use *un petit moment,* a little break. Let's attend to the meal."

She asked Katherine to go into the kitchen. "There's a small bundle of potatoes wrapped in cheesecloth on the counter. Please put them in the stockpot simmering on the stove. *Merci.*"

"My mouth is watering, Simone," Philippe expressed in a tone filled with nostalgia. "It smells like my mother's *pot au feu.* Am I right?"

Simone nodded. "With a few alterations to accommodate this old body of mine, but the taste is the same."

"Even the bone marrow?"

"Even that, if you will toast the *croûtes.*"

Kat came back into the salon, her eyes wide. "I was almost held captive by the tantalizing smells from that pot!"

"You are in for a treat, Kat!" Philippe exclaimed. "Truly a classic French meal!"

Simone added, "A classic, *oui.* But it was really a meal for poor families where everything would get thrown into the pot, which would simmer as it hung over the fire. The meat was usually so tough that it needed to cook for a long time. Sometimes my brothers would say the smell of it cooking was even better than the eating of it!"

She tapped her wrist as if to indicate a watch, which they knew she never wore. "We have twenty minutes for the potatoes to cook. Let's continue this saga."

Philippe picked up the story. "Grandpère started taking me to Paris with him when I was five. Jean-Luc was twenty-three and in medical school at that point. He would take time from his studies to take me to parks and museums—and glorious ice cream from Berthillon! He began my education of Paris and culture, and that continued for stimulating and memorable years until I was fifteen. My father disliked city life, so he was pleased for me to have that time with his father—little did he know Jean-Luc was my mentor."

Simone broke in, "And that gave Gregoire and me time alone. My mother had long since passed away."

For a moment Kat felt overwhelmed with the reminder that the love and experiences older people have lived was often discounted. Her thoughts went to her parents, whose love story was equally powerful in its own way.

Philippe added, "Jean-Luc and Grandpère were very close. I do remember that."

"Yes. That was such a joy to me. They loved each other very much. Jean-Luc somehow grew up understanding the situation and making the best of it. Gregoire was his hero. He put our son through medical school."

"I never forgot your *madeleines*, Simone, or your beauty."

"You are making this old woman blush," she scolded gently.

Philippe smiled. "*Avec plaisir.* Though I never suspected you were anyone other than a good friend. Grandpére spoke of you with such respect."

"Gregoire claimed my *madeleines* were exceptional. They were the first things he wanted to eat when we were together, no matter what time of day! Do you know, he also gave me my first *âne* and named it Victor Hugo. He thought I needed a pet here, and he just arrived with it one day. Imagine!"

They all laughed at the visual, understanding now why the tradition of keeping a donkey was so important to Simone.

She continued, "We somehow managed to celebrate only the positive in our time together, and we lived with no regrets. That is something war teaches you. We appreciated each moment of life we shared. There was much laughter in our time together."

"And then he died," Philippe said sorrowfully.

"He died in my garden of a heart attack. It was a peaceful end for him. We had spent a few days together. As I said, your *grandmère* did not like their Cap property and preferred to stay in their house in town. We were lying under the cherry tree . . ."

With that she stood and ran her fingers along the fireplace mantle over the set of initials carved into it. "He simply looked at me, smiled, and passed. Just like that. He was seventy-five and not sick a day."

Katherine was astounded at how Simone's face glowed with love instead of becoming distorted with the pain of loss. She sat in awe of her graciousness.

"And then the bickering began," Philippe muttered. "That's why the property sat neglected for twenty-five years."

Simone shook her head in disgust. "It was ridiculous."

With a wave of her hand, she motioned they should follow her to the kitchen. "This is a good time to pause in our storytelling and enjoy our lunch. Let us savor the love story before we explain the debacle. Now we will have the pleasure of a hearty meal and talk of other things."

CHAPTER THIRTY-ONE

Simone led the way and asked Kat to dress the green salad with olive oil and lemon. Philippe was instructed to transfer the meat and vegetables from the stockpot to a large serving platter.

Simone then removed a clove-studded onion from the pot. Philippe followed her instructions to pour the broth through a sieve into another warm pot. As she stirred the broth, Philippe removed the marrow from the bones.

"You have done this before," Simone commented.

"This was my assignment in my mother's kitchen," he replied with a grin, then asked Katherine to slice the baguette.

Soon everything was placed on the dining table, already set with a typical blue-and-yellow Provençal tablecloth, cutlery, and a bowl of fresh fruit. Simone beamed with pleasure as they exclaimed rapturously over the meal. "This feels like family," she responded.

"Simone, you went to so much trouble with this delicious meal," Kat complimented her.

"*Ma chérie*, this is the kind of French cooking that looks complicated but really is so simple. I will show you one day, if you like.

Monsieur Beau *le boucher* is most helpful, as he delivers the meat already tied in bundles—the most fiddly part."

"I have a long list of cooking questions already," Kat told them as she served a mouth-watering blend of potato, carrot, onion, and meat onto each plate.

"Guard those questions well, *chérie*, and we will prepare some meals together since you are back. Now let's talk about today and your plans. Happy topics only, please!"

Philippe filled each wineglass with a vintage Saint-Émilion he had brought along for the occasion. "I have saved these two bottles for years and never knew why. Now I believe it was for this auspicious *rendezvous*."

They wished each other *bon appétit*. Simone's eyes glistened.

Throughout all of their emotional conversation, Katherine had completely forgotten the exciting news about their expanded family. She gave Philippe a small prompt to announce the news, but he insisted it was hers to share.

"*Deux chiots?* Two puppies? What fun! You must bring them to visit as soon as you can!" Simone was delighted.

They talked about the work that lay ahead in training the pups. "We had planned to wait until we were living at the villa," Philippe told Simone, "but they were irresistible, those little chocolate bundles of joy."

Katherine giggled, "And we haven't come up with names. We're wracking our brains! Any ideas?"

Simone beamed at them both, shaking her head. "What lively times for you. I'm so happy to be sharing all this with you."

Katherine turned to Philippe. "Explain what's happening with the villa because I'm certain"—and now she nodded to Simone—"you must have heard a lot of noise next door over the past two weeks."

Simone clapped her hands. "What a joy to hear life there again, even if it did involve a certain amount of banging and crashing and a parade of trash bins!"

Philippe spoke of their meeting with Didier. "He had no trouble putting together his *équipe*, as I know Kat already explained. Jobs are scarce along the coast right now, so these guys are happy to have the work. His cousin, Auguste, has just arrived from Calais to help as well. He is the largest man I have ever seen. Didier says he can lift things that normally require machinery!"

Katherine added, "He's like a gentle giant from a fairy tale. Truly, Simone, you'd instantly love him. He's always whistling as he works and has a contagious laugh. Some of the other workers arrive in rather dour moods, and he has them joking in no time. So far it's a pleasure to drop by, and they seem to be making reasonable progress."

Philippe agreed, with a word of caution. "It's early days, though. This first part has been more about clearing fallen beams and crumbling walls and putting up supports. The more complicated part comes next, and we will see how long their good humor lasts!"

The meal finished with Simone's ambrosial *crème brûlée*. The crisp scorched shell shattered perfectly to mix with the rich smooth custard below. A hint of vanilla brought murmurs of delight from Kat and Philippe. Simone smiled contentedly, saying she never varied from her family's centuries-old recipe.

They returned to the comfort of the salon to continue the story. Katherine could hardly contain her curiosity.

Simone said, "Now that we have given you the history, we pick up from this point. Gregoire was indeed the father of our son Jean-Luc."

Katherine looked at Philippe. He nodded and added, "So Jean-Luc was in fact my uncle. We could also say that Simone is my *grandmère* . . ."

"By association . . ." Simone clarified, her eyes dancing with affection.

"By any means is an honor," Philippe replied.

"But I made Gregoire promise we would not make this public," Simone explained. "I did not want his sons to know, and we were able to keep the secret. As a youngster, Jean-Luc always believed that his father had been a lover of mine who died before he was born. As an adult, he figured it out and agreed it was our secret."

Katherine and Philippe empathized how difficult it must have been for Simone and Gregoire to keep that secret forever. Simone's expression clearly signaled the answer.

Philippe explained how his father had always told him that he and his brothers had divided themselves into two distinct factions in childhood. The twins had been spoiled by their mother and never forgave Gregoire for his absence in their lives. "For no good reason, they felt that he had more of a relationship with the two younger boys and held that against them. Sadly, the fractious behavior continued into adulthood, and when Gregoire passed away, the fight began over the property. My father was already deceased, but they did not want to share with Oncle François. They were so belligerent that they preferred the land to sit abandoned all those years."

Katherine shook her head. "What a shame. How crazy was that?"

Simone explained, "The history of France is filled with such family feuds. People simply dig in their heels no matter how ridiculous, and some of our archaic laws support that behavior."

Philippe continued, "It wasn't until Guy and Gaston both passed away—they were never uncles to me—within two years of each other that Oncle François became the owner. He then had to go through years and piles of paperwork to turn the property over to me. That was eight years ago. And then my late wife, Viv, died—and that's the story."

Seeing Simone slowly getting up, Philippe extended his hand to her. She walked over to a wall on one side of the salon and pressed the middle of a painting hanging on the wall; two panels of the wall slid open. They blended so well that Katherine had never noticed them before.

The open panels revealed a good-size hidden room, lined floor to ceiling on three sides with book-filled shelves. Daylight flooded in through a skylight. In the middle of the space sat an ornate French writing desk and chair. She picked up an envelope and returned to the salon. The panels slid silently closed behind her.

With a cocky grin, she walked back to the sofa. "More surprises."

Katherine and Philippe were speechless.

She held out an envelope with Philippe's name written on the front. "Here is a copy of a letter I have sent to my lawyer adjusting my will. This property will one day belong to you, Philippe, to do with as you please. And I hope that means it will belong to Katherine too, in time. I cannot adequately express what pleasure this brings to me."

"Simone, this is not necessary," Philippe protested. "It's very generous of you, but there's no need."

"You don't understand. This is the act of a selfish woman. I am doing this for me. Until you both came into my life . . . Katherine, you as a bright new spirit to bring joy to my days, and Philippe, you as someone who has returned from the past with the promise of renewal for Gregoire's property—I despaired of anyone loving this house and gardens again. In fact, I intended to leave it to charity to be used as a retreat, never to be sold for private occupation. I was afraid of a developer eventually getting his hands on it. I couldn't bear that thought. You have made my dream come true."

CHAPTER THIRTY-TWO

Two dog crates were tucked into a corner of the spacious kitchen in their apartment, along with all the other pet supplies.

Katherine and Philippe were on their way back to Mougins with two smaller pet carriers in the backseat of the Citroën.

Ever since leaving Simone's house earlier that afternoon, they'd been unable to stop exclaiming. The compelling stories and revelations that concluded with Simone's generous gift for the future had left them blown away.

Now they were grinning at the thought of the pups coming home. "But we still don't have names for them."

"C'est vrai," Philippe agreed, "but let's see if something comes to us as we watch their little personalities over the first few days."

Delphine had all the paperwork ready. There was a small fee to cover administrative costs, but Katherine and Philippe also left a generous check. This *refuge des animaux* had made an excellent impression, not only with the care of the animals but also with the way the facility was managed.

As they were preparing to leave, Delphine said, "I received a lovely e-mail from your friend Annette."

"Oh my goodness," Katherine said, "In all this excitement I forgot to tell you. Yes! Felicette has settled in very nicely. Annette says the change in her mother has been slow and steady. She already loves that cat!"

Philippe expressed amazement.

Delphine nodded solemnly. "It's not unusual for elderly people to have this response."

"And now you will have two more happy customers!" Katherine told her. *"Merci mille fois."*

"It is we who thank you," Delphine replied sweetly.

Katherine and Philippe clipped little leashes onto the collars they'd brought for the pups. Delphine walked out with them to take some marketing photos. She asked if they'd be willing to give a testimonial about the refuge.

"Any time. Gladly," they said.

As they put the pups in the carriers, a dust-covered pickup truck came screeching into the parking lot, and a middle-aged man with a serious limp hobbled over to them.

"I'm glad I arrived in time! Delphine told me the pups were leaving today, and I wanted to say good-bye to them. I am Raymond Albert, the administrator of the refuge. These pups have been with us almost since birth, and we have become attached to them. We're so happy you are taking both."

He leaned over and gave each dog a scratch around the ears. "Delphine would not tell you this, but she nursed them for weeks, sleeping here on the couch and bottle-feeding them on schedule, giving them lots of love. She has been their mother for two months. All the positives you will see in them are thanks to her."

Delphine had turned away in embarrassment, and Katherine noticed her shoulders shaking. She went to the young girl and put a hand on her back.

"Pardonnez-moi," Delphine whispered between sobs, "I just fell in love with them. You will too."

Philippe handed her his business card. "You can find me at the market in Antibes. We would be happy to have you visit the pups anytime." Katherine nodded her agreement as she handed Delphine a tissue.

The two caretakers waved good-bye as the car drove away.

The pups fussed in the carriers. Between being separated from each other and the motion of the car, they simpered and whined continuously. Philippe stopped the car, and Katherine moved to sit with the pups in the backseat, stroking them to provide comfort. She was already smitten.

"I can't wait for them to meet Picasso. After all, he's the one who taught me about the love a dog can bring to your life. He'll always be special to me."

"We will take these two on a road trip to visit Pico for sure."

They had chosen a potty place, as Kat called it, in the garden and were pleased to see Delphine had indeed already started the training process. On command, both pups piddled to great applause.

Once in the apartment, the happy new owners played and cuddled with their charges for a half hour until the pups appeared ready for a nap. In the crates, they soon fell asleep in their new home.

Katherine and Philippe knew their lives were going to be regulated by the demands of puppy training for the next little while.

Nick called a few days after the pups arrived. He gave the details of Molly's flight and the rehabilitation schedule Dr. Primeau had negotiated for her with the hospital in Nice. It would take about ten days for Molly to be properly registered into the clinic's schedule, he told them.

Her condition appeared to be improving faster than anticipated. It was all good news.

The days and nights preceding Molly's arrival were a blur of puppy parenting. Kat and Philippe shared articles on the subject, often reading to each other, and quickly filled a shelf with books about every aspect of being a dog owner. It did not take long for them to agree that it was a gratifying experience, although with patience tested from time to time, thanks to the pups' abilities to fill each day with mischief as well as joy.

They were also surprised at the amount of time and commitment involved. Katherine and Philippe were determined to keep to the schedule Delphine had sent home. They took turns when they were at home together, but Katherine insisted on getting up during the night so Philippe could get his sleep.

Delphine had told them that after a few nights of adjusting, the pups would be able to go without a trip outside from midnight to six in the morning. Both Katherine and Philippe thanked her for that after seeing it was so.

Katherine took the midnight-walk shift, and Philippe took each pup out around six before he left for the market. They had agreed to do this separately until the pups got a bit older.

The pups proved adept at pottying outdoors and found their favorite spots in the back garden by the apartment parking lot. They were growing by leaps and bounds. Their beautiful coats were becoming more soft and shiny, and Katherine swore pure love radiated from their deep and soulful dark-brown eyes—even when they were caught chewing on a slipper or a biking glove.

"We all have lessons to learn," Kat and Philippe agreed on those occasions.

Obsessed with finding names for their new charges, Kat and Philippe traded constant texts back and forth, then continued the topic during long conversations in the evenings. After many failed attempts at choosing cute combinations like Mocha and Chino and Choco and Latte, they gave up on that idea.

Philippe thought they might call the male Banon, after one of his favorite cheeses that came wrapped in aged brown grape leaves. Then they decided it might be confusing for the pup to hear the *non* part of his name all the time.

Finally, they chose Coco for the female—with thoughts of Coco Chanel and the deep brown of the pup's coat. It seemed to fit her somewhat delicate nature. Her brother became known as Rocco; he was proving himself to be a strong and assertive force.

"When we call them together, we can call them Rococo," Katherine said. "Like Brangelina! Guess where that idea came from?"

Philippe rolled his eyes and laughed. "It had to be Molly!"

March was roaring in like a lion. It was a cool, blustery day, but the sun was shining and the sky even brighter, thanks to the wind. The Monday afternoon of Molly's arrival, Kat waited at home while Philippe went to the airport.

Earlier in the week, Molly had shared her good news that she'd be arriving wheelchair-free. She still had a brace on her leg and needed to use a cane, though. Her movements were slow, but otherwise her leg had healed well. Dr. Primeau and the rehab staff had been amazed at how quickly she had improved.

Therapy would still be needed on her leg and shoulder, and it was arranged that could be done at a new facility just fifteen minutes outside Antibes that was linked to the hospital in Nice.

Katherine wanted everything to be set up so Molly would be comfortable. She also wanted the pups to have visited the potty place just before Molly's arrival so that they could greet their houseguest minus puddles of excitement.

New linens had been purchased for the bedroom Molly would use. With color advice from Simone, Philippe and Katherine had spent a

Monday painting the room a soft-eggshell tone. Katherine had been to the market that morning and gathered together a stunning bouquet of lisianthus in varying shades of pink and purple. It was quickly becoming one of Kat's favorite flowers.

Philippe phoned as they drew up to the front entrance. Then Kat flew down the stairs. "Molly, Molly! *Bienvenue!* Welcome back to Antibes," she cried excitedly. "We're so happy you're here!"

Molly's face was flushed with elation as they hugged gently. "Katski! I honestly can't believe this is happening. I wish we could jump up and down! That's what I know we both want to do. The drive along the Bord de Mer brought back such happy memories!"

Katherine laughed and jumped up and down on her own. "I'll do it for both of us! I'm so excited."

Philippe took Molly's suitcase and carry-on bag up the staircase while Katherine and Molly squeezed into the elevator.

"How charming is this?" Molly exclaimed. "I can't wait to see your new home and get a feel for your life here now. On the flight, I kept thinking of our trip here last summer and how your life changed forever after that."

"Did I ever tell you I met the Browns? The people who owned that sweet house we stayed in?" Kat reminded her.

Kat slid open the elevator door, and they followed Philippe into the apartment.

"Do you think you brought enough clothes?" Kat asked. "The weather can be quite changeable in March and April."

"I don't think I'm going to be attending too many fancy *soirées,*" Molly laughed, "unless Nick has arranged for royalty to visit while I'm here. Knowing him, anything is possible!"

Molly's eyes swept around the spacious entry. The walls, painted in a blend of pale yellows, and high ceilings, accented with the decorative millwork of another era, invited her to take a step back in time. She sighed. "This is beautiful."

Her voice caught as she saw Elisabeth's carpet hanging in a place of honor. "Oh my! It looks perfect there." She wiped her eyes, "I'm overcome to know Elisabeth and Jozsef's spirits live on here."

When Molly recovered her composure, Kat and Philippe couldn't wait to introduce her to Coco and Rocco. They felt like proud parents, they admitted. Molly squealed with delight as the dogs clambered all over her, subjecting her to a serious attack of puppy affection.

"I love them already!" Molly declared. "Can they sleep with me when I'm all better?"

Katherine and Philippe laughed at her enthusiasm. "One day at a time!"

After Molly finished investigating the apartment and got settled, they chatted through the remainder of the afternoon. With sunshine streaming in, they sat around the kitchen table enjoying a bottle of Bandol rosé and a selection of olives and a *tapenade*.

Dinner was planned earlier than usual to accommodate Molly's jet lag. Philippe grilled well-seasoned lamb chops on the new indoor grill he was trying out. Katherine prepared a simple *salade au chèvre chaude*, which she knew had been a favorite of Molly's when she had been in Antibes.

The savory, hot, melted goat's cheese served on crispy toast with walnuts over crunchy chilled salad leaves dressed with honey and French mustard was one of Katherine's favorite meals too. Fig jam was served on the side.

Philippe often brought home delicious varieties of *chèvre* to use. They had decided that the special product crafted by Jacques, near Entrevaux, was the one they liked best.

While Molly raved about the cheese, Katherine assured her that visits to Jacques's farm and to the intriguing village of Entrevaux were definitely planned for when she was ready to travel. "And our friends Véronique and David are looking forward to meeting you too!"

"You know, it won't be long before I can move about more easily. I'm feeling so fuc . . . whoa! There I go again! Almost! So frickin' good! I think I'll be able to ditch this brace soon. I'm really anxious to see what this new clinic has to say."

After dinner, Philippe left for a quick meeting on the Cap with Didier. "Minou, don't forget he wants to talk to you about the change to the kitchen that I mentioned. Can you see him tomorrow?"

Kat assured him she would make some time. "I'm so excited to see what he has in mind!"

The first appointment in the morning was at the clinic so they could assess Molly's requirements. Once her treatment schedule was set up, Kat and Molly could begin to plan other things.

Now they sat on the floor and played with the pups again. Molly said it was the most comfortable position for her, as long as she had help getting up and down.

"Katski, I have to tell you about the strangest thing that happened to me in the rehab hospital in Toronto. Since it was close to your house, Lucy took it upon herself to be a regular visitor."

"That was nice of her," Katherine remarked. "She's such a gentle soul."

"I only met her a few times with you, and she always was very sweet." Molly stopped talking and rolled her eyes in her typical way that made Kat laugh. Then she continued, "Well, it was kind of frickin' strange, that's what it was. I mean, she was giving me the heebie-jeebies."

"Why on earth would you say that?"

"Did you know she was a Reiki master?"

"Ummm, I can't say I did, but I'm not surprised, because she's so into yoga and meditation. She's such a believer in all things spiritual, astrological and, well, Zen, for lack of a better word."

"Well, she decided she was going to give me some—uh, what did she call them? Oh, yeah, attunements—when the staff weren't around. So she would stay for an hour and do her thing with her hands and say all that positive energy stuff. At first I thought she was a bit wacko, lightly placing her hands around my neck and head and leg and shoulder. But I got used to it, and then it actually sounded kind of cool."

"I guess it just depends on your attitude and beliefs. Did it make you feel any better?"

"Well, here's the really weird bit. I think it did make a difference. My shoulder seemed to stop hurting, and the staff all exclaimed how quickly it was healing. I think Lucy was helping me get better faster with all of that touching. She'd hold her hands just above where the surgery had taken place, and I actually thought it tingled there when she did it."

"I've never had any experience with Reiki, but I know several women from yoga who are involved with it. Did you feel more centered? Could you sleep better after one of her sessions?"

"Yes to both, and she listened to my music playlist and made some great suggestions for music for us to listen to sometimes while she did her things with her hands."

Katherine sat thinking for a few minutes. "I guess we just have to try all these things until we come to a conclusion that works for us."

Molly agreed. "And much to my surprise, Tony thought what Lucy was doing was a good idea too."

Katherine smiled. "He's such an interesting man. After all those years of seeing him fleetingly and thinking of him as Father DeCarlo, it was a pleasure to really get to know him. It's interesting how society tends to separate men of the cloth, as it were, from regular people. I was guilty of that, anyway."

Molly nodded and looked away for a second. "That's for sure." Yawning, she said, "I'm starting to fade. It's three in the morning my time . . ."

"Try to stay awake for another hour if you can. I'll take the pups out for their walks while you get ready for bed. See you in half an hour or so, and let me know if you need anything." They stood up and hugged again, smiling into each other's eyes.

Kat sighed happily. "It's so good to have you here, on your way back to being you. You had us seriously worried for a while."

CHAPTER THIRTY-THREE

Early Wednesday morning, Katherine and Molly went to Molly's first meeting at the physiotherapy clinic. The drive was easy, the staff professional and friendly.

Molly had been concerned about not speaking French, but Katherine had assured her that most of the staff was happy to speak English with her.

"This is still very much part of your recuperation," the physiotherapist reminded Molly. "You've been through tremendous physical and emotional trauma, and it will require more time than you realize to fully recover. Even your brain injury will take time, there is still healing going on there too."

On the way home after a three-hour session, Molly said, "Wow, Katski, you sounded so impressive when you spoke to the receptionist in French. You're really coming along with that!"

Kat sighed. "I'm getting more comfortable with the language. But I've still got a long way to go. Thank heavens for my tutor, Ida, and for patient Philippe and my friend Annette. Even Simone some days—everyone is helping!"

"It's so great to see all this familiar territory. I just want to run around and go everywhere you took me before and stroll the cobblestone lanes . . ."

"There will be no strolling the cobblestone lanes until you get the go-ahead from the clinic. Remember what the physiotherapist said as we were leaving. You have to be very careful where you walk for another couple of weeks or else you'll have to go back into a wheelchair. But don't worry, there are plenty of streets that aren't cobblestone where we can walk."

"All right! Then can we stop at Le Vieil Antibes for old times' sake and I'll have an espresso? Then next time I want to go to Choopy's and that pizza place where we met Nick and Graham and I've just got to meet Simone and what about Bernadette . . . Oh, wait, let's go to your place on the Cap, I'm dying to see that!"

"Whoa!" Katherine laughed. "Make a list and we'll do it all. We've got tons of time! I'll park at the port now, and we'll go to Le Vieil Antibes so you can have that espresso. Then we'll go to the Cap."

As they sat sipping their espresso and tea, they reminisced about their time together the previous August. Katherine was touched by how meaningful that trip had been for Molly.

Molly set her cup down. "Thanks to you, my eyes were really opened to the endless experiences travel brings. It completely changed my perspective for the future. As you well know, I'd never been out of Canada, apart from the States, and I really didn't have that big a desire or the funds to take trips. Being back here reminds me that travel is going to play a part of my life from now on. Once a year I'm going to plan a trip somewhere, and I'm excited about that."

Katherine looked thoughtful. "We're both going through major change in our lives right now. I still shake my head in amazement sometimes."

With her lips pursed, Molly nodded and gave Katherine a noticeably intense look. "So here's my question for you, Katherine Elisabeth

Price: have you accepted in your head what your heart has been telling you for some time? Before you left Toronto last month, you admitted you were still struggling with the idea that your home would be in France forever."

Katherine returned the intense look as only the best of friends can. She knew Molly was right. She knew there was no point in dragging out the process any longer.

Neither blinked. "As they say, poop or get off the pot," Molly continued. "See how I've cleaned up my act? Now, what's it going to be?

Katherine shook her head and laughed. "Trust you to take a serious moment and make me laugh."

"Never mind. That was just minor comedic relief. I'm waiting for your answer."

"I'm close to knowing. With certainty. Philippe has been patient beyond words, and after the time we spent with Simone the other day, I feel like the truth is staring me in the face."

Molly gave Kat a wide-eyed questioning look and spread her hands out, palms up. "So?"

"So, I'm glad you're here to push me."

"I'm waiting. We can talk about it anytime."

Reaching for Molly's hands, Kat clasped them in hers. "And we will."

Accepting this was the end of the conversation for now.

Molly changed her tone. "I can't believe we're sitting here chatting in this little café in the South of France, once again," she said with an enormous grin.

Katherine blew out a big sigh. "I'm so relieved you're here at all. You gave us quite a scare!"

Molly's eyes filled with tears. "How can I ever thank you for all you've done? For coming back to Toronto and making sure everything was handled properly. For taking care of me when there really was no one else. For bringing Andrea and Terrence into my life, and now

Philippe and Nick. Oh my God, dear, dear Nick. I'm so grateful to you for everything."

Katherine and Molly shared an embrace of love, friendship, and gratitude. Kat reminded herself to be gentle with Molly's still-delicate condition.

Kat smiled at her friend. "I'm going to be as trite as can be now, but that's what friends are for. We are so lucky to have each other."

Molly nodded, wiping her eyes.

"Just don't reunite us through a serious accident again, please and thank you."

"I guess that's one of the benefits of being unconscious. I didn't know how much of a scare I gave you until much later. This accident has been a game changer for me."

They talked about how the next few weeks might play out, made some plans, agreed that all plans were subject to change, and simply decided to have the best time together that they possibly could.

Katherine called Didier to say they would be over and that they would bring lunch. After picking up the requested baguette sandwiches, Katherine could not believe her eyes as they drove up the driveway to the villa.

A carpet of deep purple covered the gardens and much of the lawn, and spread like a flowing stream through the woodland. A sweet fragrance hung heavily in the air as Kat helped Molly out of the car.

"Wow! Just wow!" they exclaimed to each other. "What is that?"

Katherine quickly walked over and bent down to pick one of the delicate blooms. "Violets! I didn't know we had any on the property or that they bloomed this time of year. They've popped open in the two days since I was last here. Look at them all!"

Didier came out to greet them, touching his fingers to his beret in respect. After Kat introduced him to Molly, she raved about the abundance of violets.

Didier's enthusiasm matched hers. "*Oui! C'est magnifique!* Because the property was neglected for so many years, these violets spread with wild abandon," he explained. "Tourrettes-sur-Loup has a *fête des violettes* this month. You must go! Most of their harvest goes to the perfume makers in Grasse, as they have for centuries. They are also the official flower of Toulouse and there are many *fêtes* all around that region this month, but that's quite a drive."

"Oh! We'll go to Tourrettes for sure! It's one of my favorite villages. When Philippe takes me for a spin into the hills on his Ducati, we often stop there. The village is atmospheric and so picturesque. Molly, the first sight of it will make your jaw drop."

Katherine was still mesmerized by the purple haze that had taken over the property. "This is so dreamlike. I love it, don't you, Moll?"

"Fanfrickingtastic!" Molly exclaimed.

Katherine picked up her camera from the backseat of the car and snapped away. She kept repeating that she had never seen anything quite like it.

Didier blew his whistle and proudly assembled his team before handing out the baguette sandwiches. Then he gave Molly and Kat a tour of all that had been done so far. While Kat continued to fill her camera chip with the dreamlike purple haze carpeting the property, he showed Molly the drawings of what was to come.

Molly could not contain her enthusiasm. "Even in this state of disrepair, it's easy to see what a special place this will be. You can feel the history and the character everywhere, and the garden is magic—simply magic. I've never seen so much purple! I want to come back and help you plant and dig and weed and all that, Kat. Promise me I can do that!"

"I promise you can come back every single time you wish," Katherine assured her. "We're always going to have plenty of room for company. That's something Philippe and I both are excited about. He's such a people person and never really had the chance to enjoy that in his own home. You know how everyone loves him at the market."

Molly nodded. "Tomorrow we'll have to go there."

"For sure, we can head there after your physio," Kat agreed. "And I'm serious about you making a list. I want to do everything you want. Oh, and we've got some projects to put you to work on too. I'm not kidding!"

"Whatever you want. I'm at your disposal, *mon amie*," Molly answered.

Kat and Molly settled on a bench with their sandwiches in a sheltered sunny spot in the garden. They breathed in the fragrance of the violets, exclaiming repeatedly in pleasure.

"I guess Philippe knows about this and doesn't think it's such a big deal," Kat speculated. "It'll be interesting to see what he says."

"I bet he wanted you to be surprised," Molly suggested.

"Why didn't I think of that? That would be just like him." Kat smiled knowingly.

Molly nodded in between bites. "What is it about baguette sandwiches that makes them taste so delicious with just a simple slice of cheese and ham? Actually, I'm not looking for an answer. That was purely rhetorical. I know the French discovered the secret for the most delicious bread in the world centuries ago."

Katherine grinned and mumbled her agreement, her mouth full.

Molly went on in rapture, "Mmmmm . . . frickin'. . . mmmmm! Color me happy!"

The days passed quickly, with physiotherapy sessions every morning. Molly had bonded well with Claire, the well-trained woman in charge of her program. Her gentle persuasion kept Molly disciplined in doing interval exercises at home, and the results were showing.

Katherine was firm in reminding excitable Molly to take things slowly. Even though they were thrilled to be together and eagerly anticipated the adventures that awaited them, they also knew it was important to rest. Everything would happen in due course.

Simone asked Kat to bring Molly over for tea and *madeleines*, and that became a part of their weekly routine.

The weather had not been conducive to most excursions anyway. "Let's give spring a little more time to settle in," Kat rationalized. "I'm so glad you'll be here to experience that."

Molly had countered by saying the weather was a major improvement compared to what she'd left behind in Toronto. Philippe enjoyed agreeing thoroughly with that.

The next Monday they drove up to Tourrettes-sur-Loup with Philippe and Gilles to enjoy the *fête des violettes*. The festival lasted throughout March, with a focus on all the edible possibilities one could create with violets. Molly and Kat agreed that the violet ice cream had been their favorite.

Along the way, Kat and Philippe continued a conversation they had been having since Kat discovered the violets at the villa. Philippe hadn't told her about them because he wanted her to have precisely the reaction she did.

"You're the best surprise maker! Thank you again for that one, it was fabulous!"

Philippe grinned. "I've been thinking about your idea for a name for the villa. *Tu as raison*, Minou. You're right. I like it!"

Katherine reached over and kissed him on the cheek. "I love it too! Molly, what do you think? Gilles? Do we have a unanimous vote?"

Villa des Violettes would be the name of the restored villa.

Much of Molly's time was spent reading and relaxing while Kat worked on her photography files. They also began developing the FromageGraphie website together, and the more they planned, the more excited Kat and Philippe became about the possibilities. A summer launch was their target.

Molly was intrigued by their ideas for the website. She threw herself into investigating layouts and formats while Katherine kept busy planning for her debut in the photography exhibit. The three of them shared a lot of laughter and good ideas as they tossed around concepts that would marry the themes of cheese and photography.

Molly spoke with Tony almost every day on Skype. Often, Katherine and Philippe were invited to join in.

Katherine avoided having any discussion with Molly about Tony, other than to regularly say what an impressive man he was and how much she liked his company. Molly always agreed and then changed the subject.

"Everyone looks for happiness. I mean, why wouldn't we? But we each find it in different ways. Look at what you thought made you happy for so many years and compare it to what makes you happy now. Wow! I'm happy to simply be alive, and for now, that's all I need."

"I think she does that from habit," Katherine commented to Philippe one night in bed. "She'd had to keep him secret for so long, it just comes naturally now. Besides, she doesn't know that we're aware of their relationship."

"I think it's time you encouraged her to talk about it," Philippe said. "Let her know Tony spoke to us. I'm in touch with him a fair bit, so I'll check to see if the time is right to begin the conversation."

The opening night of André's art exhibit, titled *Les Images de Nos Rêves/ The Images of Our Dreams*, was the Friday of Molly's second week.

Invitations had been sent, but it was also open to the public so no one would feel unwelcome.

Attendance was overwhelming, and André swore every person from Antibes was there. "I always have been fortunate to have good attendance at all of our exhibits, but this is exceptional," he kept repeating.

Many of Katherine and Philippe's friends from Nice came, including the Johnstons, who brought some friends. Almost all the women from Katherine's expat walking group arrived together. She was constantly touched by enthusiastic support. They were also eager to meet Molly, inviting her to join them as soon as she could.

Henri and Sylvie drove down from Roussillon and brought best wishes from Joy and Oncle François, with instructions to take many photos and bring them back for their consideration. "François is determined for one of your photos to grace his wall, Kat."

Kat replied, "Tell him everything was sold. I'm going to do something especially for him, as a gift. But don't tell him that part."

Before the end of the evening, several pieces on display—including two of Katherine's five entries—had been purchased. She was floating on air and kept insisting Philippe assure her that he had not been the buyer.

The exhibit would last for two weeks, and Katherine had committed to spending time there each day. The more time she spent speaking with photographers and people who were interested in seeing the exhibit, the more she felt herself making her hobby a serious component of her life.

The thought excited her more than she had anticipated. Another new chapter in her life was beginning.

CHAPTER THIRTY-FOUR

By the last weekend in March, Molly was walking with just a hint of a limp. Her shoulder was also responding well to treatment, and it looked like she would have a full range of motion, after initial doubts. Her hard work was paying off.

She also was finally given permission by Claire to stroll the cobblestone streets. Molly was instructed to be careful and to bring along her cane if she felt it was necessary. They knew she wasn't about to take any foolish chances.

"There's no frickin' way I want to go through this again," Molly assured Claire and everyone else within earshot. After a few wanderings with Katherine and Rococo, she felt stable and confident.

Now Kat and Molly were able to enjoy hilltop lunches as they browsed along the cobblestone lanes of Eze and Saint-Paul-de-Vence. They lingered over portside seafood snacks in Molly's favorite town of Villefranche-sur-Mer. Often, they ambled along the Prom in Nice after meeting Véronique for coffee or took restorative strolls along the sandy beaches of Juan-les-Pins to build up Molly's strength.

"Katski, I'd forgotten how close all these exquisite places are. Why would you not want to be here, I ask you! I could be persuaded without any effort!"

There had been many opportunities for long conversations.

One day, as Molly was telling Katherine how thrilled she was that Kat and Philippe had fallen in love, Katherine broached the subject of Molly's love life.

"Molly, I know you've always told me you weren't interested in the dating scene. I didn't see you a lot for many years, and the only time you mentioned anyone in your life was, as you described him, your Italian lover, Antonio—your friend with benefits. Didn't you ever date anyone else?"

Molly said nothing for a few seconds, bobbing her head around as they continued walking. She pulled her jacket a little more tightly around her, even though it was quite a warm day.

Looking straight ahead, she began, "Okay, Katski, here's the condensed version of my dating life. Prepare to be amused."

Katherine knew if anyone could spin the dating scene into a comedy routine, it would be Molly. "I'm ready, Moll. Don't hold back."

Molly cleared her throat and took a deep breath, which she then immediately blew out. "A few years ago, I enrolled on LFL—Looking for Love—an online dating website. Besides a bunch of total assholes, there really are a lot of sincere people on the site who are looking for a good match."

She paused and met Katherine's gaze. "Even though everyone says they don't have baggage, each person lugs at least one Samsonite along with them. Anyone over six feet does not lie about his height. Otherwise, short men exaggerate by two or three inches, and you find yourself kissing the tops of their bald heads."

Kat snorted.

Molly screwed her face into an exaggerated grimace before rolling her eyes and continuing. "There are all kinds of guys looking for all kinds of different connections. Some want to book the church after the first meet and greet. Others, as soon as they meet you, give you the Italian once-over from head to toe, then their eyes glaze over and they're polite for the requisite half hour. You never hear from them again. It's a lot like high school. The ones that like you, you don't like, and the ones you don't like, stalk you. You've got to kiss a lot of frogs to get to a prince."

Katherine chuckled. "I don't know whether to laugh or cry. It sounds pretty awful."

"And don't get me started on the subject of kissing . . ." Molly opened her mouth, stuck two fingers partway in and made a loud gagging sound.

Kat was laughing again before she said, "Getting serious for a minute, Moll, I suppose it's important not to invest all your hopes in the possibilities."

"Absofrickinlutely! You really have to remember that these websites are simply an avenue to meet a person of interest and then see where that goes. A lot of the men I met told me the same stories about women not looking anything like their profile picture. That's what impressed a lot of guys about me. What they saw was what they got."

"I can only begin to imagine what it was like," Katherine said. "I'm thankful I didn't have to go through that. I'm not sure I could."

Molly looked at Katherine with a frustrated expression. "It wears you down, Katski, and within no time, it's no fun. I met some guys who looked nothing like their profile photo. Ten years older, twenty pounds heavier and—oh, you thought I wouldn't notice—half a head of hair lighter. Or they say they don't smoke, but there's a photo in their profile where they have a cigarette in their hand. Or, a real classic, the guy who posted photos of himself cleaning fish, with blood and guts all over the place—including himself."

Kat snorted at that last remark, and Molly gave her an exaggerated eye roll as she shook her head.

"But that's just me. I know a few women at work who have met great guys. Two have even gotten married."

By this time they had reached the ramparts that ran along the coast. They stopped and looked down at the Plage de La Gravette, the picturesque beach they liked best. Molly sighed and said, "You know, it looks inviting even though I know it's freezing right now. We sure had a few good days floating in that beautiful cove."

"And we'll have some more. You'll just have to come back again in the summer."

They turned and began walking along the ramparts toward the apartment. "So, getting back to online dating—did you ever meet anyone interesting?"

"Sure. I met some guys who were nice, kind, fun, even interesting . . . but not necessarily for me. Most of the time on dates I sat looking through guys, trying to be polite, so I could get out of wherever we were as soon as possible. It doesn't take great intuition to know when a guy is going to ask for another date. Whenever I sensed that coming, I would excuse myself to the ladies' room, throw cold water on my face, give myself a pep talk, and go back out with my standard response ready."

"Which was?" Katherine asked.

"After they popped the question, I would look at them sweetly and say, 'Are you fucking kidding me?'"

Kat stopped again and looked Molly in the eyes. "You did not say that! Tell me you didn't."

Molly laughed. "Well, there was a day when I might have but . . . no, I never did. I had an extremely polite response about feeling more friendship than romance for them. I might as well have said the other. It was never well received."

Katherine sympathized, "Rejection is never easy."

"That's one of the pieces of advice these dating websites stress. It's not that simple to put into practice. You learn it's hard to find someone you connect with in all three departments: head, heart, and pants. Nothing clicked for me. Certainly not Fish-gutting Guy." She sighed. "I mean, nothing."

Katherine looked at her with compassion. "Oh, Molly, it must have been depressing."

"Yup! That about sums it up. That's why I stopped."

"I can't say I blame you," Kat muttered, putting her arm around Molly. They stopped to untangle the leashes the dogs had managed to wrap around each other.

"The pups obviously need more leash training, Kat."

"Maybe we need more leash training!" Kat laughed. "We can't talk and keep Rococo untangled at the same time."

As they continued walking home, Molly picked up the conversation where they had left off.

"I have my music, and you know that comes straight from my heart. I'm so relieved my singing wasn't affected by my injuries. And I have my students. You know how I love teaching. Now I've experienced whole new dimensions of life that I hopefully can share with the kids. So screw the dating scene. I simply don't need it."

Kat debated dropping the subject. Molly sounded convincing and sure of her feelings. *Why should I push it?*

But then she did.

"So do you still have your friend with benefits? The enigmatic hot Italian lover?" Katherine asked, feeling as if she was completely crossing a line. On the other hand, as she'd told herself often during the past two months, she and Molly were true friends who cared about each other, and it was time to put all their cards on the table.

Molly stopped walking. Rocco took advantage of the halt in their stroll to engage in serious sniffing around nearby bushes, and Coco soon joined him.

Katherine spoke again. "Molly. After all these years, I think you can be honest with me. You know you can trust me."

Molly spoke slowly and clearly. "You know who my friend with benefits is, don't you?"

"I think so. I just need to hear you say it. You said this accident was a game changer for you. Why not change your life in every way? What could possibly be a better time than now?"

The two friends faced each other. Their eyes met.

"Okay," Molly said, taking a deep breath and not breaking Kat's gaze. "So all that online dating stuff happened intermittently. Tony is the lover I've had all these years, but there were times when we tried to go our separate ways."

"I can imagine," Kat said, filling in a long pause on Molly's part. Katherine could tell this was emotionally difficult for Molly.

With her voice almost a whisper, Molly said, "He means everything to me. I will never look for anyone else again. We both realized that a few years ago. The only problem is that we can never be together because of his calling in life."

Katherine continued to meet Molly's eyes. "His obvious concern for you in the hospital certainly caught my attention. Probably not everyone else's, so don't worry about that. His caring for you took precedence over everything else when your life hung in the balance. You're very fortunate to have that kind of love in your life."

This time Molly snorted. "Well, I'm not sure how fortunate a woman is when her primary competition is the Catholic Church—or God."

They began walking again, and Molly poured her heart out. She spoke of the early days of her friendship with Father DeCarlo. She first met him through the drug-addiction problems her brother, Shawn, faced and her involvement in trying to help him.

"We were friends for a few years before it evolved into a relationship. No one put more effort into helping Shawn kick his drug habit than Tony. I had—and still do have—so much respect for him. He was kind to me and spent a lot of time getting to know me and Shawn and learning the details of our past, of our childhood. I trusted and respected him before I ever realized how attracted I was to him."

"So how do you see your love affair continuing?"

"I guess we will simply carry on as we have . . . in secrecy."

"But wouldn't it be better for both of you if you could be open and honest about your love for each other?"

Molly's expression saddened as she struggled to get the words out. "Impossible. The Catholic Church would never accept our relationship. We've talked about it."

"But what if he left the church? Wouldn't that make it right for you?"

"I couldn't live with the guilt. Tony is such a . . . well, such a man of God. He lives his faith in everything he does. That's one of the reasons I love him so very much. He makes me a better person, and he even put up with my f-bomb issues for all those years."

"Philippe and I got to know him—pretty well, we think—for the short time we had in Toronto. I mean, I've known him for years, of course, but only in his role as a priest. We were able to get to know Tony DeCarlo, the regular guy, in the hospital with you. He's quite something."

Molly's face lit up. "I don't know anyone else like him. Such simple things about him are exceedingly special. I guess if I had to describe him with one sentence, I would say that he lives life in the superlative."

Kat looked amused. "I don't think I've ever heard anyone described that way. What do you mean?"

"Whenever he tells me something, it's always, 'Moll, I met the most interesting person today.' Or, 'I ate the hottest, most delicious curry for lunch.' Or 'I read the best book this week.' See what I mean? Everything is in the superlative. He sees the good in everyone and everything. Nothing is ever a problem that cannot be solved. His glass is always half full. No, let me correct that! His glass is always full . . . or, as he likes to say, his cup runneth over."

Katherine could hear the love in Molly's voice amid her restraint. "I'm sure he loves you in the superlative too!"

Molly looked at Katherine with an expression mixed with sadness and relief. "I guess I'm glad that I've told you. I'm not sure, though. Please don't let on to Tony that you know anything about our relationship . . . maybe you shouldn't tell Philippe either."

Katherine was torn between continuing the conversation and revealing all that she knew. But Tony had also spoken to her in confidence. She knew she had to respect that until he told them otherwise.

At least the door to talk about it had been opened. She hoped Molly would let her walk through again.

CHAPTER THIRTY-FIVE

As soon as the market closed the following Saturday, Philippe loaded the car while Katherine and Molly walked the pups. They were all on their way to visit Joy and the rest of the family in Sainte-Mathilde for two days.

Katherine made arrangements with André so he did not need her at the exhibit, which still had another week to run. Philippe was taking Sunday off. Molly was beside herself with anticipation. The pups were bouncing with eagerness to do everything.

Philippe gave Molly a running commentary as they drove along the route that was now so familiar to Katherine. Molly admired the beauty of the red hills of the *massif de l'Esterel*.

She became thoroughly animated as the car turned up into the countryside through vineyards, orchards, and farm fields still sleepily beginning to emerge from their hibernation.

The vineyards still wore their winter look, with no leaves evident so far.

"Our last few weeks have been rather cool. I think bud break will commence soon, though, and the vines will begin to show signs of green growth," Philippe predicted.

In contrast, the creamy drifts of the early-blooming almond trees made up for the lack of color in the fields, and pink-tinged cherry blossoms were beginning to open. Combined with the gray-green mounds of lavender plants, there was a sense of spring in the air.

Every perched village elicited moans of delight from Molly, and she made Katherine promise they would visit a few. After studying a Luberon guidebook Katherine handed her, Molly chose Roussillon and Gordes since they were not far from Joy's.

Joy had called to forewarn them that temperatures dropped significantly in the evenings, so they should bring some warm clothes. She also said the winds had died down and the rain had stopped. She felt they would have two lovely days and suggested they plan to take the dogs on some good walks.

As they pulled into the driveway of Joy's *manoir*, Molly gasped again. "I'm living the dream!"

Katherine chuckled and said, "Now you know how I felt when I arrived for my exchange! I was in that dream too."

The front door opened before they could get out of the car. Once again, Henri was the first to reach them. "Henri, you are becoming the official greeter!" Katherine said as they exchanged *bises*.

He greeted Molly warmly, having met her at André's exhibit. "*Bienvenue!* We have heard so much about you and are so happy to see you again. What better place to recuperate than with Katherine and Philippe?"

Sylvie followed closely behind Henri and, after welcoming everyone, she peered through the window into the backseat. The pups were standing in their travel crates, tails wagging as they eagerly pawed to join the welcome.

"*Quels beaux chiots!* The pups look so sweet! Should we let Picasso out? Maman is holding him in the great hall until we let her know what to do."

"*Oui,*" Philippe agreed as he unloaded the overnight bags. "Let our boy Pico out to greet us first and then we will introduce Rocco and Coco to him."

Henri whistled loudly, and Picasso burst out of the house. As always, he danced eagerly between Philippe and Katherine, happy to see them, and at the same time made Molly feel very welcome too.

Katherine got on her knees to give him a hug and receive his standard sloppy kiss.

Joy followed the dog out of the house and greeted everyone with delight. "*Bienvenue chez nous,* Molly. I know you're like a sister to Katherine, and we've all been worried about you. How nice to see you are doing well. We hope you'll feel at home here."

By this time, the pups were excitedly barking and Picasso was bouncing up and down, trying to see where the noise was coming from.

Antoine, who ran the household along with his wife, Hélène, came out to take the bags from Philippe, which freed him to release the pups. Chaos reigned for several minutes as they raced in between Picasso's legs and back and forth to their owners. Picasso took charge and ran in circles, with the pups in fierce pursuit. Every once in a while he would stop and chase them, which caused everyone to laugh uproariously.

After a few minutes, Philippe and Henri led the dogs around to the back terrace while the others went into the house.

"I'm sure you may be a bit hungry after your, drive so there's some crostini and champagne waiting in the salon. Why don't you get settled in your rooms and then we can relax together," Joy said. "Antoine has taken your bags straight up, and Katherine, you know where to take Molly."

Katherine and Joy hugged gently, as they always did, thanks to Joy's British background. "I am so thrilled to see you. It feels like forever since we were all together for Noël."

"And I you, *ma chère*. It's been too long! But I know it couldn't be helped. You must bring us up to date on everything when you come back downstairs . . . oh, but first let me see your beautiful ring."

She took Katherine's hand and examined the ring carefully, her eyes shining brightly. "*C'est magnifique!* I'm so happy for you both, and I felt so honored to play a little part in this by introducing Philippe to the jeweler. That made this old woman very thrilled to be in on the secret."

Katherine nodded. "It was only fitting that you should be involved, Joy. I was thrilled too when Philippe told me about that."

Wide-eyed, Molly followed Katherine up the grand marble staircase. She took in the portraits on the walls, commenting how they blended with the historic grandeur surrounding her. "Katski, this is even more beautiful than I imagined."

"It's truly magnificent, and the family even more so. You're going to be enchanted and love it here, as I do."

Molly came to Kat's door after she had freshened up. "*Mon* frickin' *Dieu!* Not only do I have a fireplace in my room, I have the most splendid four-poster too! It's like *Downton Abbey* with a French twist!"

They giggled together as they went back downstairs where everyone was waiting.

As they settled into the comfortable furniture in the salon, champagne was poured and toasts followed. Molly was introduced to Christian and Marie, who had stopped to pick up Oncle François on their way. Molly beamed and blushed as the patriarch kissed her hand. The mood was jovial and celebratory with so much good news to share.

Picasso was lying in his bed in the corner of the room, with two exhausted chocolate bumps snuggled beside him.

Before dinner, Molly was given a complete tour of the *manoir*. She couldn't stop asking questions. She was fascinated with the family history and the graceful particulars of the architecture. Everything—the high ceilings, wood beams, cavernous fireplace, and decorative plaster around windows and doors—elicited expressions of awe at the craftsmanship and attention to detail paid by the ancient builders.

Katherine and Oncle François slipped off to a favorite quiet corner to have one of their intimate conversations. He held Katherine's hand lightly in his and spoke of his immense happiness at how events were unfolding between her and Philippe.

From behind the sofa, Kat retrieved a sizable paper-covered gift. The kindly uncle's eyes lit with surprise and delight as he unwrapped an enlarged framed photo, which captured him sitting quietly on a rock, watching over his beloved goats in the early morning light.

Kat explained, "This was last June when I first arrived at the farmhouse, before we even knew each other. I was so taken with the peace I felt, seeing you in that soft lighting. Now I know those were some of the happiest times for you, and I hope this brings you joy."

His beaming face mirrored his emotions.

Philippe joined them after a while, and they recounted to François their conversations with Simone. François's eyes glistened as memories flooded back to him of youthful days on the Cap property.

"Of course I remember Simone, and of course I knew of her love affair with my father. However, we did not speak of those things in those days. She was always a lady, and we treated her as such on the rare occasions that we actually were in her company."

His stories ranged from the dire conditions during the Occupation, when food rationing kept them all hungry, to the gala postwar parties that were held in the gardens of the Cap property. Simone often attended those parties. "Of course, those are memories of a child, so take some of them with a grain of salt."

Much to Katherine and Molly's surprise, dinner was served outside on the terrace with the propane heaters keeping everything cozy. Hélène had prepared her prized *coq au vin* recipe, which garnered great compliments from all the diners.

As Molly exclaimed it was the best *coq au vin* she had ever tasted, Henri coyly teased her that it was probably because she'd never eaten the dish with real *coq*. Molly looked a little flustered, and he quickly apologized and explained that Hélène still insisted on using the original recipe passed along through many generations of her family—and that meant cooking rooster, not chicken.

Joy took over the details. "It's traditionally made by slowly cooking a rooster in red Burgundy wine with mushrooms, *lardons*, and pearl onions . . ."

"*Un plus delicieux braise!*" Oncle François interrupted with a dreamy expression.

There were murmurs of accord around the table, as Joy continued, "The rooster is marinated all day and then is slow-cooked overnight in our wood-fired bread oven. It's a dish we love in every season, as it's both nourishing and deeply comforting—definitely a family favorite, but mainly thanks to Hélène's magic touch."

Everyone nodded in enthusiastic agreement.

"And somehow," Philippe added, winking at Christian and Marie, who oversaw the family's vineyard and stocked their vast cave, "the kitchen in this house always manages to have the best source for excellent wines."

The evening passed quickly, filled with conversation as pleasing as the meal.

As Kat nestled drowsily in Philippe's arms in bed that night, she murmured, "*Le plaisir et la séduction*—the first time I understood the importance of those words in explaining the life, the people, the culture of France, was from Joy and her family . . . then you made that come alive for me."

"Hmmm, perhaps we should review what we know about *plaisir et séduction*, right here, right now . . ." Philippe murmured back, his voice low and husky, as his arms gently tightened around her. Kat turned her lips to meet his.

Sylvie decided to join Molly and Katherine the next day on their excursion to Roussillon and Gordes. Since she and Henri lived in Roussillon, the women would meet her there.

As they approached through the surrounding farmland and forests, Molly commented on the dramatic color changes in the soil and rocks. Ocher ridges popped out from the landscape, providing new scenery.

Katherine had pointed out the endless rows of mounds in the lavender fields on the way. "You have to come back to see them in June. This will be my first year experiencing the full whammy of lavender season, and I can hardly wait. Even André says it's truly something to which no photo can do justice. Add that to your list of reasons to return, *ma chère amie!*"

"As if I needed any more!" Molly replied.

The reds, browns, oranges, and yellow shades of ocher in the painted houses of this colorful village soon appeared on the hilltop. It was time for Molly to gasp once again. "It's simply stunning, there's no other word for it . . . the contrast of the colors with the greens beginning to show in the landscape and the blue of the sky. No wonder artists and painters found inspiration in Roussillon! Who wouldn't want to live here?

"I know! I know!" Kat agreed. "I don't have to explain why I'm in love with all of these villages and areas."

They parked on the edge of town and walked to Henri and Sylvie's house. Sylvie took them on a tour of the most beautiful nooks and crannies of Roussillon, sharing history and secret stories. She made certain they didn't miss a single captivating aspect of the village. Passing a local artist's studio, Molly couldn't resist purchasing two posters. "These are going to be framed and have a place of honor in my living room," she declared.

Next they began the winding and picturesque ten-kilometer drive to Gordes. Katherine was delighted that Sylvie had offered to drive for the remainder of the day, since she knew the back roads of her home territory intimately.

"Sylvie, I can't thank you enough. Now I won't have to subject Molly to the possibility of becoming hopelessly lost with me driving, GPS or no GPS. I've already proven that on the maze of country routes around here!"

Sylvie laughed. "*C'est mon plaisir!* It's always fun to be a guide around our beautiful countryside, which we never take for granted. There are few days when I don't smile at our good fortune to live here."

The day was mild and sunny, and at one point Sylvie suggested that Molly roll down her window and breathe in the air. "The best thing about driving here is smelling the scenery as well as seeing it."

They inhaled noisily, and Katherine was instantly reminded of how she had been charmed by the aromatic air during her first exchange. "I loved savoring the fragrant scents as I walked to Sainte-Mathilde or biked these roads. It was like having an intense aromatherapy session every time!"

"Of course, it was even better for you in June. You would have had the benefit of peak fragrance season from so many plants!" Sylvie concurred.

They stopped en route to visit Sylvie's friend's lavender farm. Molly found it intriguing to hear how that couple had packed in their professional careers in Paris to take on the challenge of their acreage. "I'm definitely coming back some year at the end of June so I can see all these fields in bloom," she promised them.

The first view of Gordes drew an actual squeal from Molly. Sylvie pulled over at the popular photo spot. Molly stood on a rocky ledge above a hundred-foot drop to take the perfect shot of the breathtaking village that tumbled from the castle on high to the valley below.

"You know," she said to Sylvie, "this would absolutely never be allowed in North America. There would be a tall fence for sure!" She couldn't stop exclaiming at the unique beauty of the area. "Sorry for repeating myself, but this is quite overwhelming."

Sylvie smiled. "I understand completely."

Katherine had already told Molly that the steep cobbled streets of Gordes would offer some challenges for her walking. "You called that right!" Molly agreed. They decided to simply take in some shops on the main square, then go into the castle. Side streets would be saved for a future visit.

Since they had the time, Sylvie took them past ancient *bories* and into the picturesque isolated valley of the Abbaye de Sénanque. Molly's face changed as the storied twelfth-century Cistercian abbey and cloisters came into view.

"It's easy to picture how this will look when all those rows of lavender are in bloom," Molly said as Katherine took photo after photo.

"I haven't been here before either, Molly. It's enchanting even without the flowers."

Sylvie had a special place to take them for lunch. They drove between high stone gates and down a long lane to a pastoral setting overlooked by a classic stone farmhouse with traditional blue shutters. Beneath the trees on the terrace, elegant tables were set with white china and yellow glassware on soft blue tablecloths that complemented the shutters. Sheep and goats grazed in a nearby field.

The setting was as idyllic as the meal was delicious.

CHAPTER THIRTY-SIX

Molly felt as though she would burst with pleasure the entire weekend. Never had she imagined how anything could match the time she'd spent with Katherine in Antibes the previous summer.

"I have to tell you, Katski, this visit is a close frickin' second! Visually, gastronomically, and socially, this is superb. There's a completely different ambiance, of course, not being on the sea. But it's a magical area, that's for sure!"

After their day spent touring with Sylvie, they returned to Joy's to discover the three dogs running about as if they were old friends. Picasso was patient with the young ones as they nipped at his ears, and he gently caught them and rolled them over from time to time.

When Katherine went outside, Pico came to her side and waited patiently for her to scratch his ears. Rocco and Coco clung to him like shadows, and their constant activity caused laughter from all who were watching. Fatigue still came upon the pups suddenly, and there were a number of spontaneous naps during the afternoon.

Before dinner they all went for a hike through the field with Oncle François's goats, now faithfully watched over by the young local Philippe. He smiled and waved as they passed by. Joy told Katherine the young man had accepted Oncle François as a mentor and spent hours talking with him, debating serious topics and discovering his own self-worth. "It has been wonderful for us to watch his transition," she told them, "and we see the benefits it brings François as well . . . it's a new lease on life for both of them."

On Sunday morning there was a *brocante* in Sainte-Mathilde, and the women all went in to browse for flea market treasures. Meanwhile, the men played a serious game of *boules* since Philippe would not be there for an afternoon game.

Molly was eagerly anticipating the lunch that Joy's brother-in-law and his wife—Jean-Pierre and Madeleine Lallibert—were hosting at their farmhouse. She had become friends with the couple when they stayed in Kat's house in Toronto on their part of the exchange with her.

"I can't wait to see this farmhouse where the dreams of your new life began," Molly said to Katherine as they walked through the vineyard.

"I'm looking forward to spending time at the house again too," Katherine said. "There are some powerful memories to relive there, that's for sure!"

A light feast of *charcuterie*, salads, and warm baguette was laid out on the dining table. Desserts were the serious items of this meal and Hélène had spent the morning preparing *chocolat fondant*, *crème brûlée*, *tarte au citron avec meringue*, and *petits beignets* filled with apple purée that simply melted in your mouth.

As it always seemed to be, conversation was light and the air filled with laughter. English, French, and something in between made it all work. Picasso and the pups provided comic relief.

In the afternoon, good-byes were said and plans made to see each other later in May, which was fast approaching. Molly was scheduled to leave before the middle of May, eager to prepare for the next school year. She was certain she would receive a full medical clearance based on how she was feeling.

The drive back to Antibes passed quickly and quietly with everyone except Philippe sound asleep. Philippe told Kat later that he'd used that quiet time to think over some details he and Katherine and Molly were discussing in preparation of launching their FromageGraphie website. They were excited that it was all coming together.

Traffic was light on this late March day, and they made good time returning to the coast. Arriving back in town, Katherine wakened just as Philippe was ending what seemed to be a brief phone conversation.

They hadn't been home more than a few minutes when the buzzer to their apartment sounded. Katherine was surprised when Philippe moved quickly to answer, though she'd been closer to the door.

Katherine continued preparing dinner; Molly was in her room unpacking her weekend bag.

Philippe spoke quietly into the intercom phone.

Moments later, he took Katherine by the hand and led her down the hall to their bedroom. As a knock lightly sounded on the front door, Philippe called out to Molly, "Would you mind getting the door please, Molly? Kat and I are busy, thanks!"

"Sure thing," Molly responded, and they heard the front door open. Silence followed.

Katherine was quizzing Philippe on what was happening, and he sat her on the bed, his finger to his lips. "Be patient for a few minutes, Minou. Then we will know what is going on."

Low voices could be heard coming from the salon. Katherine looked at Philippe in alarm, thinking she heard Molly crying softly.

"I'm worried. Please tell me who was at the door. What's going on, Philippe?"

"Tony is here. He flew to Rome last week to finalize his church business and meet with some old friends. Now he has come to spend time with Molly. And he hopes to take her back to Toronto with him."

Katherine whispered back, her voice urgent, "Oh my gosh! Do you think that's a wise idea? Surprising her like this?"

"From what Tony has said to me lately, he feels this is the best way to handle things, rather than giving Molly a chance to tell him not to come. He's in no hurry, and I told him he could stay with us as long as he wants. He insisted on booking a hotel, so I called Jean and got him a room at Le Relais du Postillon."

The charming, two-star hotel was just minutes away, with a perfect location in the heart of the old town. They were fond of the young owners and liked to support them whenever they could. Philippe always recommended it to his business contacts.

He continued, "I think it's all good, but it will be something unexpected for Molly. Tony confirmed he's completed the plan he told us about in Toronto."

Katherine stood up and paced near the bedroom door. Then she sat down quickly on the bed. "It's over? He's left the Catholic Church?"

Philippe sat next to her. "Yes. He and I have been talking during the past month. You know that he and Molly have talked pretty much every day, but he never did let on what he was doing. He has been accepted as an Anglican priest and will go through some months of transition. His superiors in the Catholic Church were not completely surprised, and although they are not happy, the break has gone as smoothly as it could."

"Should we go out there with them?" Kat asked.

"Let's give them some time. Tony was worried how Molly would take the news."

They both lay down on the bed, staring at the ceiling. Katherine slipped her hand into Philippe's. He squeezed it gently.

Katherine repeated under her breath, "Please let Molly be happy about this. Please let Molly be happy about this."

After what seemed like forever, there was a knock on the door. Molly called them to come out.

Katherine stared at Molly's tear-stained face as she stood in the hallway holding onto Tony's hand. "Oh Molly, are you okay? Tony, welcome! Philippe has just been explaining . . . kind of . . . sort of . . . Are you both okay?"

Tony smiled and nodded, still saying nothing. Molly held out her left hand to show a beautiful ring. Delicate strands of gold and diamonds twisted together to create a stunning single band. Now she was sobbing so hard, words were impossible.

"I'm so happy for you both." Katherine cried. There was a jumble of handshakes and *bises* and then joyful hugs before they all moved as one toward the salon.

"I'll get the champagne," Philippe told them.

"I'll get the tissues," Katherine said. "I have a feeling we'll need a lot of both."

CHAPTER THIRTY-SEVEN

The fifth of May had finally arrived.

Katherine took the luxury of lying in bed to think back over the past month. She decided it had been the best four weeks she ever experienced. "Love" had been the operative word.

After Tony had arrived in Antibes to ask Molly to marry him, their joy at being able to freely acknowledge their feelings gave them a new lease on life.

Katherine and Philippe convinced Tony and Molly to stay at the apartment with them for as long as they wished. Tony had a commitment in Toronto on May sixteenth, so they'd have to leave by then.

The two couples had cemented their friendship with hours of conversation about life, love, and the future, and had shared many memorable adventures. Philippe had planned day trips to all of their favorite destinations.

Then three days earlier, he sent Molly, Tony, and Katherine off to Avignon for an overnight stay. "You need more than a day there, and I'm too busy to go," he said as he waved them off.

"You're giving us a total-immersion experience of the Côte d'Azur and Provence!" Tony declared as they set out on yet another exploration.

"There's no question you're ensuring Molly and I will be back after all of these little tastes we're having."

"Mission accomplished!" Philippe replied.

Katherine's shipment from Toronto had finally arrived in the middle of April. The crate had endured a lengthy series of detours via Finland, Morocco, and Amsterdam before it eventually ended up in a storage facility in Marseille. None of the authorities could offer a reasonable explanation, but Kat was just happy to receive her possessions. She and Molly spent a few afternoons unpacking some boxes and putting others in storage until the villa restoration was completed.

As Kat placed her photos, books, and art around their apartment, she felt a growing contentment. She was home. She was happy to have these items from her past. But she knew now that she carried all the important aspects of her past inside her heart, and they would remain with her wherever she chose to live her life.

On a recent walk, she had said to Molly, "At some point when I was first back in Toronto, the words 'home is where the heart is' filtered through my mind. At the time, I was struggling with the uncertainties I was feeling about moving to France. Those words stayed with me."

Molly looked pensive. "Well, I wasn't exactly a lot of help at the time, was I?"

Kat snorted and shook her head. "You were otherwise occupied, and I wasn't about to burden you with my crazy thoughts."

"Were you ever doubting your love for Philippe, or his for you?"

"I don't think I ever doubted that. I just got hung up on the thought that by moving, I'd depend on him for my entire happiness. I thought I might not be able to truly take charge of my new life. Nick told me I had a simple case of cold feet, and I think he was right."

"Oh man, I love Nick! But, you know, it is a big deal to just up and start over in a new country with a different language, traditions, culture. How do you feel now? From what I've seen, you've done it . . . in fine style! I'm so happy for you."

"I'm happy for me too, Moll. For all of us! How cool that at this stage of our lives we can move on to new chapters and be happy in ways we never were before."

"Katski, my former self would have one word for all that is happening in our lives right now."

Kat's eyes crinkled with laughter. "I know, I know. It's fanfrickintastic!"

"Something like that," Molly laughed back.

Most mornings in April, while Philippe was at work, Tony had spent his time at the villa. He was a man of many surprises.

Shortly after arriving in Antibes, he had disclosed that his father, grandfather, and great-grandfather had been master tile craftsmen in Italy. The skill had been passed on to Tony as a child, and he often indulged in it as a hobby. Even Molly had been unaware of this interest. Through all the years they had been lovers, she had never been in his living quarters, since his apartment was in a large residence owned by the church.

"I've tiled and retiled all the bathrooms and kitchens in that residence," he had told them with a chuckle.

With Philippe and Kat's blessing, he had set to work creating a colorful fresco on a terrace wall at the villa. Filled with floral designs and birdlife patterned after the overflowing gardens on the property, it was his gift to them for taking such good care of Molly and for being so supportive of the two of them.

Didier and his *équipe* had been skeptical at first, but they soon saw Tony knew what he was doing. They made certain he had all the materials he required, and within a few days they presented him with a beret, which he proudly wore.

Katherine put an end to her reverie. It was time to start this most special day.

First, Kat and Molly drove to the Cap to pick flowers from the gardens for a bouquet. Philippe insisted they not take the pups along, as they normally would. He said he and Tony would take them for a walk instead.

The morning sun glistened on the waves that gently washed over the rocks bordering the foot of the Cap property. There was only the slightest suggestion of a breeze. The temperature was warm for the fifth of May, and poppies were blooming.

Molly was emphatic that they not even think about going into the villa, as time was of the essence. She knew Katherine was always keen to see the progress every time she was over there.

Kat was surprised to discover all the entrances sealed with caution tape. It also seemed odd that all the shutters were tightly closed. Indeed, it appeared that no one was working today.

She called Philippe to ask about it. He explained that Didier told him they had been laying tile throughout the villa, so the floors could not be walked on for several days. The men were having a well-earned day off, he said.

Kat and Molly picked a beautiful assortment of fresh blooms from the garden. From a garden tap, they filled a vase they had brought. Molly carefully placed it by the car.

Then they walked along the path Didier had uncovered and restored, over to Simone's garden. They found her outside, perched on one of her whimsical wrought-iron benches, with Victor Hugo contentedly grazing nearby.

A small easel was set up, and she was sketching a gardenia from the bush next to her. An entire hedge of the blossoms was in full bloom, perfuming the air, and the women inhaled deeply before talking.

"It's impossible to ignore this overwhelmingly beautiful fragrance," Molly proclaimed. "I've never experienced gardenia more than one bloom at a time before. This is incredible!"

Simone and Kat nodded their agreement. "There's always something to eagerly anticipate in a garden," Simone added, "but this is one of the highlights for me. I sit out here for hours."

"It's so good, it might just be illegal," Molly said, making them all laugh.

Kat looked at Simone. "We've got to dash—we just wanted to say *bonne journée*. But we'll come by tomorrow, if that's okay."

"Of course! I'll be right here and will look forward to that. Bring the pups too! I haven't seen them all week, and I miss them. So does Victor!"

They had all been amazed at how the donkey clearly liked having the pups run around and nip at his legs. He snuffled and snorted but never brayed loudly when the pups were there.

"Come for tea in the afternoon, if that suits you. Molly, you are leaving soon, *n'est-ce pas?* We must plan something special to say good-bye to you and Tony. Are you certain we cannot entice you to stay forever?"

Molly grinned. "I wish. We're leaving in three more days."

Katherine had decided to keep their plans for today to themselves. It had been difficult to keep the secret from Simone, and Kat planned to tell her as soon as it was all done. She wanted no one to know in advance except those who had to, like Molly and Tony.

Katherine paused before getting into the car back at the villa. She looked across the lawns and gardens to the sea and beyond. This view never failed to give her a thrill. Particularly on a day like this, when the weather gods appeared to join forces in the best way. The sky, the sea, the air—all of nature was in perfect harmony.

It was the kind of day Philippe described as promising: promising good weather, good crowds at the market, good laughter and ambiance, and a good end of day to be spent with his beloved Kat. Kat's heart had filled to overflowing the first time he explained his definition to her, and she smiled now. It was the perfect day to be "promising."

It was their wedding day.

CHAPTER THIRTY-EIGHT

After their visit with Simone, Katherine and Molly returned to the apartment to carefully get dressed. *Le mariage à la mairie* was to be performed by the mayor, Monsieur LeBrun, at two that afternoon.

"You know what feels great, Katski? Not having to rush around to a hairdresser, makeup person, and all that stuff you probably did the first time you got married. It's nice to feel just fine about the way we look. I've even gotten used to my short hair."

Kat agreed. "Does it go along with our age, Moll? We're not so hung up on all that anymore. Or maybe it's because it's just us and not a huge crowd."

As she looked at her friend now, Kat thought back to when Molly was in the hospital and life was in a state of flux. Molly's recovery had set many wheels in motion. After Philippe and Kat had completed the paperwork at the French consulate, the seed for today had been sown.

Once he'd cajoled her into getting married, Philippe had said to Kat, "We can do whatever you like. A big blow-out affair. A church wedding. A quiet appearance at the Hôtel de Ville. *Qu'est-ce que tu veux?* What's your pleasure?"

The only condition to Kat's hesitation had been that there was a six-month period during which they needed to marry or certain documents would have to be submitted to the government again. They agreed the wedding would happen before that.

Katherine chose a quiet civil ceremony at the Hôtel de Ville in Antibes with only four witnesses. It held a special appeal to her. She had watched many couples joyfully celebrate on that doorstep, right at the edge of the daily market.

She liked the casual air, with dress ranging from fancy to jeans, and the way everyone stood about afterward sipping champagne or wine and mingling. People passing by stopped to applaud or offer greetings. It seemed like the authentic French way to wed. Philippe was delighted with her choice.

The fact that the banns of marriage were published at the *mairie* a full ten days before the service had concerned Kat. She might not be able to keep her secret. *Who knows how many people saw them?*

So far, no one had mentioned it to her. Philippe assured her that no one had mentioned it to him either. Katherine couldn't believe that none of Philippe's customers had noticed. "Maybe it's just the French way. No one is saying anything since they weren't invited."

Philippe had simply shrugged, and Kat could see it wasn't an issue for him.

Now she turned her body this way and that in front of the mirror, hoping she looked as good as she felt. She had kept her dress a secret too. It was the palest of deep blues, almost touching on white, like some of the graceful flax blooms that had reseeded in random patches of the garden on the Cap. That plant was among her favorites. She had included a few fragile stems in the bouquet they picked.

With delicate shoulder straps, the linen sheath complemented Kat's figure. She had been carefully counting calories, knowing this day was coming at some point.

They had not settled on a date until recently. It hadn't mattered. What mattered was only that it was to be. Now it was here.

On such a promising day.

Katherine picked up her shawl. A delicate blend of silk and cashmere, it was a darker shade of the same family of blue as her dress. She and Molly had found it at the busy Friday market, across the Italian border, in Ventimiglia a month earlier.

In her usual manner, Molly had gathered a crowd that day and caused great hilarity as she haggled with the vendor. It was common knowledge that bargaining was part of the show at this popular market, as opposed to the markets in France, where that behavior was considered poor manners.

Kat, usually rendered speechless and blending in with the crowd, had never seen anyone have as much success as Molly. To top it off, along with giving her well-discounted prices, the vendors always ended up kissing Molly's cheeks passionately and declaring her *la più dolce bella donna*. Often the crowd applauded as Molly collected her purchase, and that was one of the few times when Katherine saw her friend slightly embarrassed. *But not enough to stop doing it*, Katherine chuckled to herself.

When she purchased it, Katherine didn't know that the wrap would go perfectly with the dress in which she was getting married. However, when she'd taken the dress out of her closet a few days ago, Molly had instantly retrieved the shawl.

"Bingo, *ma belle*! Look how well these go together!" Finished with a pair of pale-blue strappy stilettos, the outfit was complete. Molly had giggled as Kat asked, "Could you imagine me wearing these shoes a year ago?"

Now Molly sat on the bed and watched as Kat finished getting ready by touching up her makeup and running a brush through her hair. Molly mumbled about her envy at Katherine having the kind of hair that looked great, no matter what.

"I'm still waiting for my hair to grow long enough again to do something with it. Now all I can do is put some product in it and hope I don't look like I just survived a serious windstorm," Molly complained. No matter how sincerely Kat told her she envied Molly's curls, Molly was never happy with them.

"You look beautiful," Kat assured Molly. "That outfit looks like it was designed for you!" Her floor-length navy dress was complemented by a navy and white fitted jacket.

Ever since her physio had finished, Molly had been working not to walk with a limp. Kat reminded her now, "You're doing very well. Honestly, there's no sign of a limp. It's wonderful to see what a complete recovery you've had. Claire would be proud of you!"

The two friends hugged with great emotion.

"Molly, just imagine! A year ago today, I was still trying to adjust to my life as a single woman with, hmm, shall we say . . . equal amounts of excitement and trepidation about my upcoming home exchange in Provence."

Molly nodded, with a thoughtful expression. "I remember that well!"

Then she sang, "What a difference a year makes . . ." to the tune of the Dinah Washington hit "What a Difference a Day Makes." "It boggles my mind how the past year has brought so much change into both our lives. Who could ever have imagined any of it!"

"Well, the good news is that everything—the good and the bad—has turned out in the best possible way for both of us."

Molly stood up, and the two friends shared another hug, followed by a solid high five.

"Let's go and get you married, girlfriend."

Katherine and Molly walked out to the salon, where Philippe and Tony sat waiting for them. A bottle of champagne chilled in an ice bucket.

One of the many changes in Katherine's life was the regular occurrence of champagne. She'd grown up considering this bubbly elixir to be a rare treat for seemingly special occasions. What she had come to realize in France was that many simple events were considered special occasions.

Even more so when a day truly was celebratory. So it was no surprise that a cork would be popped and they would all toast this special day, before and after the ceremony for starters.

Molly was to be Katherine's witness at the *mairie*, along with Philippe's daughter, Adorée.

Flying in the day before, Adorée was thrilled to be involved. After a quick visit with Kat at the apartment and Philippe at the market, she went to visit some friends. She was flying back to London right after the weekend and said she wanted to make the most of her time in Antibes. She planned to stay over with her friends and would meet them at the *mairie* at the appointed time, she assured them.

Gilles would stand up for Philippe and would meet them at the *mairie* as well. Philippe had asked Tony to also be a *témoin*, or witness, as they had become very close over the previous month.

They raised their glasses now and toasted to love, to friendship, and to the fulfillment of dreams. For all of Kat's sensitivity and ease of bursting into tears, at that moment she felt happy and content. Her life had been reinvented just weeks short of a year. She felt blessed.

Turning the empty bottle upside down in the ice bucket, they prepared to leave. Molly retrieved the bouquet from the refrigerator. She had artistically arranged the blossoms and added flowing greens that Tony had picked up at the market. Thick satin ribbon wrapped around the stems to create a professionally finished look. Katherine was thrilled. "Another of your many talents! It couldn't be more beautiful."

The four celebrants strolled the ten minutes to the Hôtel de Ville. Philippe had chosen 2:00 p.m. as the time so the market would be finished and the area all cleaned up.

Everyone in the *vieille ville* knew Philippe and greeted their little group as they passed by, most unsuspecting of their ultimate destination. However, there were a few happy *"Félicitations,"* accompanied by warm smiles.

As they walked, the bells of the *mairie* tolled their joyful songs, announcing another married couple in the village. Katherine felt a tingle of excitement that those bells would soon toll the same news for her and Philippe. He squeezed her hand and smiled at her, knowing what she was thinking.

Adorée and Gilles, their eyes bright with anticipation, stood chatting near the aged wooden doors of the two-hundred-year-old building. The midafternoon sun washed over the faded finish, casting a soft glow on the pale peachy-pink walls and blue-shuttered windows. Monsieur LeBrun was inside the *salle de mariage* with his assistant, who was adjusting a stack of papers. It had been another busy day of weddings in Antibes.

The mayor's smile beamed as brightly as the shiny medal on the fancy chain of office worn around his neck along with the simple red, white, and blue sash across his chest. He welcomed Kat and Philippe to this special moment in their lives and then set about his task with an air of solemnity.

Katherine handed her bouquet to Adorée. Then she and Philippe held hands as they repeated vows and exchanged simple gold bands.

Normally, vows were not part of the civil ceremony, but Monsieur LeBrun had made an exception for them.

Holding each other's hands, Katherine spoke first, just above a whisper: "Philippe, you have filled my heart, my life, with a true love sweeter than I ever imagined. I will walk hand in hand with you wherever our journey takes us and bring that same sweet love to you in every way. With all my heart and soul, I promise you this."

Philippe's eyes closed briefly with emotion before he spoke. "Kat, you are my everything. Your love has brought me back to life. All that

I am, all that I have, all that I will ever be, is yours forever. With all my heart and soul, I promise you this."

The ceremony had to stay within their allotted twenty minutes. Katherine thought it a little odd saying *"Oui"* in the ceremony and not "I do." *But that's the French way.*

After the mayor pronounced them married, they held each other in a tender embrace, sealed with a kiss.

The newlyweds' eyes shone brightly with emotion, but neither actually shed tears. Their happiness lifted them to a state of pure joy.

Congratulating them, Monsieur LeBrun handed them their blue velvet-covered *livret de famille*, which recorded the marriage details. They joked that they didn't think the family-record part for future children would be necessary.

After signing more papers that were then witnessed by the attendants, they shook Monsieur LeBrun's hand and thanked him sincerely. He appeared somewhat overcome with emotion, saying how he'd known Philippe since childhood and had been a good friend of his parents. "I know the happiness they would feel today, Philippe. My heart is as full as theirs would be."

With a warm smile, Adorée returned the bouquet to Katherine. Her voice caught with elation as she said, "Now we are a family."

The three women shared an emotional hug. Tony and Philippe shook hands, paused, and then warmly *bised*. Philippe told him he was now officially French. Gilles and Philippe *bised* along with their handshake. Gilles wiped his eyes and blew his nose. Then they all exchanged *bises* with each other one more time, laughing as they did.

They all walked out together as the bells pealed. Katherine felt she would burst with joy at the sound. She and Philippe stopped on the step for a moment and gazed at each other, lost in happiness.

In planning Kat's quiet day, Philippe said they would go across the street to one of the bistros they frequented and perhaps have some more champagne and a small bite to eat.

He told Kat that he had a special dinner arranged for them later in the day, but he was keeping that a surprise. He'd been so supportive in letting Katherine arrange the few details of her wedding as she wanted, she was happy to hear he'd planned something special for them too.

Standing in the bright sunshine after the dim lighting inside the *mairie*, it took Kat's eyes a minute to adjust. When they did, she blinked several times. She couldn't believe what was before her.

On the street, directly in front of them, stood a beaming Bernadette on precarious sparkly stilettos, next to a highly polished vintage Rolls Royce. On its hood was a magnificent and intensely fragrant floral arrangement that included lilies, roses, lisianthus, gardenia, stock, jasmine, and agapanthus, secured with flowing pale-blue and white satin ribbons.

Katherine became aware of cheering and clapping and looked beyond the Rolls. She recognized many of the local townspeople, and it slowly dawned on her who else she was seeing.

Nick stood with Simone holding on to his arm, and beside them she saw Tim and Twig. Next to them were many of the women from her expat group in Nice with their partners. Then she spotted more familiar faces: Annette and Thibaud, Véronique and David, the cycling club members, some of the staff from the bakeries, restaurants, and shops they frequented who were more like family, Beau *le boucher*, Anouk her yogi, Ida her French teacher . . . and, to her even greater pleasure, Joy and Oncle François, along with the rest of the family and Mirella and her husband.

Standing to one side, Delphine waved shyly. She was looking after the dogs for the day. Rocco and Coco sat on command, each wearing a pale-blue bow on their collar. Katherine swallowed hard as she realized Delphine held one more leash. Dear, dear Pico was standing next to them, also wearing a bow and wagging his tail as he looked straight at her. He was so much a part of her love story. She chuckled as Philippe commented the bows wouldn't last long.

Then, as if on cue, the group parted in the middle, and from behind them appeared Andrea and Terence with their three children, as well as Lucy and Laura, and Dr. H. and Susan Henderson.

Now Kat was overcome. There was no controlling it. She burst into tears.

She found it difficult to speak, and simply walked around hugging, grinning, and shaking her head in delight. Every time she tried to say something, she could feel tears well up and her voice catch. She waved her hands in front of her eyes and whispered that she would come back to each person she greeted.

Trays filled with flutes of champagne appeared from the bistro across the street, and everyone spread out in the empty market area to chat and congratulate the newlyweds.

Nick had transported the Canadian contingent in a private plane. He had booked every room in the small hotel where Tony had stayed, Le Relais du Postillon, for them to spend the weekend. They had arrived the morning before and told Kat how Nick had organized a van to take them on a tour of the coast and up into the hills for that afternoon. They were all abuzz with excitement and so thrilled to be there.

Katherine recovered her composure, and her glee was contagious. Spirits were high. Philippe was beside himself with pleasure at how everything had worked out. Kat kept going back to kiss and hug him and say how she could never imagine anything more wonderful. Nick received his share of hugs and thanks as well.

After an hour of mingling and sipping champagne, Nick announced that everyone should follow him to a place outside the ancient town walls, just a few minutes down the street by the port. There, limos would pick up the group for the next stage of the afternoon. Kat gave Philippe a questioning look; he simply grinned.

Bernadette opened the door of the Rolls and, with a flourish, invited the bride and groom to climb in. *"Félicitations, Madame et*

Monsieur Dufours! Meilleurs voeux pour votre mariage. Je vous souhaites tout le bonheur du monde!"

All the happiness in the world, Katherine thought. *Yes, I would agree that we couldn't be off to a better beginning.*

The stately vehicle did a small tour of the town's wider streets, horn honking, as the French loved to do. Then, to Kat's surprise, they turned up the road to the Cap. She wondered where Bernadette was taking them on such a circuitous route. "She probably wants to show off this fantastic car to everyone," she commented to Philippe. He smiled and nodded. *"Bien sûr!"*

To Kat's surprise, Bernadette headed toward their property. The gates were wide open and festooned with floral ropes and lavish wreaths. This was almost more than Katherine could handle, "You mean those tapes this morning . . . your story about floor tiles . . . none of it was true?"

Philippe's eyes crinkled with delight. *"Attends, mon amour.* Just wait."

Time stood still for Kat. She found herself lost in Philippe's gaze. Every nerve tingled with delight, assuring her she had never felt so loved or been so in love before. Her fingers lingered on his cheek. The familiar touch of the light stubble on his face excited her, and she suddenly was reminded that she would wake up beside this beautiful man every day for the rest of her life.

Philippe took her hand, slowly kissing each fingertip before their lips pressed hotly together. Kat gasped as his fingers curled into her hair and he pulled her to him. Her arms went around him. She could feel his muscles, hard and strong, as their bodies melted into each other. Katherine felt intoxicated as their lips continued a delicious dance of ecstasy. Slowly, they pulled away from each other and leaned back against the seat.

Katherine rested her head on Philippe's shoulder, catching her breath.

"Je t'aime, je t'aime . . ." Philippe whispered, his lips brushing her hair. Katherine repeated his words, and they sat in luscious silence.

As the car slowly came to a stop at the front entrance, Katherine fixed her hair and straightened her dress. Philippe brushed a few strands from her face as she straightened his jacket and tie. They could not stop smiling.

Bernadette announced that they had arrived. *"Alors, nous sommes chez vous!"*

Kat could see the villa had been transformed since that morning. Enormous urns, overflowing with flowers and vines, lined the entrance. A long, beautifully painted banner reading *"Villa des Violettes ~ Amour Vit Ici*/Love Lives Here" hung across the double doors.

Standing on the front terrace were Didier and his *équipe*: Auguste, Alphonse, and Alesander, all spruced up in ironed jeans and dress shirts. All wearing new berets.

Didier proudly attended to the car door, while Auguste rolled out a carpet over the tiles. With a grand sweep of their arms, the brothers threw open the doors to the villa.

A loud "Surprise!" in both French and English rang through the air as Kat and Philippe walked into the entrance hall and main salon. The limos had obviously gone straight to the property and dropped everyone there.

The space had been transformed into a magical forest of trees and plants. The theme had been painted in *trompe l'oeil* over the walls.

The party was on.

André wandered through the crowd, taking photos. Adorée's friends were circulating with trays of appetizers and drinks. Emile waved from behind a table where crostini, *tapenades*, and *foie gras* were being served.

Philippe whispered to Katherine, "This is where Adorée and her friends were all night. Some of them came here during the week and worked with Didier and the guys. I had no idea what they were up to with all these decorations. Véronique oversaw everything, and Simone even came over to help with some painting ideas. *C'est fantastique!*"

"So that's why Molly and Tony insisted I go on the road trip to Avignon with them this week. You were all plotting behind my back."

Kat hugged Philippe with all of her might as every emotion she could imagine swirled through her. "For the lack of surprises in my life before you, you have more than made up for them. I can never thank you enough. *Je t'adore . . . tu es l'amour de ma vie.*"

"You've thanked me for everything by becoming my wife. Madame Katherine Dufours, *pour toujours et à jamais*, forever and always." They lingered in an embrace before mingling with their guests.

Katherine, Andrea, and Molly found a quiet corner to share hugs. Holding their hands, Kat said, "There are moments when I have to remind myself I'm not dreaming. I can't believe the three of us are here, living this day together."

Molly was struggling to control her emotions as Andrea replied, "When I think back to this time last year, I'm reminded that we never know where life is going to lead us. I couldn't be more thrilled for you, Kat. I feel your true destiny is just beginning. This kind of happiness was a long time coming."

Katherine kissed her cousin's cheek before the three friends squeezed each other tightly. Then she turned to Molly, who was still fighting back tears. "Molly! No more tears. I've been the crybaby lately, not you!"

Molly bit her lower lip and nodded vigorously before she spoke. "Right, Katski. I haven't cried these kind of happy tears in all my life. It's just all been so fu . . . so frickin' beautiful."

Andrea took tissues from her purse and passed them around. Katherine murmured, "I've learned so much from both of you this past year. You helped me to believe in life again, to believe in myself, and to take chances. True friends—that's what you are. I'm so lucky to have you in my life, and that's never going to change."

"Never," they all said in unison.

"I love you guys," Kat said, her voice quivering.

"Me more," Andrea insisted with a grin.

"Fuckin' A!" was Molly's response, through her tears. They all laughed uproariously as she explained, "I just said that for effect; one last f-bomb, for old times' sake."

Molly wiped her eyes, blew her nose, and continued, "Remember when you were so conflicted about making your home here?"

Katherine nodded.

"Well, I've watched you for the last two months, and may I just say this. Your. Home. Is. Here. No question! And it's a home with more affection, tenderness, joy, and fun—more *amour*—than I've ever seen. I love it . . . and I love you and I love Philippe and I love that at this stage in our lives we can begin again."

Now Kat and Molly hugged each other and rocked back and forth before they pulled Andrea into their arms.

"It's a hell of a story, Katski. I can't wait to see what happens next."

After an hour or so, the sound of a soft gong interrupted the festivities. Giving it one more tap as he stood in the middle of the room, Didier announced, *"Le repas de noce."*

The painted papers that covered the doors to the back gardens were taken down by assorted guests obviously in the know, and the shutters were opened.

A fairy-tale setting greeted Kat's eyes. On the lawn, three long tables were covered in white linen and set for a meal with colorful Provençal dishes and rainbow-hued glassware from Biot. Stunning floral arrangements overflowed from pots and containers on the ground as well as hanging from hooked holders.

White fabric-covered chairs, trimmed with blue ribbon, lined the tables. Some chairs were also scattered in groupings about the garden to create intimate spaces. On one corner of the terrace, Katherine and Philippe's bicycles were looped together and festooned with ribbons and flowers. Not a detail had been missed.

Kat could not stop gasping as she and Philippe stood arm in arm. "This is my simple *mariage à la mairie?*"

"*Oui, mon amour*, Minou, Madame Dufours . . . *c'est ça!*" His smile expressed his joy.

The air was scented with the sweet fragrance of lilacs, peonies, and gardenias from the garden combined with the vases of *les muguets*—lily of the valley—decorating the tables.

Nick invited everyone to search for their place cards. Seating had been carefully arranged so that the guests were placed both with someone they knew and with someone they didn't. He wanted them to mix, and so far that had been very successful.

Mouthwatering aromas drifted from large grills set up on a far section of the lawn and Katherine gasped as Antoine and Hélène waved to her, obviously busy supervising cooking staff.

When people had discovered their chairs and the laughter eased, Adorée welcomed them all and introduced Nick as the master of ceremonies. Nick gave a brief introduction of how he, Katherine, and Philippe all became friends. As usual, he had everyone laughing in no time. Then they all cheered as he invited them to toast the newlyweds one more time. Next, he introduced Tony and asked him to give thanks for this day and for the meal.

Platters of food arrived at each table. The service was family style, which only increased the level of conversation and laughter. Gasps of delight could be heard throughout the garden as delectable offerings arrived. Artistic presentations tempted the eye, and irresistible aromas wafted through the air.

Grilled fish, chicken, and lamb were accompanied by roasted vegetables and an assortment of green salads. Baguette, olive oil, and olives were within easy reach of every diner. Umbrellas provided shade for those who wished it, and the late-afternoon sun warmed the bucolic scene. Conversation and laughter filled the air, and Kat and Philippe took turns sitting in chairs left empty for them at each table.

As the sun began to set, candlelight created an even more romantic mood, and heaters kept the temperature comfortable. Mother Nature appeared to be an invited guest, as conditions were faultless.

The cheese course was served on olivewood boards and accompanied by bravos of admiration. Philippe had outdone himself and proudly stood to take a few bows.

Soon after, the fading light was suddenly ablaze with sparklers and on cue, a chant arose. *"Le gâteau! Le gâteau! Le gâteau!"*

Bearing a large silver tray on each of their shoulders, Auguste, Alfonso, and Alesander paraded around the tables with this spectacular traditional finale to the wedding feast. Antoine and Hélène modestly waved from the terrace as everyone recognized their artistry.

The guests cheered and applauded the three elaborate, towering *croquembouche*, dripping in caramelized spun sugar. Small fireworks shot up from the trays, and sparklers were set in between the *crème*-filled puff pastries. A tray was set on each table as the fireworks slowly fizzled.

"The surprises never stop!" Katherine exclaimed, beaming. Philippe took her hand to stand with him, and they fed a few pieces to each other—to more cheers—before the dessert was served to the rest of the celebrants.

Nick invited anyone who wished to give a speech to do so. "However, I'll warn you that a three-minute time limit will be seriously monitored by Mademoiselle Molly Malone. We all know you don't mess with Molly!" he finished with a wide grin as Molly stood and flexed her muscles.

There were memories, good wishes, and toasts shared by many, in both languages and sometimes with hilarious translation. Tissues were passed around to wipe tears that alternated between laughter and the warmest of sentiments. Katherine was filled with bliss. She and Philippe could barely look at each other, their emotions were so charged.

The simple act of having their arms around each other or holding hands transferred ecstasy between them beyond any words.

Finally, it was their turn.

"We thank each and every one of you for being here with us today. Your presence and your friendship have made this the most special day." Katherine's heart swelled with gratitude. Her face glowed. She had a sense of floating above the magical setting, as if in a dream. She paused to collect herself and contain the elation flooding through her. "I had no inkling my extraordinary husband, *mon mari extraordinaire*, had planned this unforgettable surprise. Thank you to everyone who transformed our construction site into this enchanting experience. Being here with all of you and marrying this man I adore is the best and most meaningful time of my life." She finished with two sentences in her new language, thanking their French friends and family for welcoming her into their hearts.

As they stood arm in arm, Philippe spoke next. His eyes sparkled as he eloquently expressed the elation he was feeling, alternating in French and English. "There's a Provençal saying, '*Au mois de mai, fais ce qu'il te plait*. In the month of May, do what pleases you.' I promise you this: nothing will ever please me more than marrying this most special woman today. She is beautiful both inside and out. We will never forget these moments we are celebrating with you now. Thank you for sharing our joy."

Taking Kat's hand, he led her to the terrace, near where a small jazz combo had set up. Molly walked over to the band and picked up a microphone. The first notes of "Have I Told You Lately" began, then Molly's mellifluous voice resonated across the garden. A perfect cicada chorus provided quintessential Provençal harmony.

After a few moments, everyone was invited to join in on the dance floor.

For Philippe to have chosen this song, the moment could not have been more exquisite for Kat. No other words could have captured her feelings.

As the newlyweds danced cheek to cheek, Katherine's eyes flickered across the terrace.

Beyond the swaying couples twirling around them, filling this moment with such love, she envisioned gossamer illusions of her mother and father dancing sweetly together. Elisabeth's eyes met Kat's as a smile lit her face and her head nodded in approval.

Katherine tried not to blink. She didn't want to lose the scene her imagination was creating. She felt her parents' presence.

Her heart was full. She felt calm, strong, and eager.

Music floated through the air and down to the sea as a brilliant pink sunset foretold the perfect ending to this day. Dawn would herald the promise of all her tomorrows.

She was home.

EPILOGUE

Her breathing became labored. "No pain, no gain," she repeated from time to time.

Katherine could feel her muscles straining as she left the route along the coast and cycled higher into the hills above Cannes.

She and Philippe had gotten back into a regular riding schedule in the month since their wedding. Every week he pushed her to make the ride more challenging, and she was beginning to see results. She had to admit there had been times she struggled.

After the excitement of their wedding and the departure of their houseguests, life was settling into a comfortable rhythm. Kat and Philippe agreed they missed having Molly and Tony around, but they were also reveling in the privacy and quiet of their own routines.

The work on the property on the Cap was proceeding well, in spite of inevitable glitches. Kat's photography was on permanent exhibit in André's gallery. She and Philippe were getting closer to launching their website. For the moment, everything and everyone in her world seemed to be on a very even keel.

Today she was heading for a spot they called their "secret," on a wild piece of vacant property tucked into a fairly built-up residential area. Vehicle traffic was minimal on the steep, narrow streets, and the view was stunning—definitely worth the effort to get there. They had yet to encounter anyone else on the land.

Kat didn't often cycle out this way on her own, but Philippe was busy with meetings all afternoon, and she knew he might be too tired when he got home. The urge had been too strong for her to resist the ride today. Something was telling her to go.

Dripping with sweat, she reached the viewpoint and took a long swig from the water tube of her hydration pack. After peeling off her gloves and removing her helmet, she pushed her sunglasses back on her head and sprayed water on her face. It would soon be too hot for midday rides.

She took an apple and a chunk of cheese from her pack. Then she unfolded a small towel, laid it on the ground and sat on it. Alternating bites of apple and cheese, Kat felt hypnotized by the view and the contentment she felt.

From the first day she Kat arrived in the South of France, the Mediterranean had captivated her. As she often did, she allowed herself to feel like she was floating over the red-tile rooftops below her that cascaded down to the coast.

Then the hypnotic effect of the colors of the Med took hold. There was never anything ho-hum about it. The rich, vibrant azure hues ranged from the shimmering gemlike turquoise near the shore to deep cobalt as far as the eye could see. Kat was certain this feeling of wonder at the beauty she lived with daily would never fade.

She was filled with a sense of being blessed. Validation for all the decisions she had made in the preceding year and a half. From those crushing first days of shock and despair when she felt alone and confused to this blissful time of love and renewal, a metamorphosis had been achieved.

She had opened herself to opportunities that fate presented to her, and as a result, her life had changed.

"What doesn't kill us makes us stronger," her mother had taught her. But she had never truly appreciated those words until James left her and she had to search for her inner strength.

"Take a chance. Make a choice to change your life," Andrea and Terrence had said to her when they encouraged her to go on her first home exchange. And so she did.

During the hours of talks shared as she recuperated from her accident, Molly repeatedly said, "Every day is a frickin' gift, Katski. We need to wake up every morning with that thought. Your mother told us that too." And Kat saw that as a wake-up call.

And recently Simone—dear Simone—grasping Kat's hand as they parted after a chat over tea, had said, "Once you choose to do what you really want to do, you will begin living a different kind of life. It will be the life you are meant to be living in that moment of time. That is what truly matters. I learned that lesson when I first chose to be in the Resistance, and it has driven my life ever since." So Kat committed to live the life that she felt truly mattered.

Fear, insecurity, and doubt had plagued her at times. It had taken hard work to conquer them, but she had learned how—and knew she could do it again.

Katherine's choices were made. She had discovered she was strong. She had discovered how to take chances. No one would ever take that away from her.

The love and respect she and Philippe gave to each other were the finishing touches to all this change.

The sun warmed her face. Her thoughts warmed her heart.

As Kat finished her apple and prepared for the thrilling descent, she smiled to herself and gave thanks for her good fortune. She had been given a second chance and was eager to embrace the possibilities that lay ahead.

Life was moving forward.

The first guests to stay at the Villa des Violettes would be arriving in August. New adventures were waiting to unfold.

Kat was ready.

AUTHOR'S NOTE

I Promise You This is the last book in the Love In Provence trilogy. I've loved writing each of these novels and I'm delighted that you have become so engaged with Katherine's story. It's most satisfying to hear people say they felt they were right there in France with her. The particular part of the world, with its beauty, culture, and history has become a character in its own right.

I'm excited to continue writing about the characters and the settings, and I'm full of ideas for what happens next. Sometimes I feel I'm simply a bystander who has been invited along on an ongoing adventure. The stories will continue until they . . . or you . . . let me know they are over.

Thank you to every single person who has written to me through the years or messaged me on social media. I'm also grateful to the many reviewers and bloggers who have taken the time to read my novels and write about them. I value your thoughts and opinion, so please continue to share them with me at patriciasandsauthor@gmail.com.

Have you signed up for my newsletter? It goes out once a month with all sorts of contests and information about what's coming next. Just click on "subscribe" at my website http://patriciasandsauthor.com.

Any time you have a moment to write a review, please know your efforts are appreciated. Comments from readers are helpful and inspiring to me. You are the reason I write and your words encourage others to read my books. *Merci mille fois!* Thanks a million!

And now . . . on to the next book . . .

ACKNOWLEDGEMENTS

It takes a village, as the saying goes. In order to reach that exciting point where a manuscript is finally ready to publish, a great deal of support and assistance is essential. I'm grateful to everyone who contributed in his or her own personal way to bringing *I Promise You This* to readers. The Love In Provence series will always hold a special place in my heart.

Friends and family are my rocks. My husband's patient support, encouragement, and eager first look at my words means everything to me. I feel so fortunate to have advance readers who offer honest, helpful comments and read all my rewrites without losing their sense of humor. In particular, I owe big bouquets of gratitude to Gail Johnston, Pat MacDonald, May Anis and Susan Baldwin Mayfield. Ida Young-Bondi, my friend and French instructor from Nice, applies her expertise where needed and knows how much it is appreciated. *Merci mille fois,* Ida!

My invitation from Amazon Publishing to join their Lake Union imprint continues to be an exciting and fulfilling opportunity. The support, experience, and enthusiasm offered by my developmental editor,

Amara Holstein and senior editors, Danielle Marshall and Miriam Juskowicz, and the entire Lake Union team is priceless.

Thanks once again to Amy Cooper and Barb Drozdowich (my tech angel), for their dedication, wise advice, and active involvement in all I do. Bravo to Scott Collie for another original watercolor book cover.

None of this would happen without the amazing community of authors and readers, bloggers and reviewers who make me proud, happy and inspired to keep writing.

ABOUT THE AUTHOR

Patricia Sands lives in Toronto, but her heart's other home is the South of France. An avid traveler, she spends part of each year on the Côte d'Azur and occasionally leads groups of women on tours of the Riviera and Provence. Her award-winning 2010 debut novel, *The Bridge Club*, is a book-group favorite, and *The Promise of Provence*, which launched her three-part Love in Provence series, was a finalist for a 2013 USA Best Book Award and a 2014 National Indie Excellence Award, an Amazon Hot New Release in April 2013, and a 2015 nominee for a #RBRT Golden Rose award in the category of romance. Sands also contributes to such Francophile websites as The Good Life France and Perfectly Provence and appears as a public speaker for women's groups. Celebrating the power of friendship and the courage to embrace change, her writings draw personal responses from male and female readers alike. Visit her online at www.patriciasandsauthor.com.